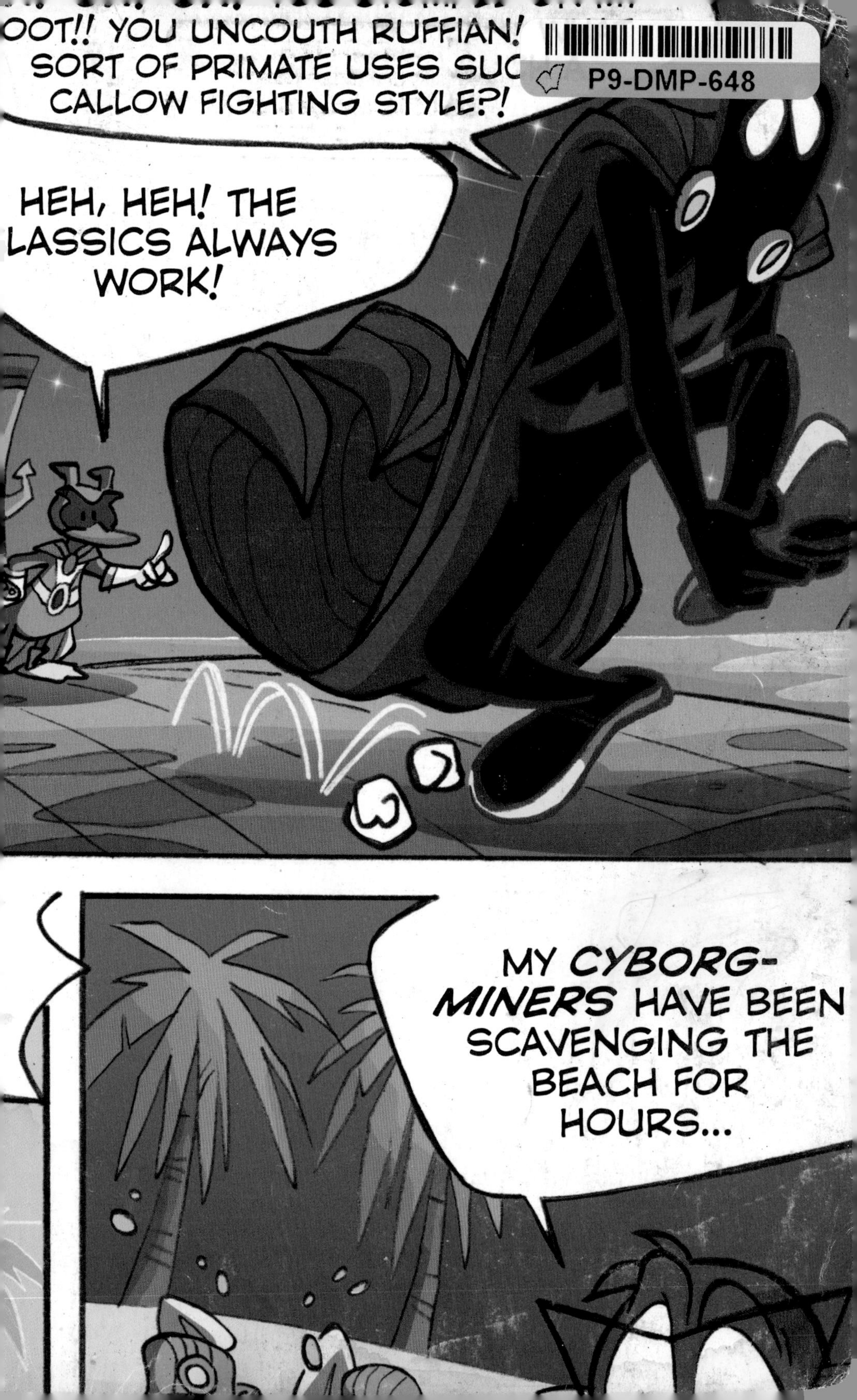
OOT!! YOU UNCOUTH RUFFIAN! SORT OF PRIMATE USES SUC CALLOW FIGHTING STYLE?!
HEH, HEH! THE LASSICS ALWAYS WORK!
MY CYBORG-MINERS HAVE BEEN SCAVENGING THE BEACH FOR HOURS...

ROSS RICHIE
chief executive officer

MARK WAID
editor-in-chief

ADAM FORTIER
vice president,
new business

WES HARRIS
vice president,
publishing

LANCE KREITER
vice president,
licensing & merchandising

CHIP MOSHER
marketing director

MATT GAGNON
managing editor

FIRST EDITION: MAY 2010

10 9 8 7 6 5 4 3 2 1
FOR INFORMATION REGARDING THE CPSIA ON THIS PRINTED MATERIAL
CALL: 203-595-3636 AND PROVIDE REFERENCE # EAST – 66642

DISNEY'S HERO SQUAD: ULTRAHEROES VOLUME TWO - RACE FOR THE ULTRAPODS –
published by BOOM Kids!, a division of Boom Entertainment, Inc. All contents © 2010 Walt Disney
Company. BOOM Kids! and the BOOM Kids! logo are trademarks of Boom Entertainment, Inc.,
registered in various countries and categories. All rights reserved.

Office of publication: 6310 San Vicente Blvd Ste 404, Los Angeles, CA 90048-5457.

A catalog record for this book is available from OCLC and on our website www.boom-kids.com on the
Librarians page.

WRITERS:
GIORGIO SALATI & ALESSANDRO FERRARI

ARTISTS:
ROBERTA MIGHELI & ANTONELLO DALENA

TRANSLATOR:
SAIDA TEMOFONTE

EDITORS:
AARON SPARROW &
CHRISTOPHER MEYER

LETTERERS:
DERON BENNETT &
JOSE MACASOCOL, JR.

COVER:
MAGIC EYE STUDIOS

ASSISTANT EDITOR:
CHRISTOPHER BURNS

ORIGIN OF SUPER GOOF:
THE THIEF OF ZANZIPAR
WRITER:
BOB OGLE
ARTIST:
PAUL MURRY

ORIGIN OF THE RED BAT
WRITER:
IVAN SAIDENBERG
ARTIST:
CARLOS EDGARD HERRERO
TRANSLATOR:
STEFANIA BRONZONI
LETTERER:
JOSE MACASOCOL, JR.

SPECIAL THANKS:
JESSE POST, LAUREN
KRESSEL & ELENA GARBO

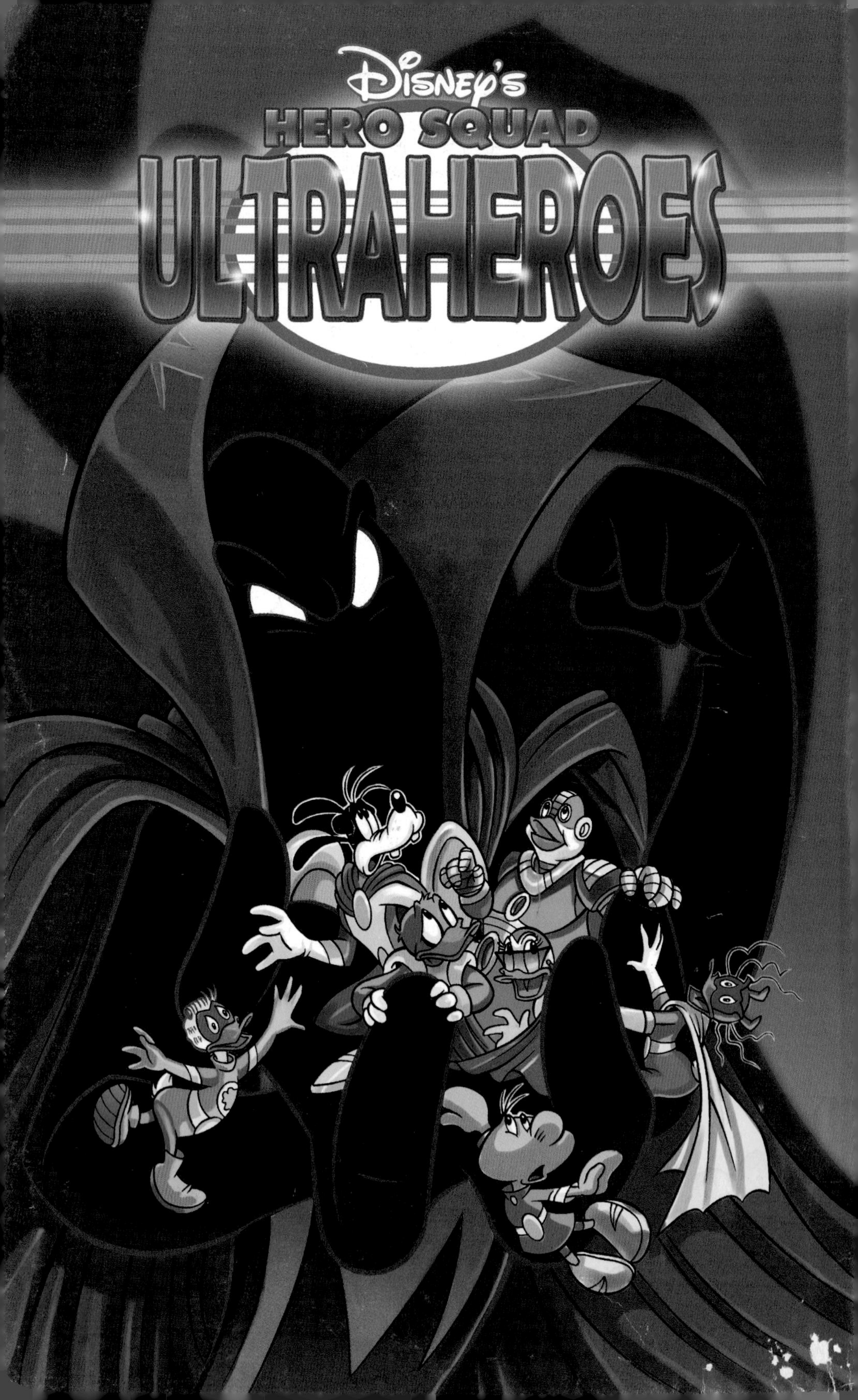
Disney's
HERO SQUAD
ULTRAHEROES

WALT DISNEY COMICS AND STORIES #699-702 RECAP:

EEGA BEEVA AND THE ULTRAHEROES HAVE BEEN IN A RACE AGAINST EMIL EAGLE AND THE SINISTER 7 TO RECOVER THE SEVEN ULTRAPODS, THE COMPONENTS NECESSARY FOR REBUILDING THE ULTRAMACHINE--A DEVICE THAT COULD GIVE ITS OWNER THE POWER TO RULE THE WORLD. THUS FAR, THE ULTRAHEROES ARE IN A DEAD HEAT WITH THEIR EVIL COUNTERPARTS AS BOTH SIDES HAVE RECOVERED TWO ULTRAPODS EACH. MEANWHILE, MICKEY'S INVESTIGATION INTO THE MYSTERIOUS DISAPPEARANCE OF SCROOGE MCDUCK AND HIS MONEY BIN HAS LED HIM TO THE PONGA ISLANDS. NOW WE RETURN TO WHERE WE LAST LEFT OUR HEROES, AS THE RED BAT STARTS HIS BATTLE WITH THE INFAMOUS PHANTOM BLOT FOR THE FIFTH ULTRAPOD...

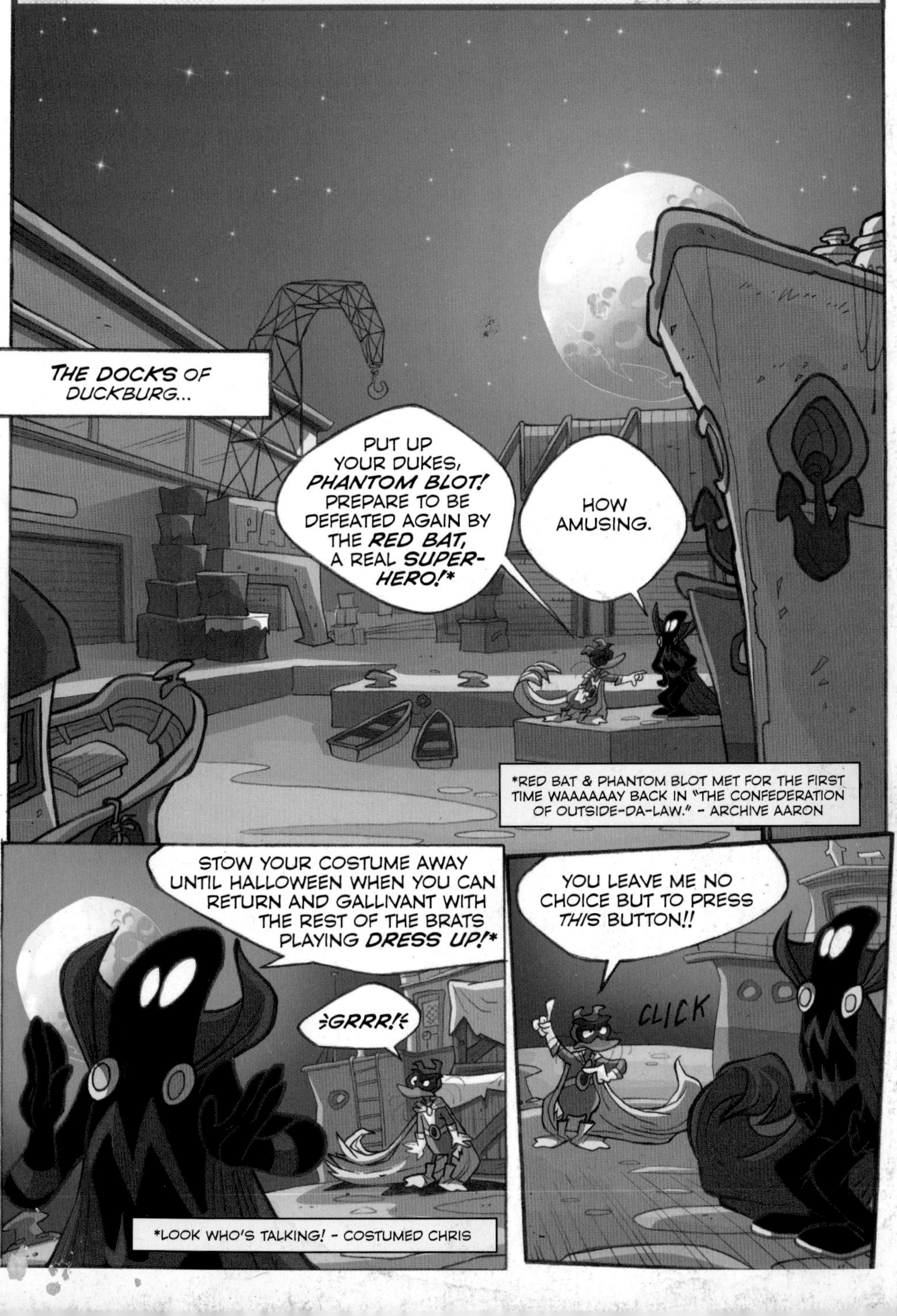
THE DOCKS OF DUCKBURG...
PUT UP YOUR DUKES, PHANTOM BLOT! PREPARE TO BE DEFEATED AGAIN BY THE RED BAT, A REAL SUPER-HERO!*
HOW AMUSING.
*RED BAT & PHANTOM BLOT MET FOR THE FIRST TIME WAAAAAAY BACK IN "THE CONFEDERATION OF OUTSIDE-DA-LAW." - ARCHIVE AARON
STOW YOUR COSTUME AWAY UNTIL HALLOWEEN WHEN YOU CAN RETURN AND GALLIVANT WITH THE REST OF THE BRATS PLAYING DRESS UP!*
GRRR!
*LOOK WHO'S TALKING! - COSTUMED CHRIS
YOU LEAVE ME NO CHOICE BUT TO PRESS THIS BUTTON!!
CLICK

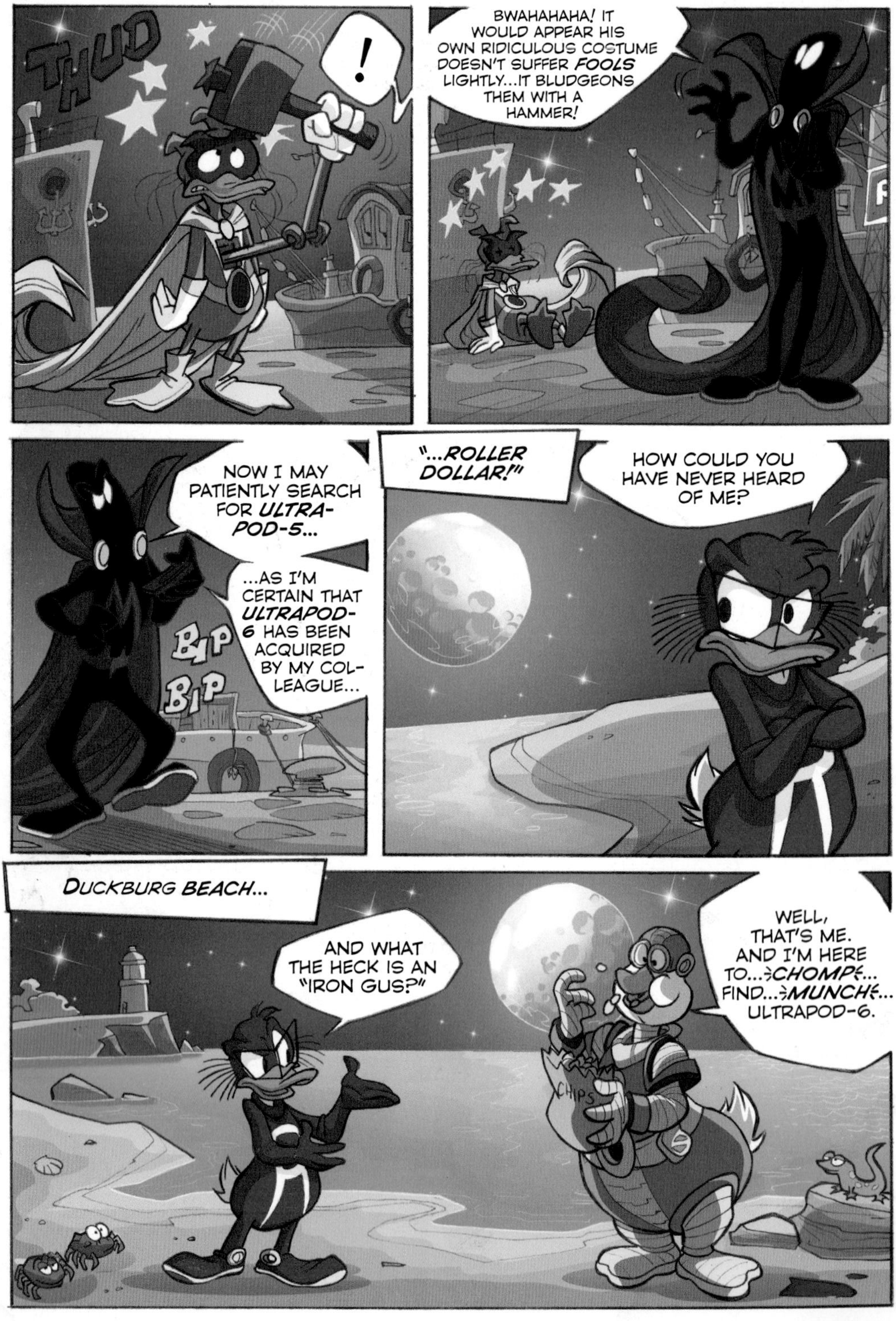
THUD
!
BWAHAHAHA! IT WOULD APPEAR HIS OWN RIDICULOUS COSTUME DOESN'T SUFFER *FOOLS* LIGHTLY...IT BLUDGEONS THEM WITH A HAMMER!
NOW I MAY PATIENTLY SEARCH FOR *ULTRA-POD-5*...
...AS I'M CERTAIN THAT *ULTRAPOD-6* HAS BEEN ACQUIRED BY MY COL-LEAGUE...
BIP BIP
"...*ROLLER DOLLAR!*"
HOW COULD YOU HAVE NEVER HEARD OF ME?
DUCKBURG *BEACH*...
AND WHAT THE HECK IS AN "IRON GUS?"
WELL, THAT'S ME. AND I'M HERE TO...*CHOMP*... FIND...*MUNCH*... ULTRAPOD-6.
CHIPS

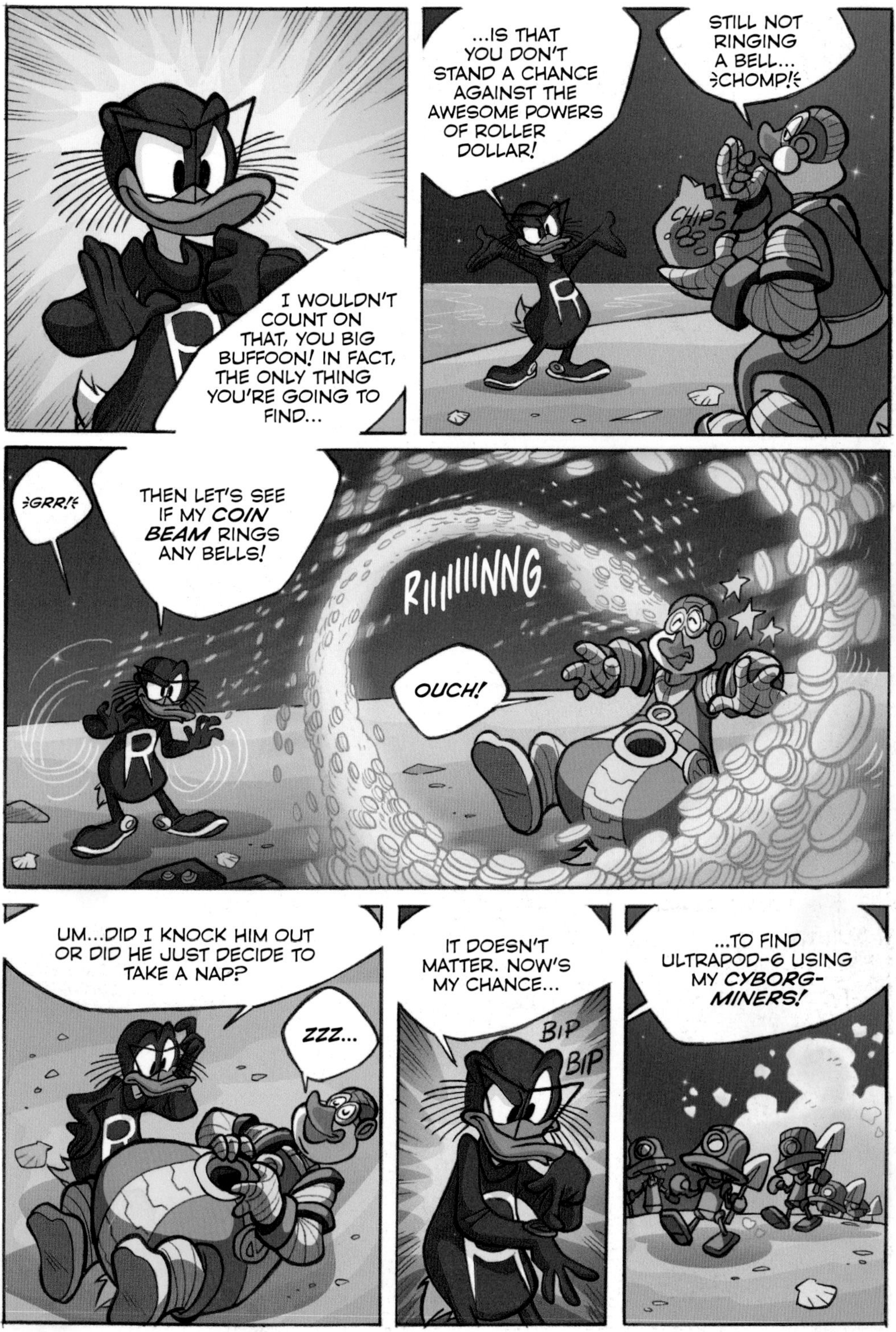
I WOULDN'T COUNT ON THAT, YOU BIG BUFFOON! IN FACT, THE ONLY THING YOU'RE GOING TO FIND...
...IS THAT YOU DON'T STAND A CHANCE AGAINST THE AWESOME POWERS OF ROLLER DOLLAR!
STILL NOT RINGING A BELL... CHOMP!
CHIPS
GRR!
THEN LET'S SEE IF MY COIN BEAM RINGS ANY BELLS!
RIIIIIINNG
OUCH!
UM...DID I KNOCK HIM OUT OR DID HE JUST DECIDE TO TAKE A NAP?
ZZZ...
IT DOESN'T MATTER. NOW'S MY CHANCE...
BIP BIP
...TO FIND ULTRAPOD-6 USING MY CYBORG-MINERS!

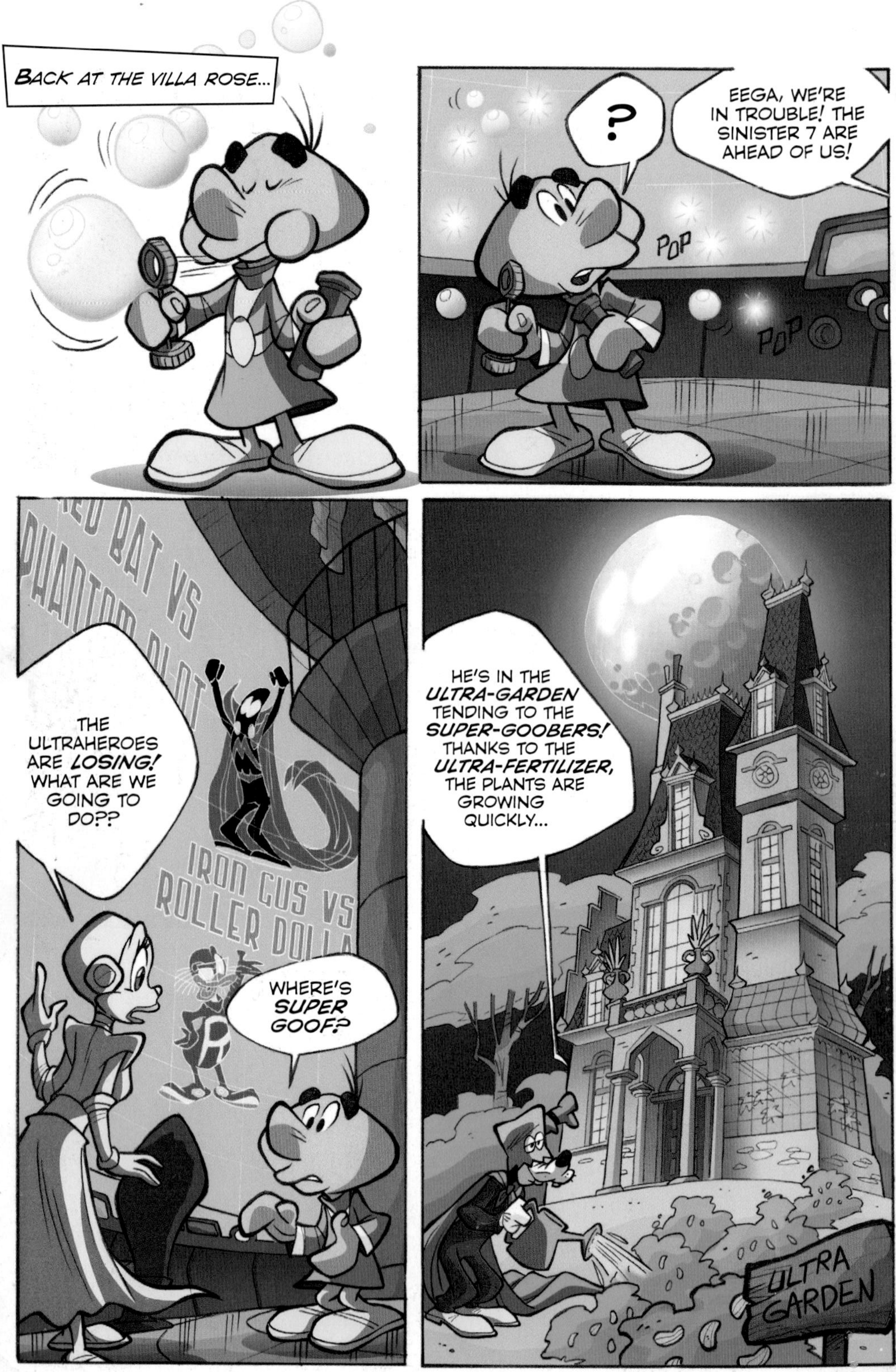

BACK AT THE VILLA ROSE...
?
EEGA, WE'RE IN TROUBLE! THE SINISTER 7 ARE AHEAD OF US!
POP
POP
RED BAT VS PHANTOM BLOT
IRON GUS VS ROLLER DOLLA
THE ULTRAHEROES ARE LOSING! WHAT ARE WE GOING TO DO??
WHERE'S SUPER GOOF?
HE'S IN THE ULTRA-GARDEN TENDING TO THE SUPER-GOOBERS! THANKS TO THE ULTRA-FERTILIZER, THE PLANTS ARE GROWING QUICKLY...
ULTRA GARDEN

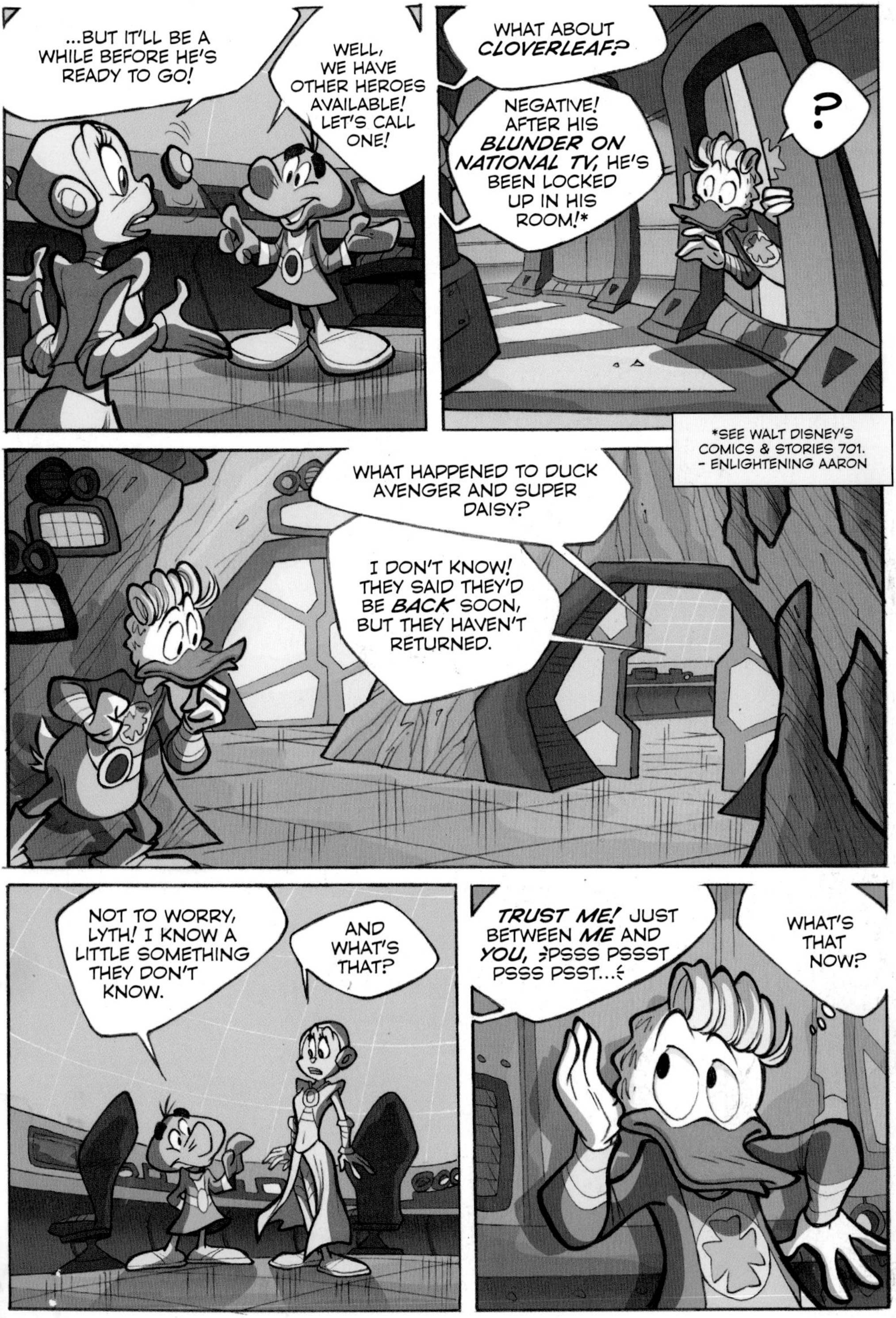
...BUT IT'LL BE A WHILE BEFORE HE'S READY TO GO!
WELL, WE HAVE OTHER HEROES AVAILABLE! LET'S CALL ONE!
WHAT ABOUT CLOVERLEAF?
NEGATIVE! AFTER HIS BLUNDER ON NATIONAL TV, HE'S BEEN LOCKED UP IN HIS ROOM!*
?
*SEE WALT DISNEY'S COMICS & STORIES 701. - ENLIGHTENING AARON
WHAT HAPPENED TO DUCK AVENGER AND SUPER DAISY?
I DON'T KNOW! THEY SAID THEY'D BE BACK SOON, BUT THEY HAVEN'T RETURNED.
NOT TO WORRY, LYTH! I KNOW A LITTLE SOMETHING THEY DON'T KNOW.
AND WHAT'S THAT?
TRUST ME! JUST BETWEEN ME AND YOU, PSSS PSSST PSSS PSST...
WHAT'S THAT NOW?

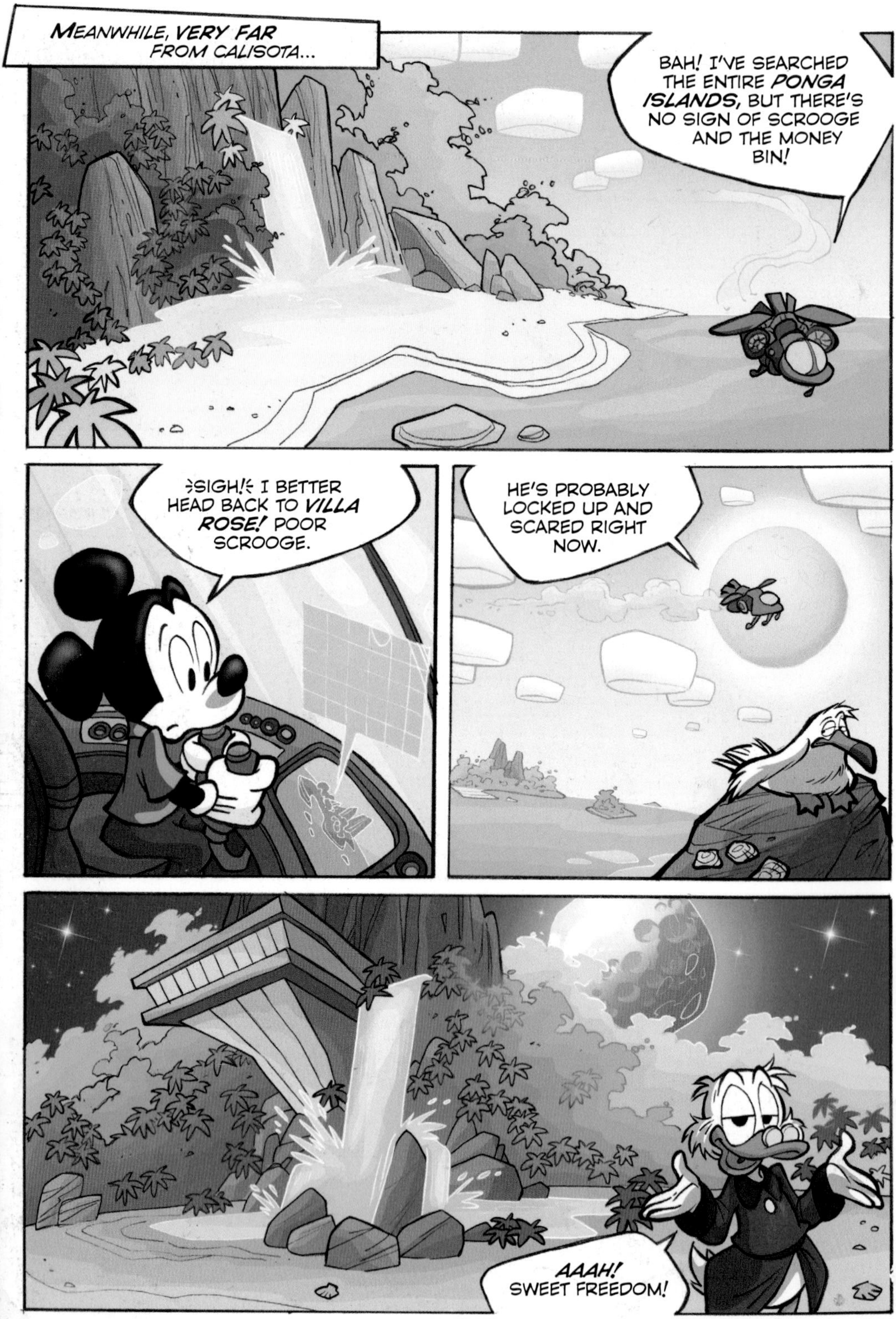
MEANWHILE, VERY FAR FROM CALISOTA...
BAH! I'VE SEARCHED THE ENTIRE PONGA ISLANDS, BUT THERE'S NO SIGN OF SCROOGE AND THE MONEY BIN!
SIGH! I BETTER HEAD BACK TO VILLA ROSE! POOR SCROOGE.
HE'S PROBABLY LOCKED UP AND SCARED RIGHT NOW.
AAAH! SWEET FREEDOM!

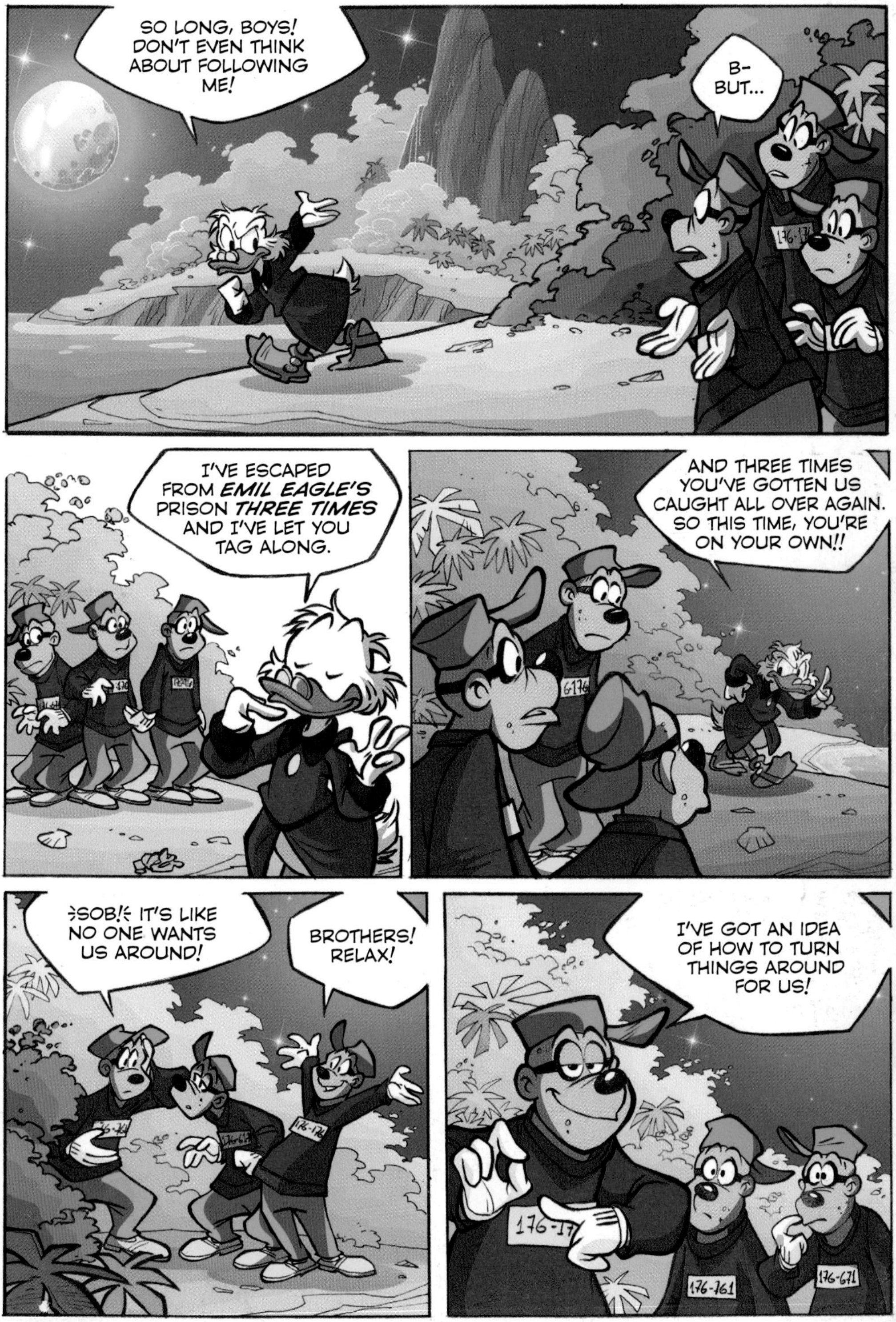

SO LONG, BOYS! DON'T EVEN THINK ABOUT FOLLOWING ME!
B-BUT...
I'VE ESCAPED FROM EMIL EAGLE'S PRISON THREE TIMES AND I'VE LET YOU TAG ALONG.
AND THREE TIMES YOU'VE GOTTEN US CAUGHT ALL OVER AGAIN. SO THIS TIME, YOU'RE ON YOUR OWN!!
SOB! IT'S LIKE NO ONE WANTS US AROUND!
BROTHERS! RELAX!
I'VE GOT AN IDEA OF HOW TO TURN THINGS AROUND FOR US!

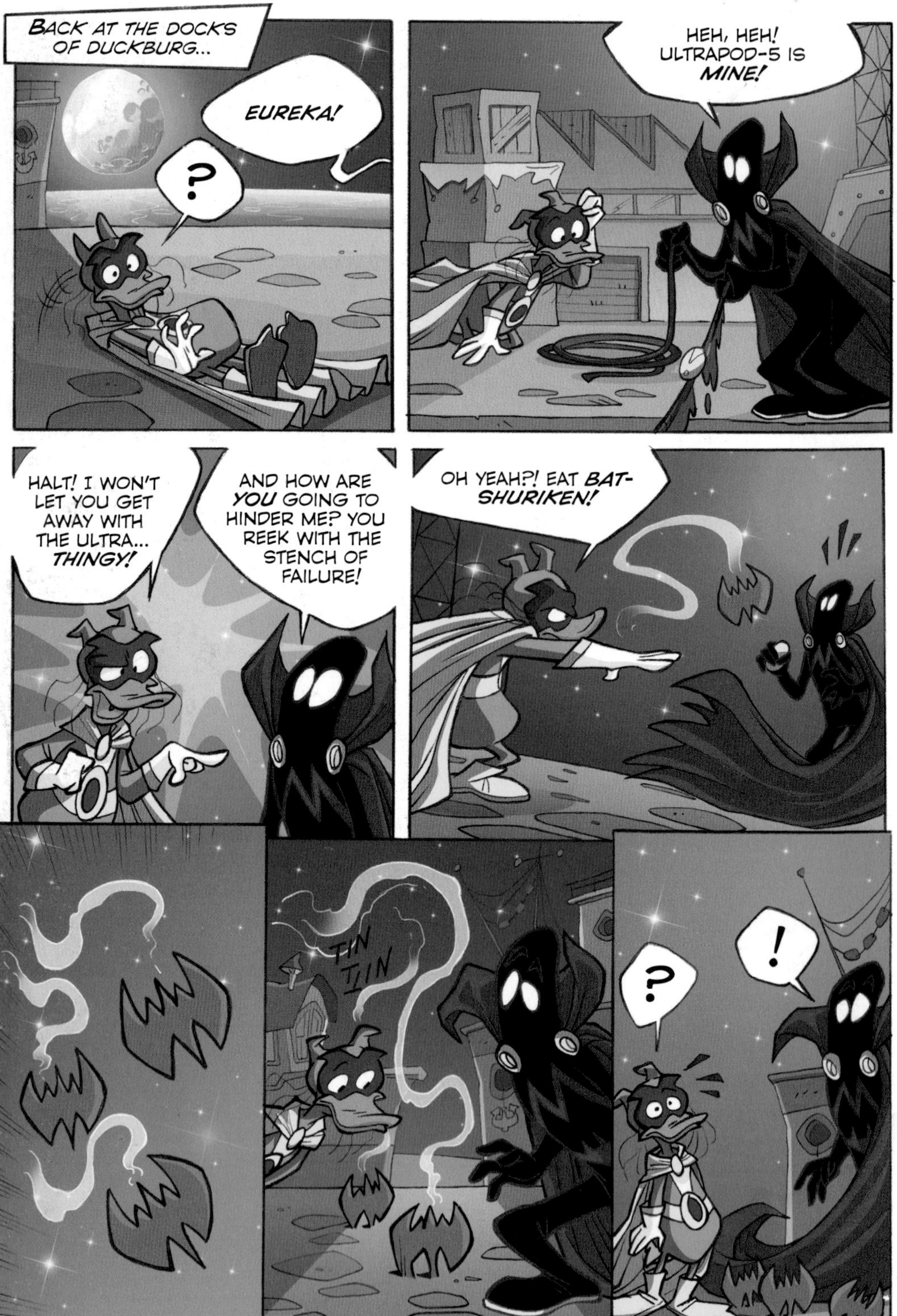
BACK AT THE DOCKS OF DUCKBURG...
EUREKA!
?
HEH, HEH! ULTRAPOD-5 IS MINE!
HALT! I WON'T LET YOU GET AWAY WITH THE ULTRA... THINGY!
AND HOW ARE YOU GOING TO HINDER ME? YOU REEK WITH THE STENCH OF FAILURE!
OH YEAH?! EAT BAT-SHURIKEN!
TIN TIIN
?
!

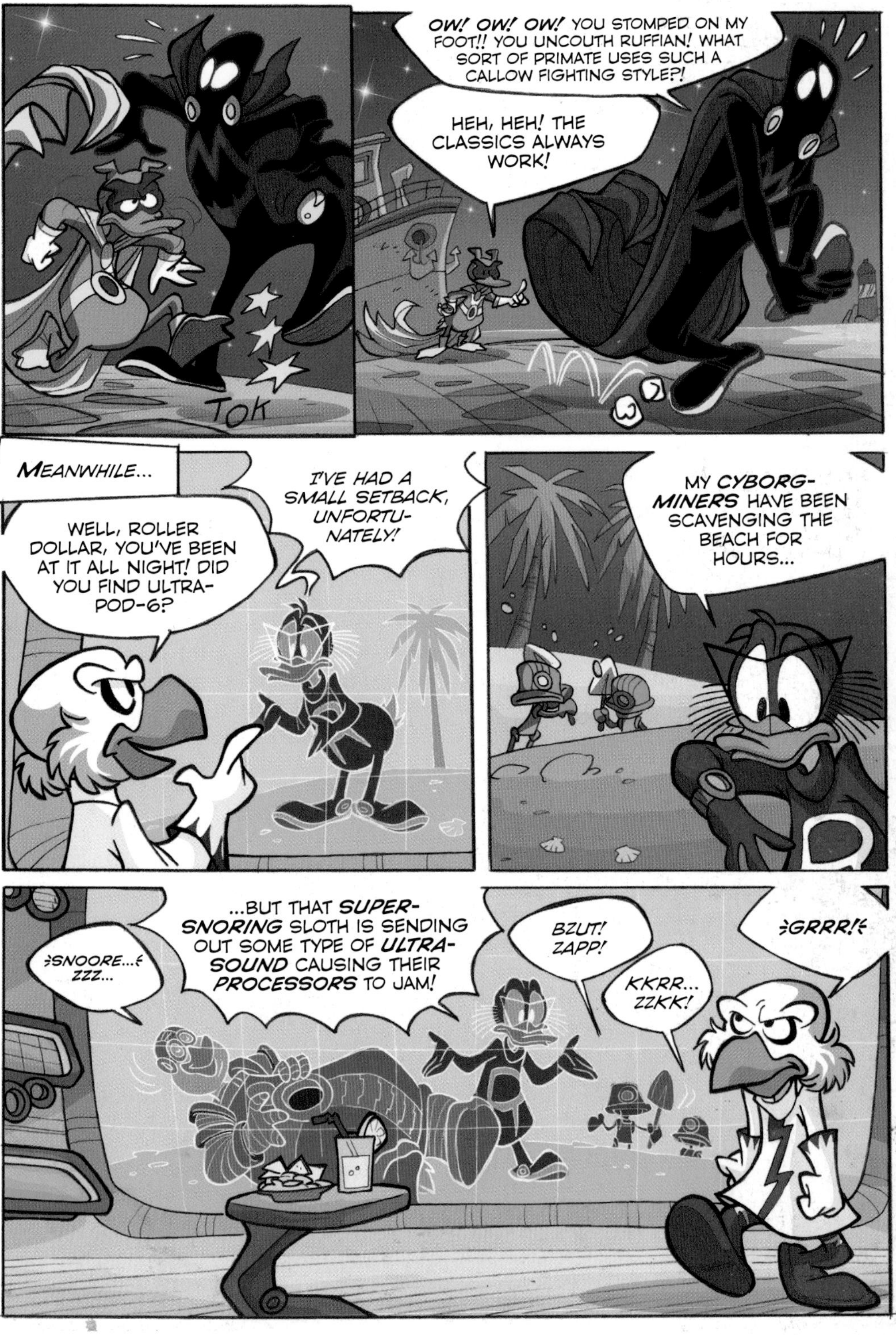
TOK
OW! OW! OW! YOU STOMPED ON MY FOOT!! YOU UNCOUTH RUFFIAN! WHAT SORT OF PRIMATE USES SUCH A CALLOW FIGHTING STYLE?!
HEH, HEH! THE CLASSICS ALWAYS WORK!
MEANWHILE...
WELL, ROLLER DOLLAR, YOU'VE BEEN AT IT ALL NIGHT! DID YOU FIND ULTRA-POD-6?
I'VE HAD A SMALL SETBACK, UNFORTU-NATELY!
MY CYBORG-MINERS HAVE BEEN SCAVENGING THE BEACH FOR HOURS...
...BUT THAT SUPER-SNORING SLOTH IS SENDING OUT SOME TYPE OF ULTRA-SOUND CAUSING THEIR PROCESSORS TO JAM!
SNOORE... ZZZ...
BZUT! ZAPP!
KKRR... ZZKK!
GRRR!

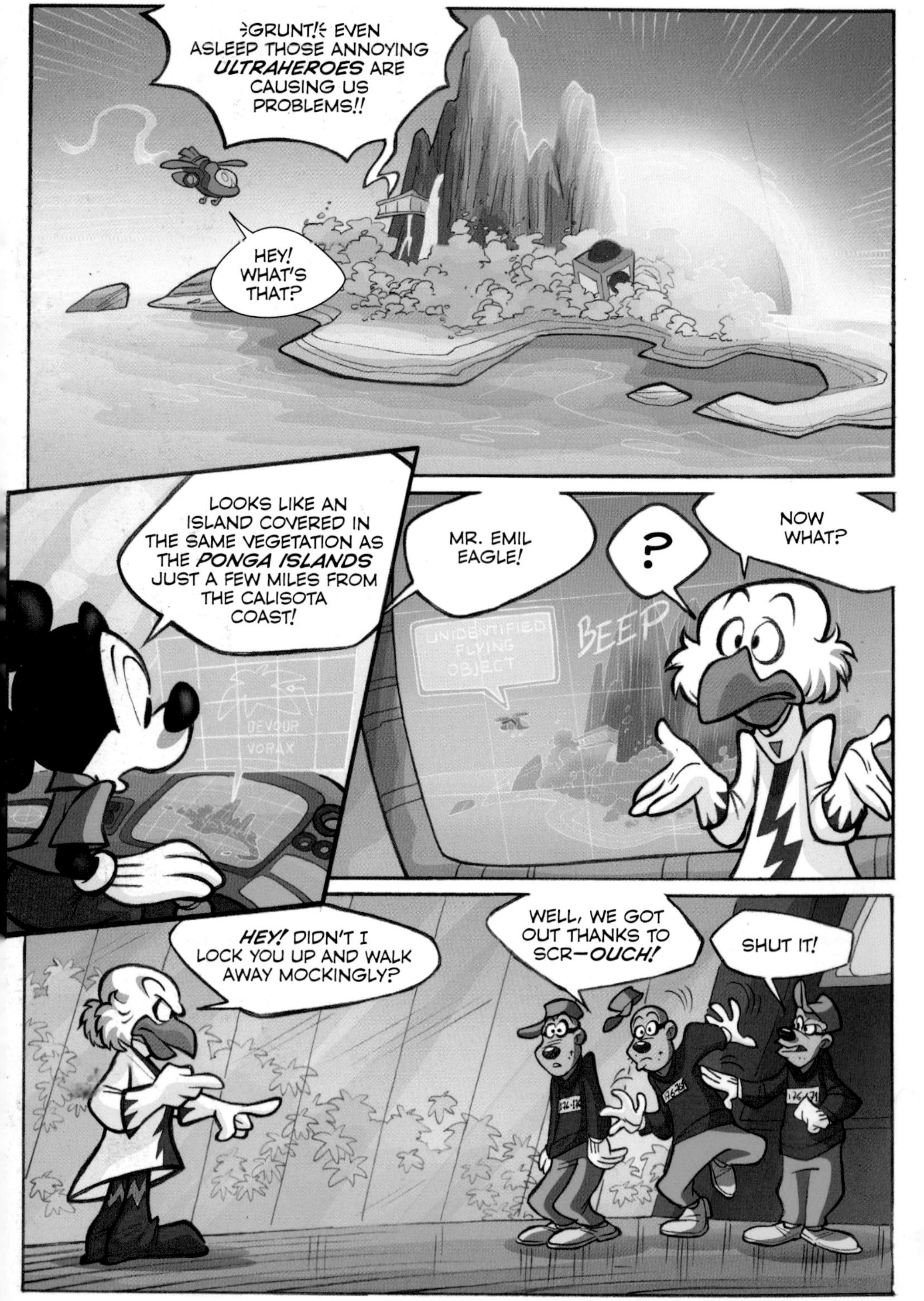
GRUNT! EVEN ASLEEP THOSE ANNOYING ULTRAHEROES ARE CAUSING US PROBLEMS!!
HEY! WHAT'S THAT?
LOOKS LIKE AN ISLAND COVERED IN THE SAME VEGETATION AS THE PONGA ISLANDS JUST A FEW MILES FROM THE CALISOTA COAST!
MR. EMIL EAGLE!
?
NOW WHAT?
UNIDENTIFIED FLYING OBJECT
BEEP
DEVOUR
VORAX
HEY! DIDN'T I LOCK YOU UP AND WALK AWAY MOCKINGLY?
WELL, WE GOT OUT THANKS TO SCR—OUCH!
SHUT IT!

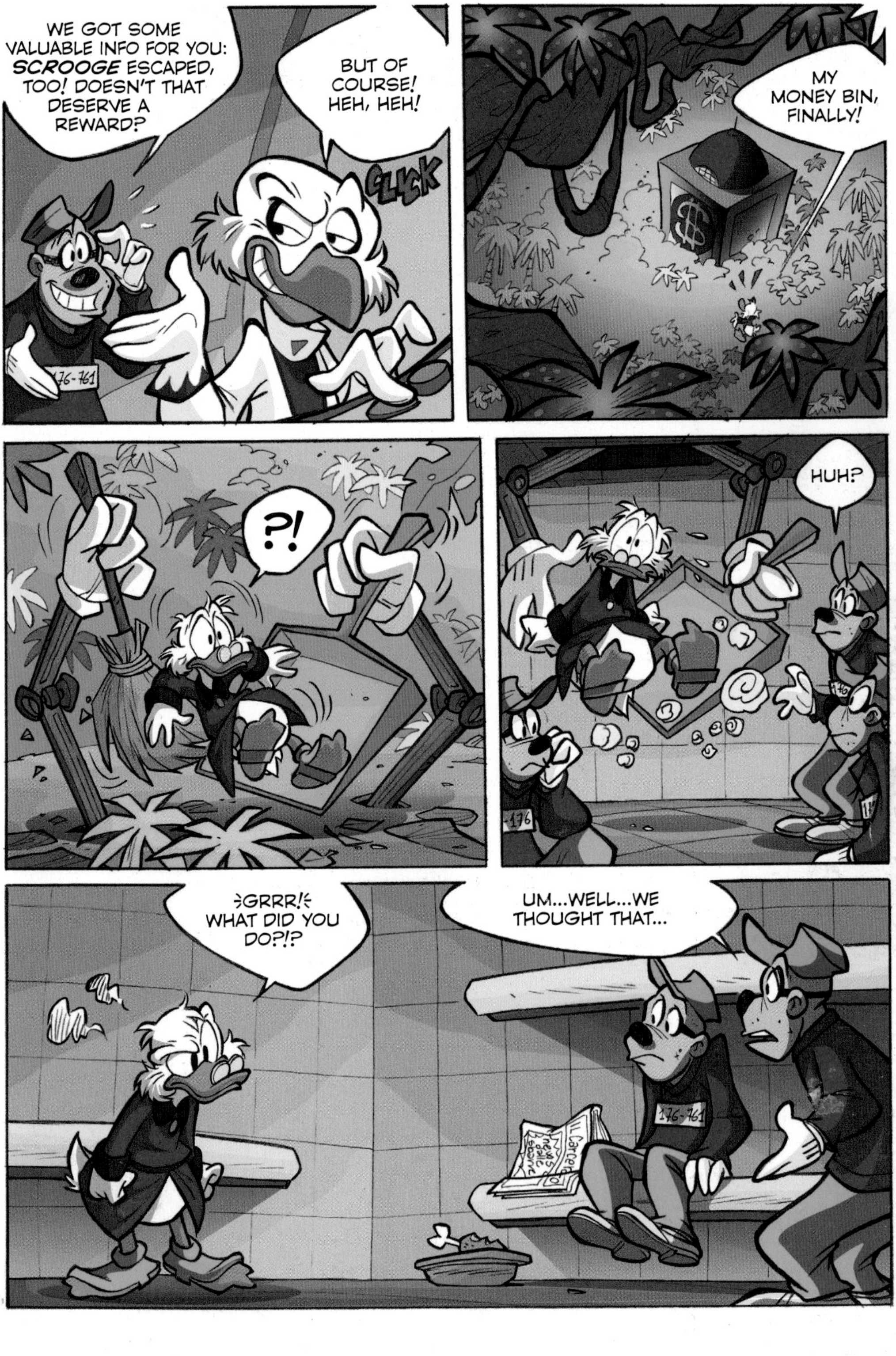

WE GOT SOME VALUABLE INFO FOR YOU: SCROOGE ESCAPED, TOO! DOESN'T THAT DESERVE A REWARD?
BUT OF COURSE! HEH, HEH!
CLICK
MY MONEY BIN, FINALLY!
?!
HUH?
GRRR! WHAT DID YOU DO?!?
UM...WELL...WE THOUGHT THAT...

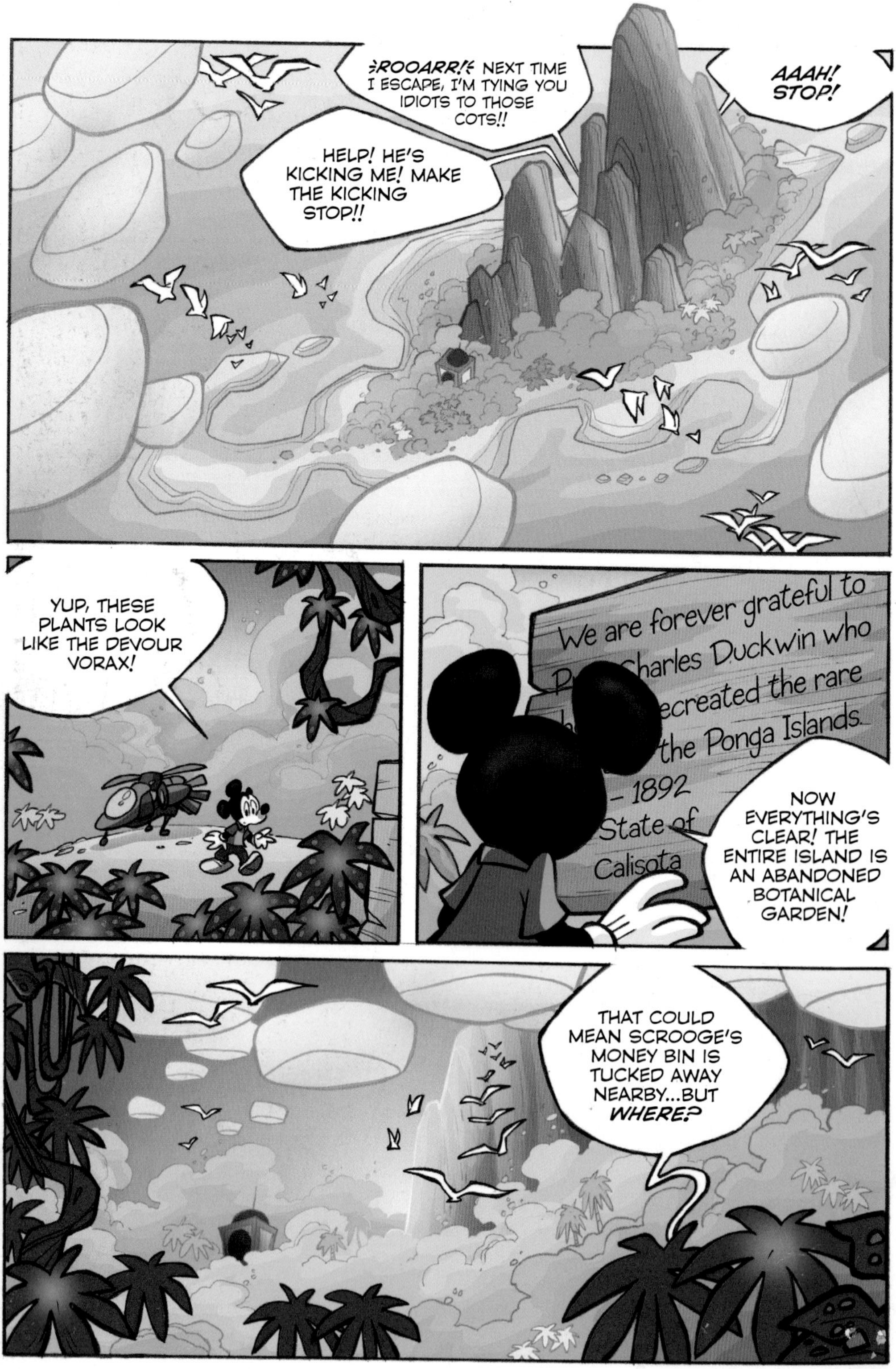

ROOARR! NEXT TIME I ESCAPE, I'M TYING YOU IDIOTS TO THOSE COTS!!
AAAH! STOP!
HELP! HE'S KICKING ME! MAKE THE KICKING STOP!!
YUP, THESE PLANTS LOOK LIKE THE DEVOUR VORAX!
We are forever grateful to
Charles Duckwin who
ecreated the rare
the Ponga Islands.
– 1892
State of
Calisota
NOW EVERYTHING'S CLEAR! THE ENTIRE ISLAND IS AN ABANDONED BOTANICAL GARDEN!
THAT COULD MEAN SCROOGE'S MONEY BIN IS TUCKED AWAY NEARBY...BUT WHERE?

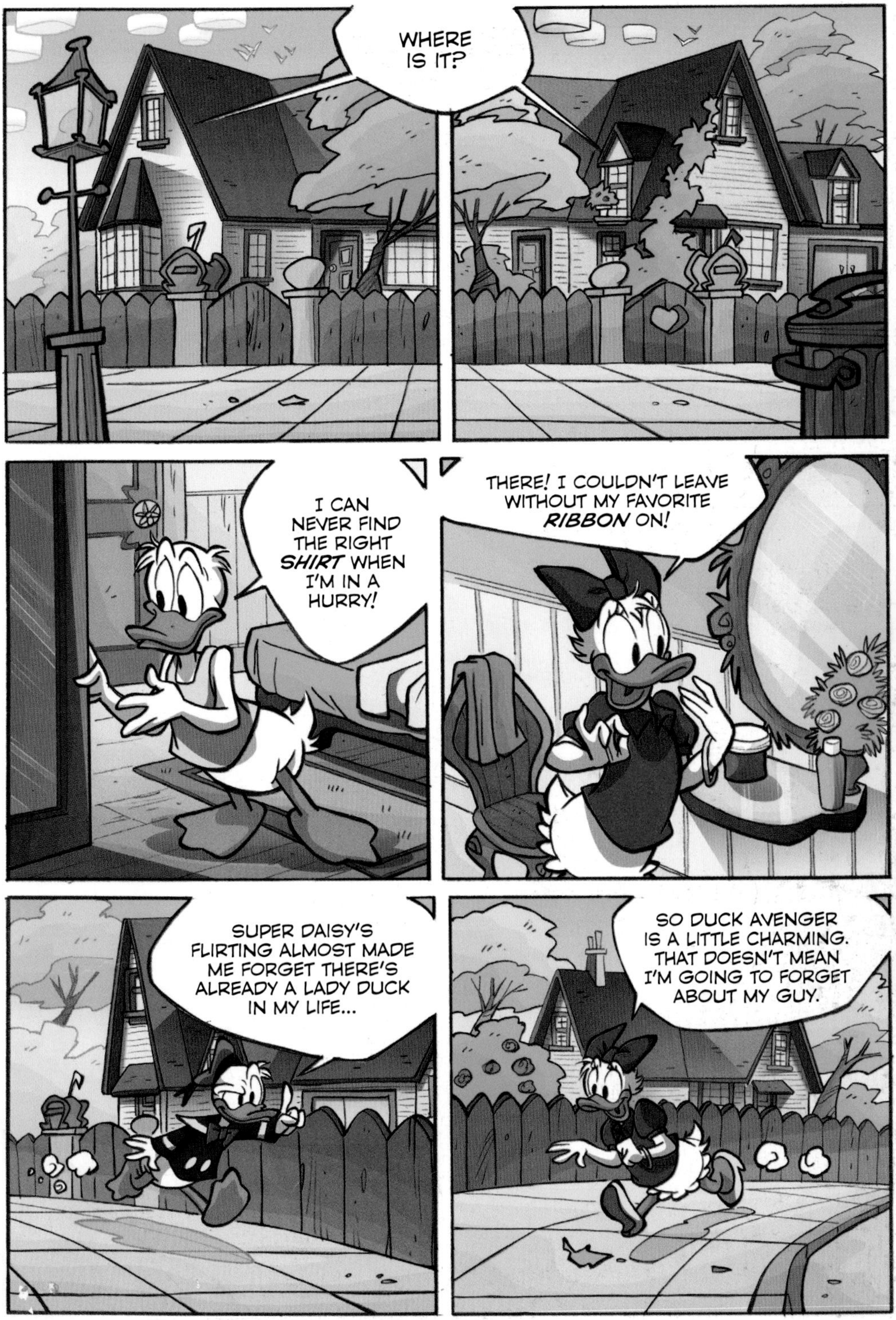
WHERE IS IT?
I CAN NEVER FIND THE RIGHT SHIRT WHEN I'M IN A HURRY!
THERE! I COULDN'T LEAVE WITHOUT MY FAVORITE RIBBON ON!
SUPER DAISY'S FLIRTING ALMOST MADE ME FORGET THERE'S ALREADY A LADY DUCK IN MY LIFE...
SO DUCK AVENGER IS A LITTLE CHARMING. THAT DOESN'T MEAN I'M GOING TO FORGET ABOUT MY GUY.

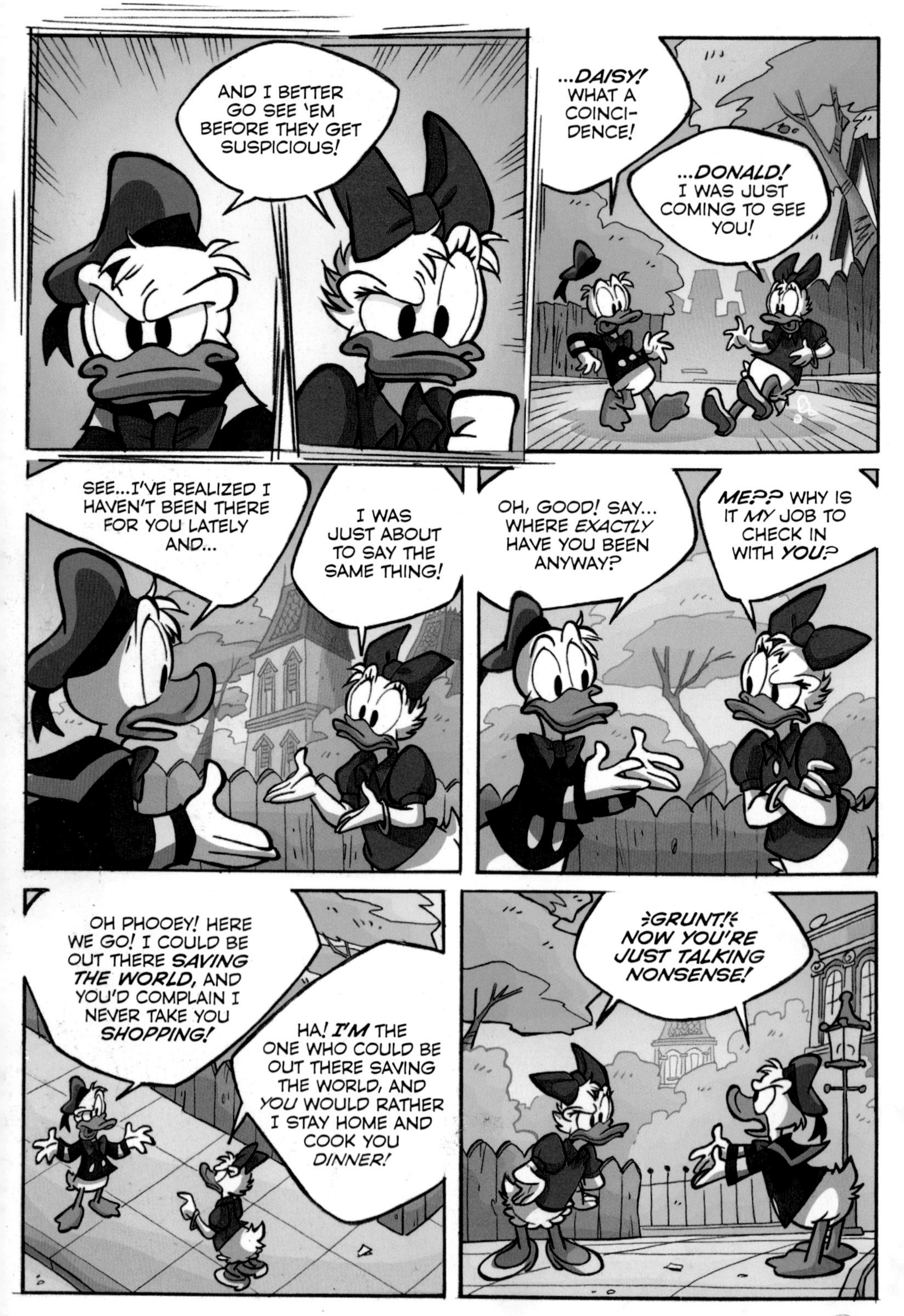
AND I BETTER GO SEE 'EM BEFORE THEY GET SUSPICIOUS!
...DAISY! WHAT A COINCI-DENCE!
...DONALD! I WAS JUST COMING TO SEE YOU!
SEE...I'VE REALIZED I HAVEN'T BEEN THERE FOR YOU LATELY AND...
I WAS JUST ABOUT TO SAY THE SAME THING!
OH, GOOD! SAY... WHERE EXACTLY HAVE YOU BEEN ANYWAY?
ME?? WHY IS IT MY JOB TO CHECK IN WITH YOU?
OH PHOOEY! HERE WE GO! I COULD BE OUT THERE SAVING THE WORLD, AND YOU'D COMPLAIN I NEVER TAKE YOU SHOPPING!
HA! I'M THE ONE WHO COULD BE OUT THERE SAVING THE WORLD, AND YOU WOULD RATHER I STAY HOME AND COOK YOU DINNER!
GRUNT! NOW YOU'RE JUST TALKING NONSENSE!

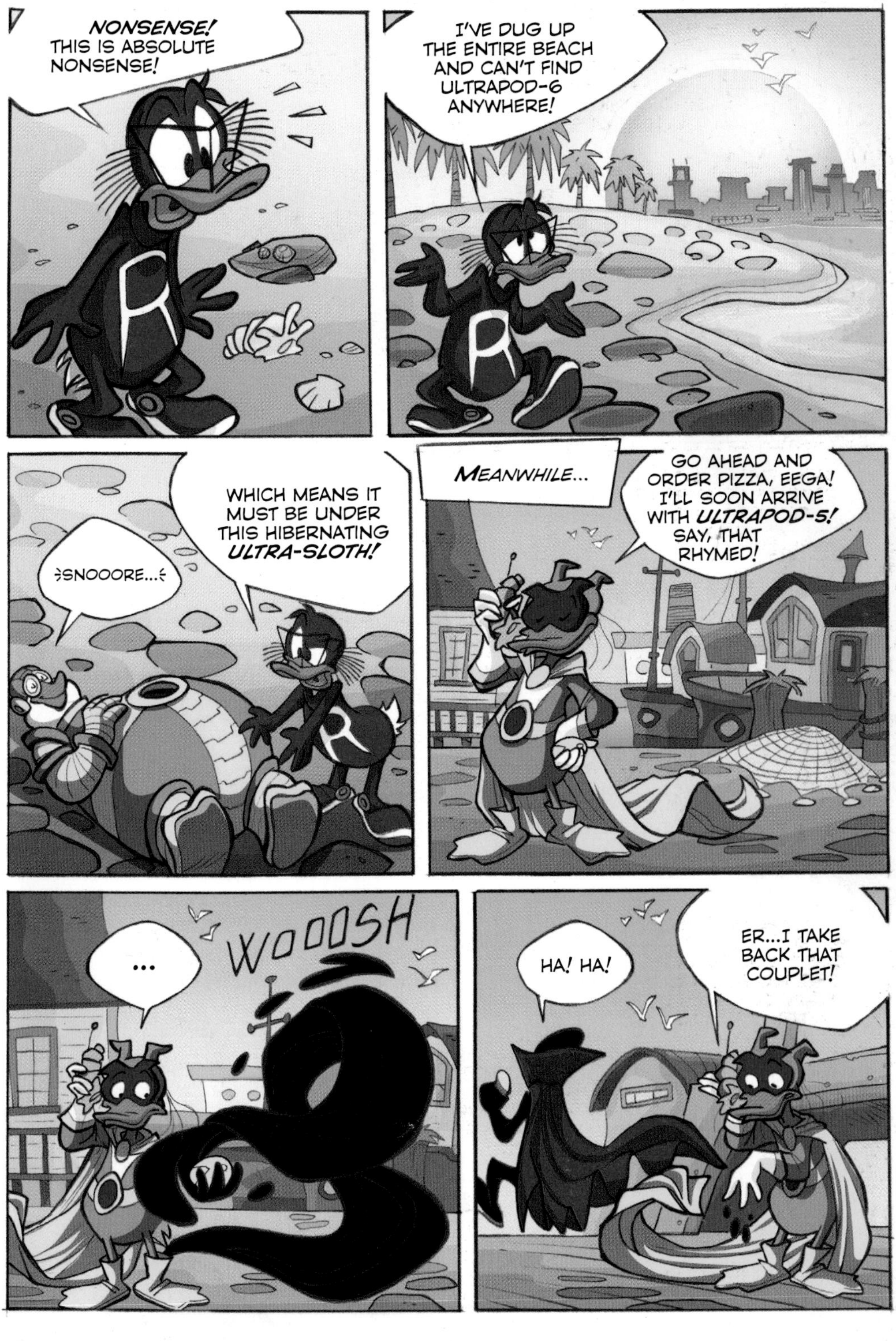
NONSENSE! THIS IS ABSOLUTE NONSENSE!
I'VE DUG UP THE ENTIRE BEACH AND CAN'T FIND ULTRAPOD-6 ANYWHERE!
WHICH MEANS IT MUST BE UNDER THIS HIBERNATING ULTRA-SLOTH!
SNOOORE...
MEANWHILE...
GO AHEAD AND ORDER PIZZA, EEGA! I'LL SOON ARRIVE WITH ULTRAPOD-5! SAY, THAT RHYMED!
...
WOOOSH
HA! HA!
ER...I TAKE BACK THAT COUPLET!

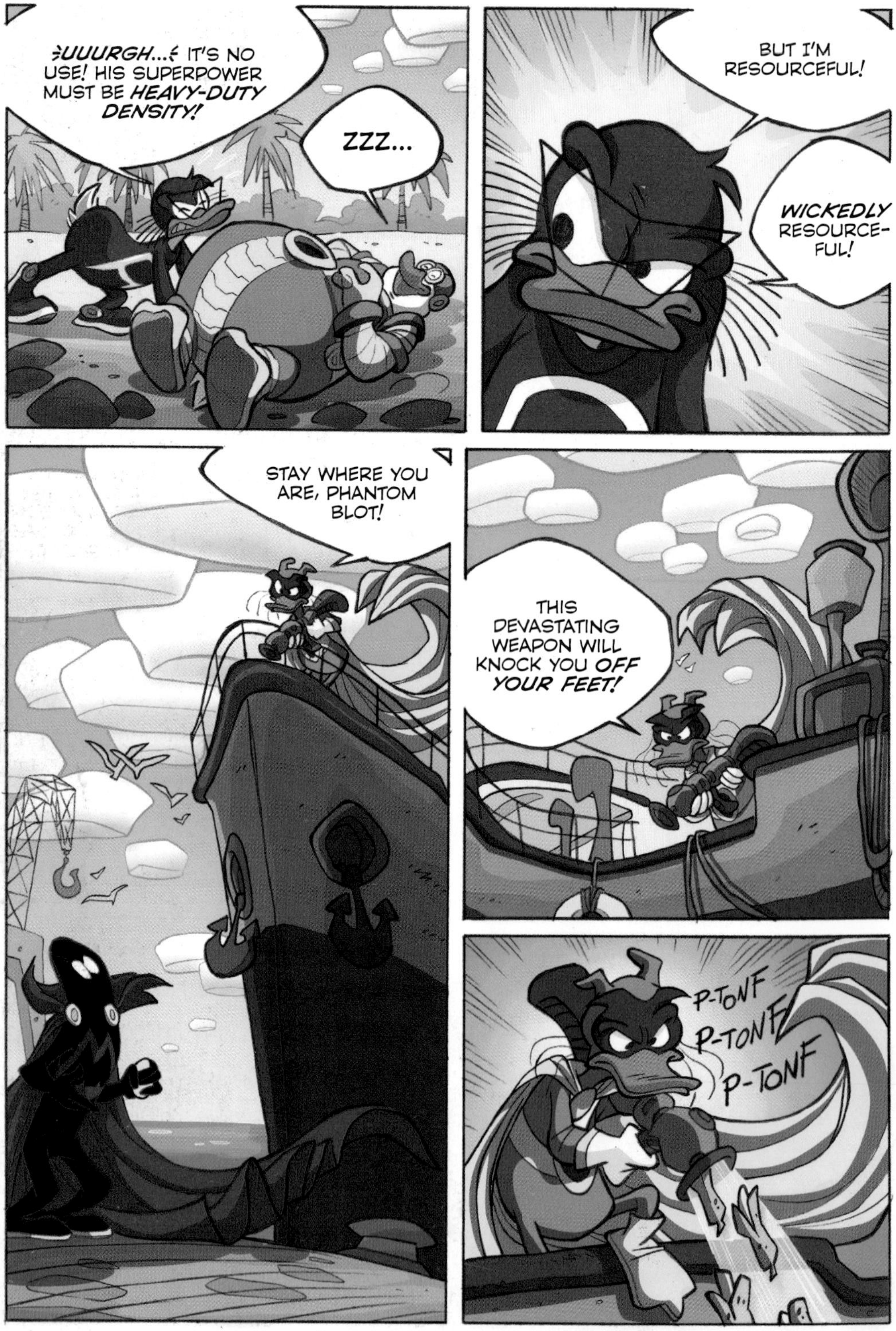
UUURGH... IT'S NO USE! HIS SUPERPOWER MUST BE HEAVY-DUTY DENSITY!
ZZZ...
BUT I'M RESOURCEFUL!
WICKEDLY RESOURCEFUL!
STAY WHERE YOU ARE, PHANTOM BLOT!
THIS DEVASTATING WEAPON WILL KNOCK YOU OFF YOUR FEET!
P-TONF
P-TONF
P-TONF

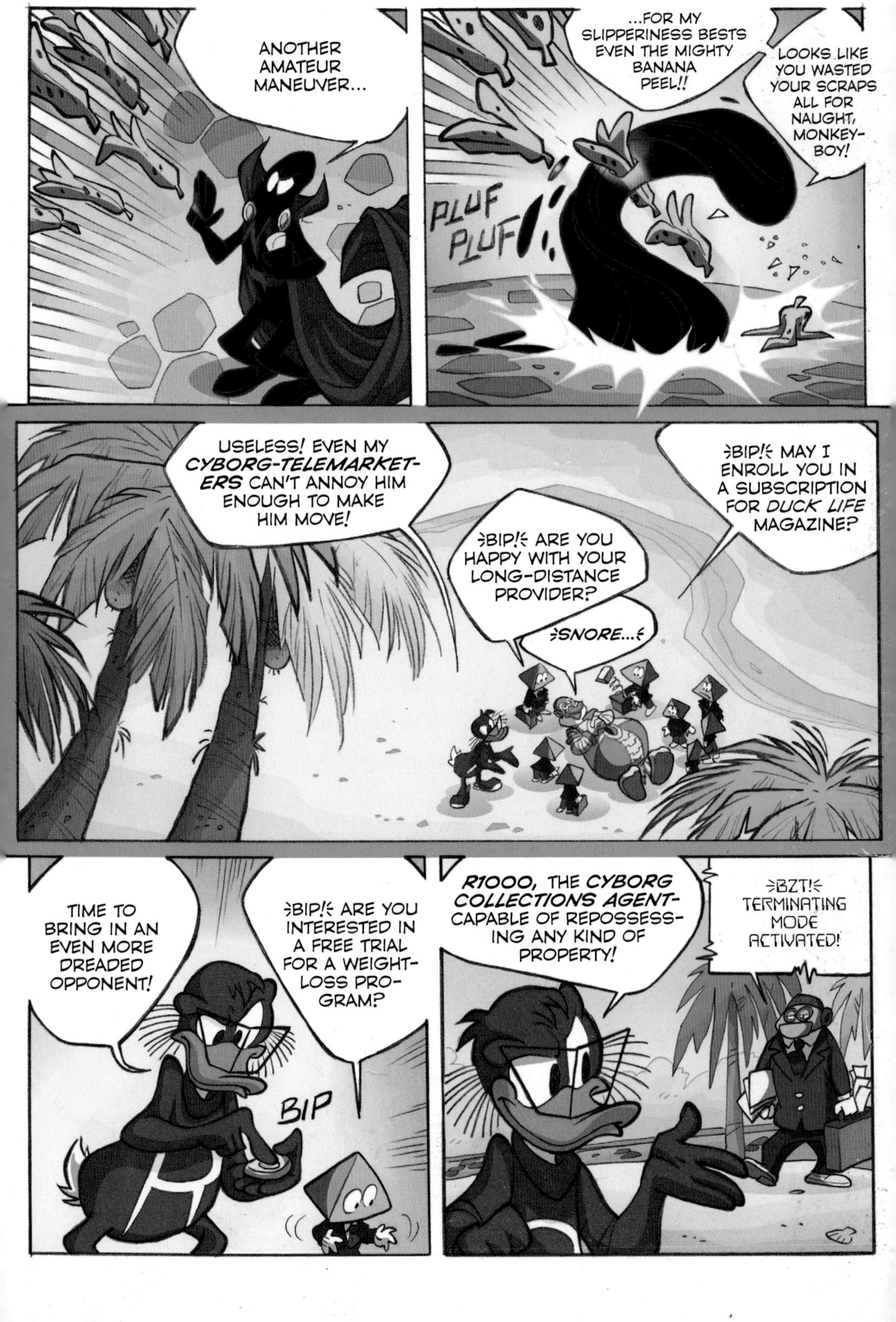
ANOTHER AMATEUR MANEUVER...
...FOR MY SLIPPERINESS BESTS EVEN THE MIGHTY BANANA PEEL!!
LOOKS LIKE YOU WASTED YOUR SCRAPS ALL FOR NAUGHT, MONKEY-BOY!
PLUF PLUF
USELESS! EVEN MY CYBORG-TELEMARKETERS CAN'T ANNOY HIM ENOUGH TO MAKE HIM MOVE!
BIP! ARE YOU HAPPY WITH YOUR LONG-DISTANCE PROVIDER?
BIP! MAY I ENROLL YOU IN A SUBSCRIPTION FOR DUCK LIFE MAGAZINE?
SNORE...
TIME TO BRING IN AN EVEN MORE DREADED OPPONENT!
BIP! ARE YOU INTERESTED IN A FREE TRIAL FOR A WEIGHT-LOSS PROGRAM?
BIP
R1000, THE CYBORG COLLECTIONS AGENT-CAPABLE OF REPOSSESSING ANY KIND OF PROPERTY!
BZT! TERMINATING MODE ACTIVATED!

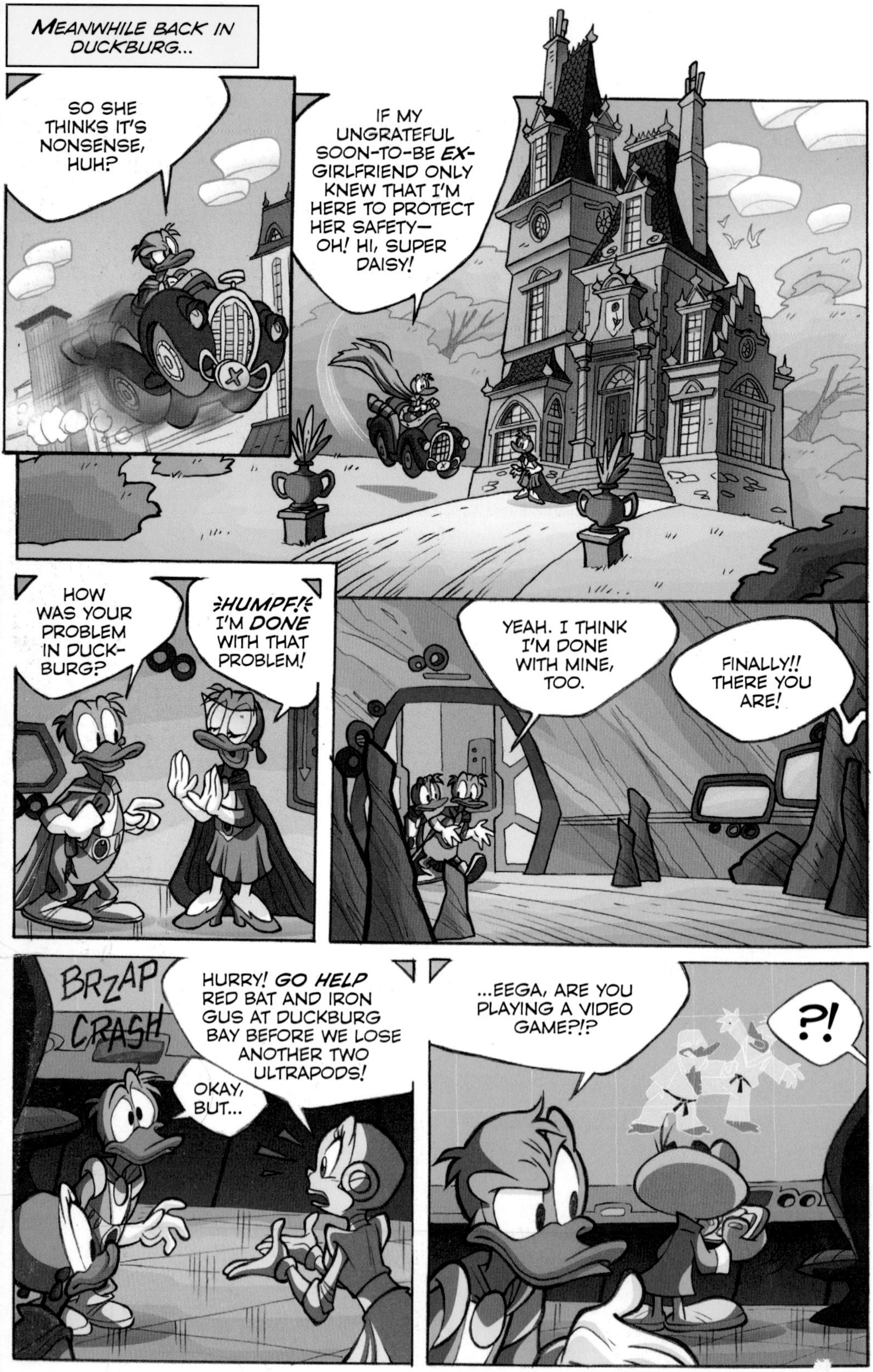
MEANWHILE BACK IN DUCKBURG...
SO SHE THINKS IT'S NONSENSE, HUH?
IF MY UNGRATEFUL SOON-TO-BE EX-GIRLFRIEND ONLY KNEW THAT I'M HERE TO PROTECT HER SAFETY— OH! HI, SUPER DAISY!
HOW WAS YOUR PROBLEM IN DUCK-BURG?
HUMPF! I'M DONE WITH THAT PROBLEM!
YEAH. I THINK I'M DONE WITH MINE, TOO.
FINALLY!! THERE YOU ARE!
BRZAP
CRASH
HURRY! GO HELP RED BAT AND IRON GUS AT DUCKBURG BAY BEFORE WE LOSE ANOTHER TWO ULTRAPODS!
OKAY, BUT...
...EEGA, ARE YOU PLAYING A VIDEO GAME?!?
?!

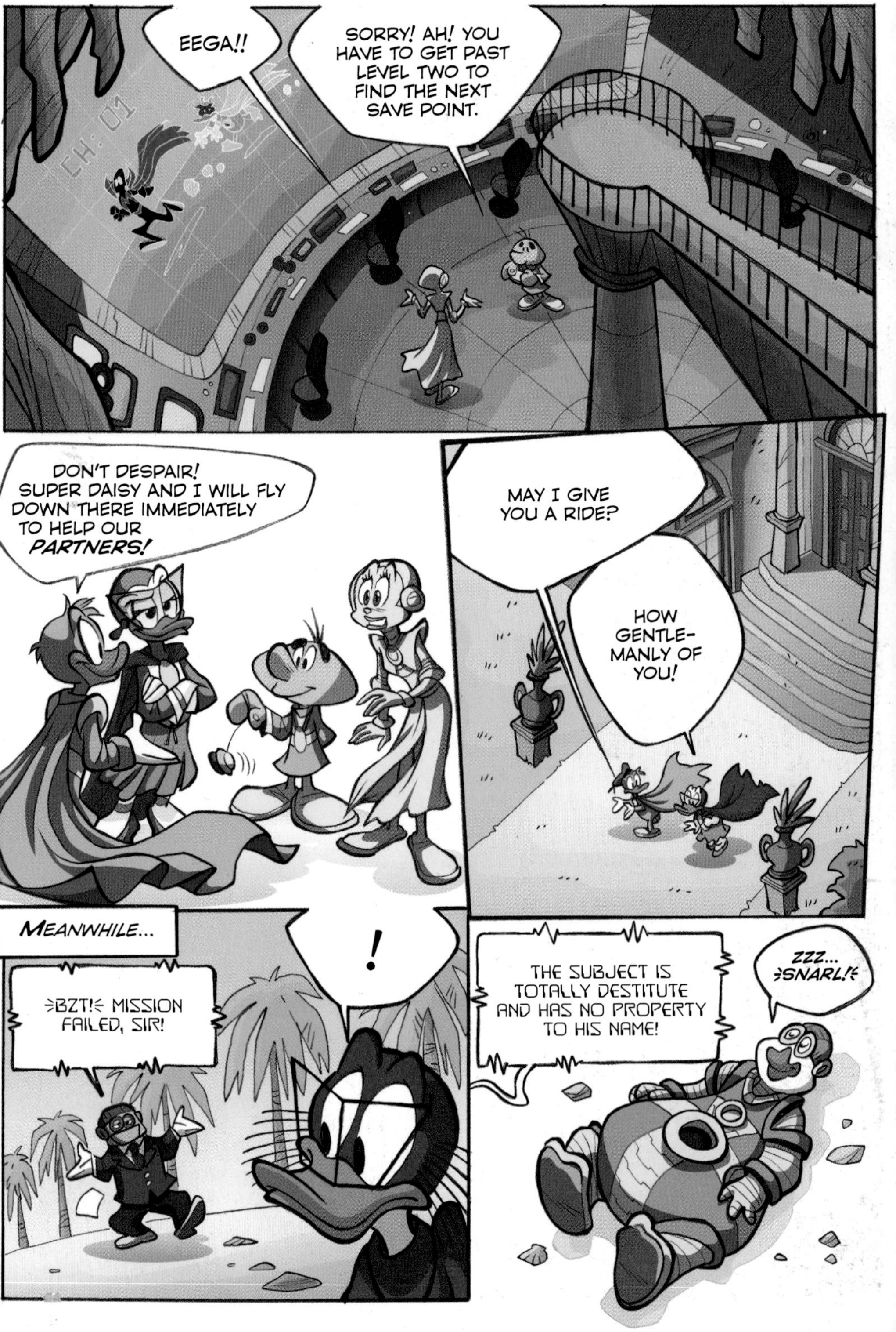

EEGA!!
SORRY! AH! YOU HAVE TO GET PAST LEVEL TWO TO FIND THE NEXT SAVE POINT.
DON'T DESPAIR! SUPER DAISY AND I WILL FLY DOWN THERE IMMEDIATELY TO HELP OUR PARTNERS!
MAY I GIVE YOU A RIDE?
HOW GENTLE-MANLY OF YOU!
MEANWHILE...
!
>BZT!< MISSION FAILED, SIR!
THE SUBJECT IS TOTALLY DESTITUTE AND HAS NO PROPERTY TO HIS NAME!
ZZZ... >SNARL!<

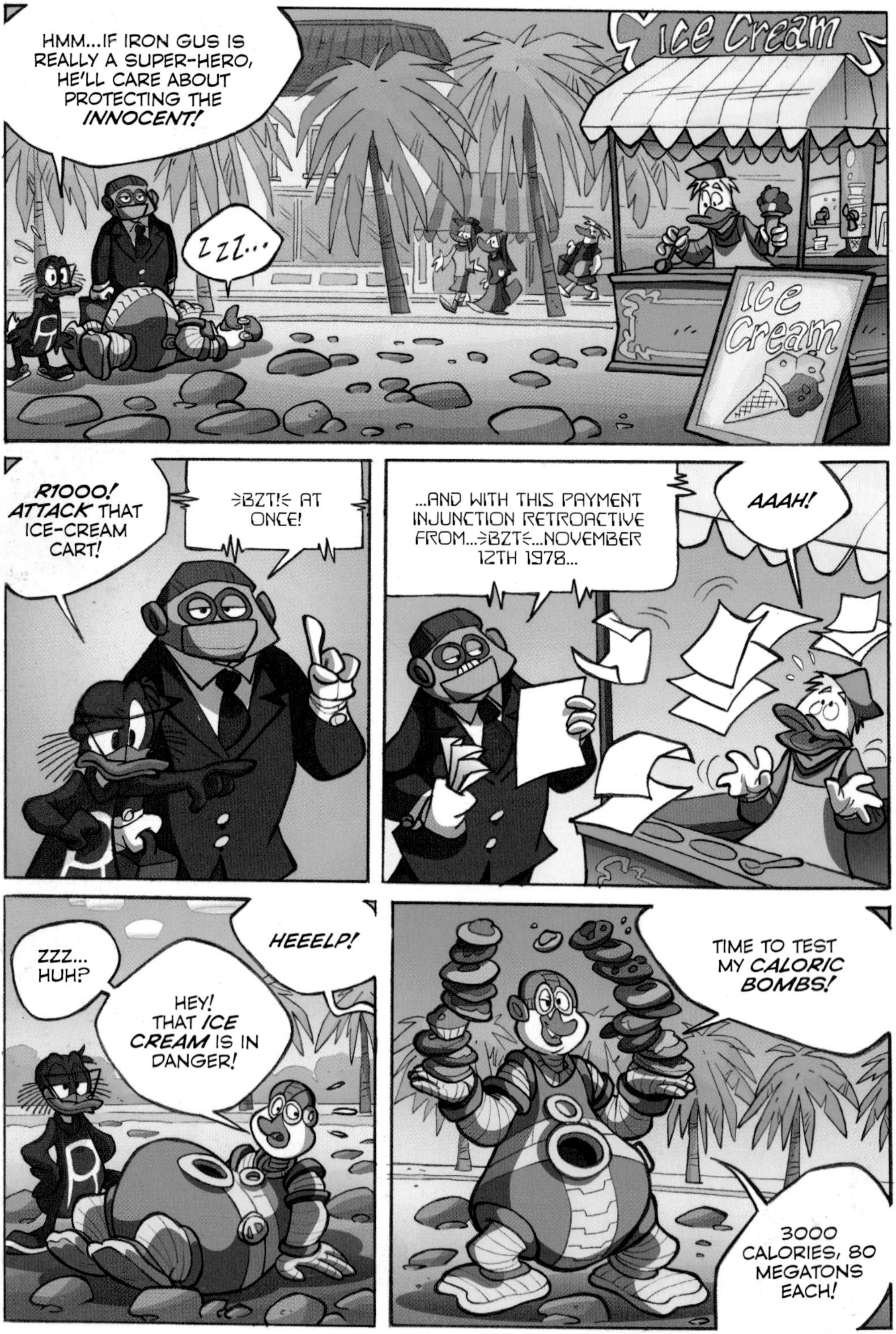
Ice Cream
HMM...IF IRON GUS IS REALLY A SUPER-HERO, HE'LL CARE ABOUT PROTECTING THE *INNOCENT!*
ZZZ...
Ice Cream
R1000! ATTACK THAT ICE-CREAM CART!
≥BZT!≤ AT ONCE!
...AND WITH THIS PAYMENT INJUNCTION RETROACTIVE FROM...≥BZT≤...NOVEMBER 12TH 1978...
AAAH!
ZZZ... HUH?
HEEELP!
HEY! THAT *ICE CREAM* IS IN DANGER!
TIME TO TEST MY *CALORIC BOMBS!*
3000 CALORIES, 80 MEGATONS EACH!

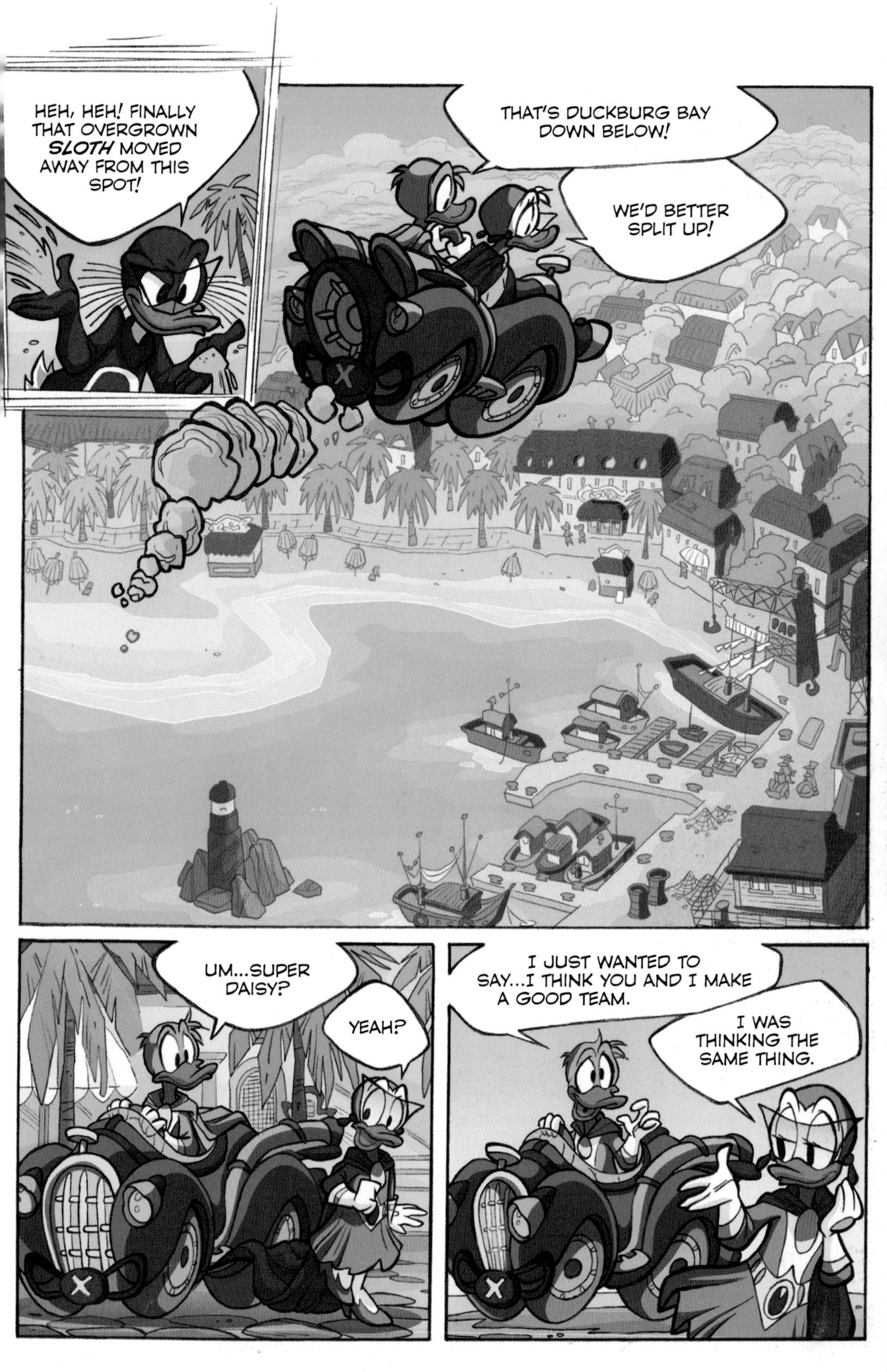
HEH, HEH! FINALLY THAT OVERGROWN SLOTH MOVED AWAY FROM THIS SPOT!
THAT'S DUCKBURG BAY DOWN BELOW!
WE'D BETTER SPLIT UP!
UM...SUPER DAISY?
YEAH?
I JUST WANTED TO SAY...I THINK YOU AND I MAKE A GOOD TEAM.
I WAS THINKING THE SAME THING.

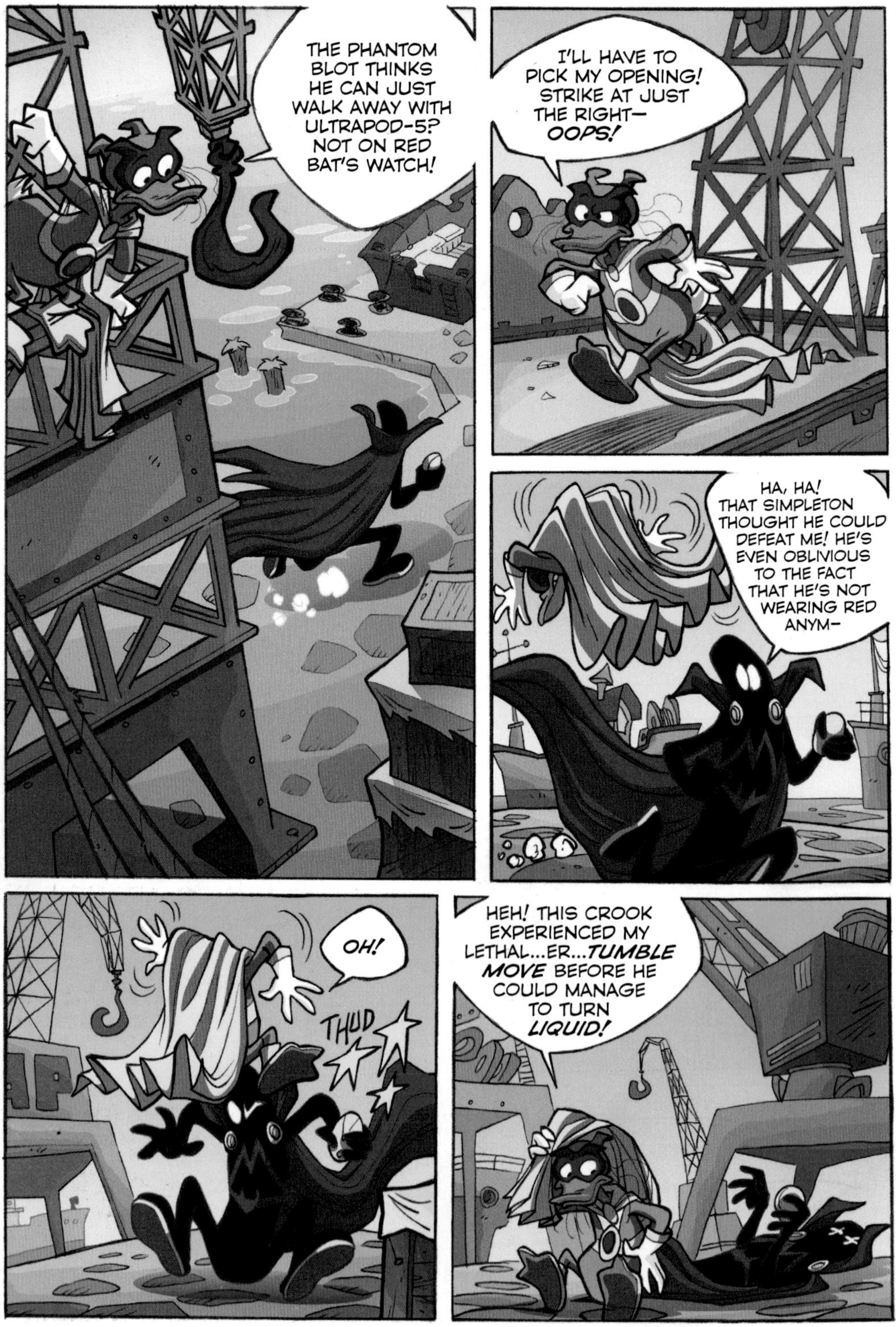
THE PHANTOM BLOT THINKS HE CAN JUST WALK AWAY WITH ULTRAPOD-5? NOT ON RED BAT'S WATCH!
I'LL HAVE TO PICK MY OPENING! STRIKE AT JUST THE RIGHT— OOPS!
HA, HA! THAT SIMPLETON THOUGHT HE COULD DEFEAT ME! HE'S EVEN OBLIVIOUS TO THE FACT THAT HE'S NOT WEARING RED ANYM—
OH!
THUD
HEH! THIS CROOK EXPERIENCED MY LETHAL...ER...TUMBLE MOVE BEFORE HE COULD MANAGE TO TURN LIQUID!

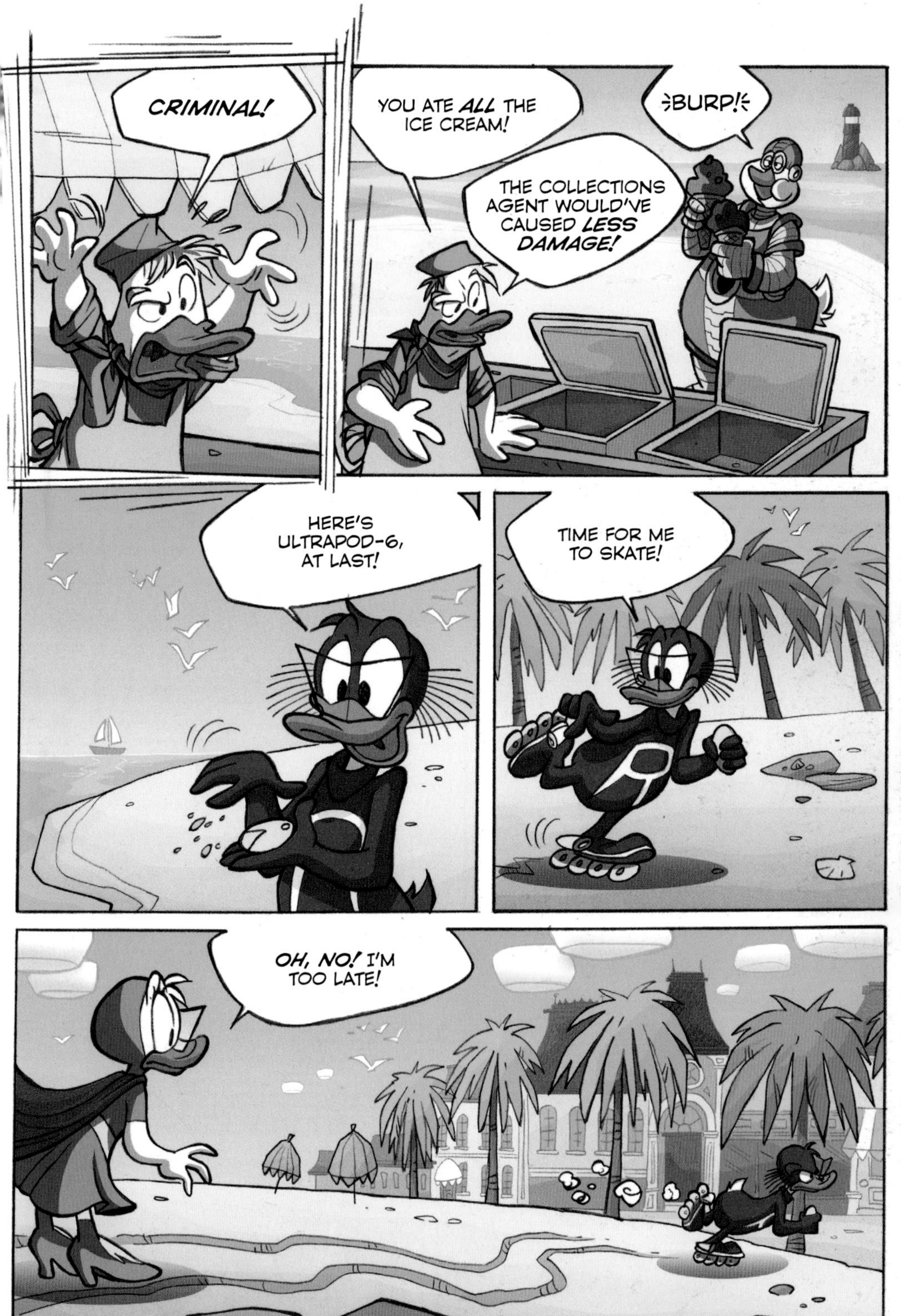
CRIMINAL!
YOU ATE ALL THE ICE CREAM!
THE COLLECTIONS AGENT WOULD'VE CAUSED LESS DAMAGE!
BURP!
HERE'S ULTRAPOD-6, AT LAST!
TIME FOR ME TO SKATE!
OH, NO! I'M TOO LATE!

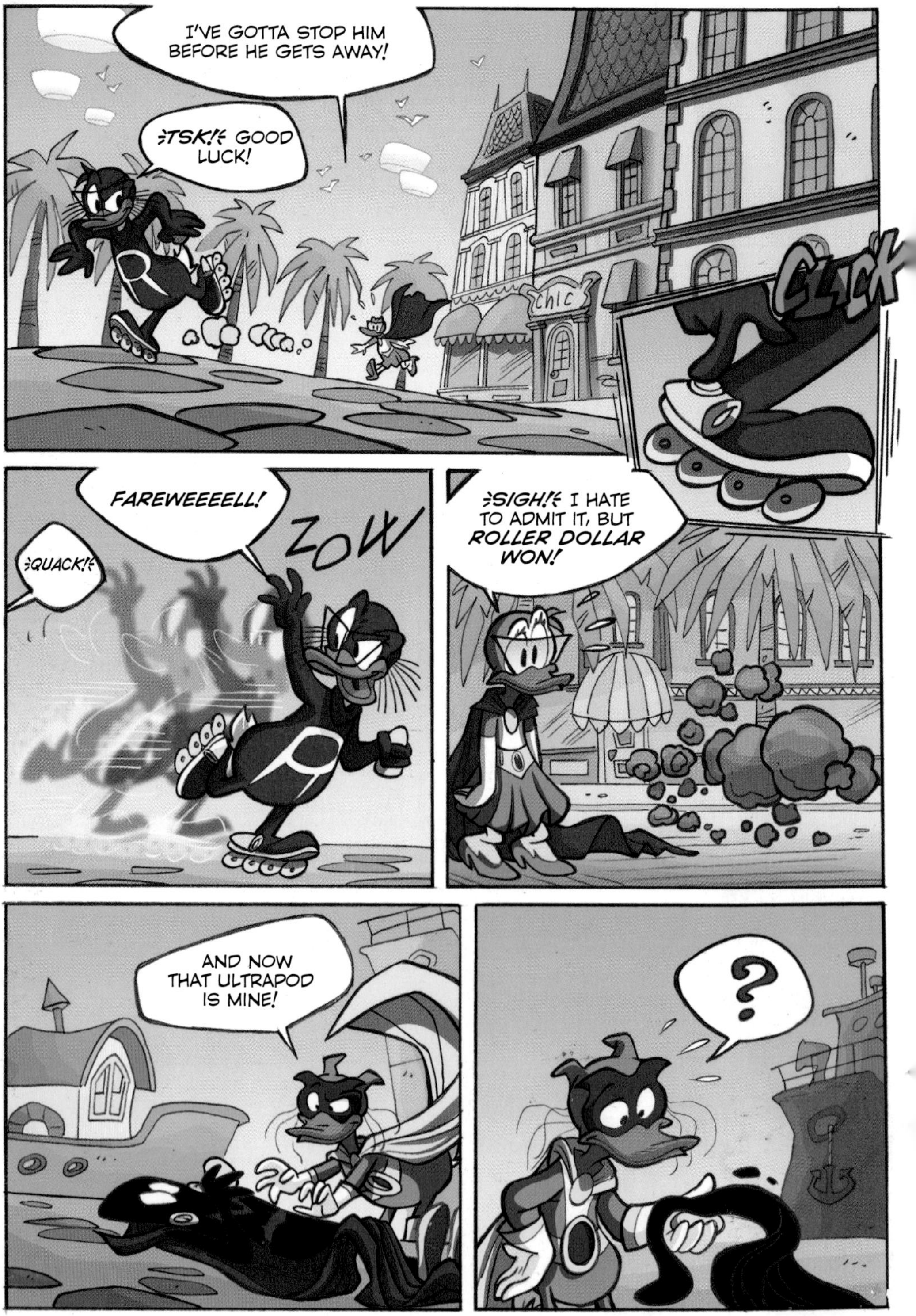
I'VE GOTTA STOP HIM BEFORE HE GETS AWAY!
TSK! GOOD LUCK!
CLICK
FAREWEEEELL!
QUACK!
ZOW
SIGH! I HATE TO ADMIT IT, BUT ROLLER DOLLAR WON!
CHIC
AND NOW THAT ULTRAPOD IS MINE!
?

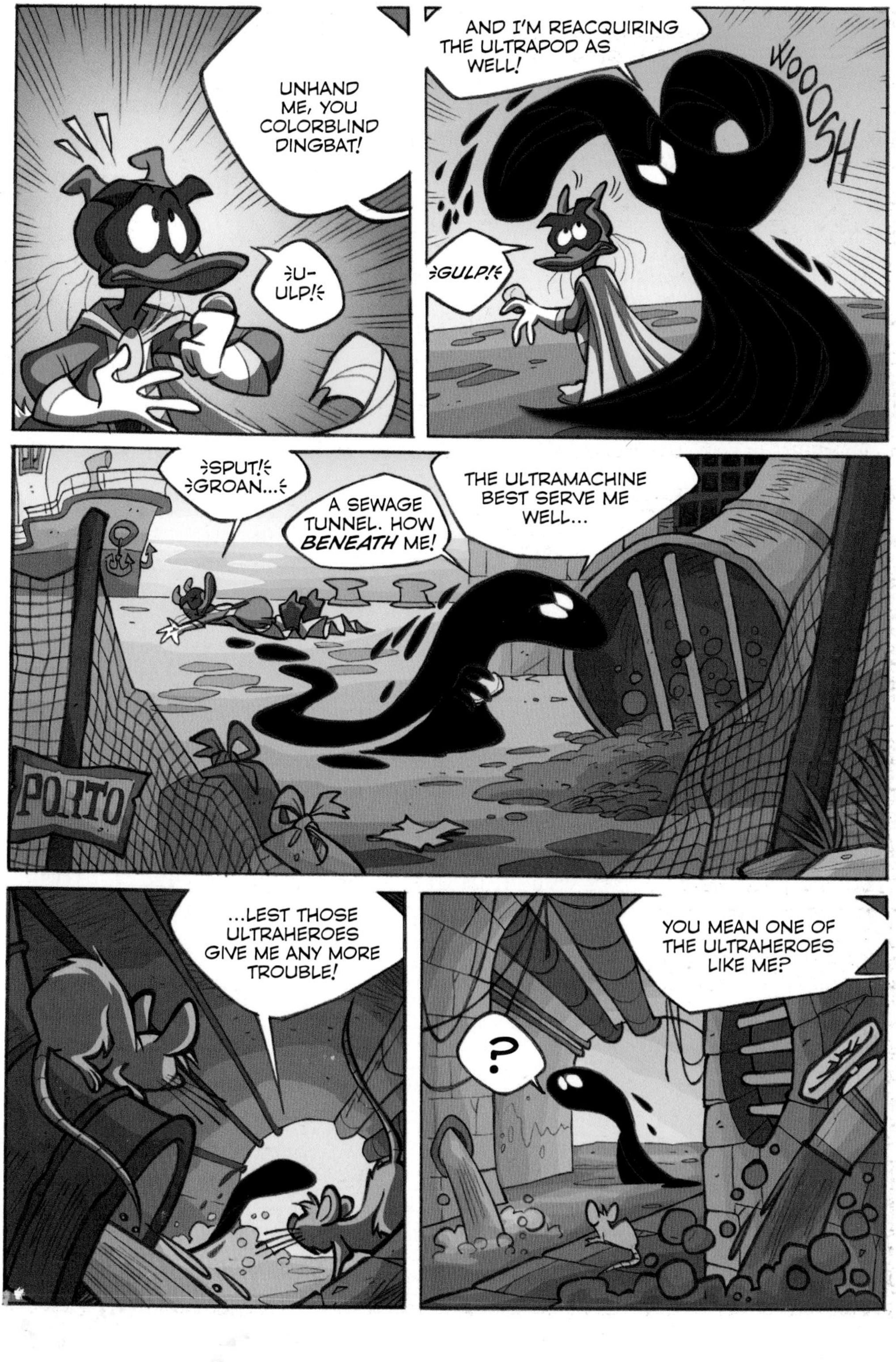
UNHAND ME, YOU COLORBLIND DINGBAT!
U-ULP!
AND I'M REACQUIRING THE ULTRAPOD AS WELL!
WOOOSH
GULP!
SPUT! GROAN...
A SEWAGE TUNNEL. HOW *BENEATH* ME!
THE ULTRAMACHINE BEST SERVE ME WELL...
PORTO
...LEST THOSE ULTRAHEROES GIVE ME ANY MORE TROUBLE!
YOU MEAN ONE OF THE ULTRAHEROES LIKE ME?
?

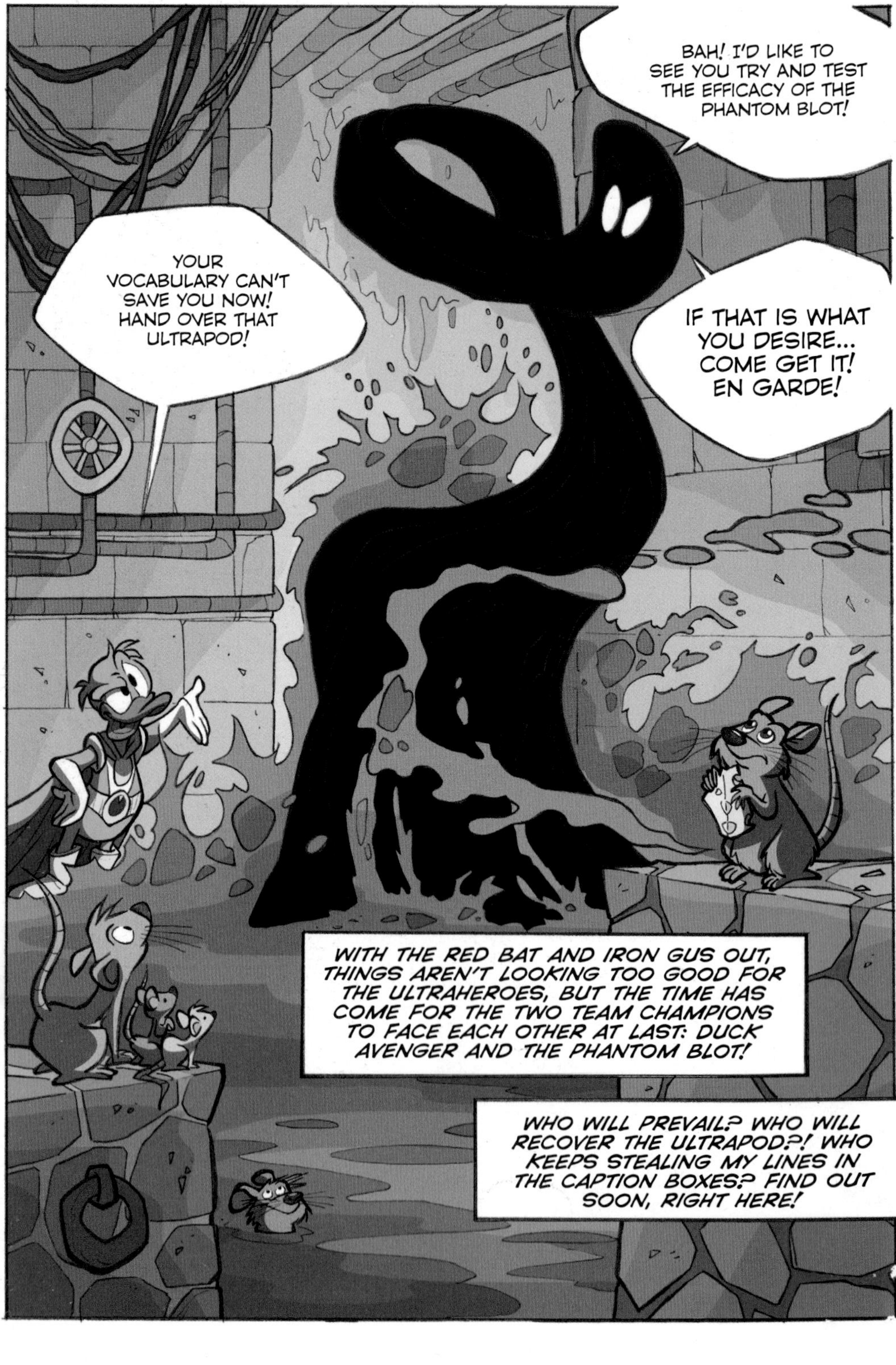
BAH! I'D LIKE TO SEE YOU TRY AND TEST THE EFFICACY OF THE PHANTOM BLOT!
YOUR VOCABULARY CAN'T SAVE YOU NOW! HAND OVER THAT ULTRAPOD!
IF THAT IS WHAT YOU DESIRE... COME GET IT! EN GARDE!
WITH THE RED BAT AND IRON GUS OUT, THINGS AREN'T LOOKING TOO GOOD FOR THE ULTRAHEROES, BUT THE TIME HAS COME FOR THE TWO TEAM CHAMPIONS TO FACE EACH OTHER AT LAST: DUCK AVENGER AND THE PHANTOM BLOT!
WHO WILL PREVAIL? WHO WILL RECOVER THE ULTRAPOD?! WHO KEEPS STEALING MY LINES IN THE CAPTION BOXES? FIND OUT SOON, RIGHT HERE!

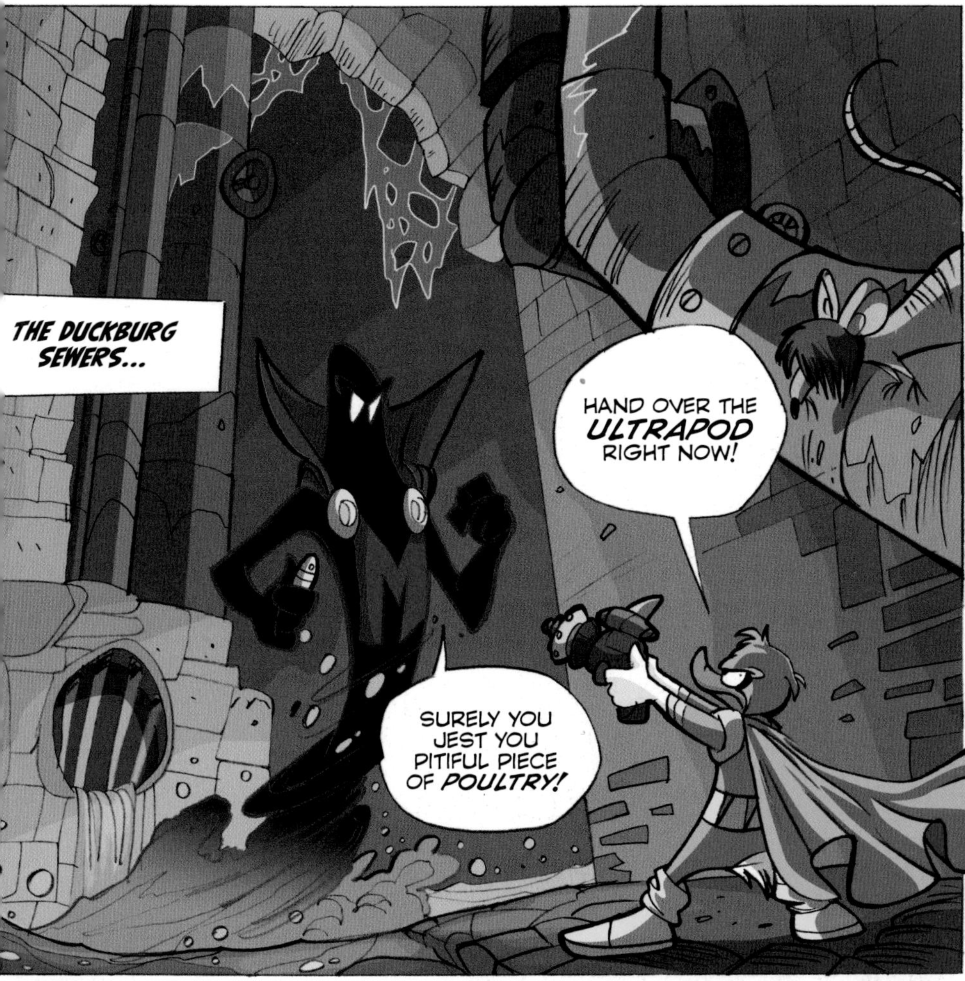
THE DUCKBURG SEWERS...
HAND OVER THE ULTRAPOD RIGHT NOW!
SURELY YOU JEST YOU PITIFUL PIECE OF POULTRY!

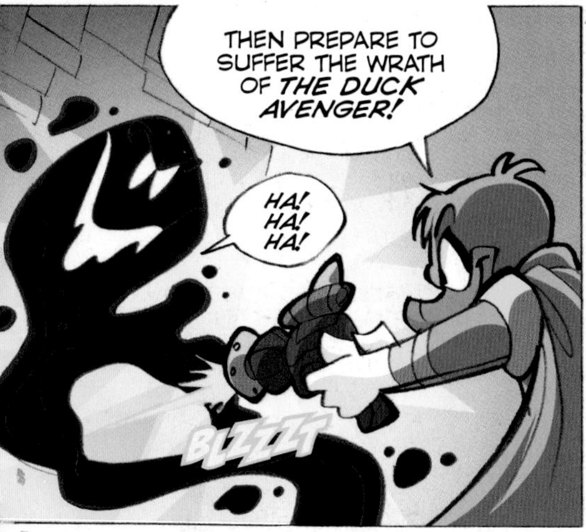
THEN PREPARE TO SUFFER THE WRATH OF THE DUCK AVENGER!
HA! HA! HA!
BLZZZT

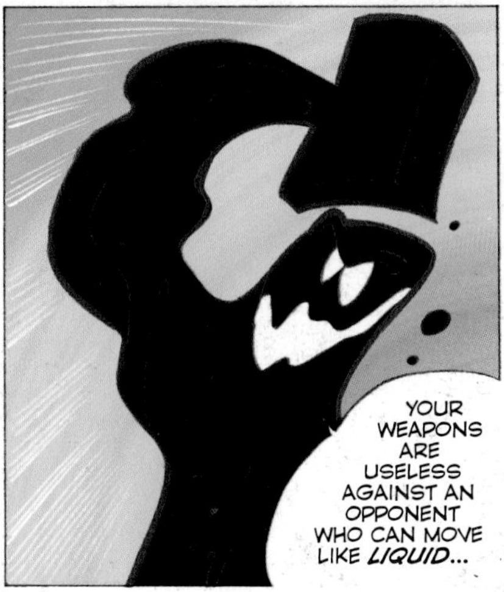
YOUR WEAPONS ARE USELESS AGAINST AN OPPONENT WHO CAN MOVE LIKE LIQUID...

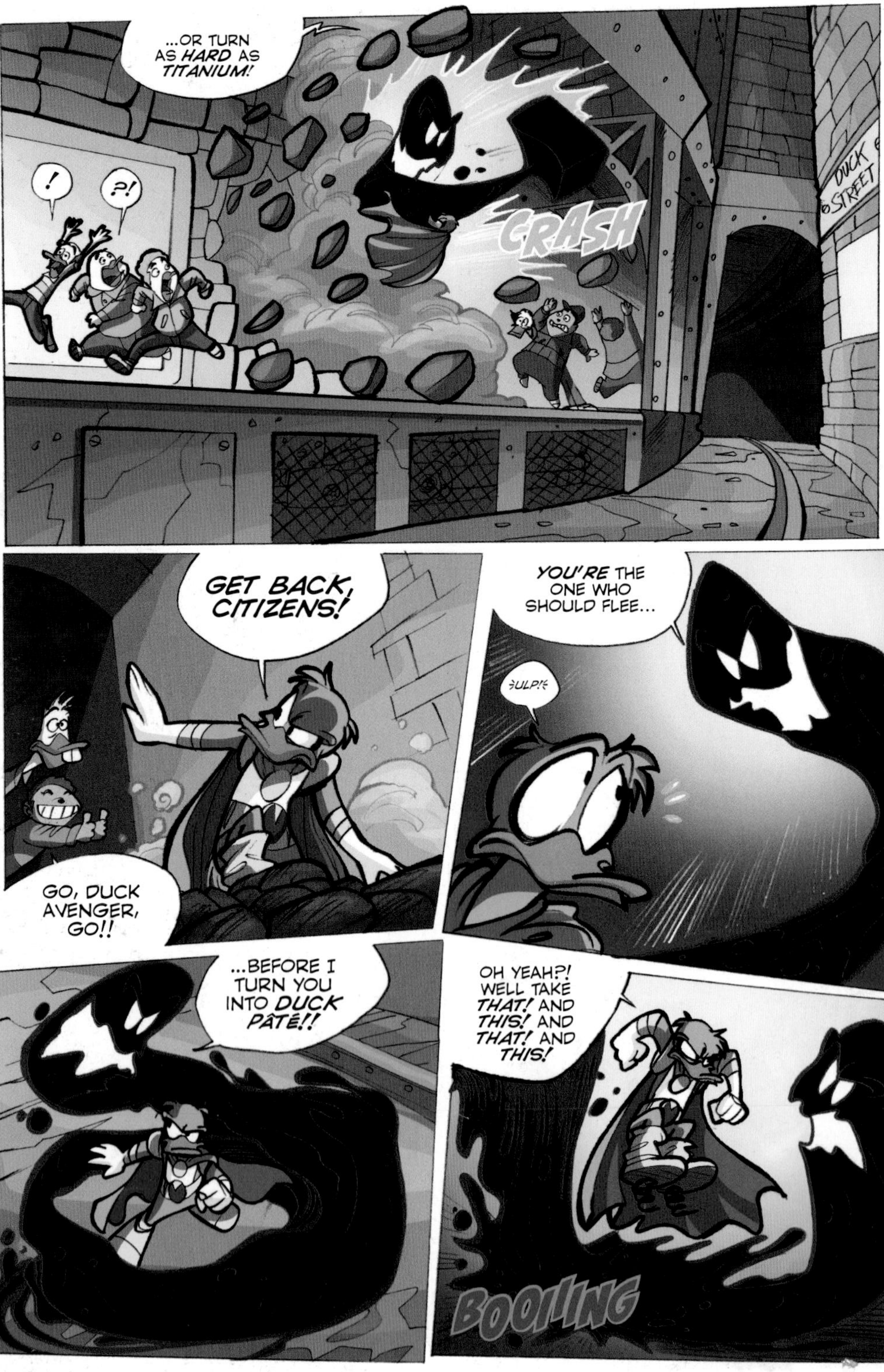
...OR TURN AS HARD AS TITANIUM!
!
?!
CRASH
DUCK STREET
GET BACK, CITIZENS!
GO, DUCK AVENGER, GO!!
YOU'RE THE ONE WHO SHOULD FLEE...
GULP!
...BEFORE I TURN YOU INTO DUCK PÂTÉ!!
OH YEAH?! WELL TAKE THAT! AND THIS! AND THAT! AND THIS!
BOOIIING

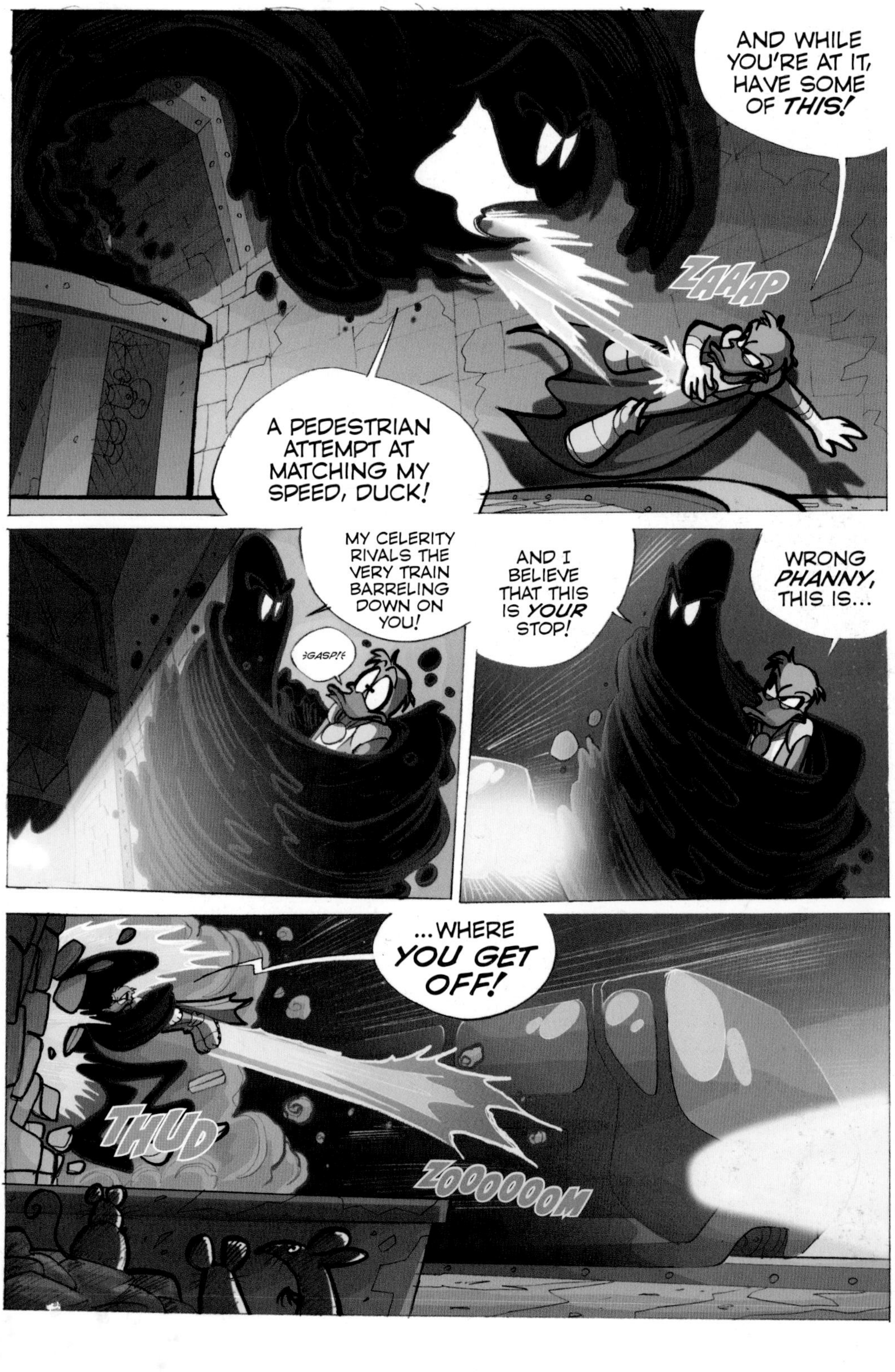
AND WHILE YOU'RE AT IT, HAVE SOME OF THIS!
ZAAAP
A PEDESTRIAN ATTEMPT AT MATCHING MY SPEED, DUCK!
MY CELERITY RIVALS THE VERY TRAIN BARRELING DOWN ON YOU!
GASP!
AND I BELIEVE THAT THIS IS YOUR STOP!
WRONG PHANNY, THIS IS...
...WHERE YOU GET OFF!
THUD
ZOOOOOOM

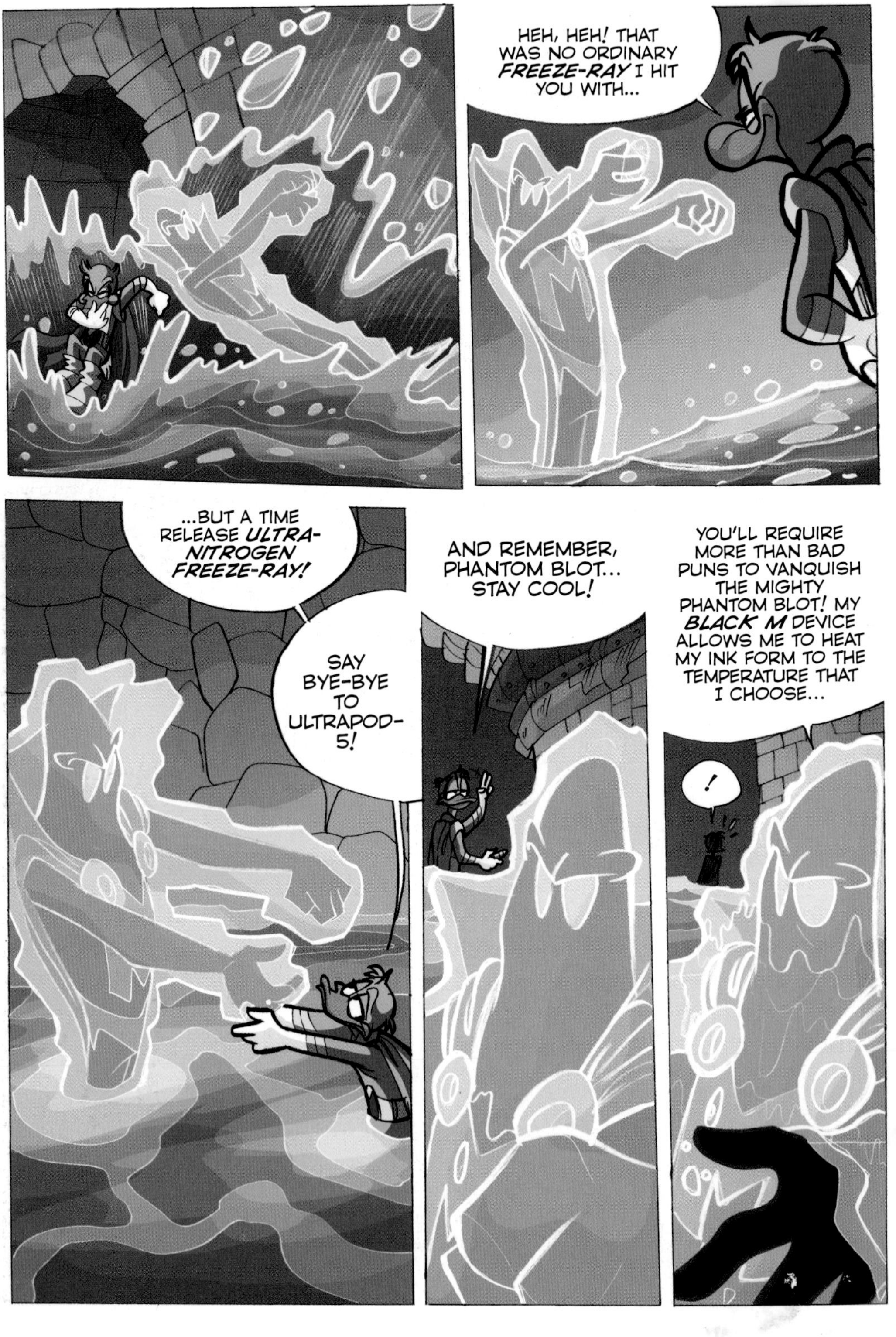
HEH, HEH! THAT WAS NO ORDINARY FREEZE-RAY I HIT YOU WITH...
...BUT A TIME RELEASE ULTRA-NITROGEN FREEZE-RAY!
SAY BYE-BYE TO ULTRAPOD-5!
AND REMEMBER, PHANTOM BLOT... STAY COOL!
YOU'LL REQUIRE MORE THAN BAD PUNS TO VANQUISH THE MIGHTY PHANTOM BLOT! MY BLACK M DEVICE ALLOWS ME TO HEAT MY INK FORM TO THE TEMPERATURE THAT I CHOOSE...
!

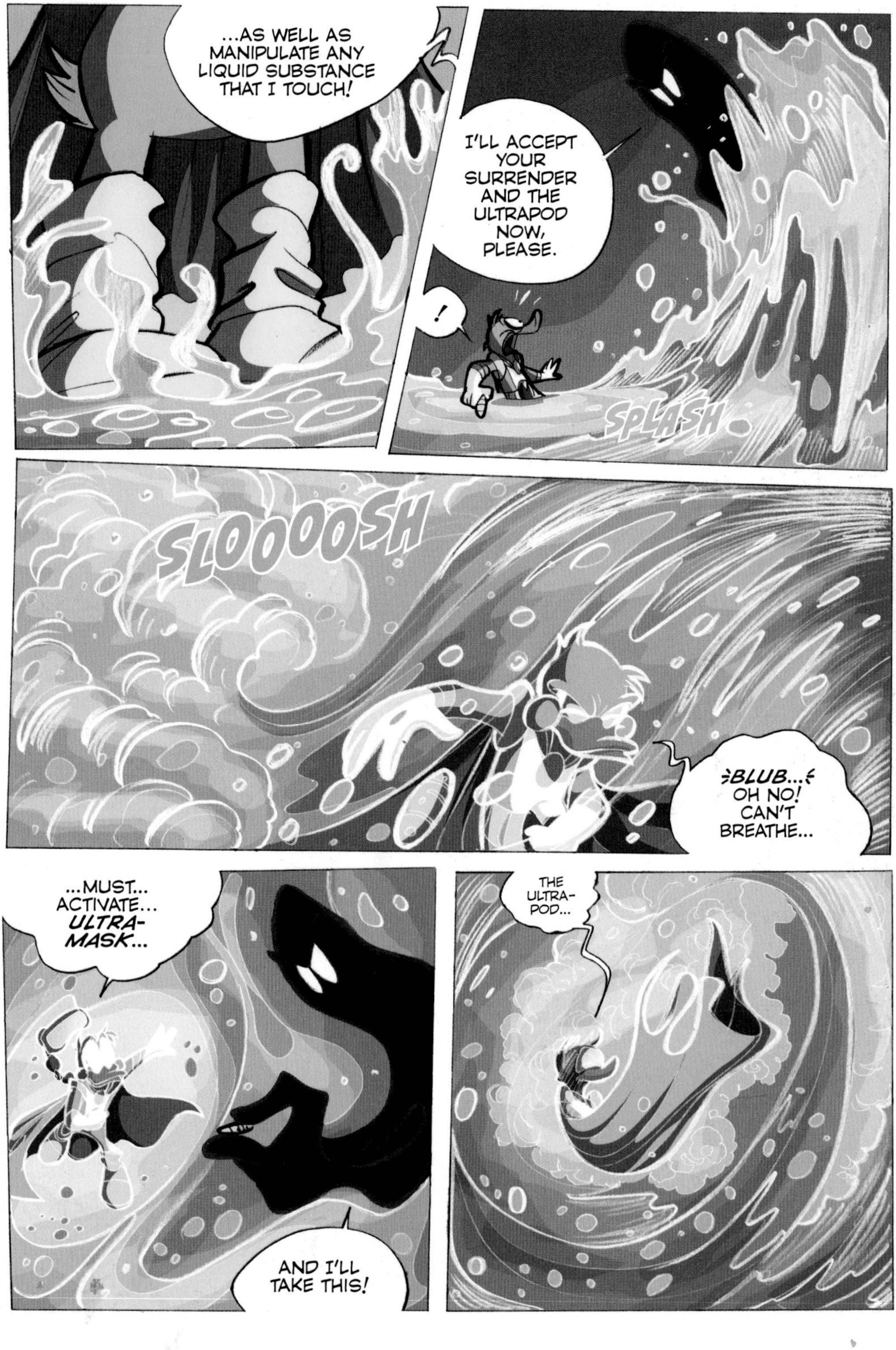
...AS WELL AS MANIPULATE ANY LIQUID SUBSTANCE THAT I TOUCH!
I'LL ACCEPT YOUR SURRENDER AND THE ULTRAPOD NOW, PLEASE.
!
SPLASH
SLOOOOSH
BLUB... OH NO! CAN'T BREATHE...
...MUST... ACTIVATE... ULTRA-MASK...
AND I'LL TAKE THIS!
THE ULTRA-POD...

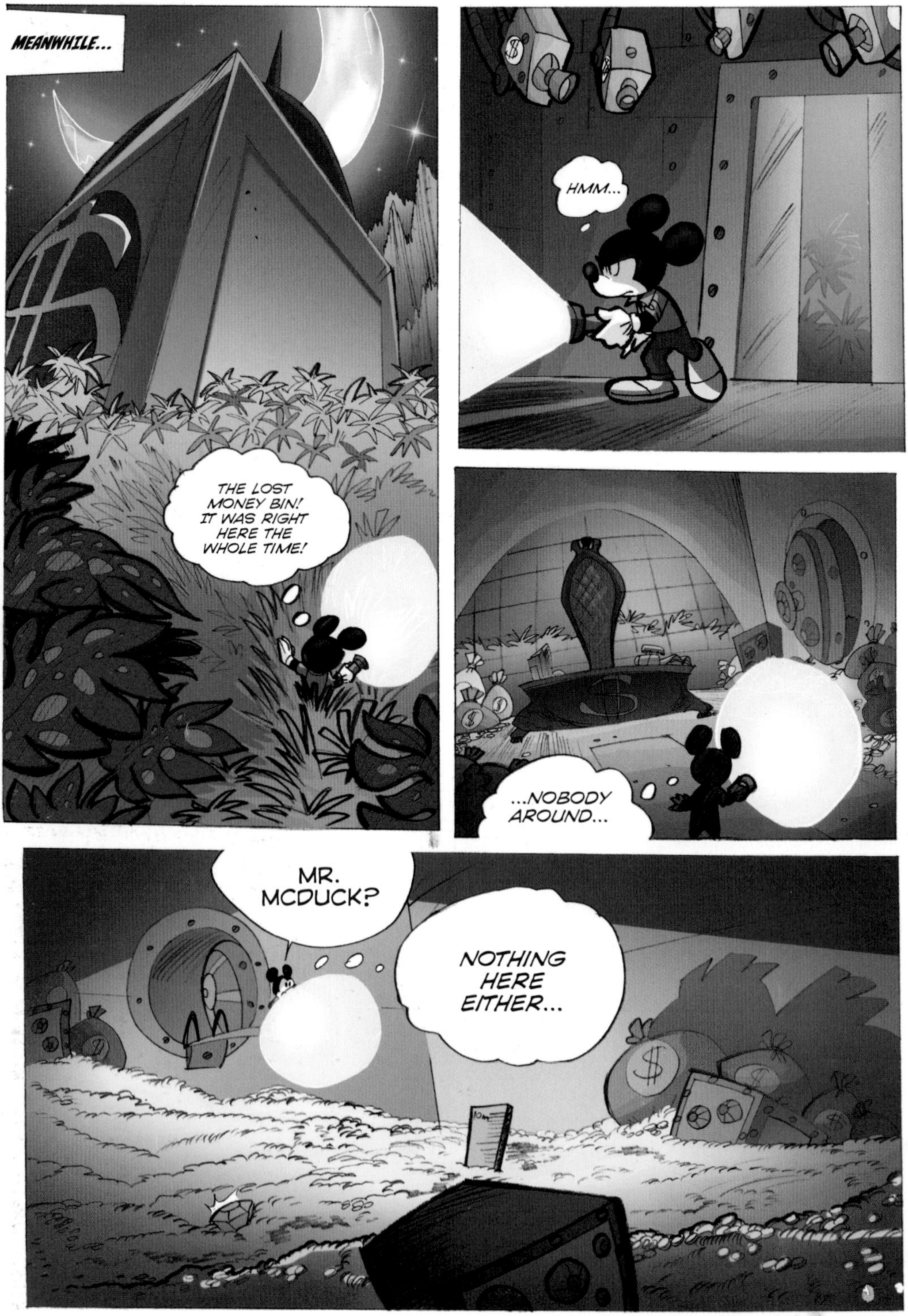
MEANWHILE...
THE LOST MONEY BIN! IT WAS RIGHT HERE THE WHOLE TIME!
HMM...
...NOBODY AROUND...
MR. MCDUCK?
NOTHING HERE EITHER...

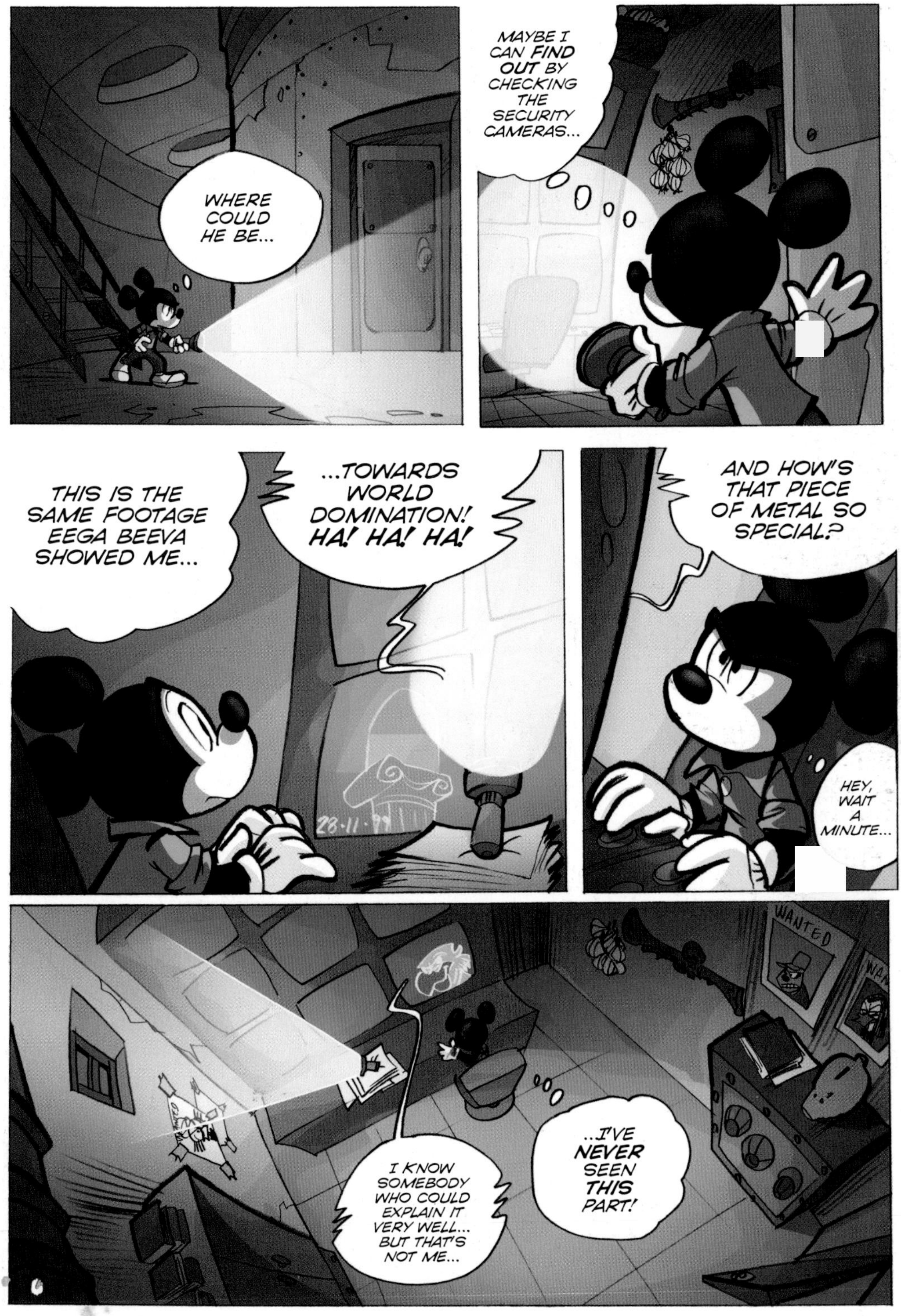
WHERE COULD HE BE...
MAYBE I CAN FIND OUT BY CHECKING THE SECURITY CAMERAS...
THIS IS THE SAME FOOTAGE EEGA BEEVA SHOWED ME...
...TOWARDS WORLD DOMINATION! HA! HA! HA!
28-11-99
AND HOW'S THAT PIECE OF METAL SO SPECIAL?
HEY, WAIT A MINUTE...
WANTED
I KNOW SOMEBODY WHO COULD EXPLAIN IT VERY WELL... BUT THAT'S NOT ME...
..I'VE NEVER SEEN THIS PART!

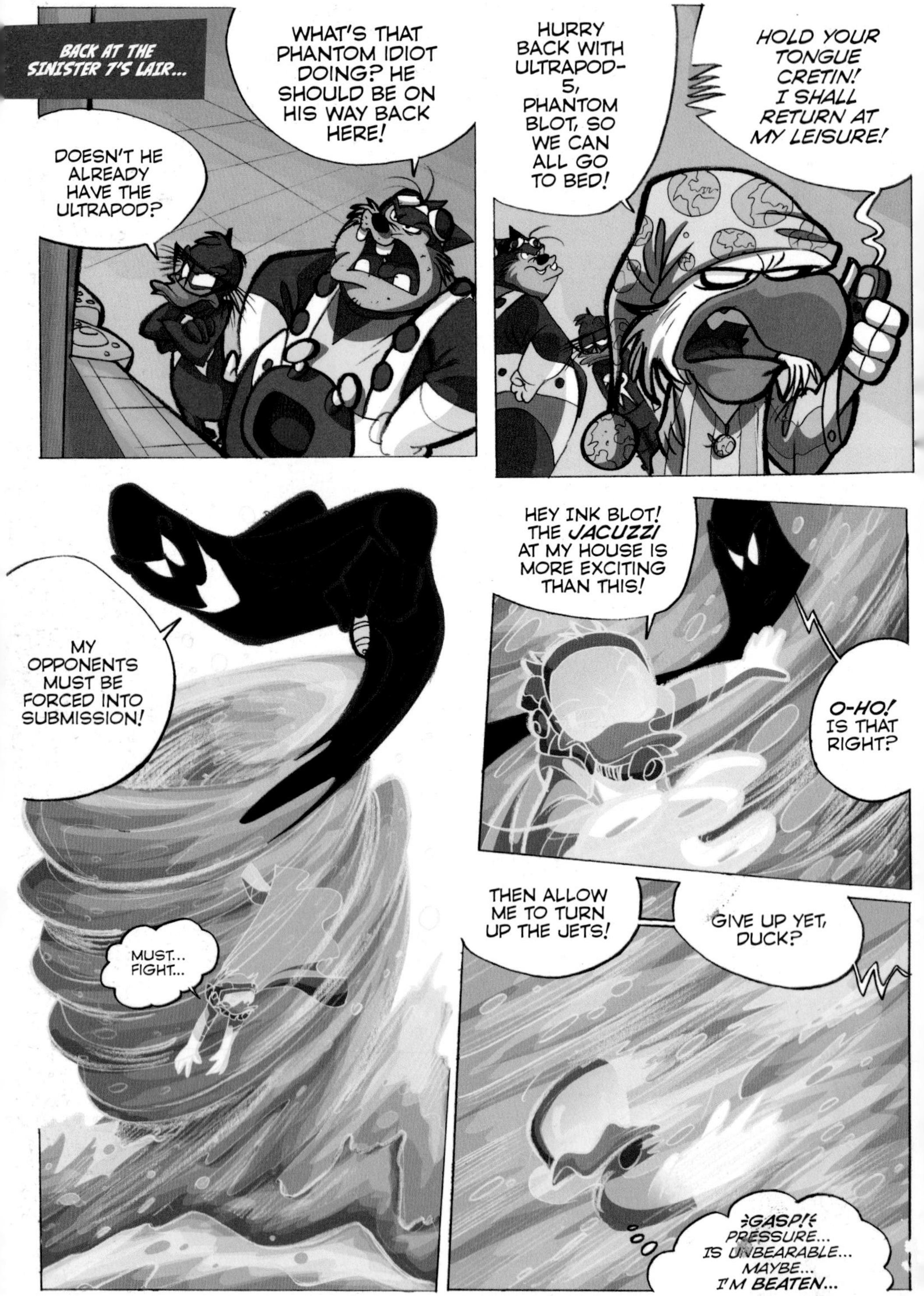
BACK AT THE SINISTER 7'S LAIR...
WHAT'S THAT PHANTOM IDIOT DOING? HE SHOULD BE ON HIS WAY BACK HERE!
DOESN'T HE ALREADY HAVE THE ULTRAPOD?
HURRY BACK WITH ULTRAPOD-5, PHANTOM BLOT, SO WE CAN ALL GO TO BED!
HOLD YOUR TONGUE CRETIN! I SHALL RETURN AT MY LEISURE!
MY OPPONENTS MUST BE FORCED INTO SUBMISSION!
MUST... FIGHT...
HEY INK BLOT! THE JACUZZI AT MY HOUSE IS MORE EXCITING THAN THIS!
O-HO! IS THAT RIGHT?
THEN ALLOW ME TO TURN UP THE JETS!
GIVE UP YET, DUCK?
GASP! PRESSURE... IS UNBEARABLE... MAYBE... I'M BEATEN...

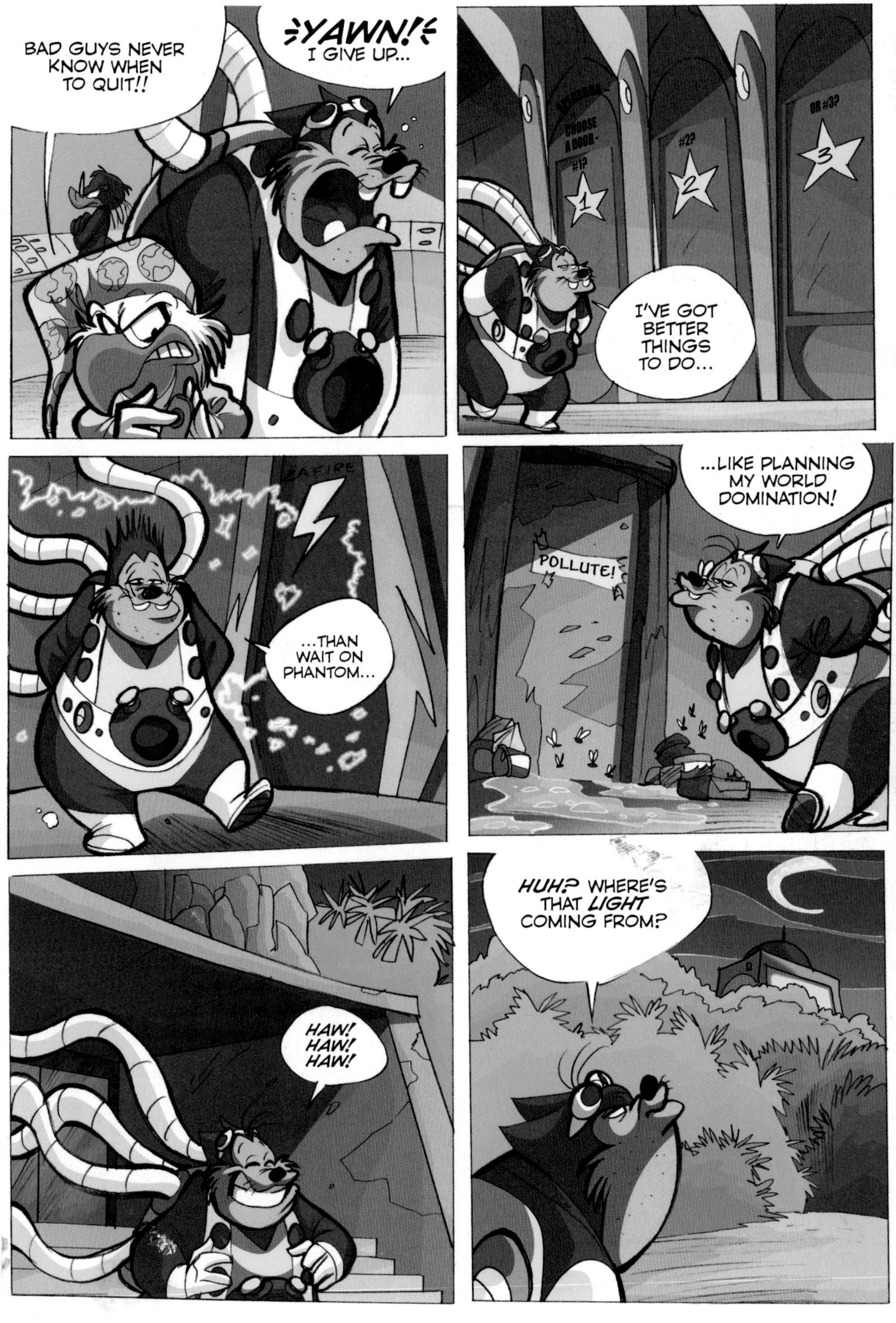
BAD GUYS NEVER KNOW WHEN TO QUIT!!
YAWN!
I GIVE UP...
CHOOSE A DOOR -
#1?
#2?
OR #3?
1
2
3
I'VE GOT BETTER THINGS TO DO...
ZAFIRE
...THAN WAIT ON PHANTOM...
...LIKE PLANNING MY WORLD DOMINATION!
POLLUTE!
HAW! HAW! HAW!
HUH? WHERE'S THAT LIGHT COMING FROM?

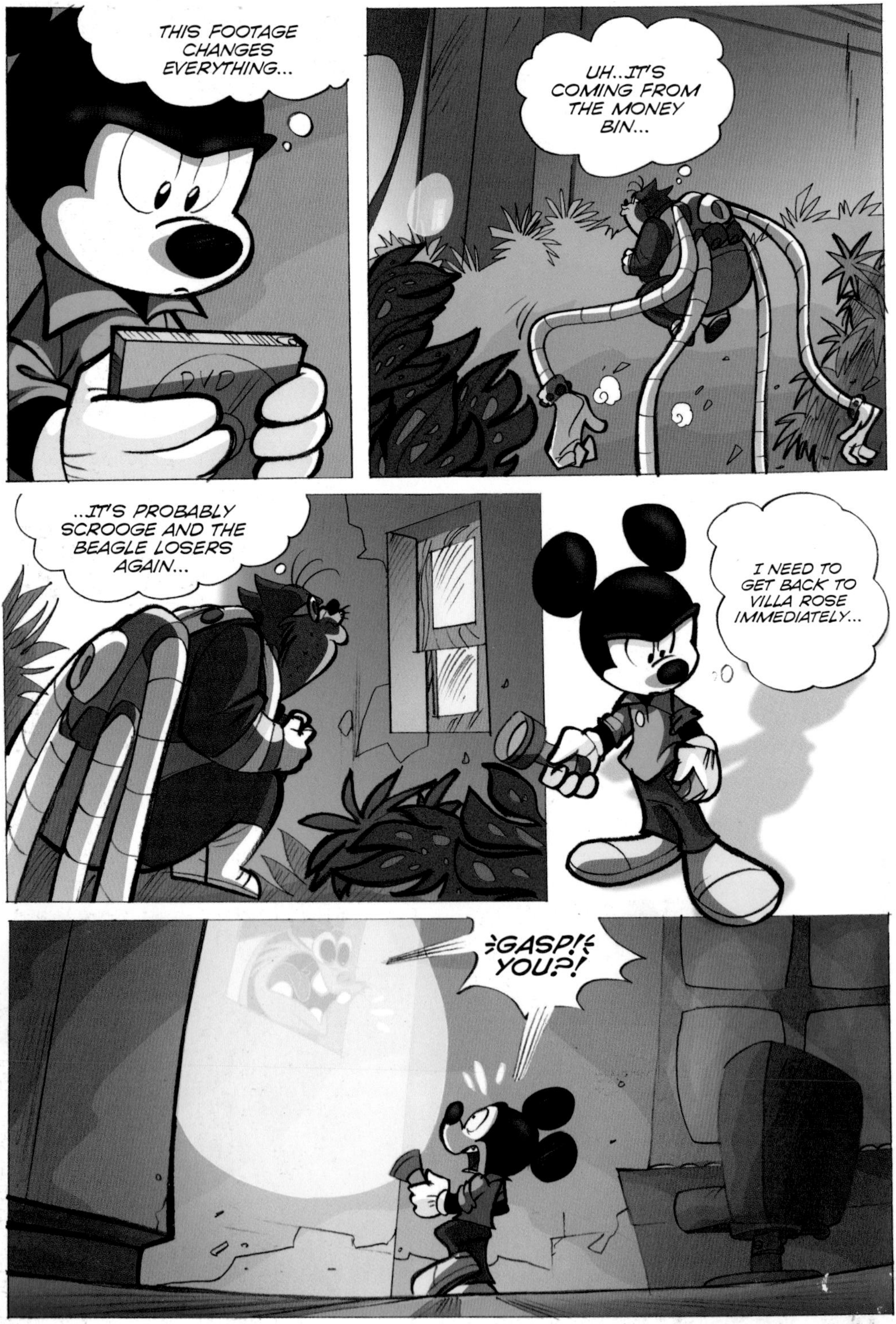
THIS FOOTAGE CHANGES EVERYTHING...
DVD
UH..IT'S COMING FROM THE MONEY BIN...
...IT'S PROBABLY SCROOGE AND THE BEAGLE LOSERS AGAIN...
I NEED TO GET BACK TO VILLA ROSE IMMEDIATELY...
GASP! YOU?!

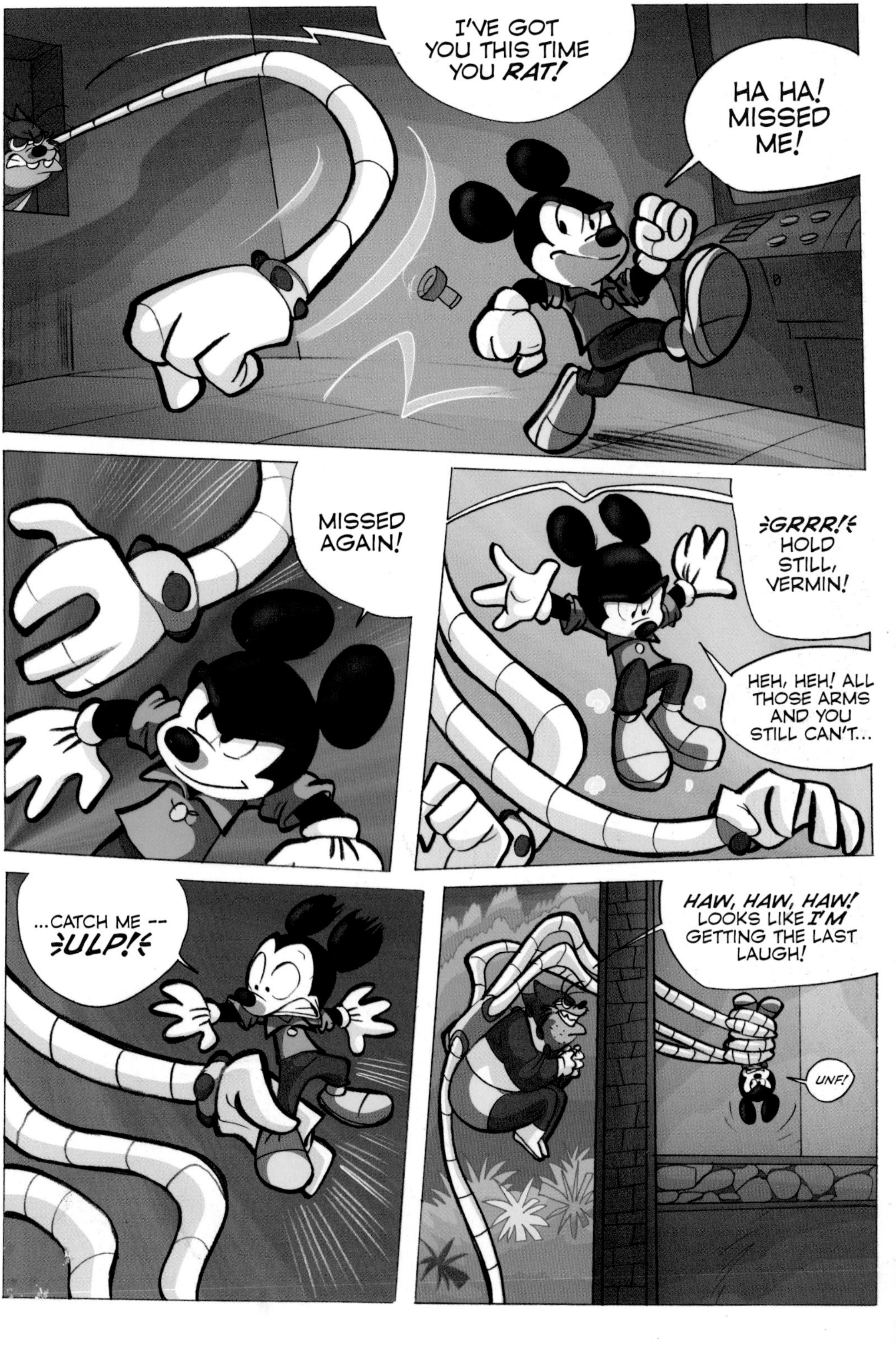
I'VE GOT YOU THIS TIME YOU RAT!
HA HA! MISSED ME!
MISSED AGAIN!
GRRR! HOLD STILL, VERMIN!
HEH, HEH! ALL THOSE ARMS AND YOU STILL CAN'T...
...CATCH ME -- ULP!
HAW, HAW, HAW! LOOKS LIKE I'M GETTING THE LAST LAUGH!
UNF!

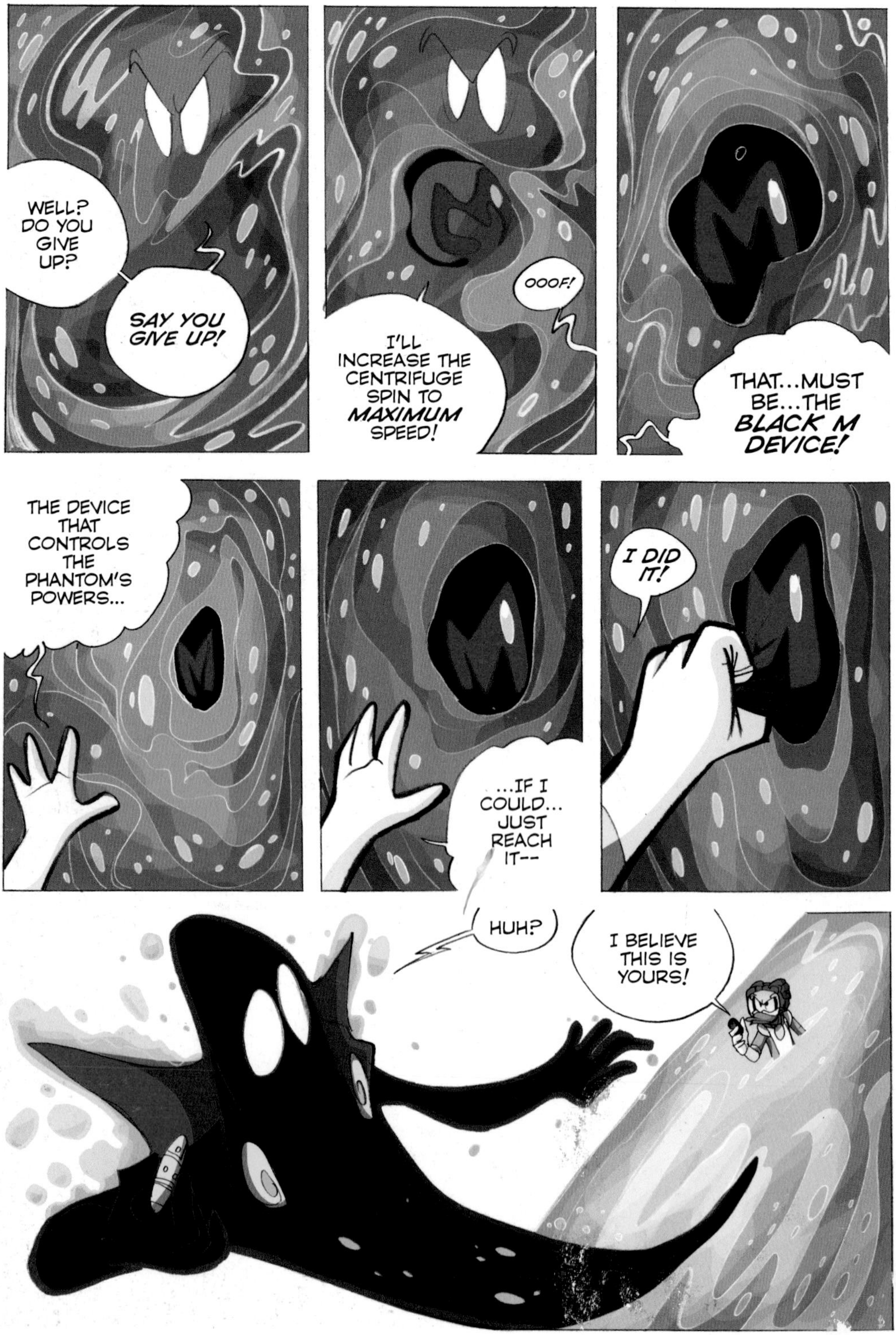
WELL? DO YOU GIVE UP?
SAY YOU GIVE UP!
OOOF!
I'LL INCREASE THE CENTRIFUGE SPIN TO MAXIMUM SPEED!
THAT...MUST BE...THE BLACK M DEVICE!
THE DEVICE THAT CONTROLS THE PHANTOM'S POWERS...
...IF I COULD... JUST REACH IT--
I DID IT!
HUH?
I BELIEVE THIS IS YOURS!

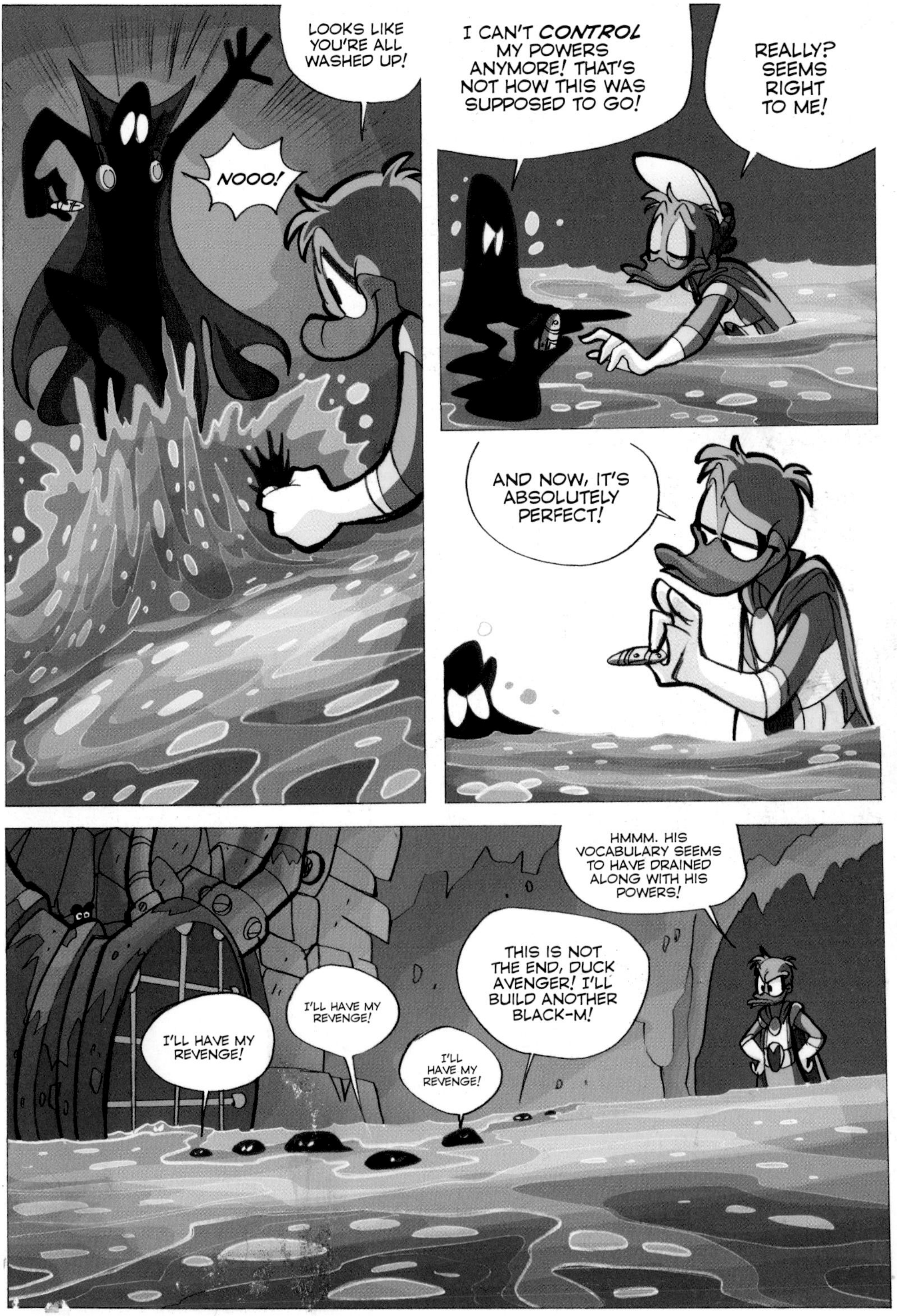
LOOKS LIKE YOU'RE ALL WASHED UP!
NOOO!
I CAN'T *CONTROL* MY POWERS ANYMORE! THAT'S NOT HOW THIS WAS SUPPOSED TO GO!
REALLY? SEEMS RIGHT TO ME!
AND NOW, IT'S ABSOLUTELY PERFECT!
HMMM. HIS VOCABULARY SEEMS TO HAVE DRAINED ALONG WITH HIS POWERS!
THIS IS NOT THE END, DUCK AVENGER! I'LL BUILD ANOTHER BLACK-M!
I'LL HAVE MY REVENGE!
I'LL HAVE MY REVENGE!
I'LL HAVE MY REVENGE!

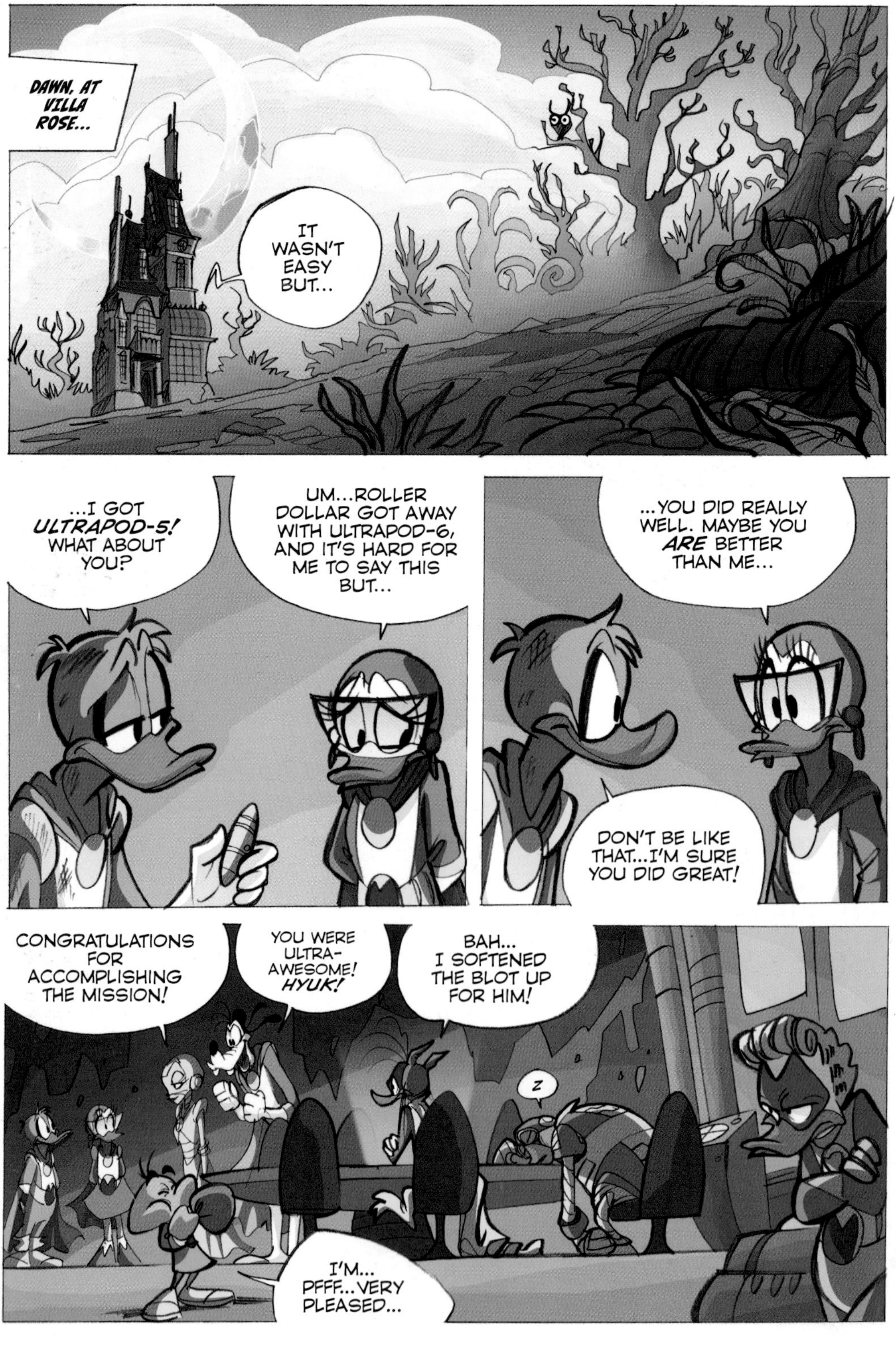
DAWN, AT VILLA ROSE...
IT WASN'T EASY BUT...
...I GOT ULTRAPOD-5! WHAT ABOUT YOU?
UM...ROLLER DOLLAR GOT AWAY WITH ULTRAPOD-6, AND IT'S HARD FOR ME TO SAY THIS BUT...
...YOU DID REALLY WELL. MAYBE YOU ARE BETTER THAN ME...
DON'T BE LIKE THAT...I'M SURE YOU DID GREAT!
CONGRATULATIONS FOR ACCOMPLISHING THE MISSION!
YOU WERE ULTRA-AWESOME! HYUK!
BAH... I SOFTENED THE BLOT UP FOR HIM!
Z
I'M... PFFF...VERY PLEASED...

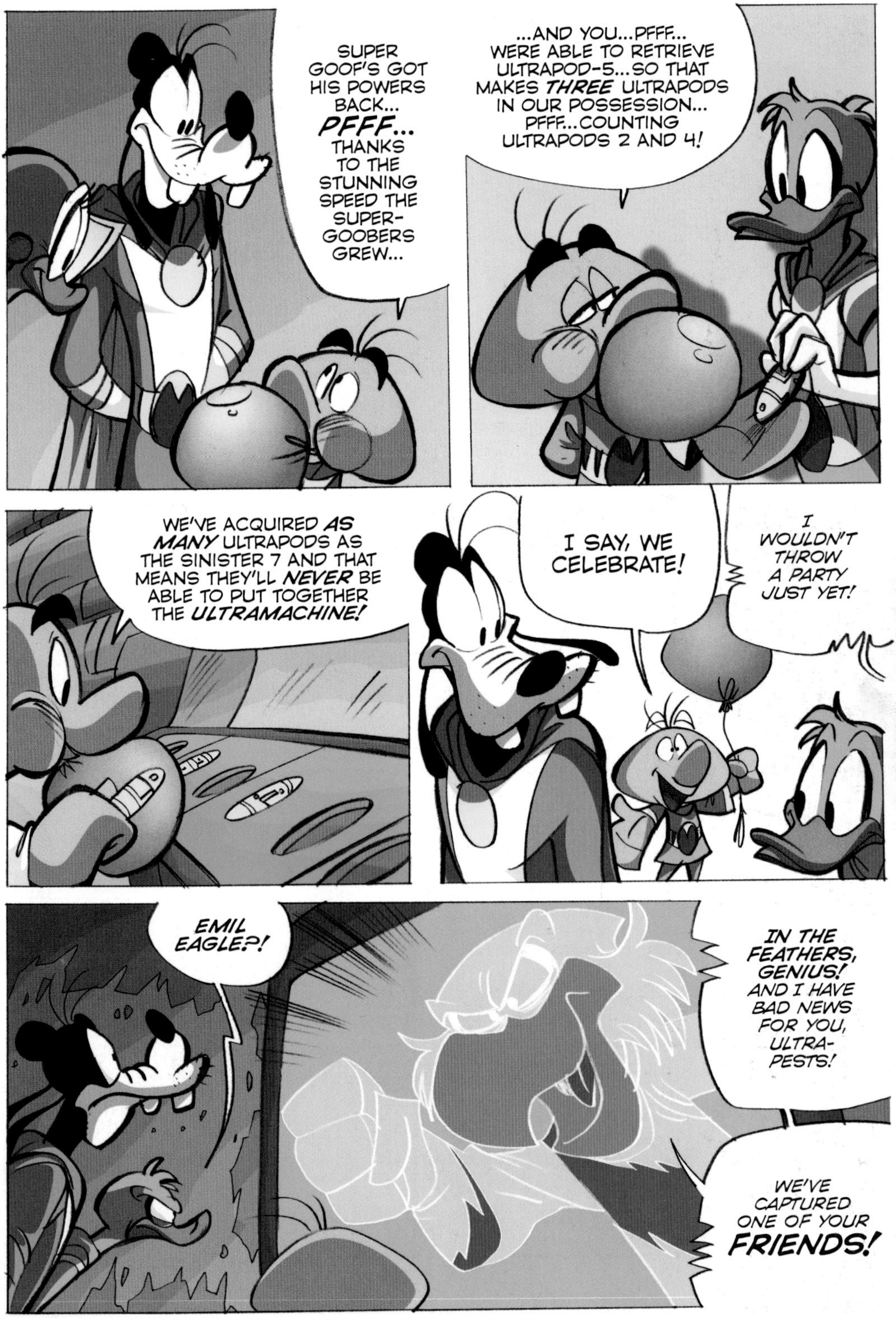

SUPER GOOF'S GOT HIS POWERS BACK... PFFF... THANKS TO THE STUNNING SPEED THE SUPER-GOOBERS GREW...
...AND YOU...PFFF... WERE ABLE TO RETRIEVE ULTRAPOD-5...SO THAT MAKES THREE ULTRAPODS IN OUR POSSESSION... PFFF...COUNTING ULTRAPODS 2 AND 4!
WE'VE ACQUIRED AS MANY ULTRAPODS AS THE SINISTER 7 AND THAT MEANS THEY'LL NEVER BE ABLE TO PUT TOGETHER THE ULTRAMACHINE!
I SAY, WE CELEBRATE!
I WOULDN'T THROW A PARTY JUST YET!
EMIL EAGLE?!
IN THE FEATHERS, GENIUS! AND I HAVE BAD NEWS FOR YOU, ULTRA-PESTS!
WE'VE CAPTURED ONE OF YOUR FRIENDS!

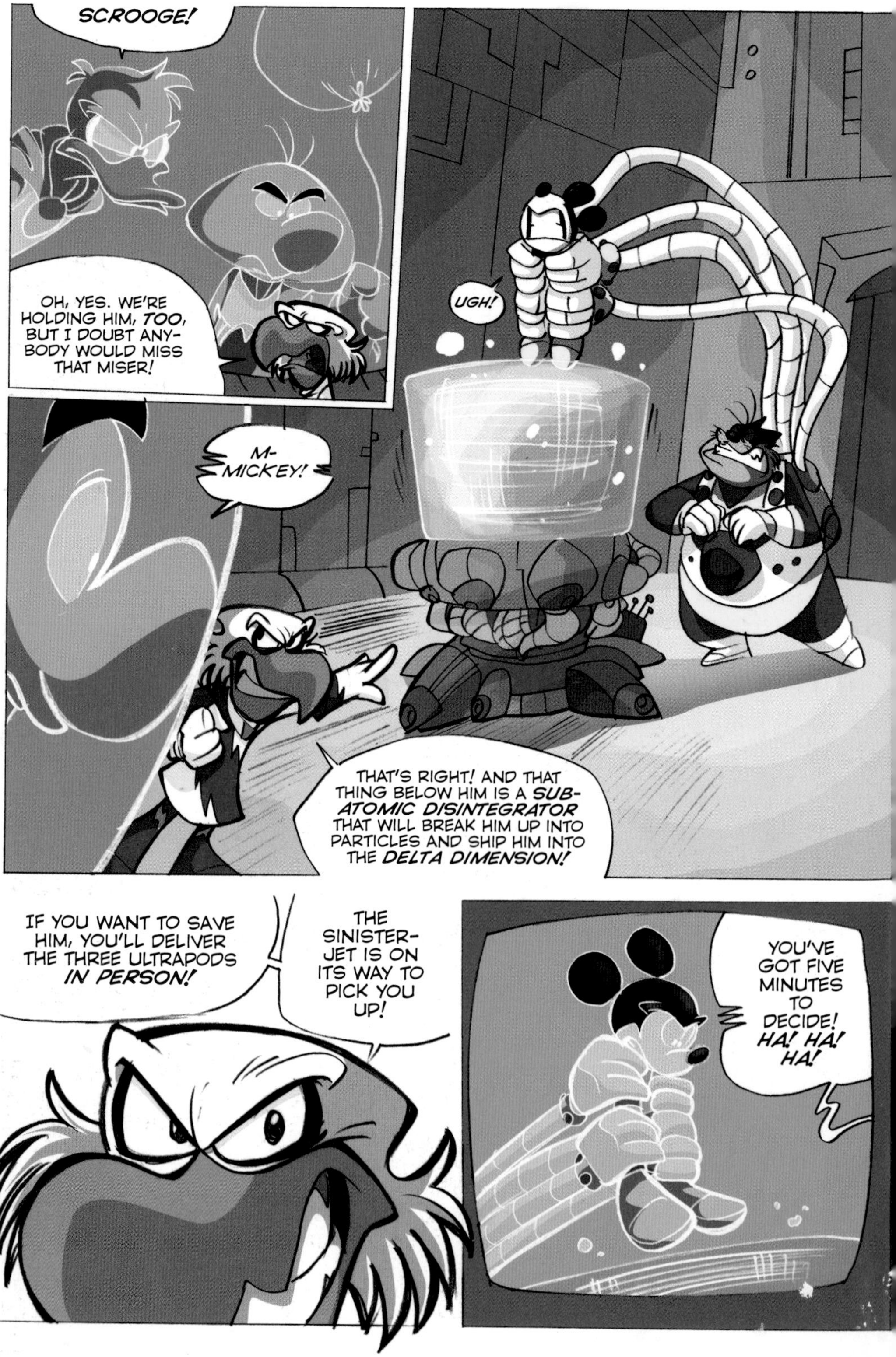
SCROOGE!
OH, YES. WE'RE HOLDING HIM, *TOO*, BUT I DOUBT ANYBODY WOULD MISS THAT MISER!
UGH!
M-MICKEY!
THAT'S RIGHT! AND THAT THING BELOW HIM IS A *SUB-ATOMIC DISINTEGRATOR* THAT WILL BREAK HIM UP INTO PARTICLES AND SHIP HIM INTO THE *DELTA DIMENSION!*
IF YOU WANT TO SAVE HIM, YOU'LL DELIVER THE THREE ULTRAPODS *IN PERSON!*
THE SINISTER-JET IS ON ITS WAY TO PICK YOU UP!
YOU'VE GOT FIVE MINUTES TO DECIDE! *HA! HA! HA!*

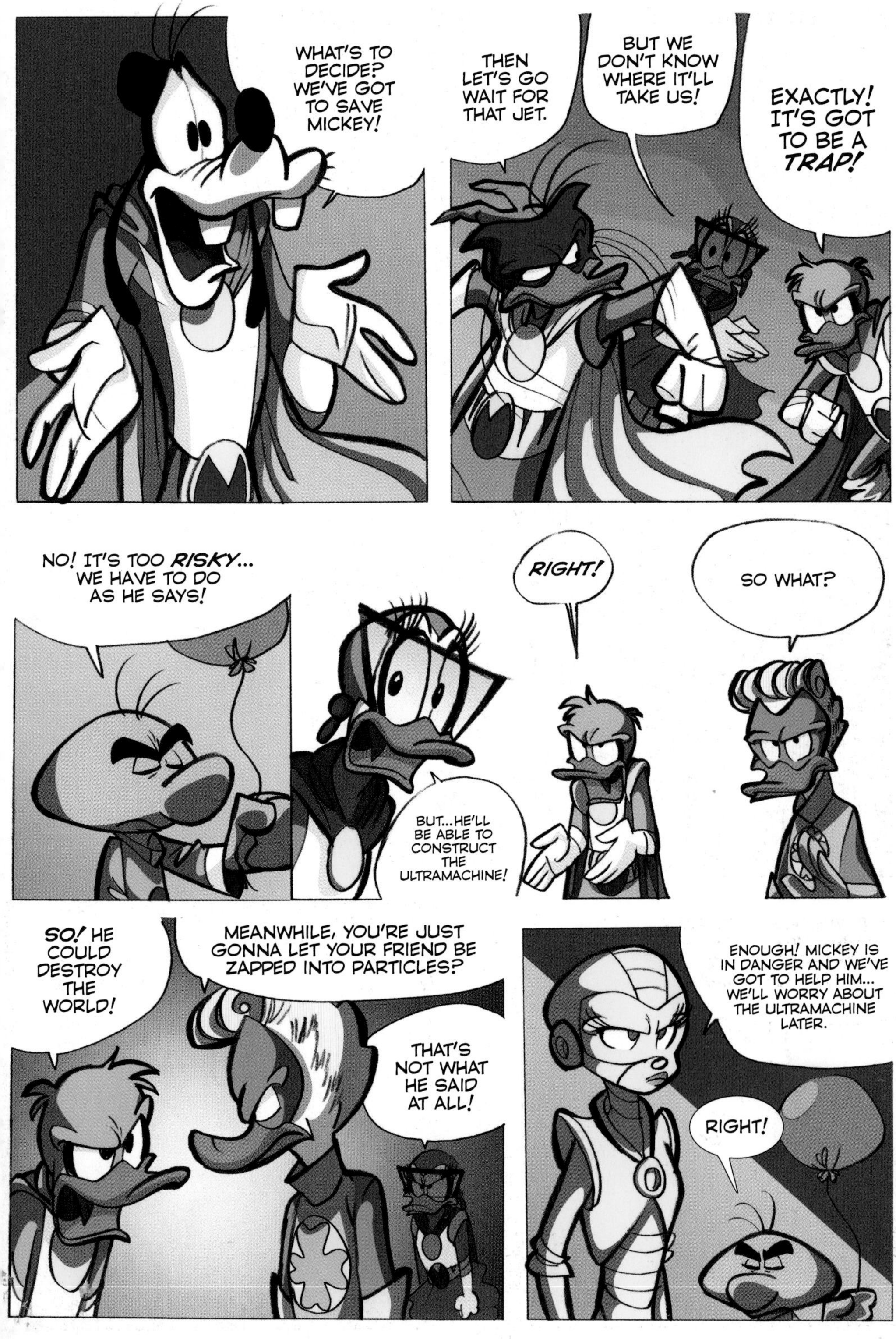
WHAT'S TO DECIDE? WE'VE GOT TO SAVE MICKEY!
THEN LET'S GO WAIT FOR THAT JET.
BUT WE DON'T KNOW WHERE IT'LL TAKE US!
EXACTLY! IT'S GOT TO BE A *TRAP!*
NO! IT'S TOO *RISKY*... WE HAVE TO DO AS HE SAYS!
BUT...HE'LL BE ABLE TO CONSTRUCT THE ULTRAMACHINE!
RIGHT!
SO WHAT?
SO! HE COULD DESTROY THE WORLD!
MEANWHILE, YOU'RE JUST GONNA LET YOUR FRIEND BE ZAPPED INTO PARTICLES?
THAT'S NOT WHAT HE SAID AT ALL!
ENOUGH! MICKEY IS IN DANGER AND WE'VE GOT TO HELP HIM... WE'LL WORRY ABOUT THE ULTRAMACHINE LATER.
RIGHT!

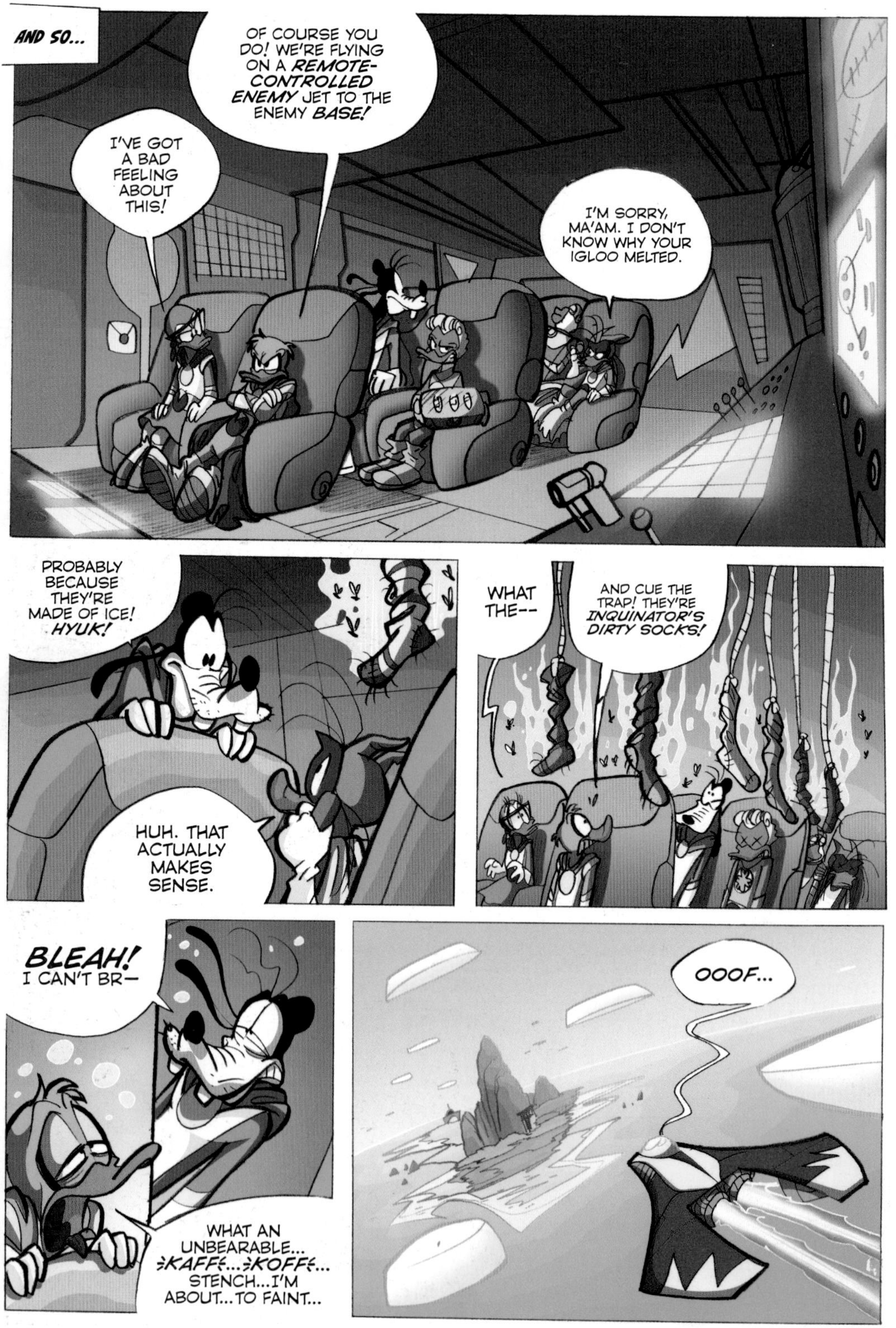
AND SO...
I'VE GOT A BAD FEELING ABOUT THIS!
OF COURSE YOU DO! WE'RE FLYING ON A *REMOTE-CONTROLLED ENEMY* JET TO THE ENEMY *BASE!*
I'M SORRY, MA'AM. I DON'T KNOW WHY YOUR IGLOO MELTED.
PROBABLY BECAUSE THEY'RE MADE OF ICE! *HYUK!*
HUH. THAT ACTUALLY MAKES SENSE.
WHAT THE--
AND CUE THE TRAP! THEY'RE *INQUINATOR'S DIRTY SOCKS!*
BLEAH! I CAN'T BR—
WHAT AN UNBEARABLE... *KAFF*... *KOFF*... STENCH...I'M ABOUT...TO FAINT...
OOOF...

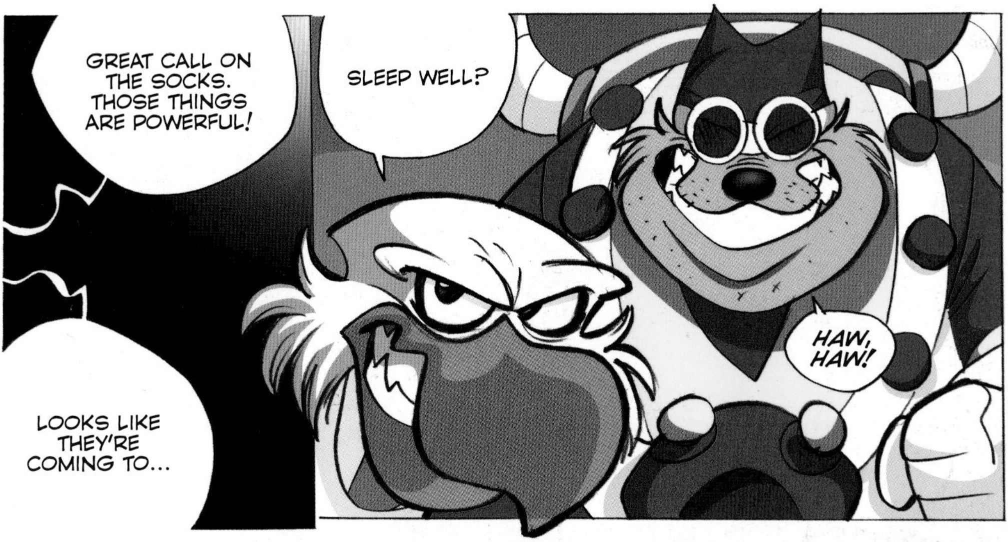
GREAT CALL ON THE SOCKS. THOSE THINGS ARE POWERFUL!
LOOKS LIKE THEY'RE COMING TO...
SLEEP WELL?
HAW, HAW!

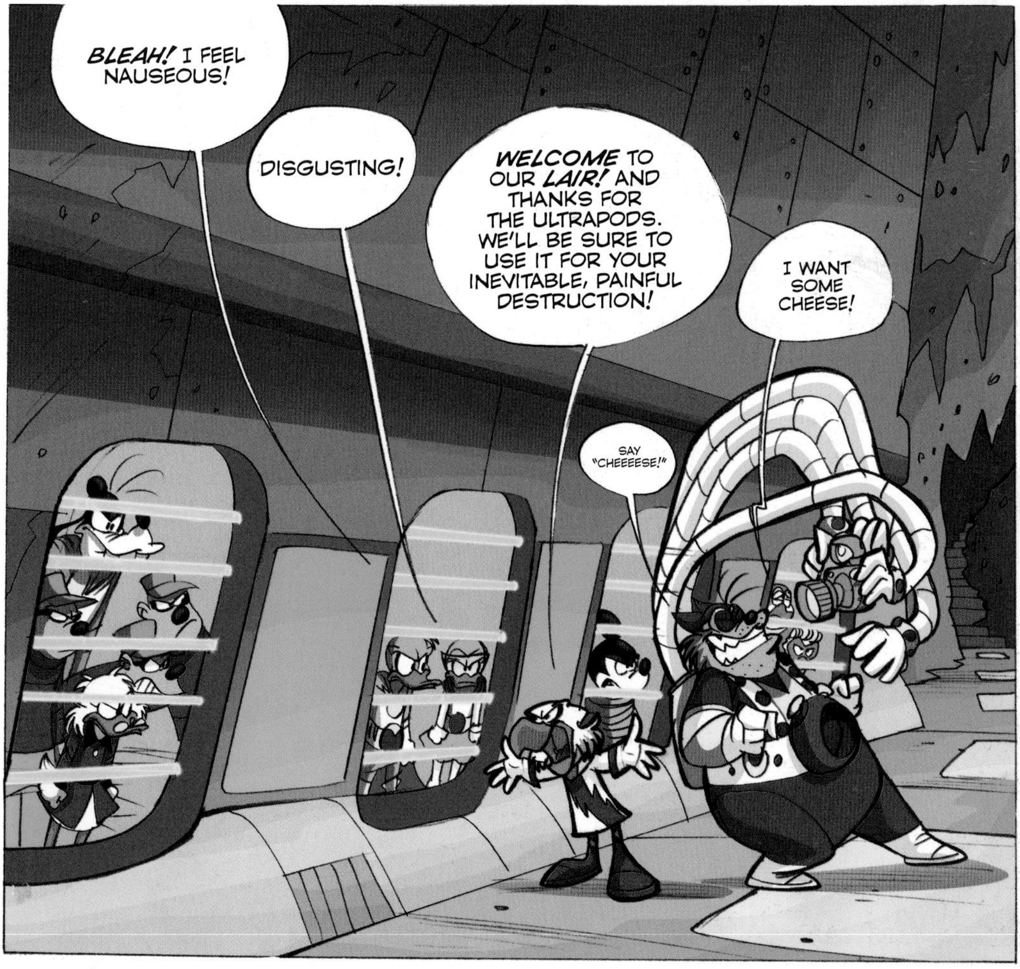
BLEAH! I FEEL NAUSEOUS!
DISGUSTING!
WELCOME TO OUR LAIR! AND THANKS FOR THE ULTRAPODS. WE'LL BE SURE TO USE IT FOR YOUR INEVITABLE, PAINFUL DESTRUCTION!
SAY "CHEEEESE!"
I WANT SOME CHEESE!

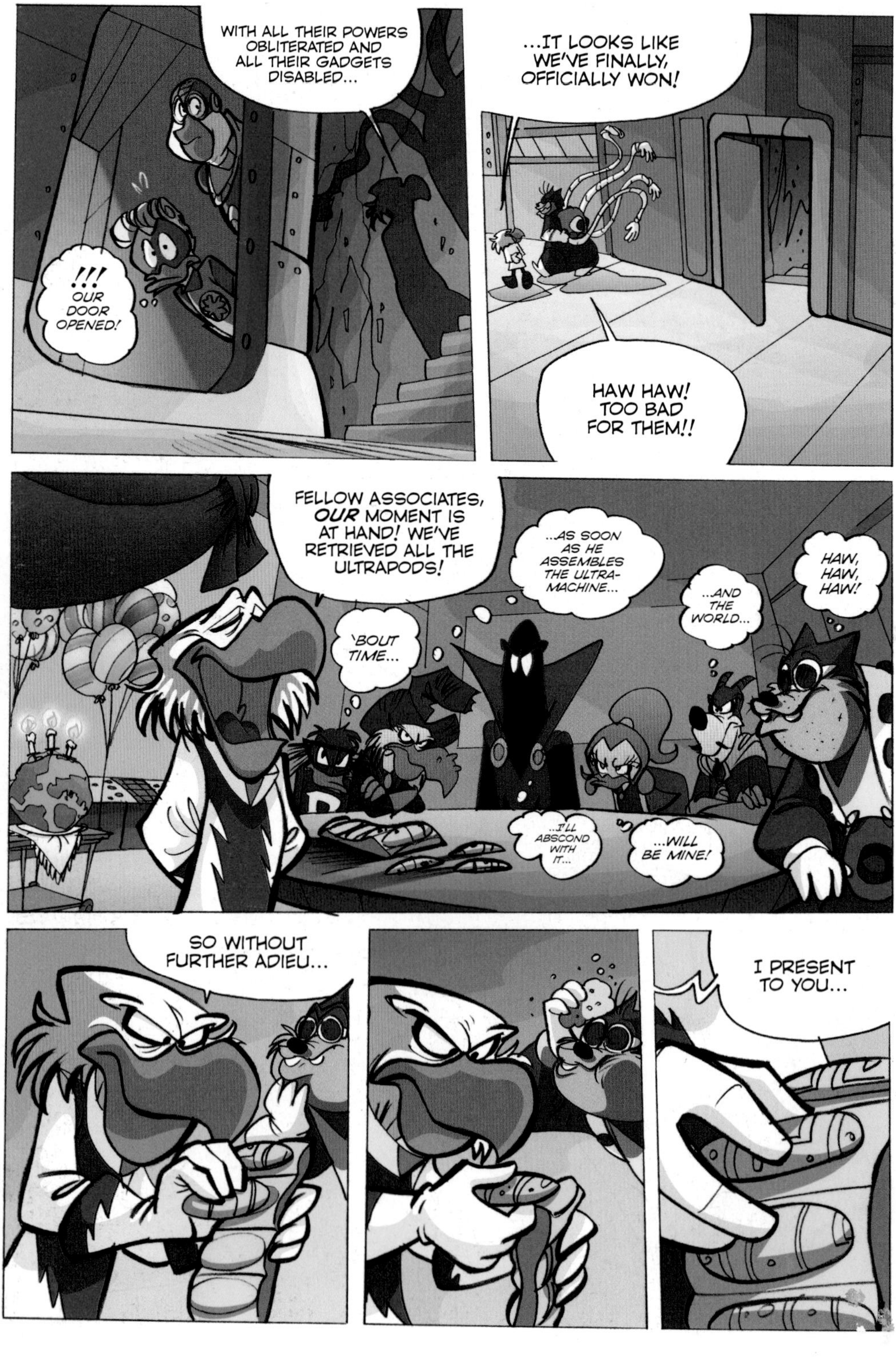
WITH ALL THEIR POWERS OBLITERATED AND ALL THEIR GADGETS DISABLED...
!!! OUR DOOR OPENED!
...IT LOOKS LIKE WE'VE FINALLY, OFFICIALLY WON!
HAW HAW! TOO BAD FOR THEM!!
FELLOW ASSOCIATES, OUR MOMENT IS AT HAND! WE'VE RETRIEVED ALL THE ULTRAPODS!
'BOUT TIME...
...AS SOON AS HE ASSEMBLES THE ULTRA-MACHINE...
...I'LL ABSCOND WITH IT...
...AND THE WORLD...
...WILL BE MINE!
HAW, HAW, HAW!
SO WITHOUT FURTHER ADIEU...
I PRESENT TO YOU...

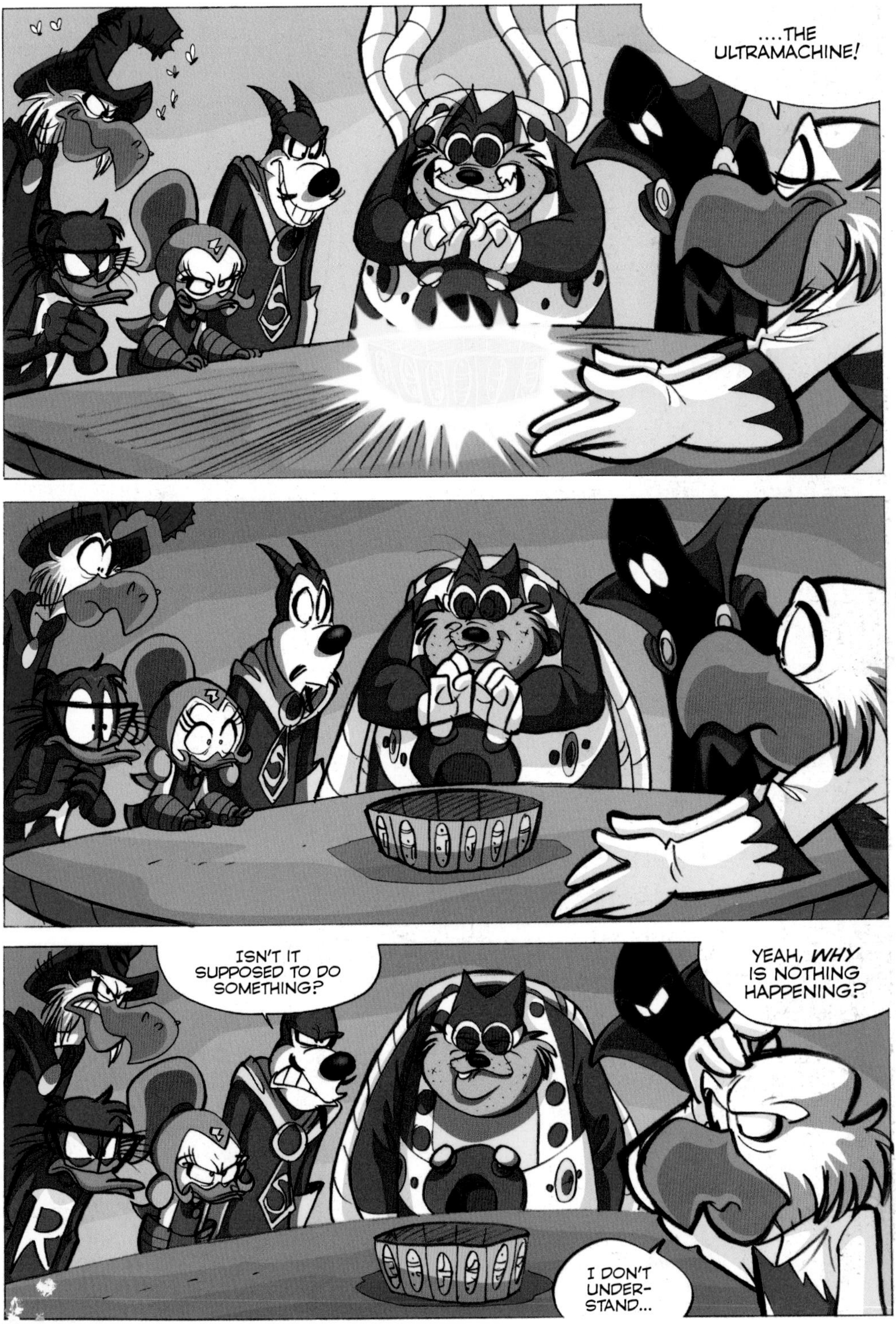
....THE
ULTRAMACHINE!
ISN'T IT SUPPOSED TO DO SOMETHING?
YEAH, WHY IS NOTHING HAPPENING?
I DON'T UNDER-STAND...

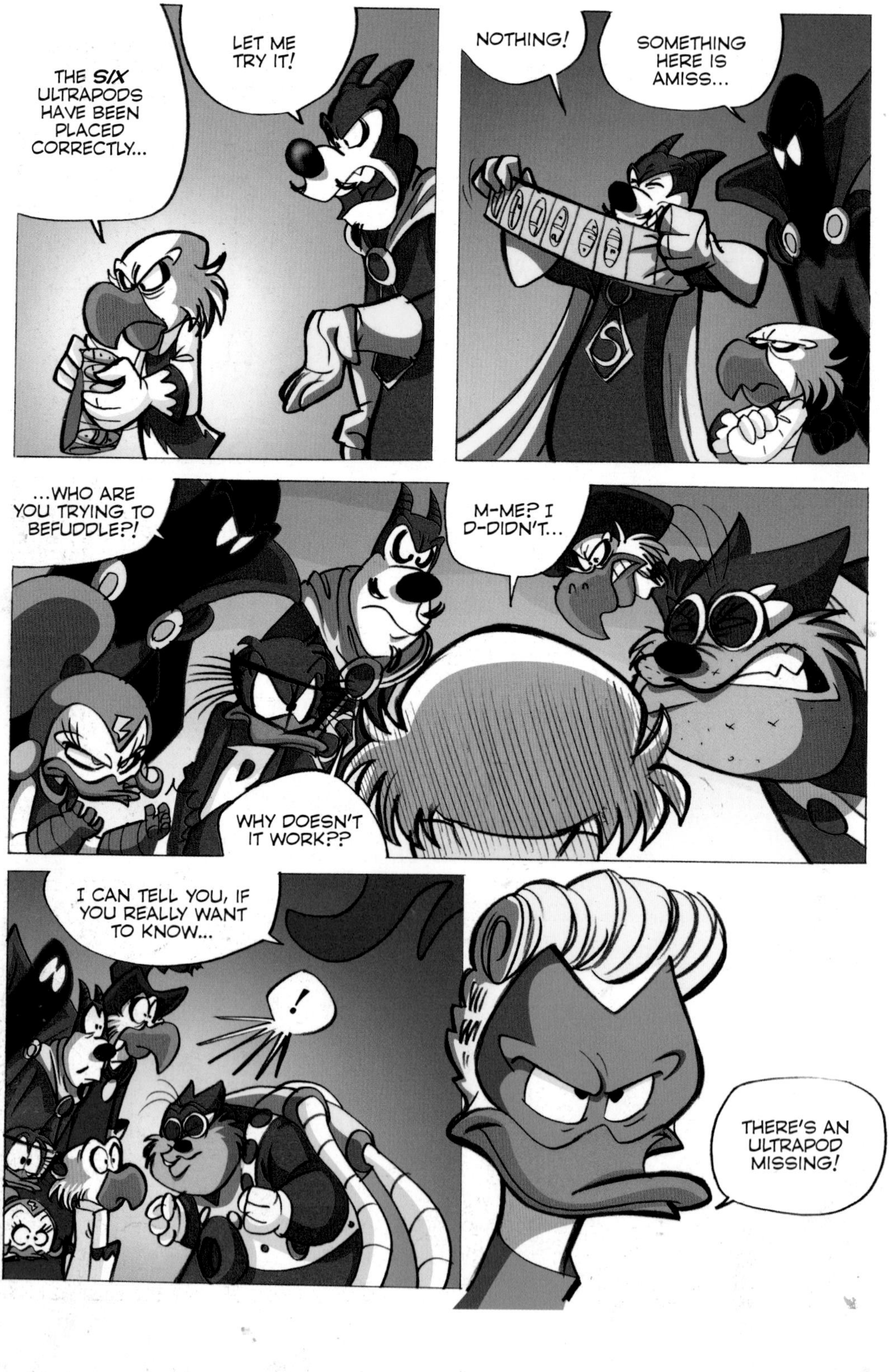
THE SIX ULTRAPODS HAVE BEEN PLACED CORRECTLY...
LET ME TRY IT!
NOTHING!
SOMETHING HERE IS AMISS...
...WHO ARE YOU TRYING TO BEFUDDLE?!
M-ME? I D-DIDN'T...
WHY DOESN'T IT WORK??
I CAN TELL YOU, IF YOU REALLY WANT TO KNOW...
!
THERE'S AN ULTRAPOD MISSING!

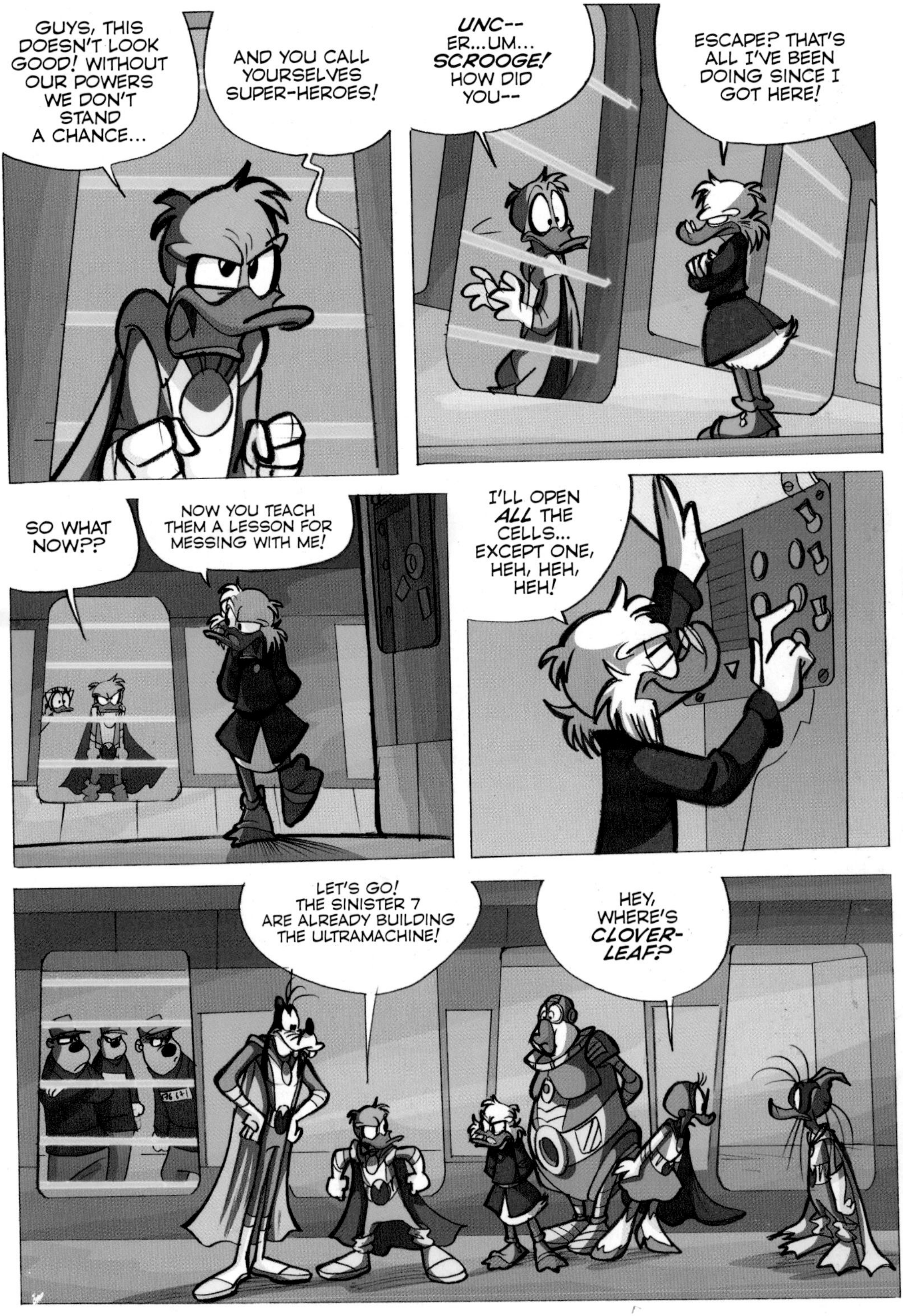
GUYS, THIS DOESN'T LOOK GOOD! WITHOUT OUR POWERS WE DON'T STAND A CHANCE...
AND YOU CALL YOURSELVES SUPER-HEROES!
UNC-- ER...UM... SCROOGE! HOW DID YOU--
ESCAPE? THAT'S ALL I'VE BEEN DOING SINCE I GOT HERE!
SO WHAT NOW??
NOW YOU TEACH THEM A LESSON FOR MESSING WITH ME!
I'LL OPEN ALL THE CELLS... EXCEPT ONE, HEH, HEH, HEH!
LET'S GO! THE SINISTER 7 ARE ALREADY BUILDING THE ULTRAMACHINE!
HEY, WHERE'S CLOVER-LEAF?

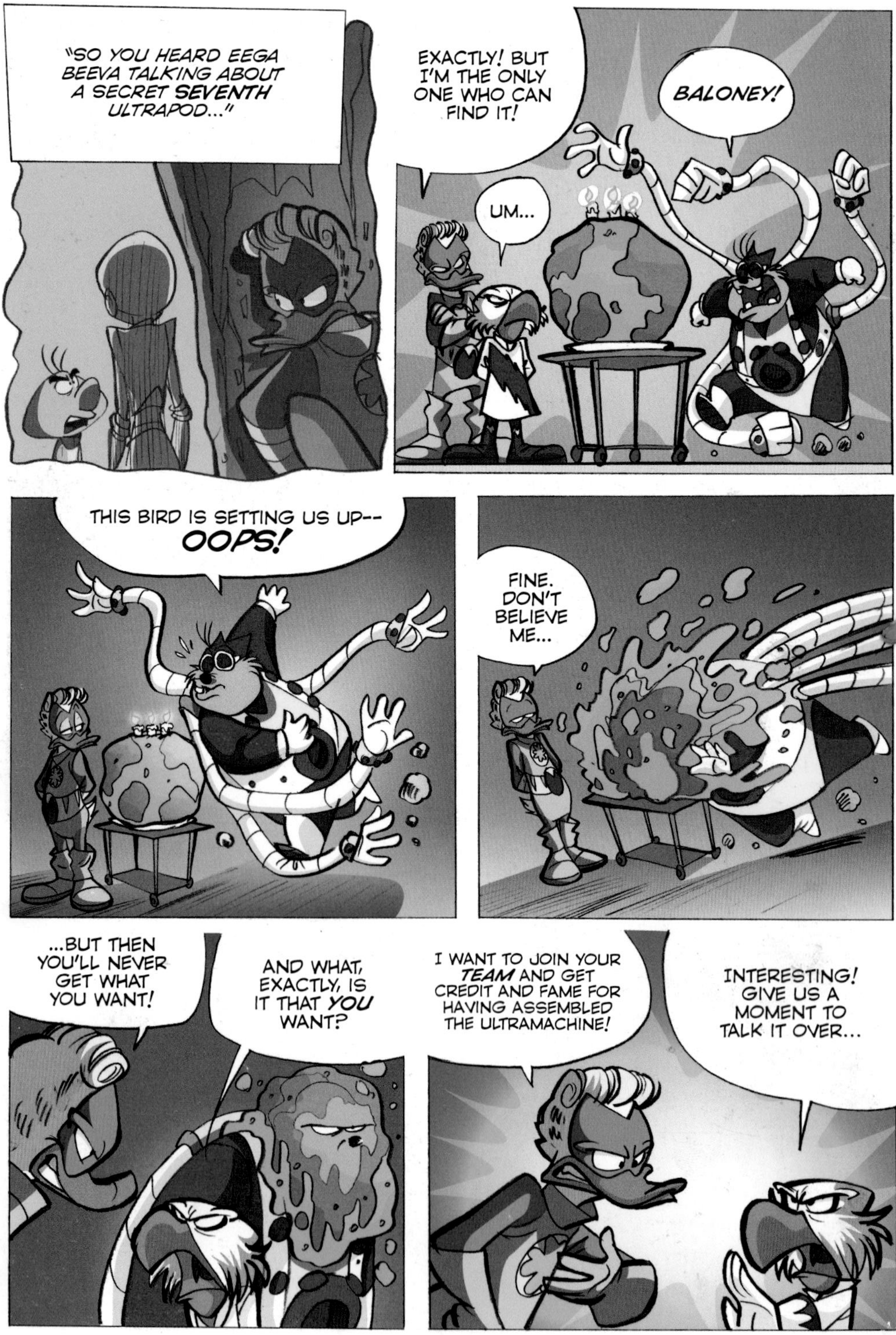
"SO YOU HEARD EEGA BEEVA TALKING ABOUT A SECRET **SEVENTH** ULTRAPOD..."
EXACTLY! BUT I'M THE ONLY ONE WHO CAN FIND IT!
UM...
BALONEY!
THIS BIRD IS SETTING US UP-- ***OOPS!***
FINE. DON'T BELIEVE ME...
...BUT THEN YOU'LL NEVER GET WHAT YOU WANT!
AND WHAT, EXACTLY, IS IT THAT ***YOU*** WANT?
I WANT TO JOIN YOUR ***TEAM*** AND GET CREDIT AND FAME FOR HAVING ASSEMBLED THE ULTRAMACHINE!
INTERESTING! GIVE US A MOMENT TO TALK IT OVER...

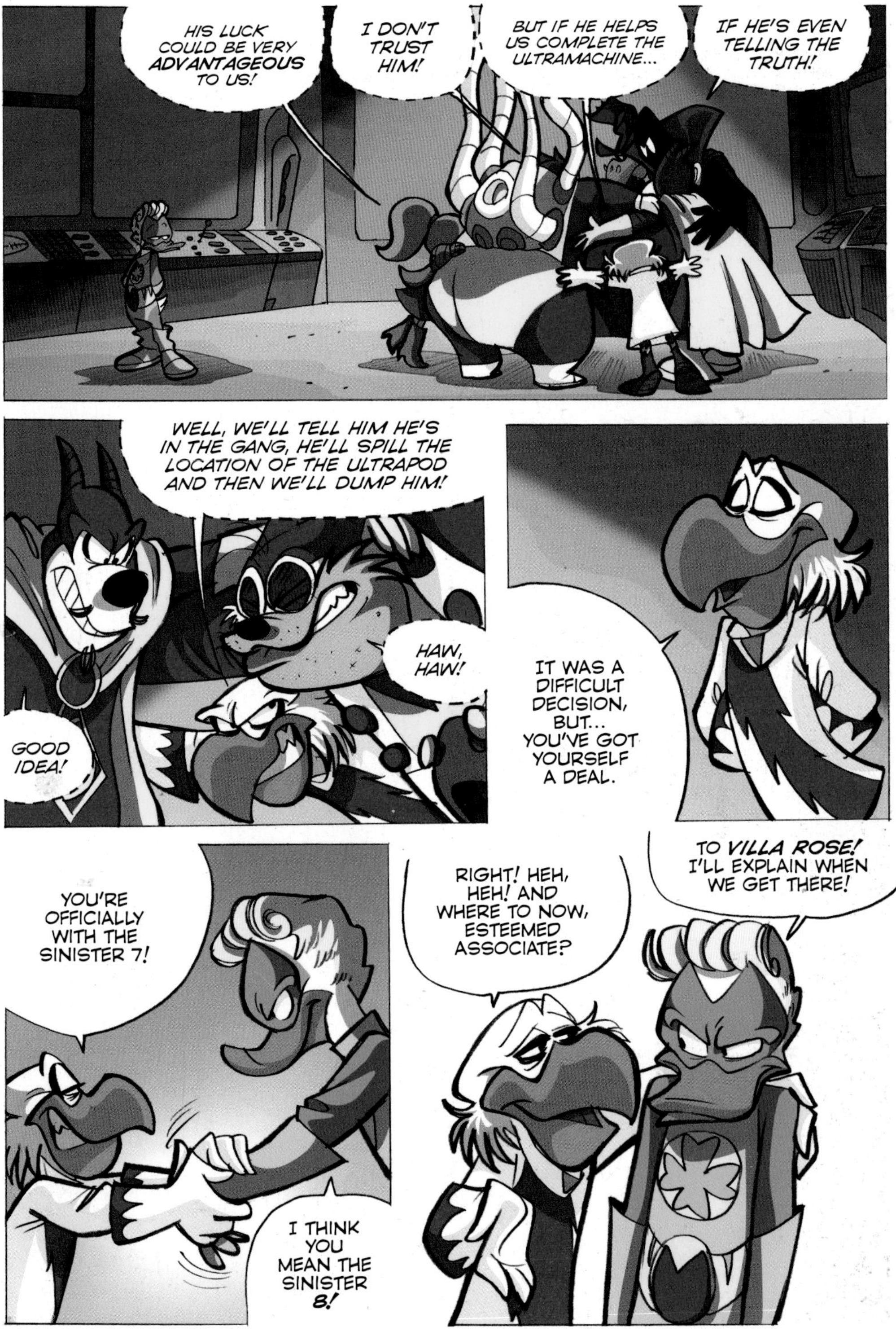
HIS LUCK COULD BE VERY ADVANTAGEOUS TO US!
I DON'T TRUST HIM!
BUT IF HE HELPS US COMPLETE THE ULTRAMACHINE...
IF HE'S EVEN TELLING THE TRUTH!
WELL, WE'LL TELL HIM HE'S IN THE GANG, HE'LL SPILL THE LOCATION OF THE ULTRAPOD AND THEN WE'LL DUMP HIM!
HAW, HAW!
GOOD IDEA!
IT WAS A DIFFICULT DECISION, BUT... YOU'VE GOT YOURSELF A DEAL.
YOU'RE OFFICIALLY WITH THE SINISTER 7!
I THINK YOU MEAN THE SINISTER 8!
RIGHT! HEH, HEH! AND WHERE TO NOW, ESTEEMED ASSOCIATE?
TO VILLA ROSE! I'LL EXPLAIN WHEN WE GET THERE!

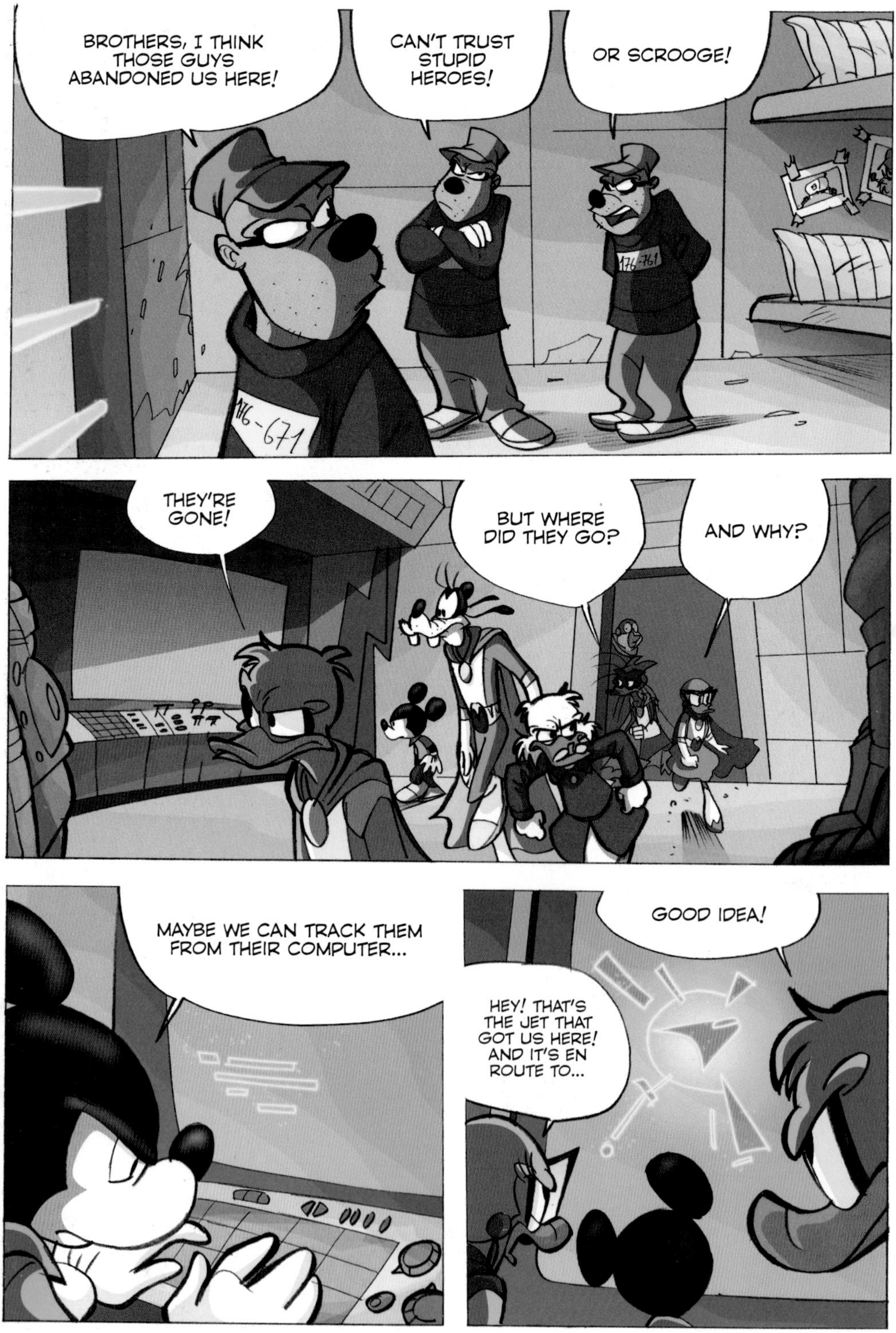
BROTHERS, I THINK THOSE GUYS ABANDONED US HERE!
CAN'T TRUST STUPID HEROES!
OR SCROOGE!
176-671
176-761
THEY'RE GONE!
BUT WHERE DID THEY GO?
AND WHY?
MAYBE WE CAN TRACK THEM FROM THEIR COMPUTER...
GOOD IDEA!
HEY! THAT'S THE JET THAT GOT US HERE! AND IT'S EN ROUTE TO...

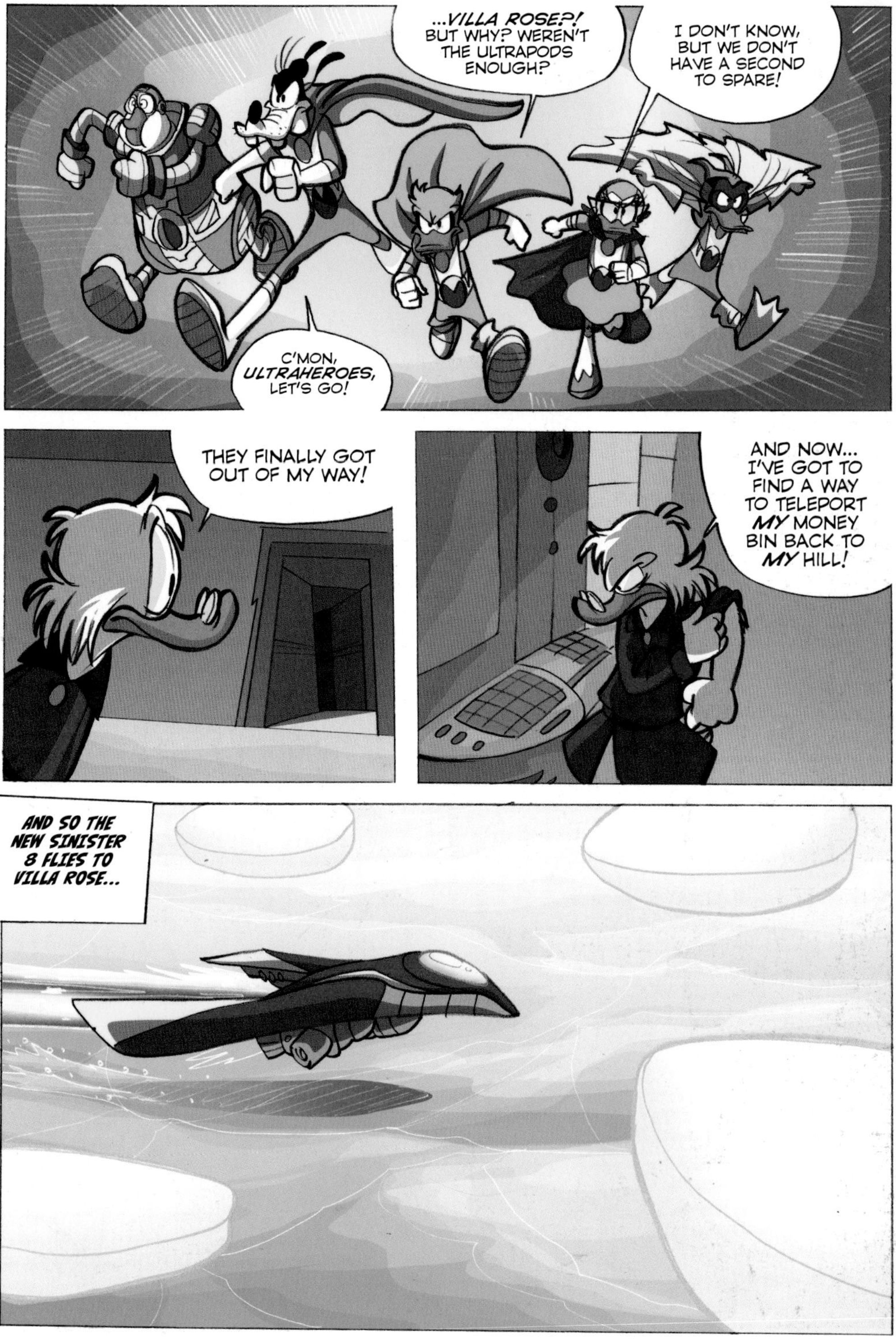
...VILLA ROSE?! BUT WHY? WEREN'T THE ULTRAPODS ENOUGH?
I DON'T KNOW, BUT WE DON'T HAVE A SECOND TO SPARE!
C'MON, ULTRAHEROES, LET'S GO!
THEY FINALLY GOT OUT OF MY WAY!
AND NOW... I'VE GOT TO FIND A WAY TO TELEPORT MY MONEY BIN BACK TO MY HILL!
AND SO THE NEW SINISTER 8 FLIES TO VILLA ROSE...

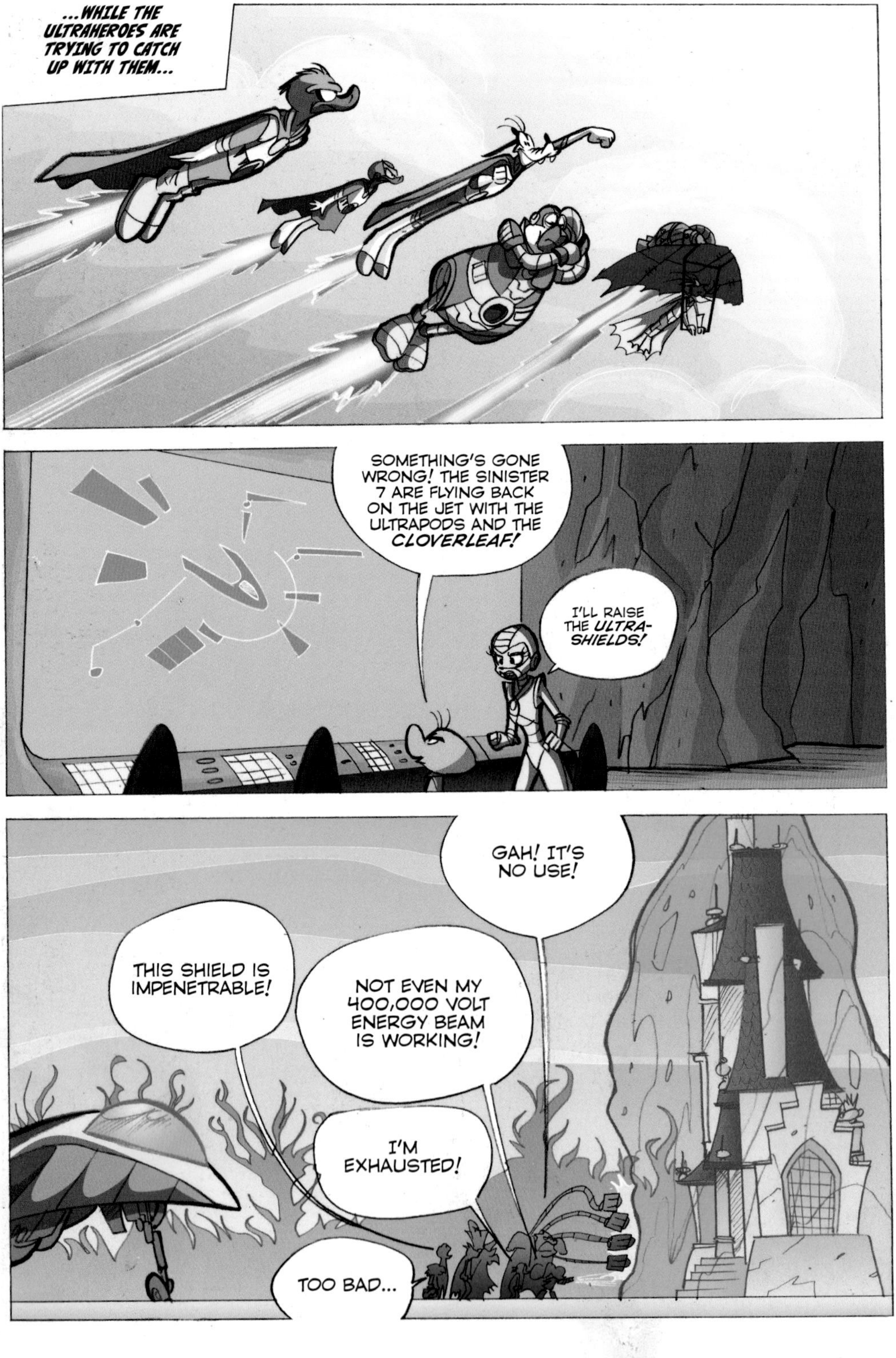
...WHILE THE ULTRAHEROES ARE TRYING TO CATCH UP WITH THEM...
SOMETHING'S GONE WRONG! THE SINISTER 7 ARE FLYING BACK ON THE JET WITH THE ULTRAPODS AND THE CLOVERLEAF!
I'LL RAISE THE ULTRA-SHIELDS!
GAH! IT'S NO USE!
THIS SHIELD IS IMPENETRABLE!
NOT EVEN MY 400,000 VOLT ENERGY BEAM IS WORKING!
I'M EXHAUSTED!
TOO BAD...

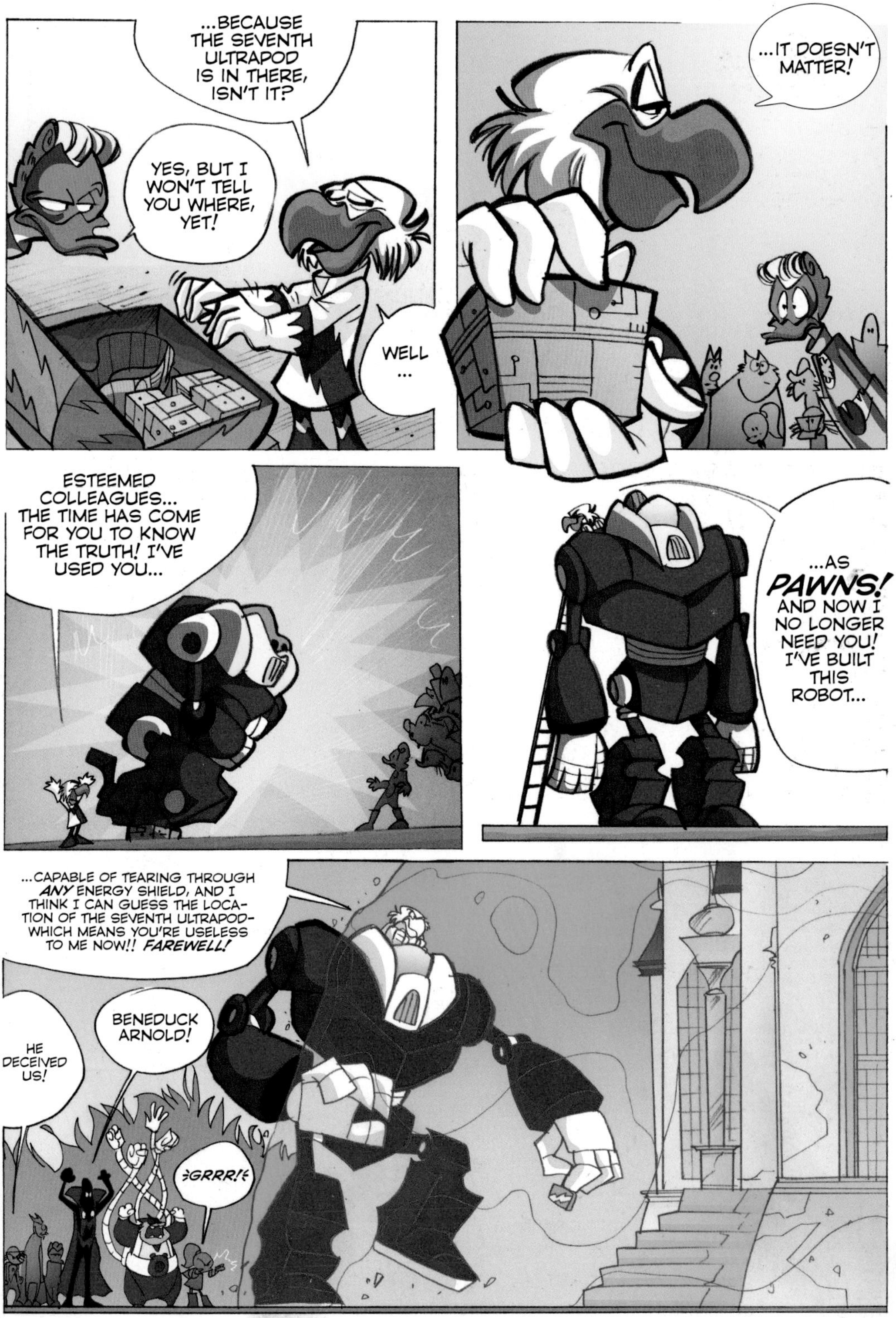
...BECAUSE THE SEVENTH ULTRAPOD IS IN THERE, ISN'T IT?
YES, BUT I WON'T TELL YOU WHERE, YET!
WELL ...
...IT DOESN'T MATTER!
ESTEEMED COLLEAGUES... THE TIME HAS COME FOR YOU TO KNOW THE TRUTH! I'VE USED YOU...
...AS PAWNS! AND NOW I NO LONGER NEED YOU! I'VE BUILT THIS ROBOT...
...CAPABLE OF TEARING THROUGH ANY ENERGY SHIELD, AND I THINK I CAN GUESS THE LOCATION OF THE SEVENTH ULTRAPOD-WHICH MEANS YOU'RE USELESS TO ME NOW!! FAREWELL!
HE DECEIVED US!
BENEDUCK ARNOLD!
GRRR!

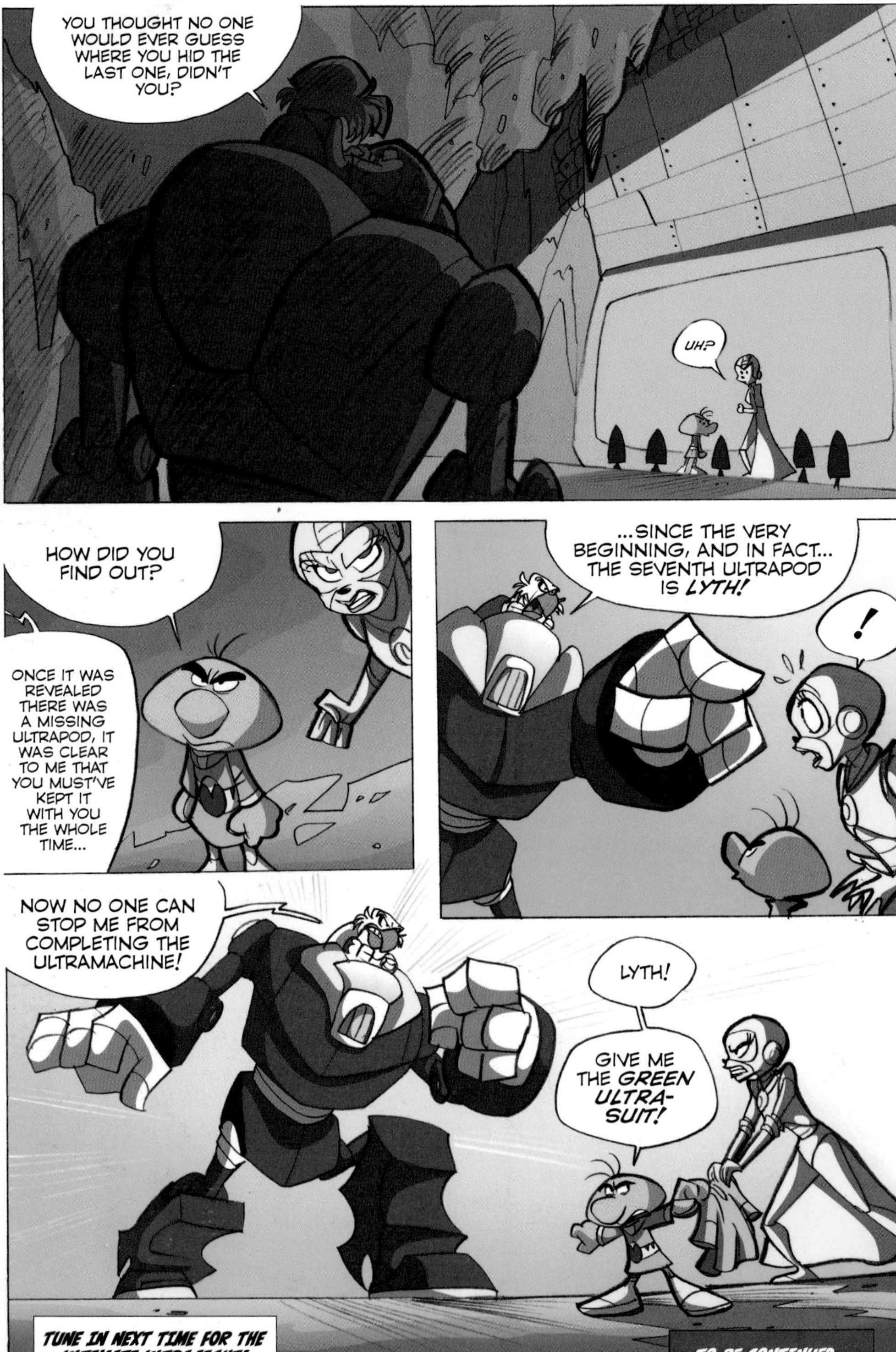

YOU THOUGHT NO ONE WOULD EVER GUESS WHERE YOU HID THE LAST ONE, DIDN'T YOU?
UH?
HOW DID YOU FIND OUT?
ONCE IT WAS REVEALED THERE WAS A MISSING ULTRAPOD, IT WAS CLEAR TO ME THAT YOU MUST'VE KEPT IT WITH YOU THE WHOLE TIME...
...SINCE THE VERY BEGINNING, AND IN FACT... THE SEVENTH ULTRAPOD IS LYTH!
!
NOW NO ONE CAN STOP ME FROM COMPLETING THE ULTRAMACHINE!
LYTH!
GIVE ME THE GREEN ULTRA-SUIT!
TUNE IN NEXT TIME FOR THE ULTIMATE ULTRA-FIGHT!
TO BE CONTINUED...

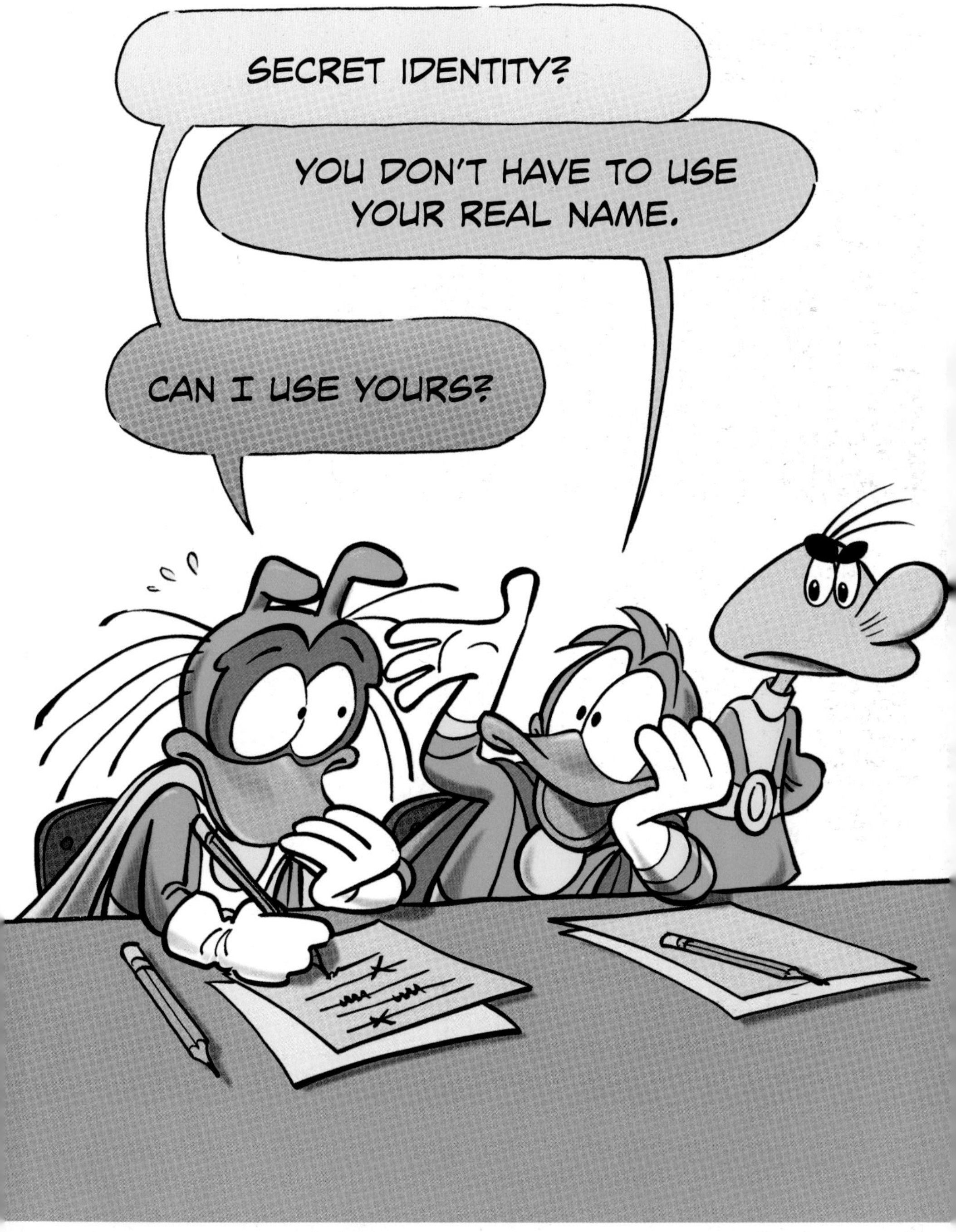
SECRET IDENTITY?
YOU DON'T HAVE TO USE YOUR REAL NAME.
CAN I USE YOURS?

ONE DRAWBACK OF SUPER HEROISM...
IS THE PAPERWORK!

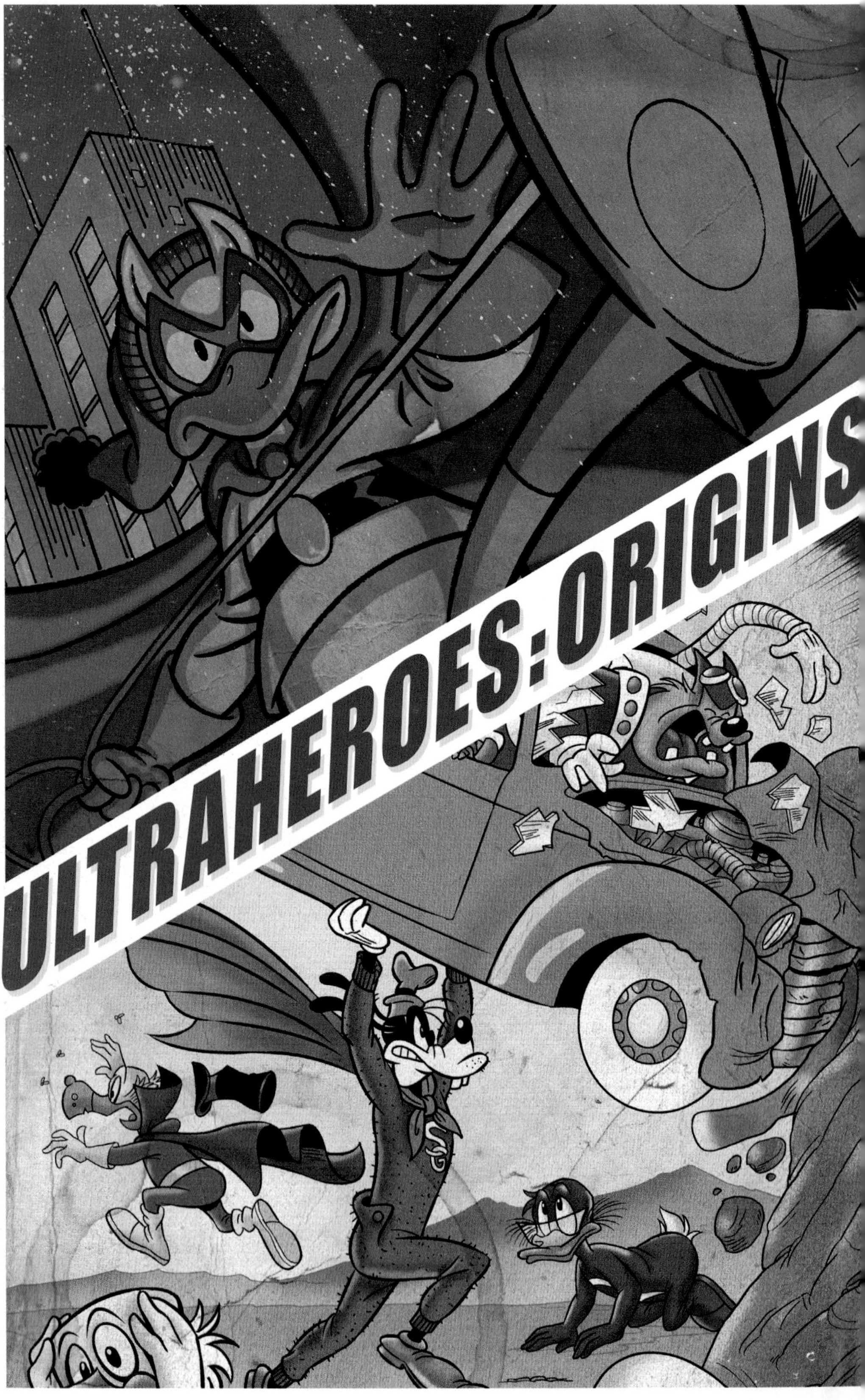
ULTRAHEROES: ORIGINS

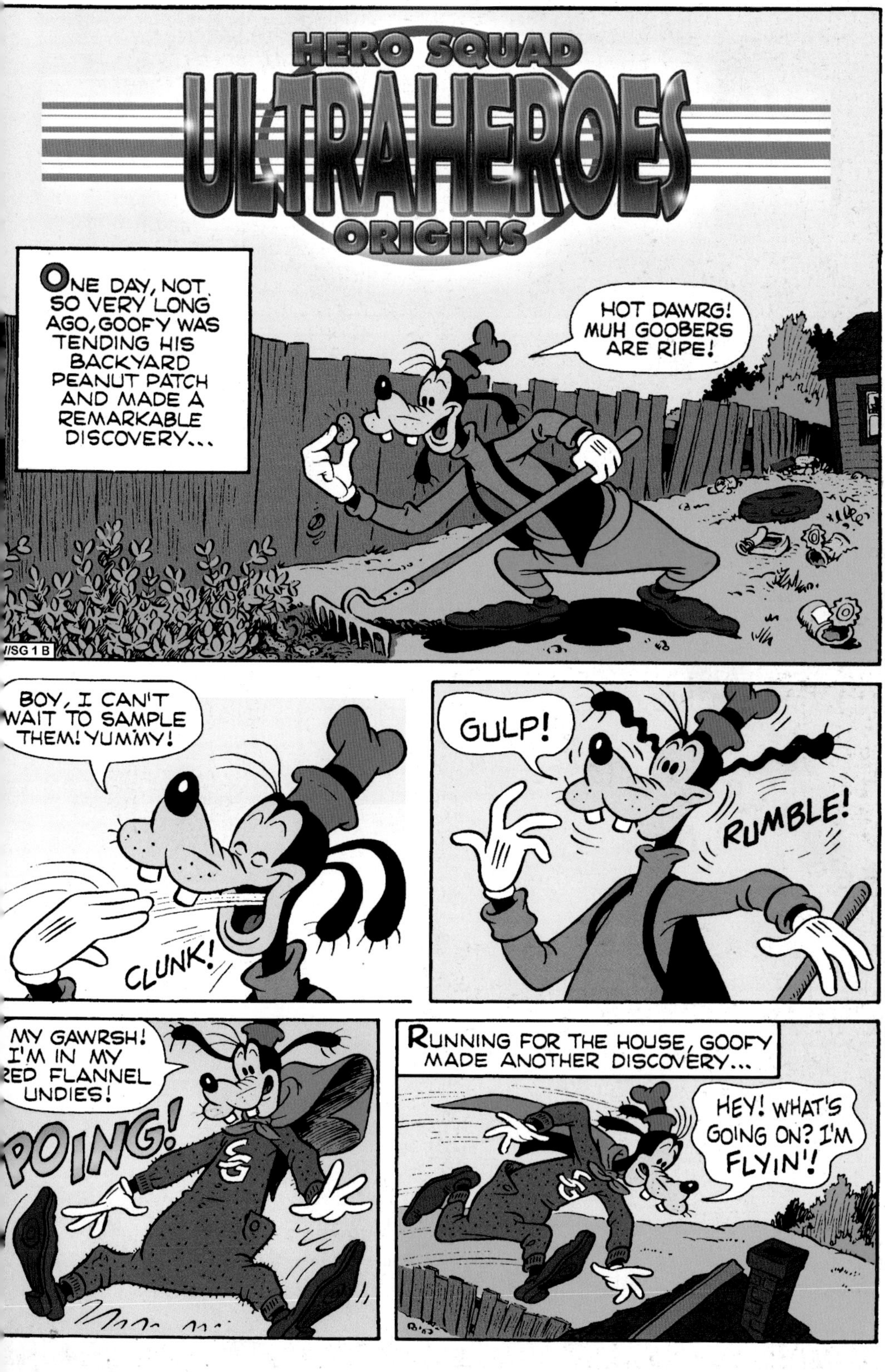
HERO SQUAD
ULTRAHEROES
ORIGINS
ONE DAY, NOT SO VERY LONG AGO, GOOFY WAS TENDING HIS BACKYARD PEANUT PATCH AND MADE A REMARKABLE DISCOVERY...
HOT DAWRG! MUH GOOBERS ARE RIPE!
W/SG 1 B
BOY, I CAN'T WAIT TO SAMPLE THEM! YUMMY!
CLUNK!
GULP!
RUMBLE!
MY GAWRSH! I'M IN MY RED FLANNEL UNDIES!
POING!
RUNNING FOR THE HOUSE, GOOFY MADE ANOTHER DISCOVERY...
HEY! WHAT'S GOING ON? I'M FLYIN'!

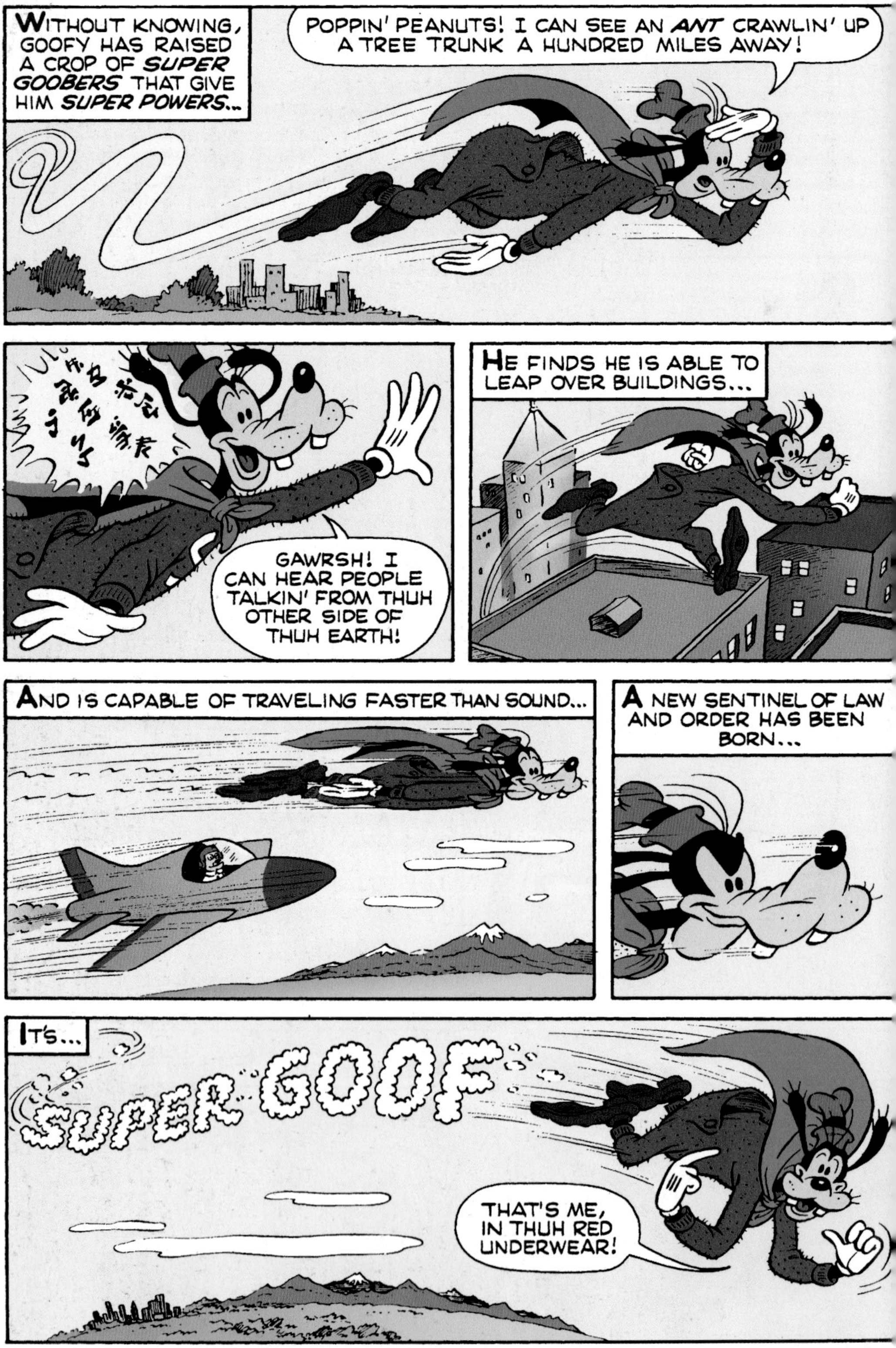
WITHOUT KNOWING, GOOFY HAS RAISED A CROP OF SUPER GOOBERS THAT GIVE HIM SUPER POWERS...
POPPIN' PEANUTS! I CAN SEE AN ANT CRAWLIN' UP A TREE TRUNK A HUNDRED MILES AWAY!
GAWRSH! I CAN HEAR PEOPLE TALKIN' FROM THUH OTHER SIDE OF THUH EARTH!
HE FINDS HE IS ABLE TO LEAP OVER BUILDINGS...
AND IS CAPABLE OF TRAVELING FASTER THAN SOUND...
A NEW SENTINEL OF LAW AND ORDER HAS BEEN BORN...
IT'S...
SUPER GOOF
THAT'S ME, IN THUH RED UNDERWEAR!

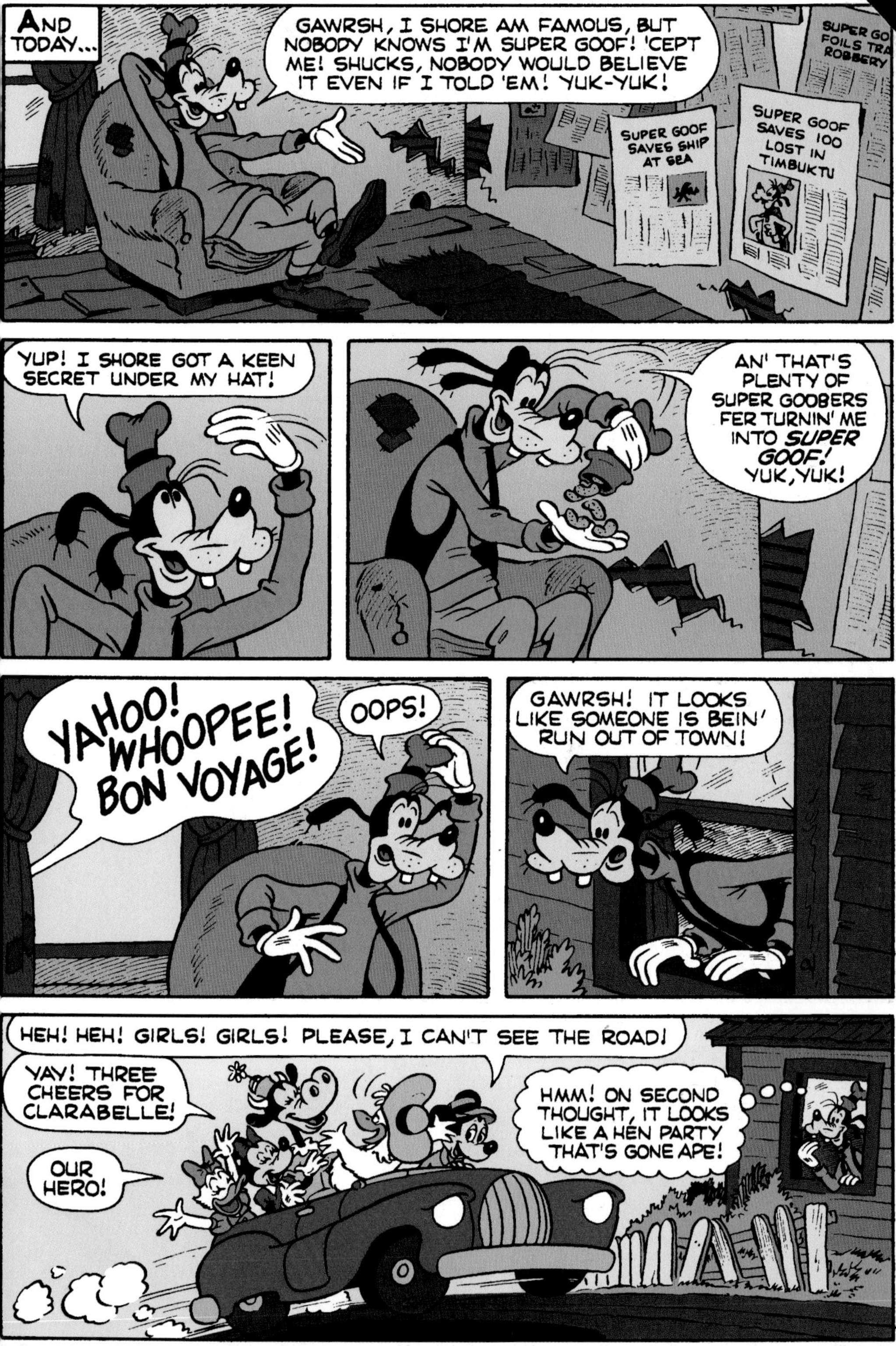
AND TODAY...
GAWRSH, I SHORE AM FAMOUS, BUT NOBODY KNOWS I'M SUPER GOOF! 'CEPT ME! SHUCKS, NOBODY WOULD BELIEVE IT EVEN IF I TOLD 'EM! YUK-YUK!
SUPER GOOF SAVES SHIP AT SEA
SUPER GOOF SAVES 100 LOST IN TIMBUKTU
SUPER GO FOILS TRA ROBBERY
YUP! I SHORE GOT A KEEN SECRET UNDER MY HAT!
AN' THAT'S PLENTY OF SUPER GOOBERS FER TURNIN' ME INTO SUPER GOOF! YUK, YUK!
YAHOO! WHOOPEE! BON VOYAGE!
OOPS!
GAWRSH! IT LOOKS LIKE SOMEONE IS BEIN' RUN OUT OF TOWN!
HEH! HEH! GIRLS! GIRLS! PLEASE, I CAN'T SEE THE ROAD!
YAY! THREE CHEERS FOR CLARABELLE!
OUR HERO!
HMM! ON SECOND THOUGHT, IT LOOKS LIKE A HEN PARTY THAT'S GONE APE!

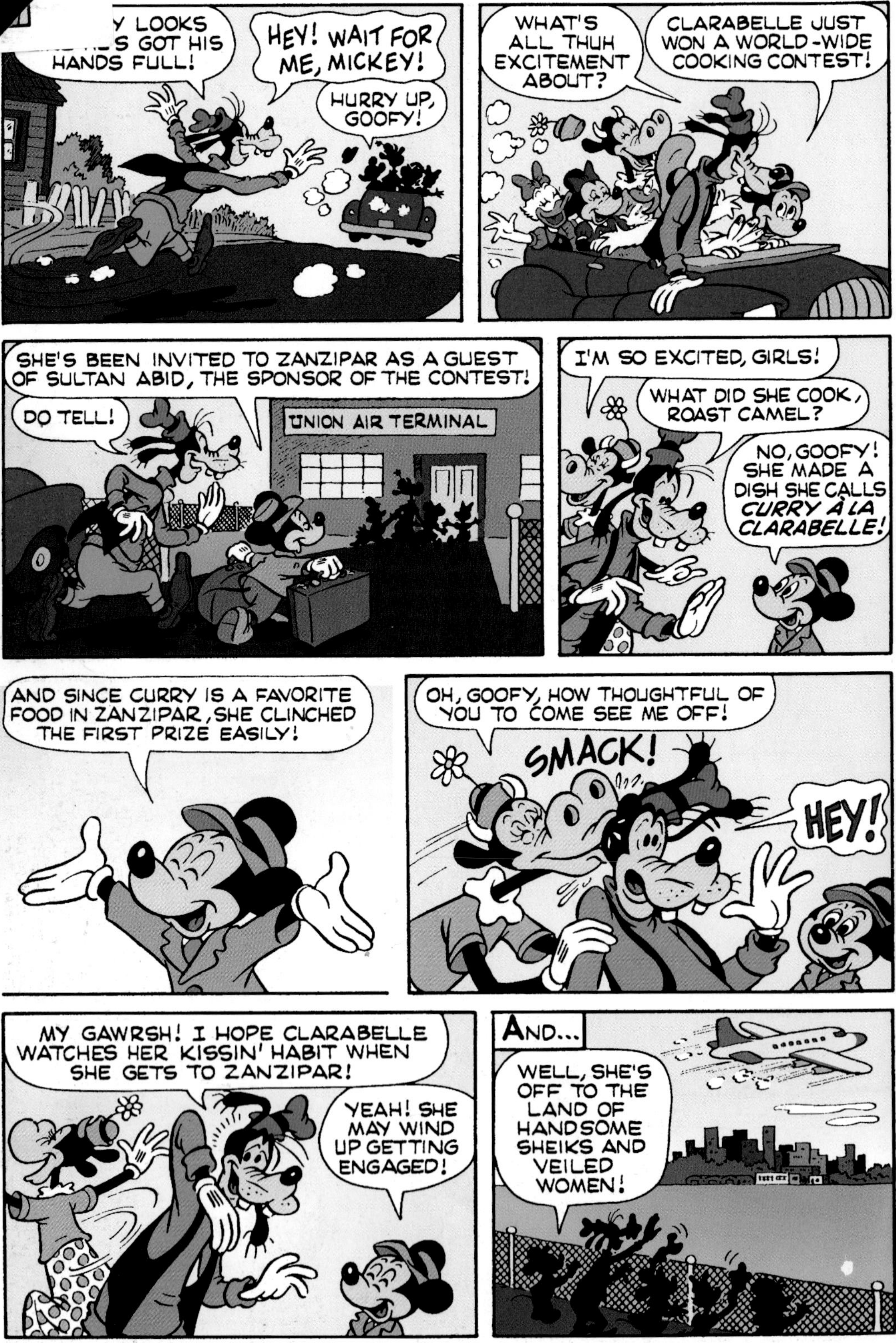
Y LOOKS S GOT HIS HANDS FULL!
HEY! WAIT FOR ME, MICKEY!
HURRY UP, GOOFY!
WHAT'S ALL THUH EXCITEMENT ABOUT?
CLARABELLE JUST WON A WORLD-WIDE COOKING CONTEST!
SHE'S BEEN INVITED TO ZANZIPAR AS A GUEST OF SULTAN ABID, THE SPONSOR OF THE CONTEST!
DO TELL!
UNION AIR TERMINAL
I'M SO EXCITED, GIRLS!
WHAT DID SHE COOK, ROAST CAMEL?
NO, GOOFY! SHE MADE A DISH SHE CALLS *CURRY À LA CLARABELLE!*
AND SINCE CURRY IS A FAVORITE FOOD IN ZANZIPAR, SHE CLINCHED THE FIRST PRIZE EASILY!
OH, GOOFY, HOW THOUGHTFUL OF YOU TO COME SEE ME OFF!
SMACK!
HEY!
MY GAWRSH! I HOPE CLARABELLE WATCHES HER KISSIN' HABIT WHEN SHE GETS TO ZANZIPAR!
YEAH! SHE MAY WIND UP GETTING ENGAGED!
AND...
WELL, SHE'S OFF TO THE LAND OF HANDSOME SHEIKS AND VEILED WOMEN!

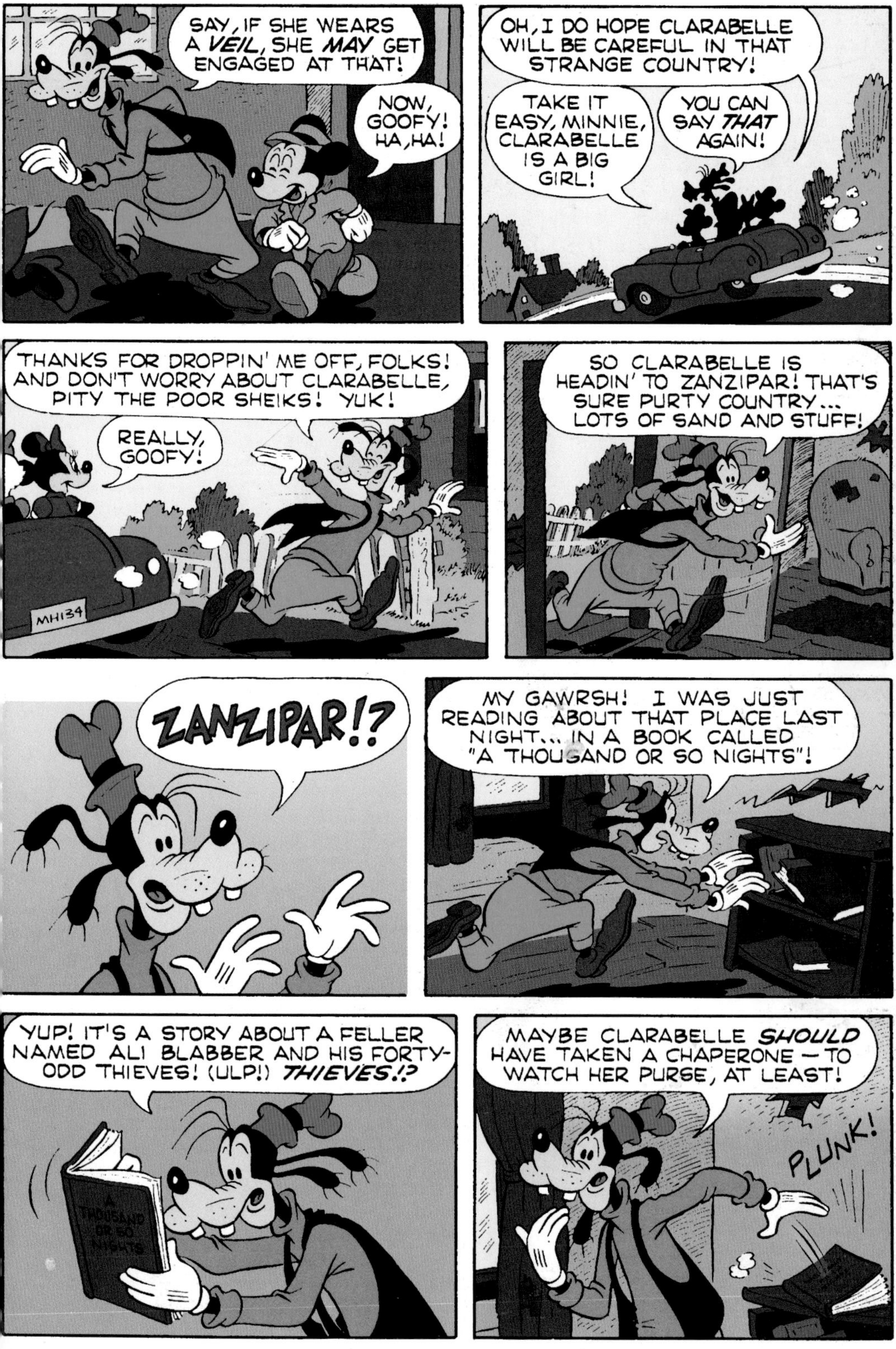
SAY, IF SHE WEARS A VEIL, SHE MAY GET ENGAGED AT THAT!
NOW, GOOFY! HA, HA!
OH, I DO HOPE CLARABELLE WILL BE CAREFUL IN THAT STRANGE COUNTRY!
TAKE IT EASY, MINNIE, CLARABELLE IS A BIG GIRL!
YOU CAN SAY THAT AGAIN!
THANKS FOR DROPPIN' ME OFF, FOLKS! AND DON'T WORRY ABOUT CLARABELLE, PITY THE POOR SHEIKS! YUK!
REALLY, GOOFY!
MH134
SO CLARABELLE IS HEADIN' TO ZANZIPAR! THAT'S SURE PURTY COUNTRY... LOTS OF SAND AND STUFF!
ZANZIPAR!?
MY GAWRSH! I WAS JUST READING ABOUT THAT PLACE LAST NIGHT... IN A BOOK CALLED "A THOUSAND OR SO NIGHTS"!
YUP! IT'S A STORY ABOUT A FELLER NAMED ALI BLABBER AND HIS FORTY-ODD THIEVES! (ULP!) THIEVES!?
A THOUSAND OR SO NIGHTS
MAYBE CLARABELLE SHOULD HAVE TAKEN A CHAPERONE — TO WATCH HER PURSE, AT LEAST!
PLUNK!

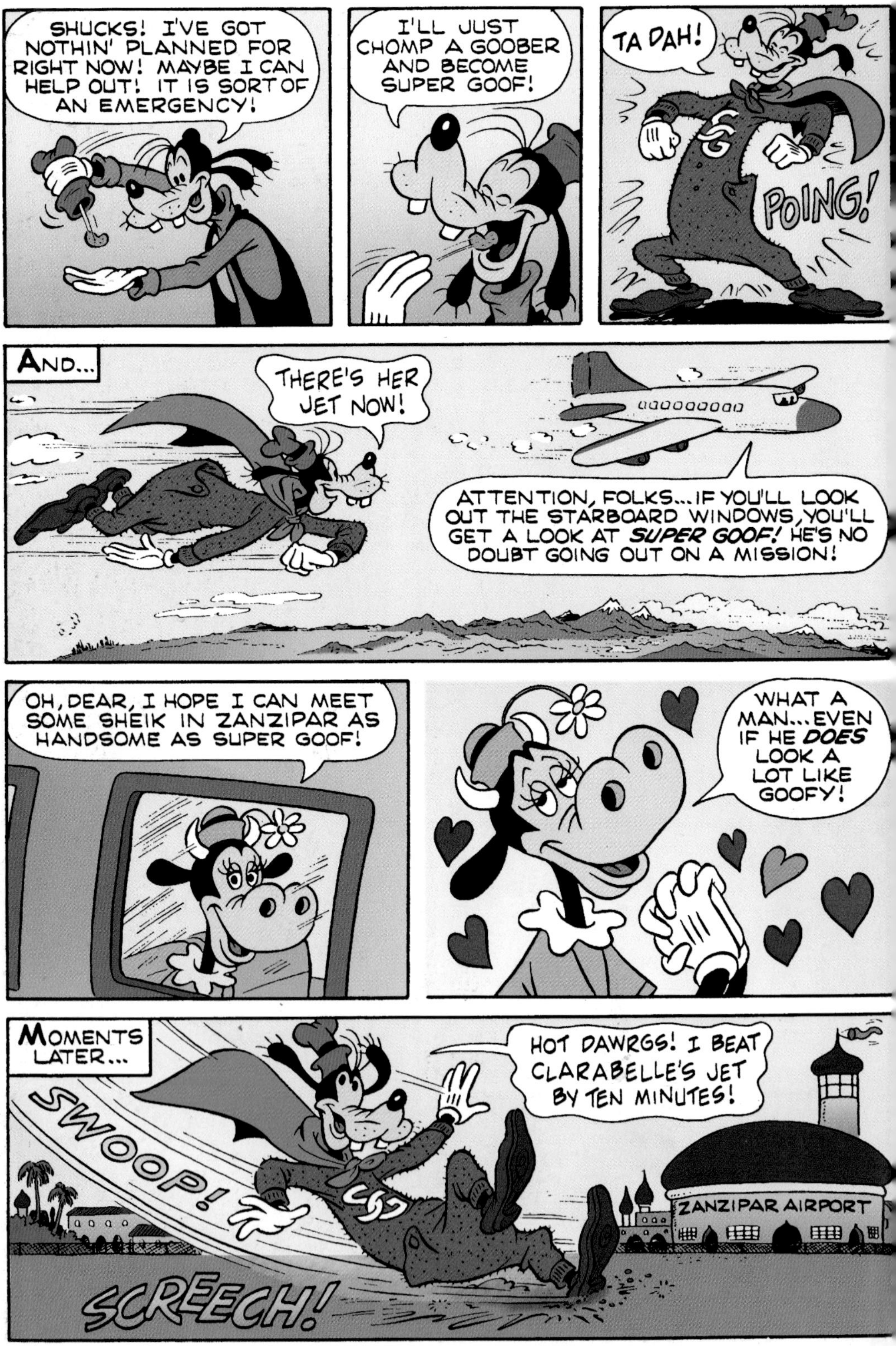
SHUCKS! I'VE GOT NOTHIN' PLANNED FOR RIGHT NOW! MAYBE I CAN HELP OUT! IT IS SORT OF AN EMERGENCY!
I'LL JUST CHOMP A GOOBER AND BECOME SUPER GOOF!
TA DAH!
POING!
AND...
THERE'S HER JET NOW!
ATTENTION, FOLKS...IF YOU'LL LOOK OUT THE STARBOARD WINDOWS, YOU'LL GET A LOOK AT SUPER GOOF! HE'S NO DOUBT GOING OUT ON A MISSION!
OH, DEAR, I HOPE I CAN MEET SOME SHEIK IN ZANZIPAR AS HANDSOME AS SUPER GOOF!
WHAT A MAN...EVEN IF HE DOES LOOK A LOT LIKE GOOFY!
MOMENTS LATER...
HOT DAWRGS! I BEAT CLARABELLE'S JET BY TEN MINUTES!
SWOOP!
ZANZIPAR AIRPORT
SCREECH!

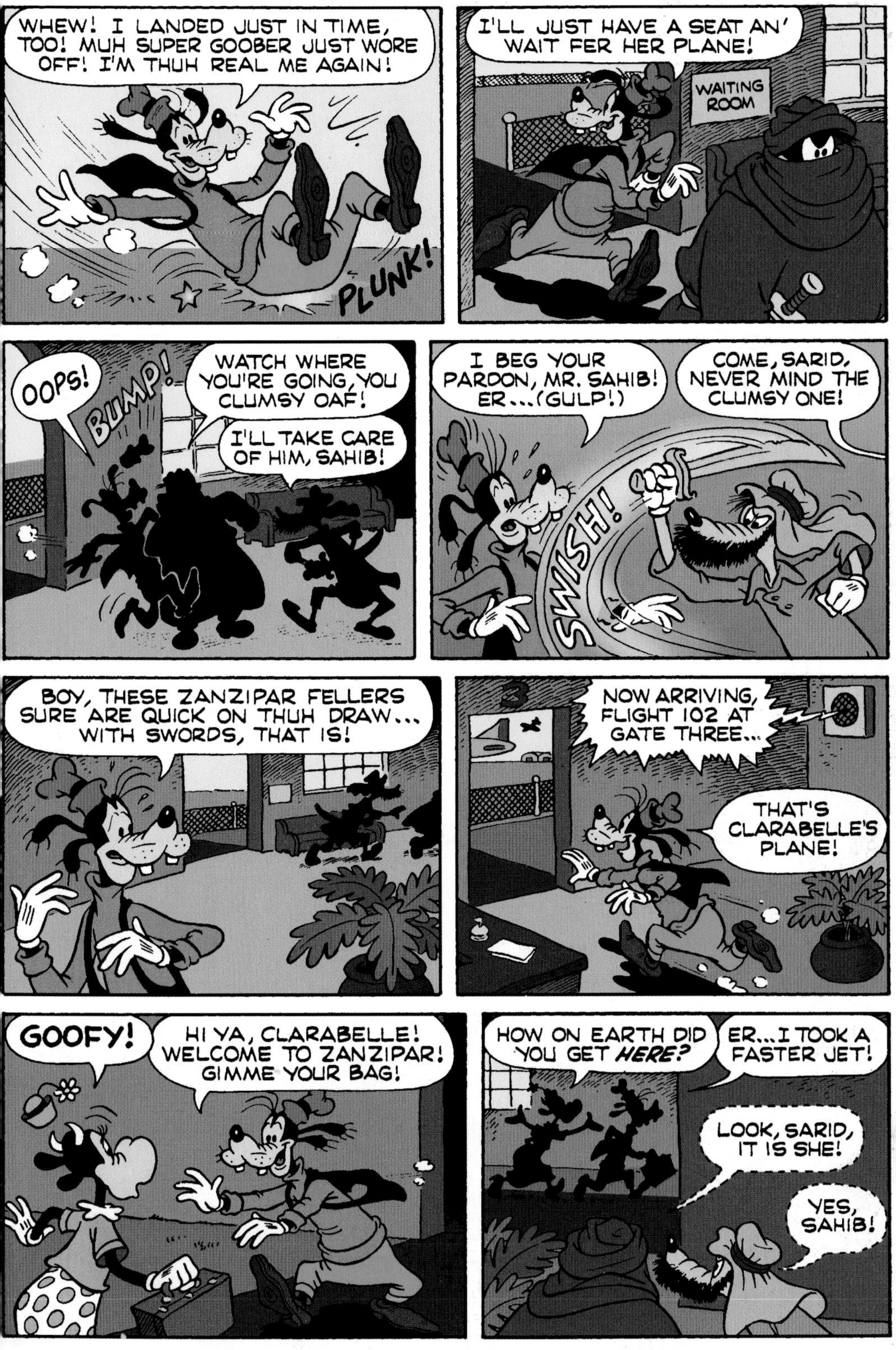
WHEW! I LANDED JUST IN TIME, TOO! MUH SUPER GOOBER JUST WORE OFF! I'M THUH REAL ME AGAIN!
PLUNK!
I'LL JUST HAVE A SEAT AN' WAIT FER HER PLANE!
WAITING ROOM
OOPS!
BUMP!
WATCH WHERE YOU'RE GOING, YOU CLUMSY OAF!
I'LL TAKE CARE OF HIM, SAHIB!
I BEG YOUR PARDON, MR. SAHIB! ER...(GULP!)
COME, SARID, NEVER MIND THE CLUMSY ONE!
SWISH!
BOY, THESE ZANZIPAR FELLERS SURE ARE QUICK ON THUH DRAW... WITH SWORDS, THAT IS!
NOW ARRIVING, FLIGHT 102 AT GATE THREE...
THAT'S CLARABELLE'S PLANE!
GOOFY!
HI YA, CLARABELLE! WELCOME TO ZANZIPAR! GIMME YOUR BAG!
HOW ON EARTH DID YOU GET HERE?
ER...I TOOK A FASTER JET!
LOOK, SARID, IT IS SHE!
YES, SAHIB!

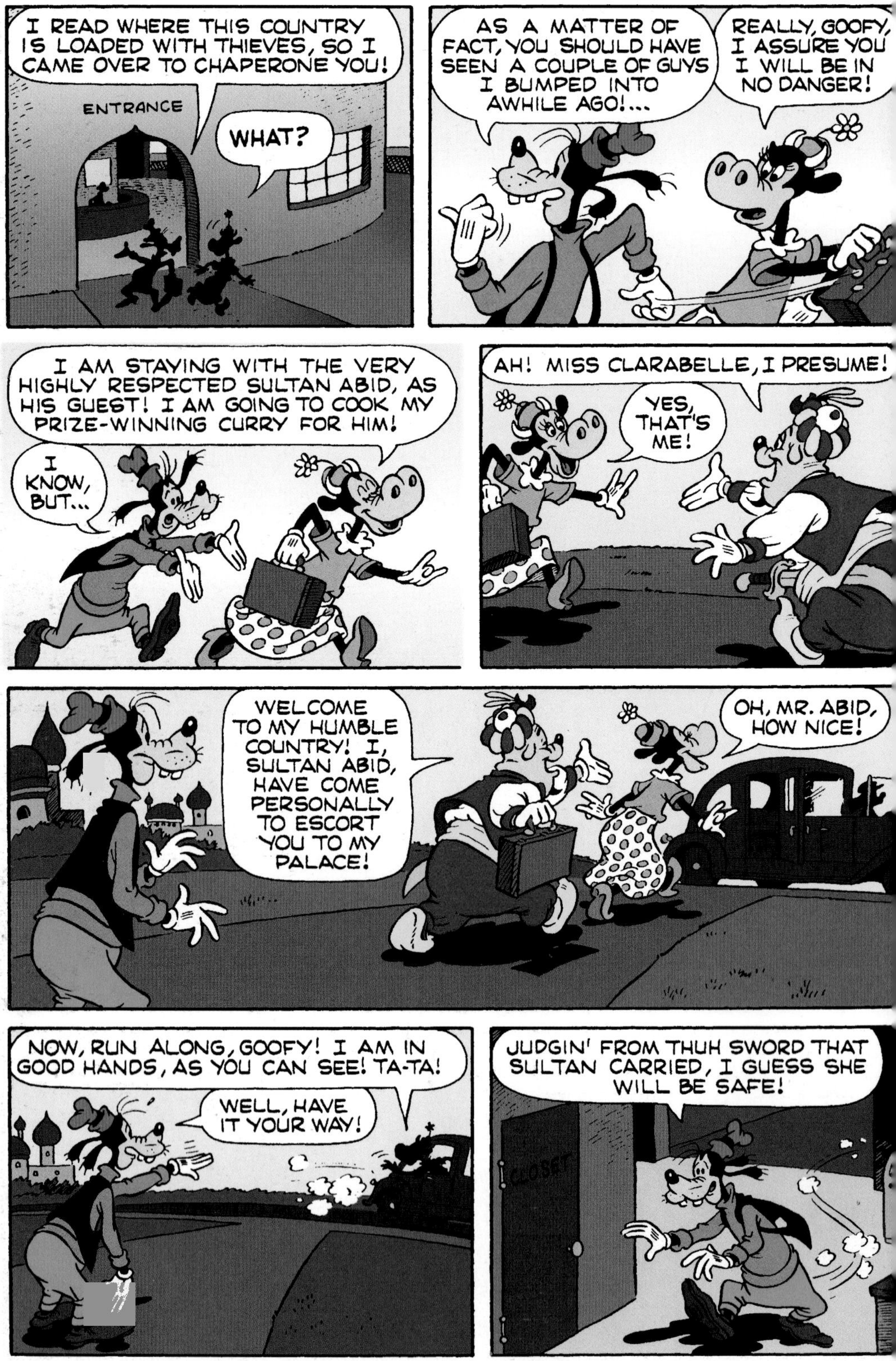
I READ WHERE THIS COUNTRY IS LOADED WITH THIEVES, SO I CAME OVER TO CHAPERONE YOU!
ENTRANCE
WHAT?
AS A MATTER OF FACT, YOU SHOULD HAVE SEEN A COUPLE OF GUYS I BUMPED INTO AWHILE AGO!...
REALLY, GOOFY, I ASSURE YOU I WILL BE IN NO DANGER!
I AM STAYING WITH THE VERY HIGHLY RESPECTED SULTAN ABID, AS HIS GUEST! I AM GOING TO COOK MY PRIZE-WINNING CURRY FOR HIM!
I KNOW, BUT...
AH! MISS CLARABELLE, I PRESUME!
YES, THAT'S ME!
WELCOME TO MY HUMBLE COUNTRY! I, SULTAN ABID, HAVE COME PERSONALLY TO ESCORT YOU TO MY PALACE!
OH, MR. ABID, HOW NICE!
NOW, RUN ALONG, GOOFY! I AM IN GOOD HANDS, AS YOU CAN SEE! TA-TA!
WELL, HAVE IT YOUR WAY!
JUDGIN' FROM THUH SWORD THAT SULTAN CARRIED, I GUESS SHE WILL BE SAFE!
CLOSET

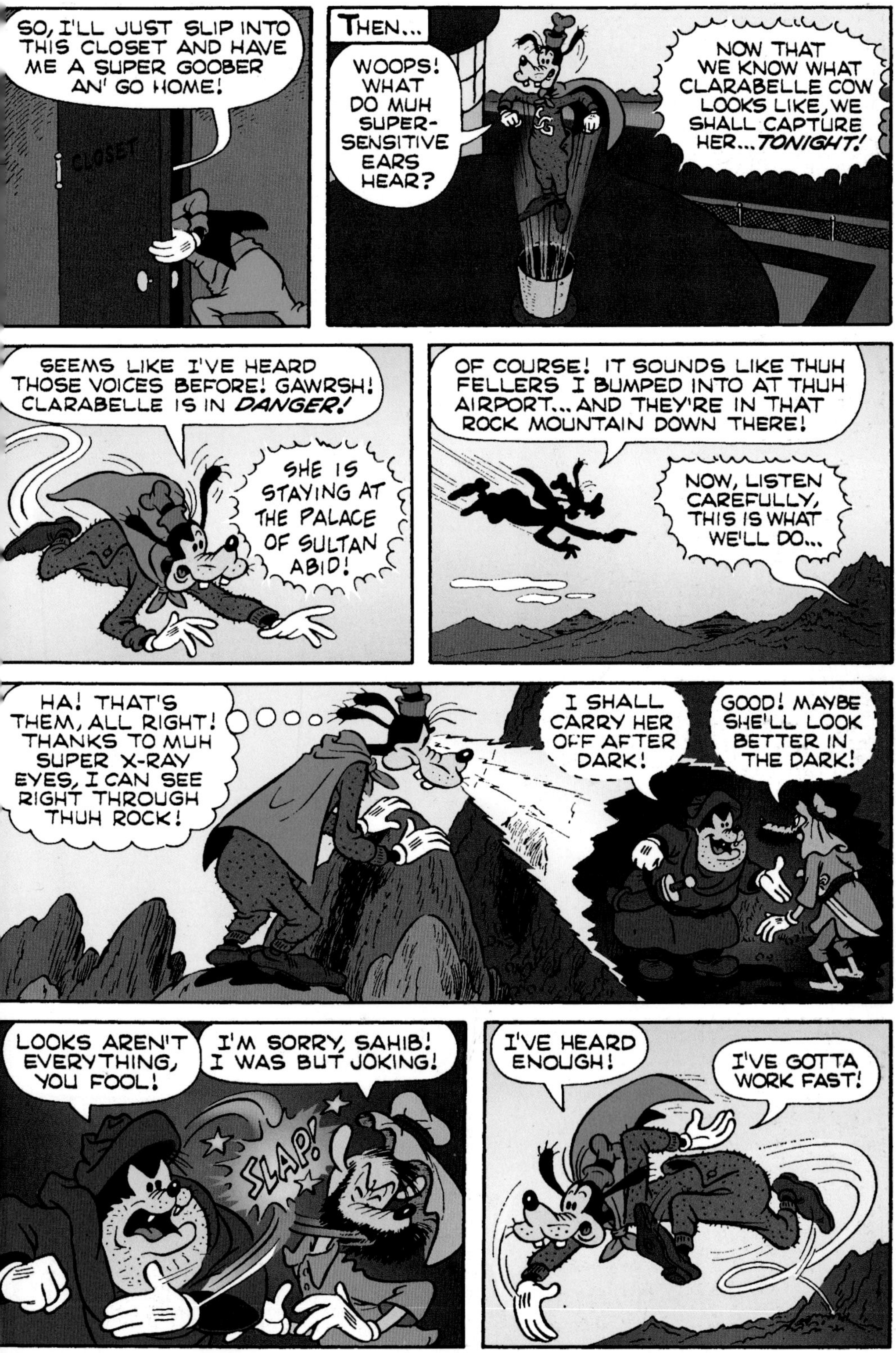

SO, I'LL JUST SLIP INTO THIS CLOSET AND HAVE ME A SUPER GOOBER AN' GO HOME!
CLOSET
THEN...
WOOPS! WHAT DO MUH SUPER-SENSITIVE EARS HEAR?
NOW THAT WE KNOW WHAT CLARABELLE COW LOOKS LIKE, WE SHALL CAPTURE HER... TONIGHT!
SEEMS LIKE I'VE HEARD THOSE VOICES BEFORE! GAWRSH! CLARABELLE IS IN DANGER!
SHE IS STAYING AT THE PALACE OF SULTAN ABID!
OF COURSE! IT SOUNDS LIKE THUH FELLERS I BUMPED INTO AT THUH AIRPORT... AND THEY'RE IN THAT ROCK MOUNTAIN DOWN THERE!
NOW, LISTEN CAREFULLY, THIS IS WHAT WE'LL DO...
HA! THAT'S THEM, ALL RIGHT! THANKS TO MUH SUPER X-RAY EYES, I CAN SEE RIGHT THROUGH THUH ROCK!
I SHALL CARRY HER OFF AFTER DARK!
GOOD! MAYBE SHE'LL LOOK BETTER IN THE DARK!
LOOKS AREN'T EVERYTHING, YOU FOOL!
SLAP!
I'M SORRY, SAHIB! I WAS BUT JOKING!
I'VE HEARD ENOUGH!
I'VE GOTTA WORK FAST!

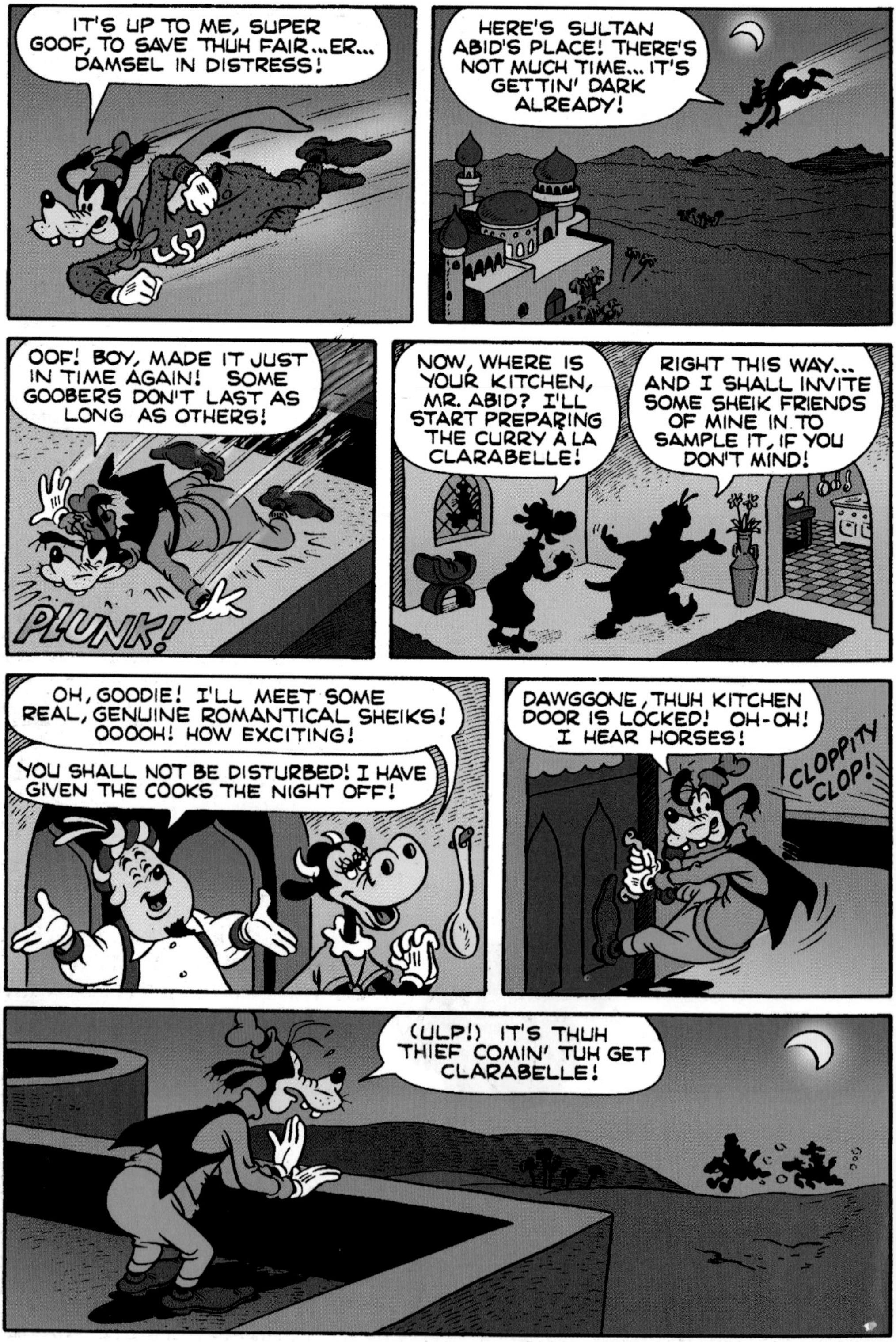
IT'S UP TO ME, SUPER GOOF, TO SAVE THUH FAIR...ER... DAMSEL IN DISTRESS!
HERE'S SULTAN ABID'S PLACE! THERE'S NOT MUCH TIME... IT'S GETTIN' DARK ALREADY!
OOF! BOY, MADE IT JUST IN TIME AGAIN! SOME GOOBERS DON'T LAST AS LONG AS OTHERS!
PLUNK!
NOW, WHERE IS YOUR KITCHEN, MR. ABID? I'LL START PREPARING THE CURRY À LA CLARABELLE!
RIGHT THIS WAY... AND I SHALL INVITE SOME SHEIK FRIENDS OF MINE IN TO SAMPLE IT, IF YOU DON'T MIND!
OH, GOODIE! I'LL MEET SOME REAL, GENUINE ROMANTICAL SHEIKS! OOOOH! HOW EXCITING!
YOU SHALL NOT BE DISTURBED! I HAVE GIVEN THE COOKS THE NIGHT OFF!
DAWGGONE, THUH KITCHEN DOOR IS LOCKED! OH-OH! I HEAR HORSES!
CLOPPITY CLOP!
(ULP!) IT'S THUH THIEF COMIN' TUH GET CLARABELLE!

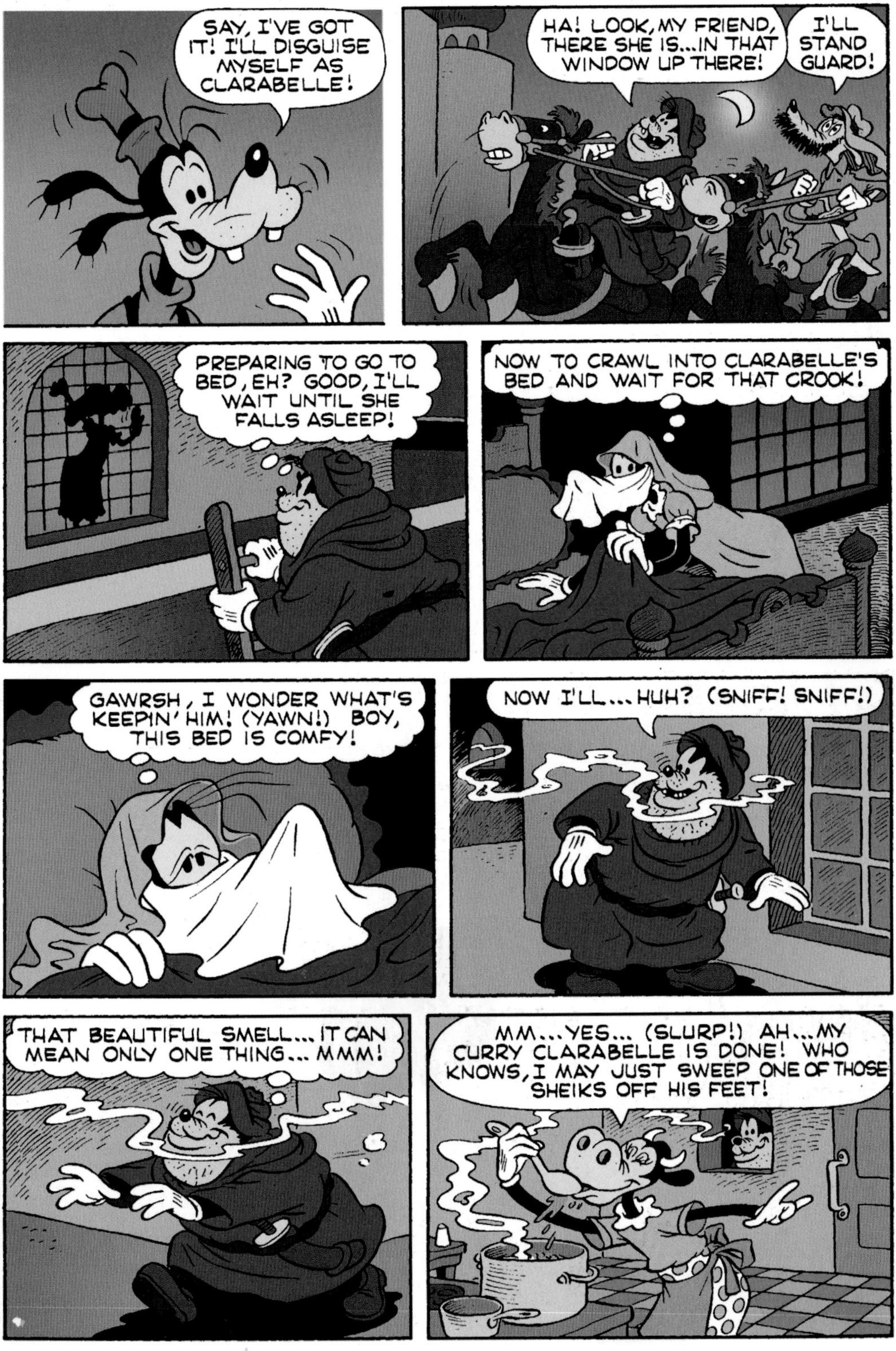
SAY, I'VE GOT IT! I'LL DISGUISE MYSELF AS CLARABELLE!
HA! LOOK, MY FRIEND, THERE SHE IS...IN THAT WINDOW UP THERE!
I'LL STAND GUARD!
PREPARING TO GO TO BED, EH? GOOD, I'LL WAIT UNTIL SHE FALLS ASLEEP!
NOW TO CRAWL INTO CLARABELLE'S BED AND WAIT FOR THAT CROOK!
GAWRSH, I WONDER WHAT'S KEEPIN' HIM! (YAWN!) BOY, THIS BED IS COMFY!
NOW I'LL... HUH? (SNIFF! SNIFF!)
THAT BEAUTIFUL SMELL... IT CAN MEAN ONLY ONE THING... MMM!
MM... YES... (SLURP!) AH... MY CURRY CLARABELLE IS DONE! WHO KNOWS, I MAY JUST SWEEP ONE OF THOSE SHEIKS OFF HIS FEET!

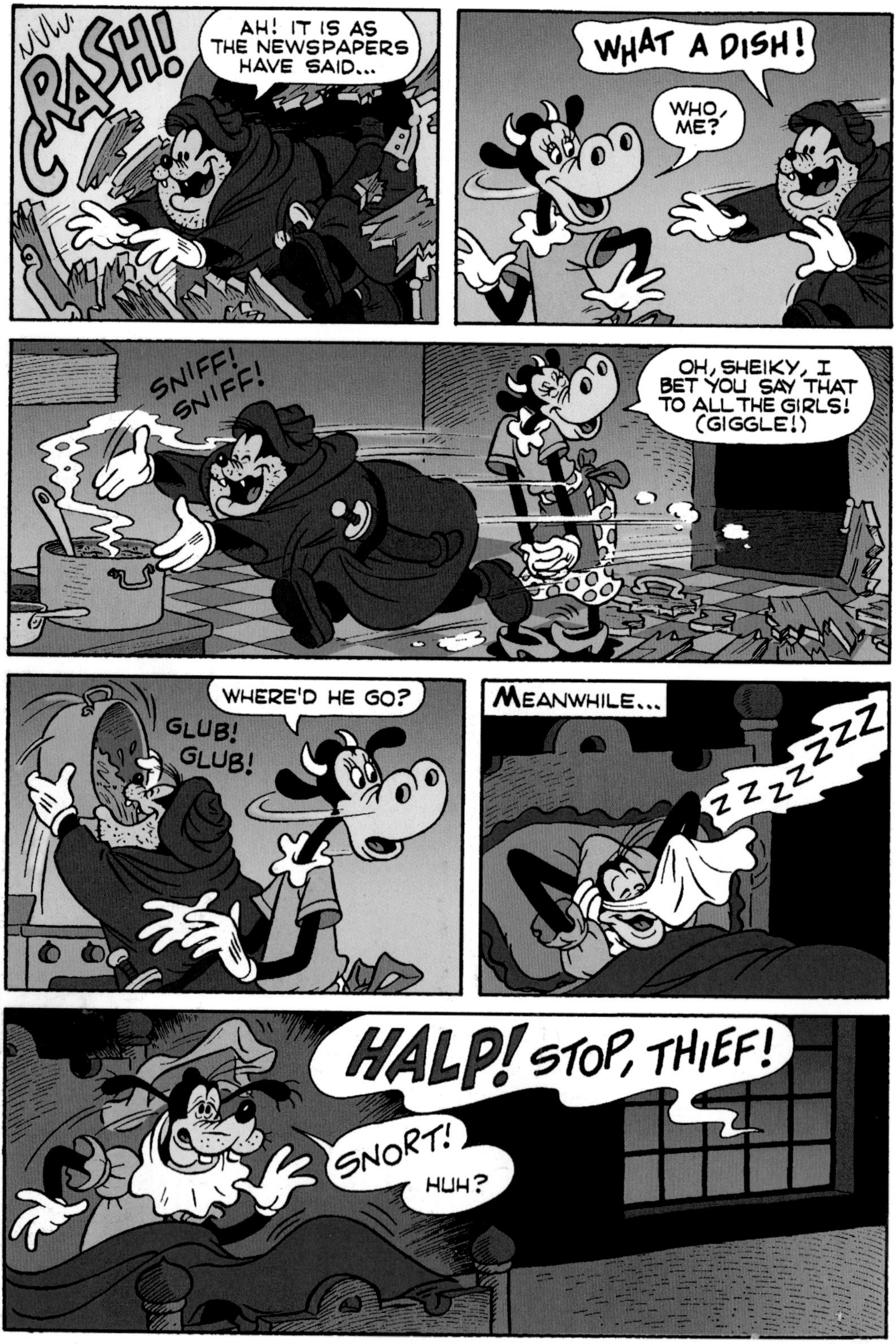
CRASH!
AH! IT IS AS THE NEWSPAPERS HAVE SAID...
WHAT A DISH!
WHO, ME?
SNIFF! SNIFF!
OH, SHEIKY, I BET YOU SAY THAT TO ALL THE GIRLS! (GIGGLE!)
WHERE'D HE GO?
GLUB! GLUB!
MEANWHILE...
ZZZZZZZZ
HALP! STOP, THIEF!
SNORT!
HUH?

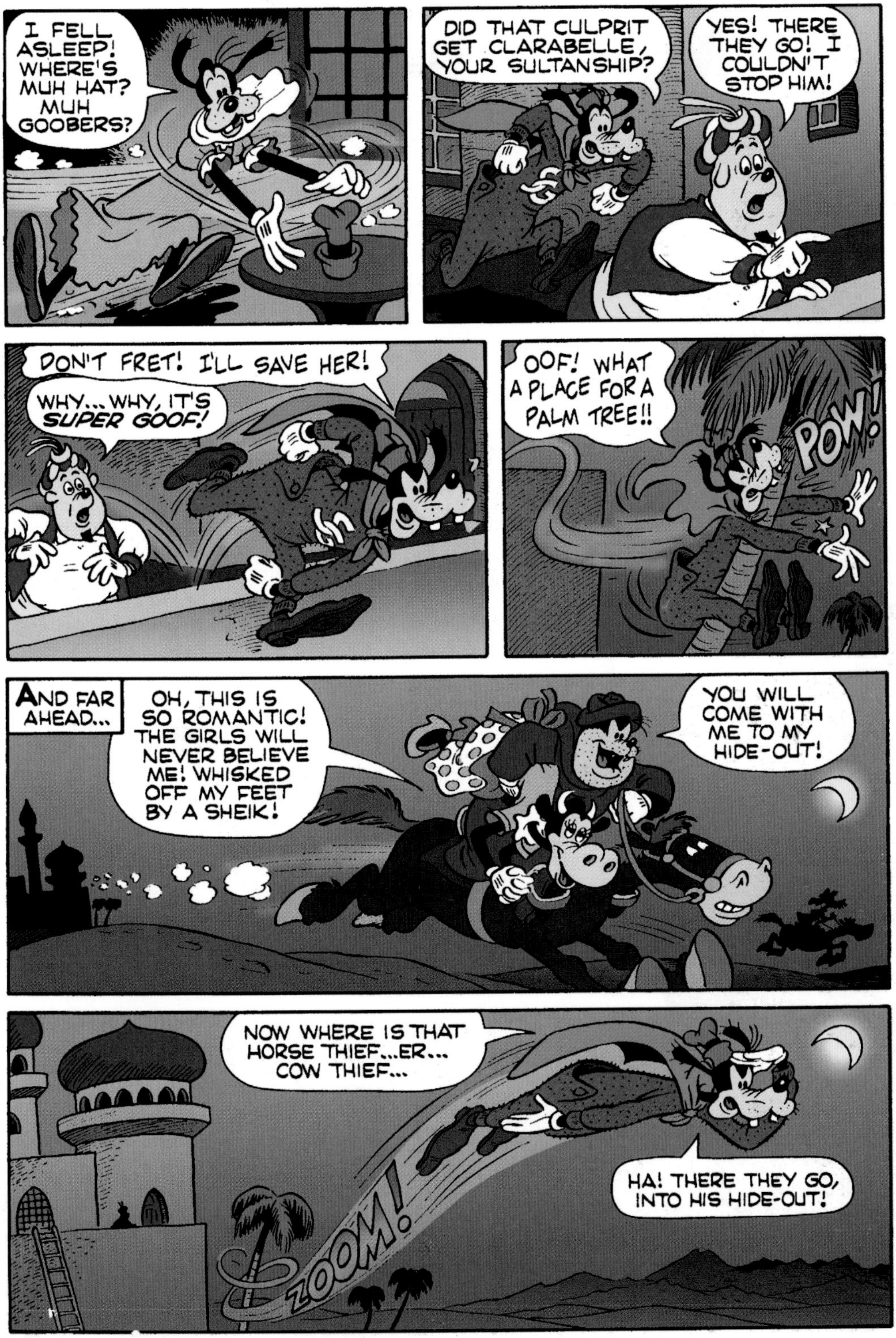
I FELL ASLEEP! WHERE'S MUH HAT? MUH GOOBERS?
DID THAT CULPRIT GET CLARABELLE, YOUR SULTANSHIP?
YES! THERE THEY GO! I COULDN'T STOP HIM!
DON'T FRET! I'LL SAVE HER!
WHY... WHY, IT'S SUPER GOOF!
OOF! WHAT A PLACE FOR A PALM TREE!!
POW!
AND FAR AHEAD...
OH, THIS IS SO ROMANTIC! THE GIRLS WILL NEVER BELIEVE ME! WHISKED OFF MY FEET BY A SHEIK!
YOU WILL COME WITH ME TO MY HIDE-OUT!
NOW WHERE IS THAT HORSE THIEF...ER... COW THIEF...
HA! THERE THEY GO, INTO HIS HIDE-OUT!
ZOOM!

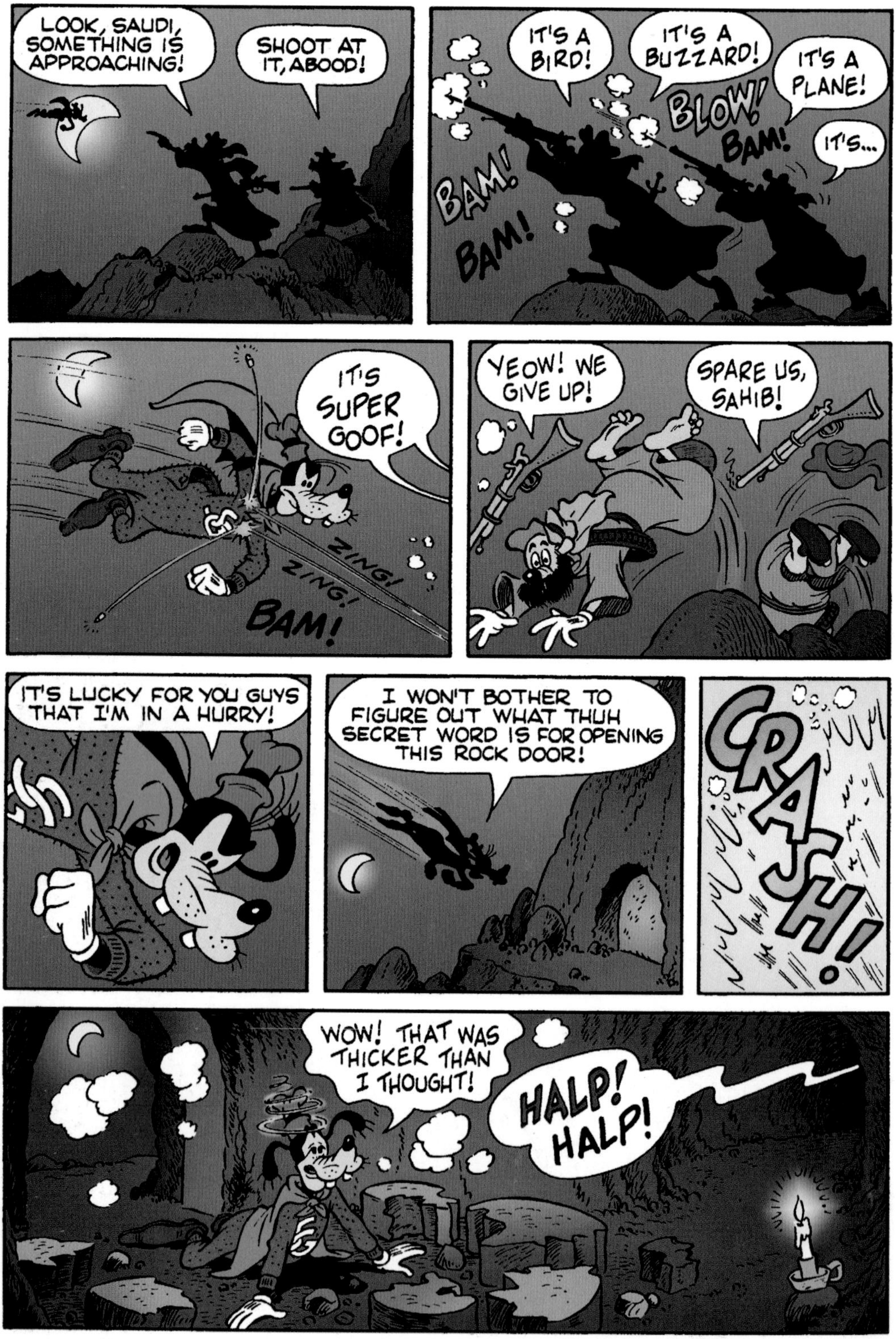
LOOK, SAUDI, SOMETHING IS APPROACHING!
SHOOT AT IT, ABOOD!
IT'S A BIRD!
IT'S A BUZZARD!
IT'S A PLANE!
BLOW!
BAM!
IT'S...
BAM!
BAM!
IT'S SUPER GOOF!
ZING!
ZING!
BAM!
YEOW! WE GIVE UP!
SPARE US, SAHIB!
IT'S LUCKY FOR YOU GUYS THAT I'M IN A HURRY!
I WON'T BOTHER TO FIGURE OUT WHAT THUH SECRET WORD IS FOR OPENING THIS ROCK DOOR!
CRASH!
WOW! THAT WAS THICKER THAN I THOUGHT!
HALP! HALP!

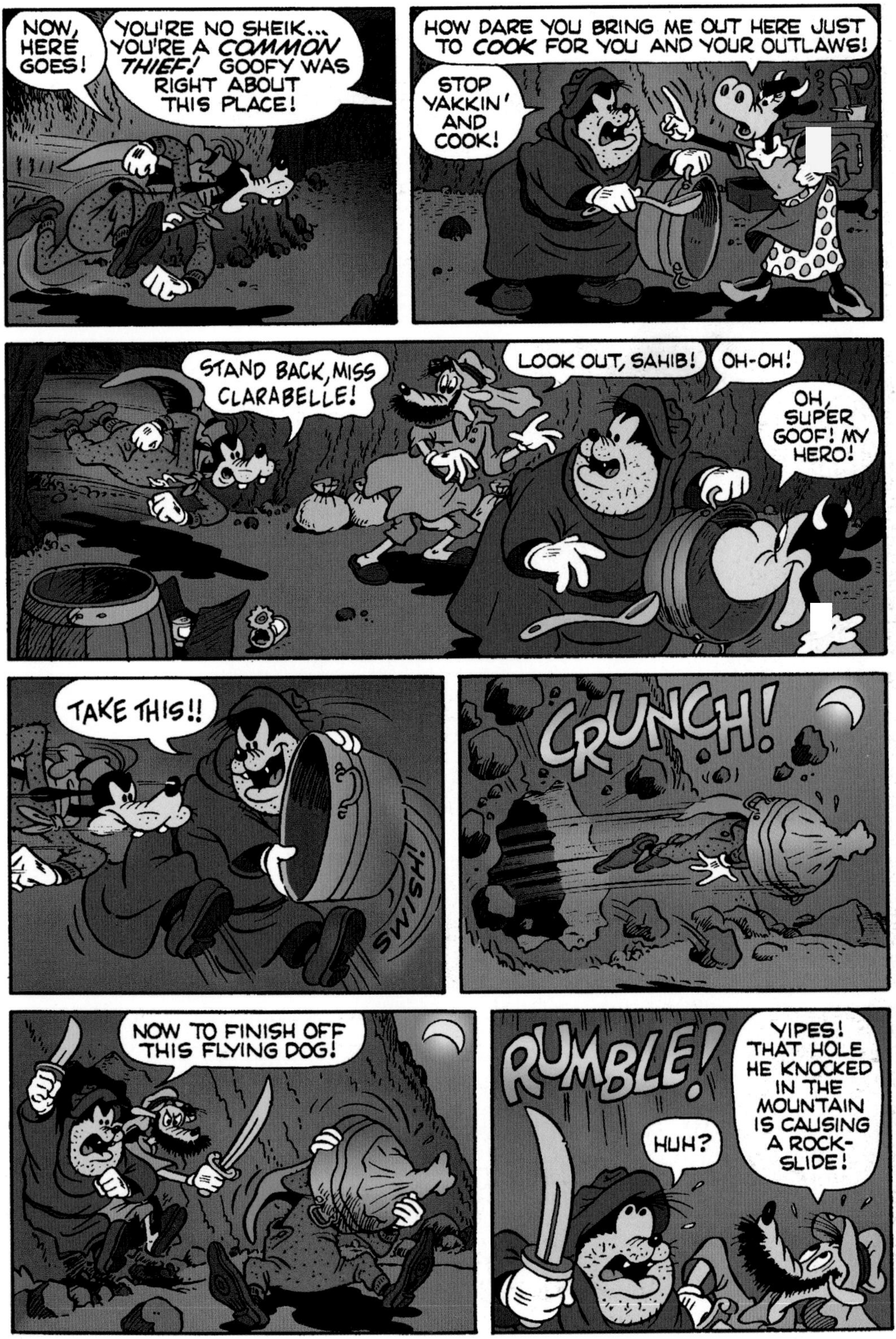

NOW, HERE GOES!
YOU'RE NO SHEIK... YOU'RE A COMMON THIEF! GOOFY WAS RIGHT ABOUT THIS PLACE!
HOW DARE YOU BRING ME OUT HERE JUST TO COOK FOR YOU AND YOUR OUTLAWS!
STOP YAKKIN' AND COOK!
STAND BACK, MISS CLARABELLE!
LOOK OUT, SAHIB!
OH-OH!
OH, SUPER GOOF! MY HERO!
TAKE THIS!!
SWISH!
CRUNCH!
NOW TO FINISH OFF THIS FLYING DOG!
RUMBLE!
HUH?
YIPES! THAT HOLE HE KNOCKED IN THE MOUNTAIN IS CAUSING A ROCK-SLIDE!

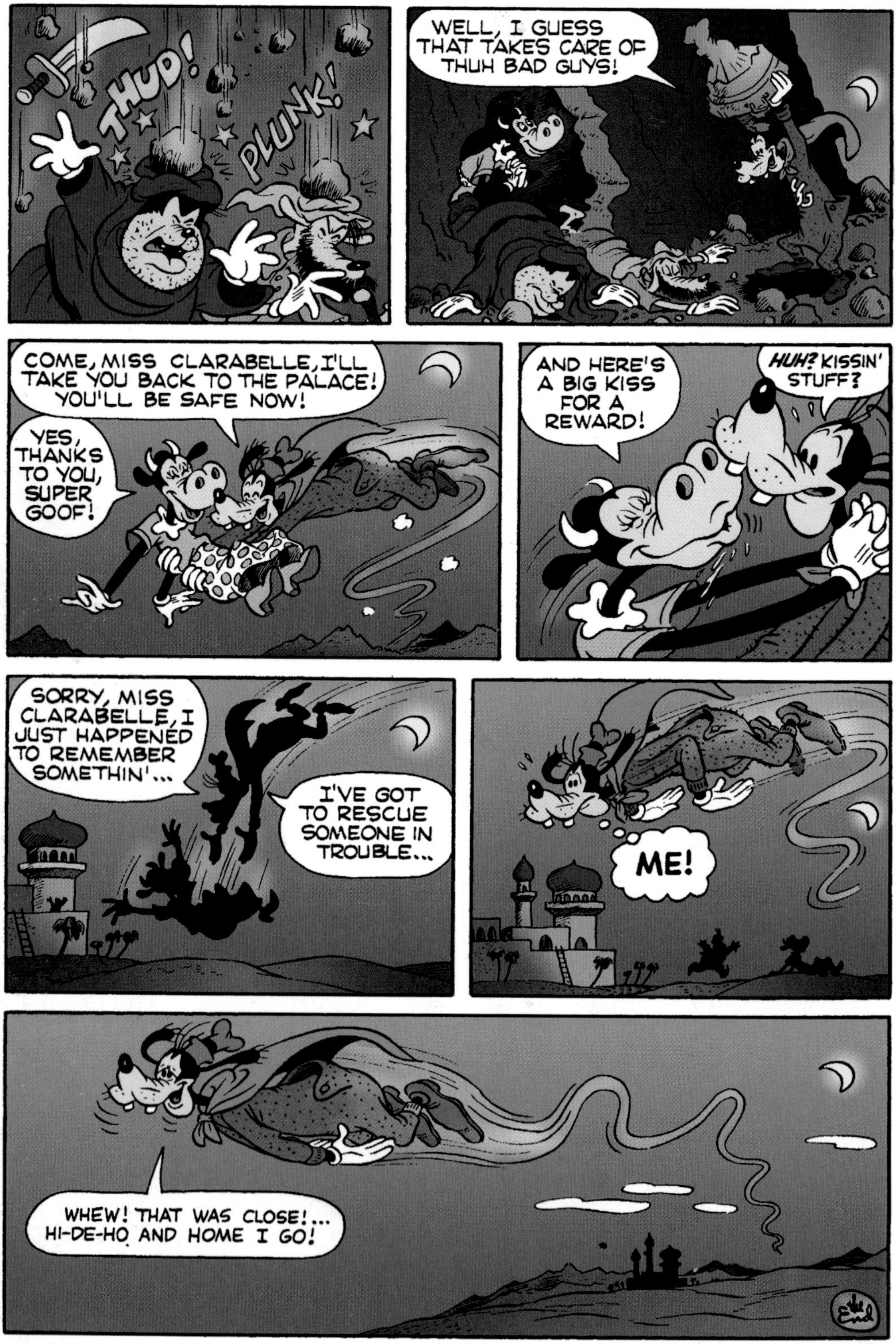
THUD!
PLUNK!
WELL, I GUESS THAT TAKES CARE OF THUH BAD GUYS!
COME, MISS CLARABELLE, I'LL TAKE YOU BACK TO THE PALACE! YOU'LL BE SAFE NOW!
YES, THANKS TO YOU, SUPER GOOF!
AND HERE'S A BIG KISS FOR A REWARD!
HUH? KISSIN' STUFF?
SORRY, MISS CLARABELLE, I JUST HAPPENED TO REMEMBER SOMETHIN'...
I'VE GOT TO RESCUE SOMEONE IN TROUBLE...
ME!
WHEW! THAT WAS CLOSE!... HI-DE-HO AND HOME I GO!
The End

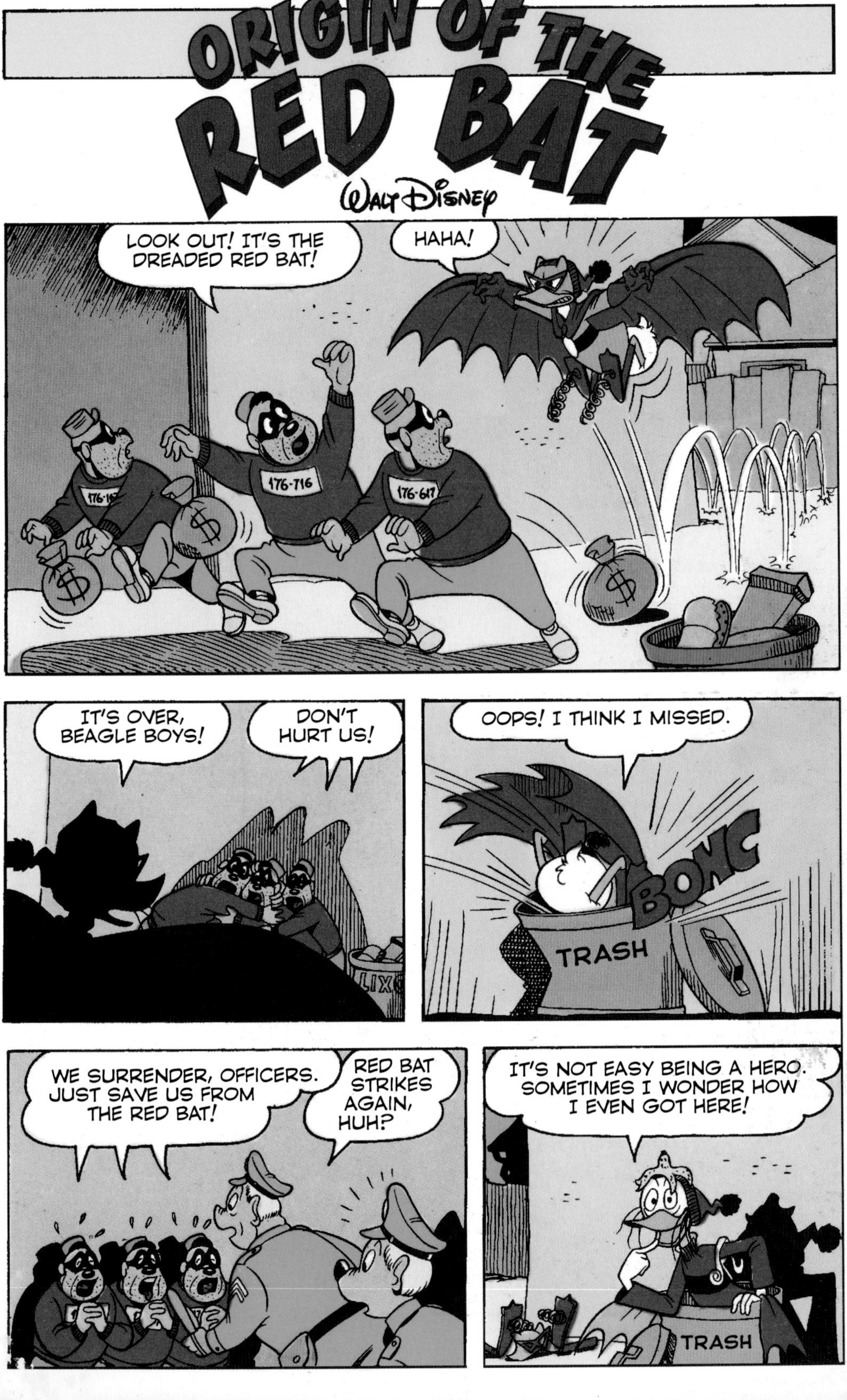
ORIGIN OF THE RED BAT
WALT DISNEY
LOOK OUT! IT'S THE DREADED RED BAT!
HAHA!
176-716
176-617
IT'S OVER, BEAGLE BOYS!
DON'T HURT US!
OOPS! I THINK I MISSED.
BONC
TRASH
WE SURRENDER, OFFICERS. JUST SAVE US FROM THE RED BAT!
RED BAT STRIKES AGAIN, HUH?
IT'S NOT EASY BEING A HERO. SOMETIMES I WONDER HOW I EVEN GOT HERE!
TRASH

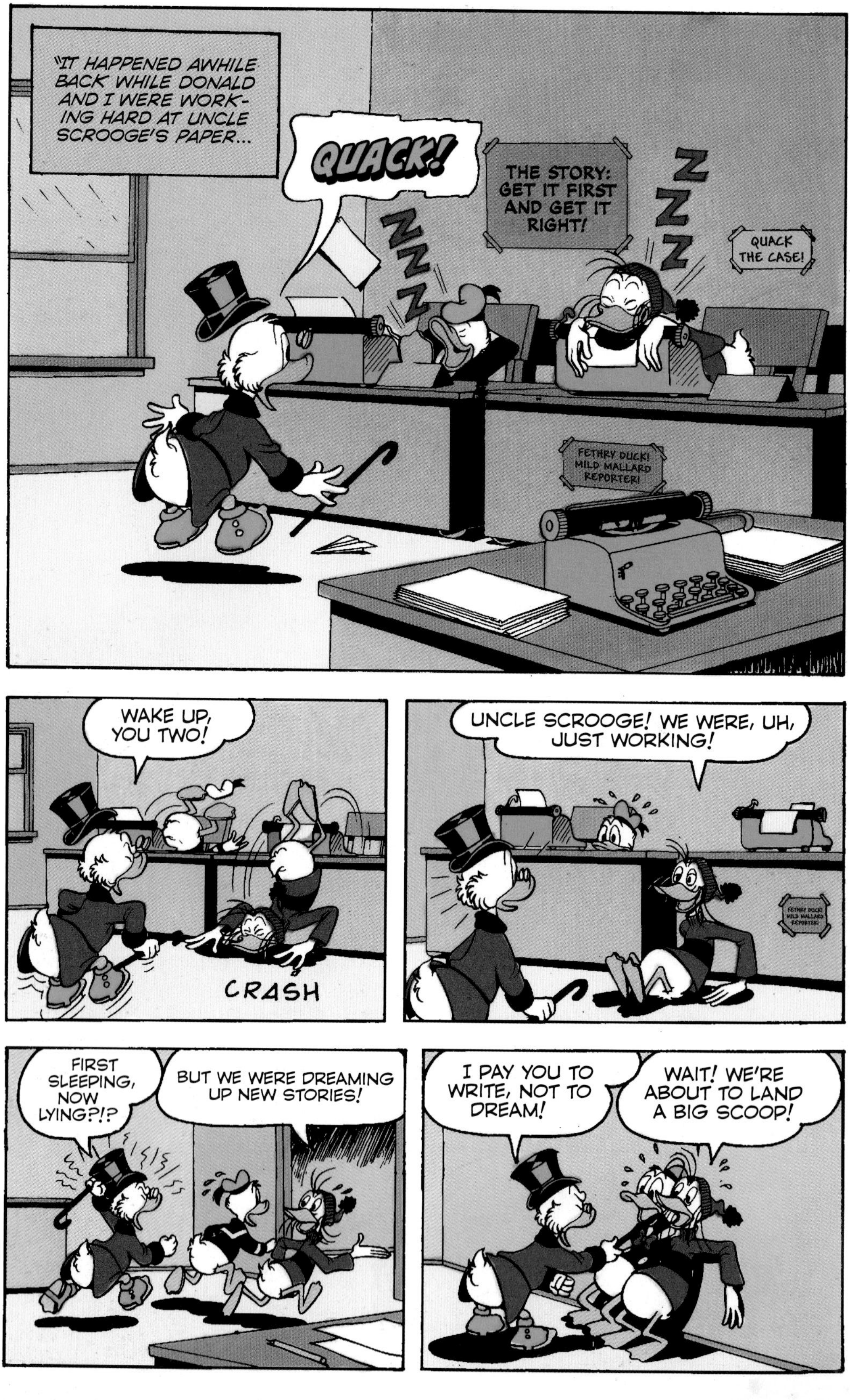
"IT HAPPENED AWHILE BACK WHILE DONALD AND I WERE WORKING HARD AT UNCLE SCROOGE'S PAPER...
QUACK!
ZZZ
THE STORY: GET IT FIRST AND GET IT RIGHT!
ZZZ
QUACK THE CASE!
FETHRY DUCK! MILD MALLARD REPORTER!
WAKE UP, YOU TWO!
CRASH
UNCLE SCROOGE! WE WERE, UH, JUST WORKING!
FETHRY DUCK! MILD MALLARD REPORTER!
FIRST SLEEPING, NOW LYING?!?
BUT WE WERE DREAMING UP NEW STORIES!
I PAY YOU TO WRITE, NOT TO DREAM!
WAIT! WE'RE ABOUT TO LAND A BIG SCOOP!

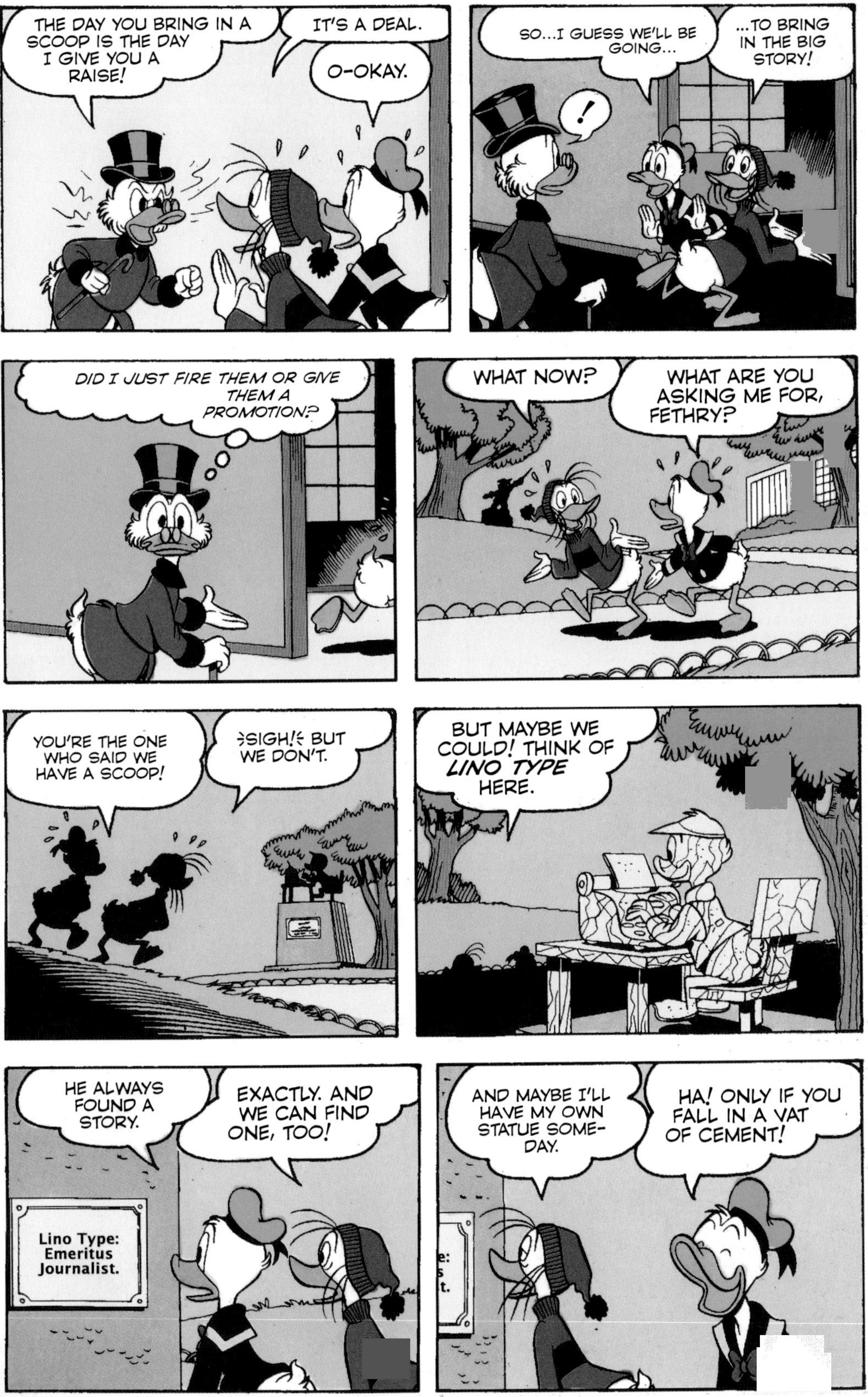
THE DAY YOU BRING IN A SCOOP IS THE DAY I GIVE YOU A RAISE!
IT'S A DEAL.
O-OKAY.
SO...I GUESS WE'LL BE GOING...
...TO BRING IN THE BIG STORY!
!
DID I JUST FIRE THEM OR GIVE THEM A PROMOTION?
WHAT NOW?
WHAT ARE YOU ASKING ME FOR, FETHRY?
YOU'RE THE ONE WHO SAID WE HAVE A SCOOP!
SIGH! BUT WE DON'T.
BUT MAYBE WE COULD! THINK OF LINO TYPE HERE.
HE ALWAYS FOUND A STORY.
EXACTLY. AND WE CAN FIND ONE, TOO!
Lino Type: Emeritus Journalist.
AND MAYBE I'LL HAVE MY OWN STATUE SOME-DAY.
HA! ONLY IF YOU FALL IN A VAT OF CEMENT!

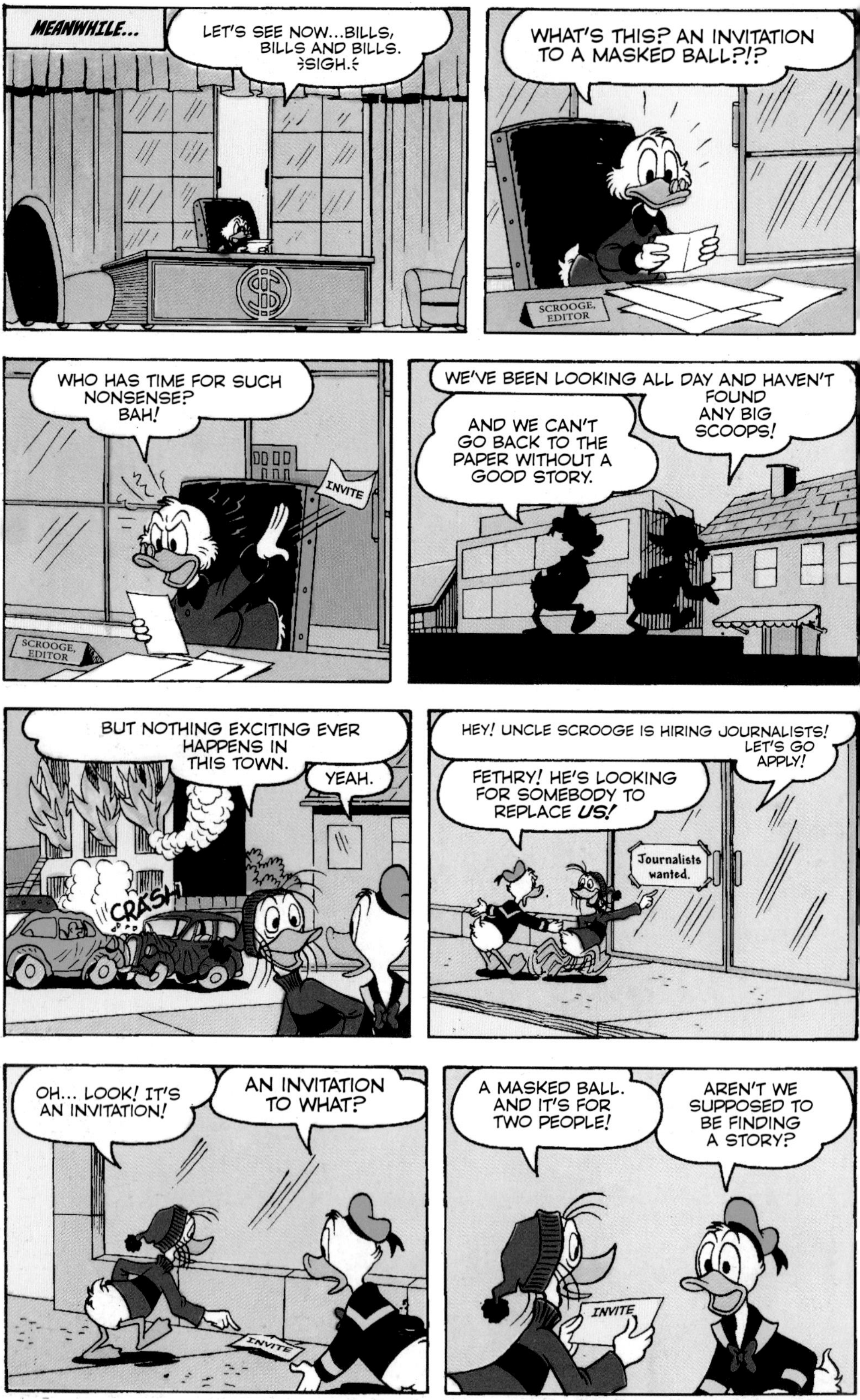
MEANWHILE...
LET'S SEE NOW...BILLS, BILLS AND BILLS. ⋛SIGH.⋚
WHAT'S THIS? AN INVITATION TO A MASKED BALL?!?
SCROOGE, EDITOR
WHO HAS TIME FOR SUCH NONSENSE? BAH!
INVITE
SCROOGE, EDITOR
WE'VE BEEN LOOKING ALL DAY AND HAVEN'T FOUND ANY BIG SCOOPS!
AND WE CAN'T GO BACK TO THE PAPER WITHOUT A GOOD STORY.
BUT NOTHING EXCITING EVER HAPPENS IN THIS TOWN.
YEAH.
CRASH
HEY! UNCLE SCROOGE IS HIRING JOURNALISTS! LET'S GO APPLY!
FETHRY! HE'S LOOKING FOR SOMEBODY TO REPLACE US!
Journalists wanted.
OH... LOOK! IT'S AN INVITATION!
AN INVITATION TO WHAT?
INVITE
A MASKED BALL. AND IT'S FOR TWO PEOPLE!
AREN'T WE SUPPOSED TO BE FINDING A STORY?
INVITE

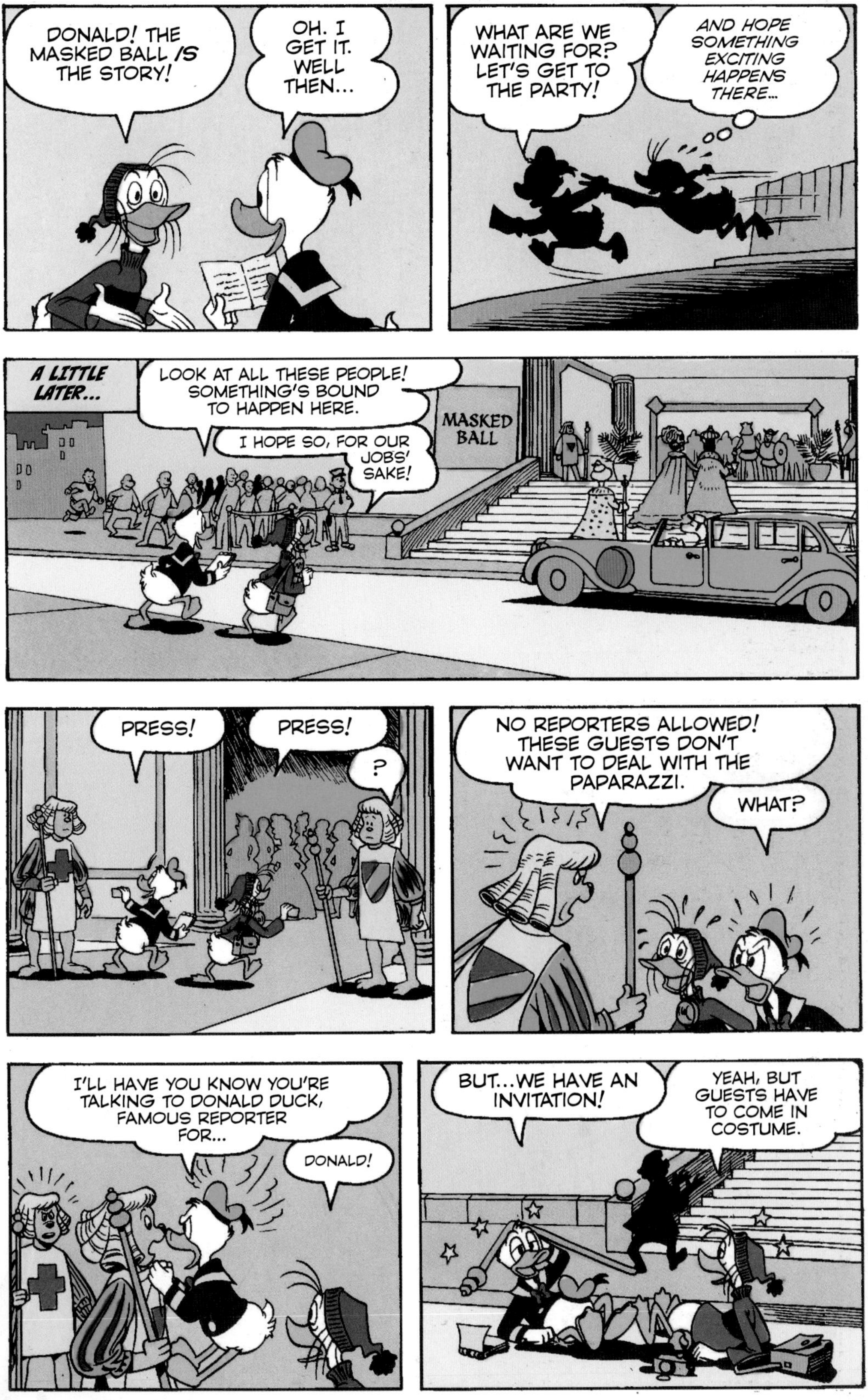
DONALD! THE MASKED BALL *IS* THE STORY!
OH. I GET IT. WELL THEN...
WHAT ARE WE WAITING FOR? LET'S GET TO THE PARTY!
AND HOPE SOMETHING EXCITING HAPPENS THERE...
A LITTLE LATER...
LOOK AT ALL THESE PEOPLE! SOMETHING'S BOUND TO HAPPEN HERE.
I HOPE SO, FOR OUR JOBS' SAKE!
MASKED BALL
PRESS!
PRESS!
?
NO REPORTERS ALLOWED! THESE GUESTS DON'T WANT TO DEAL WITH THE PAPARAZZI.
WHAT?
I'LL HAVE YOU KNOW YOU'RE TALKING TO DONALD DUCK, FAMOUS REPORTER FOR...
DONALD!
BUT...WE HAVE AN INVITATION!
YEAH, BUT GUESTS HAVE TO COME IN COSTUME.

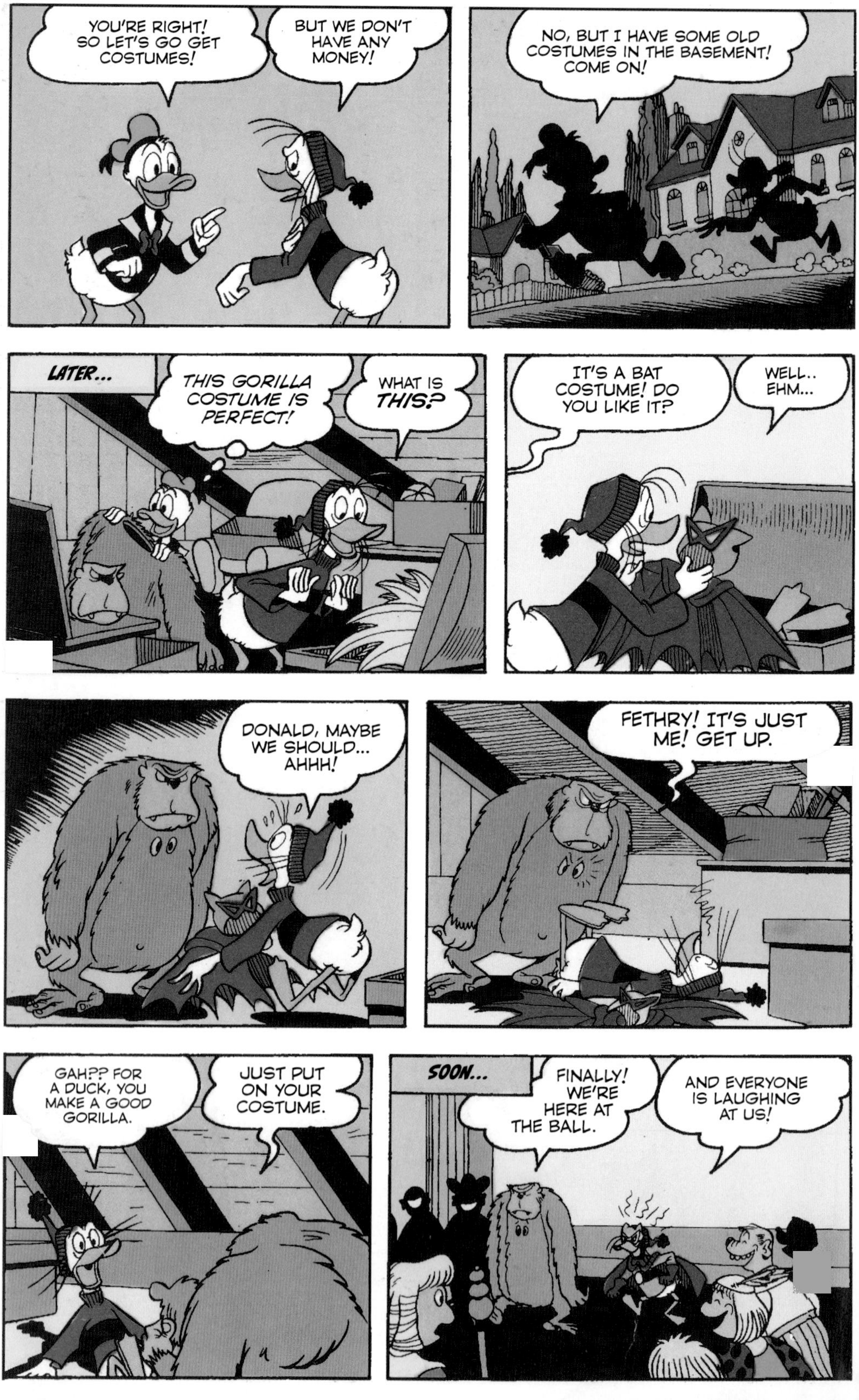

YOU'RE RIGHT! SO LET'S GO GET COSTUMES!
BUT WE DON'T HAVE ANY MONEY!
NO, BUT I HAVE SOME OLD COSTUMES IN THE BASEMENT! COME ON!
LATER...
THIS GORILLA COSTUME IS PERFECT!
WHAT IS THIS?
IT'S A BAT COSTUME! DO YOU LIKE IT?
WELL.. EHM...
DONALD, MAYBE WE SHOULD... AHHH!
FETHRY! IT'S JUST ME! GET UP.
GAH?? FOR A DUCK, YOU MAKE A GOOD GORILLA.
JUST PUT ON YOUR COSTUME.
SOON...
FINALLY! WE'RE HERE AT THE BALL.
AND EVERYONE IS LAUGHING AT US!

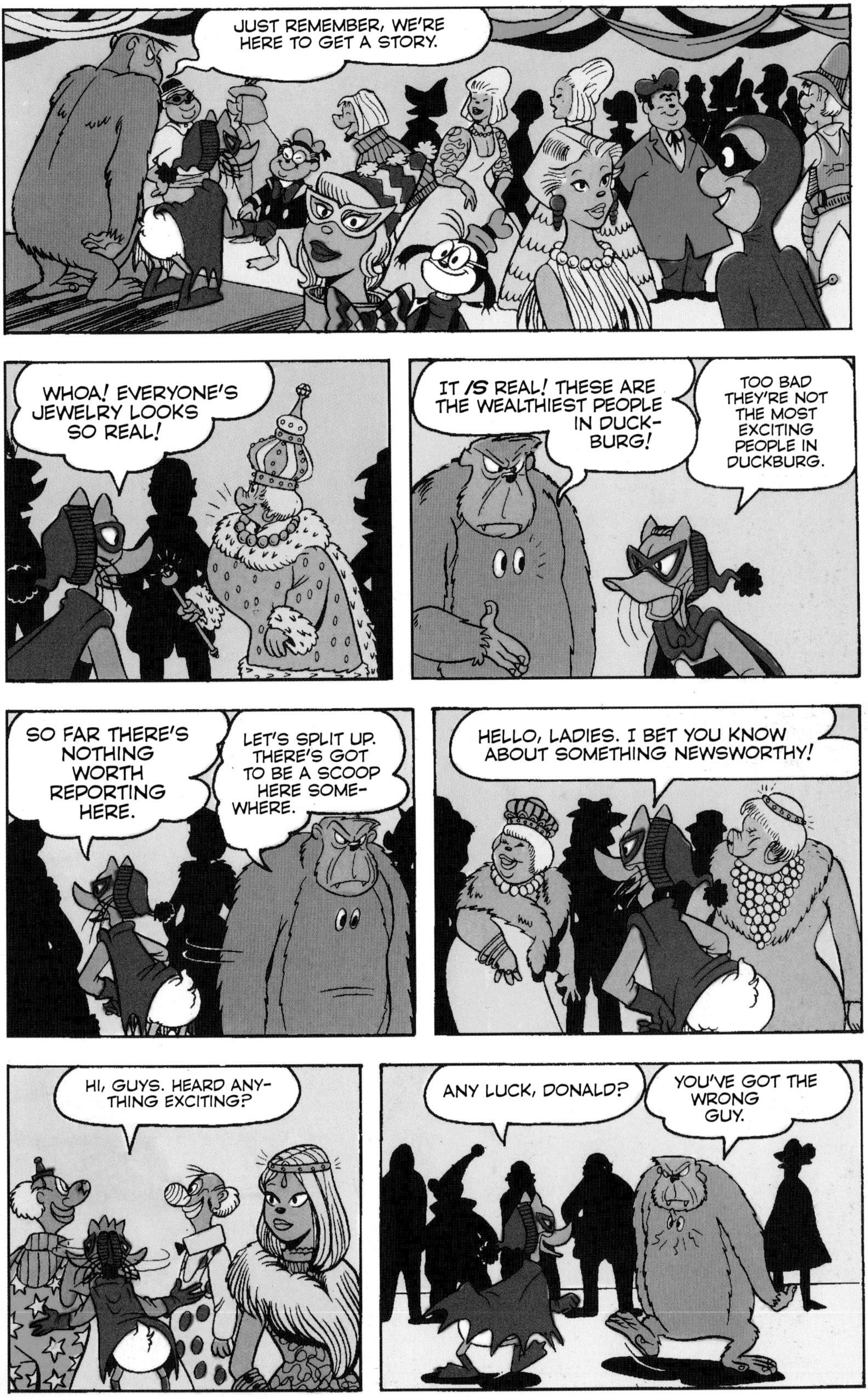

JUST REMEMBER, WE'RE HERE TO GET A STORY.
WHOA! EVERYONE'S JEWELRY LOOKS SO REAL!
IT IS REAL! THESE ARE THE WEALTHIEST PEOPLE IN DUCKBURG!
TOO BAD THEY'RE NOT THE MOST EXCITING PEOPLE IN DUCKBURG.
SO FAR THERE'S NOTHING WORTH REPORTING HERE.
LET'S SPLIT UP. THERE'S GOT TO BE A SCOOP HERE SOMEWHERE.
HELLO, LADIES. I BET YOU KNOW ABOUT SOMETHING NEWSWORTHY!
HI, GUYS. HEARD ANYTHING EXCITING?
ANY LUCK, DONALD?
YOU'VE GOT THE WRONG GUY.

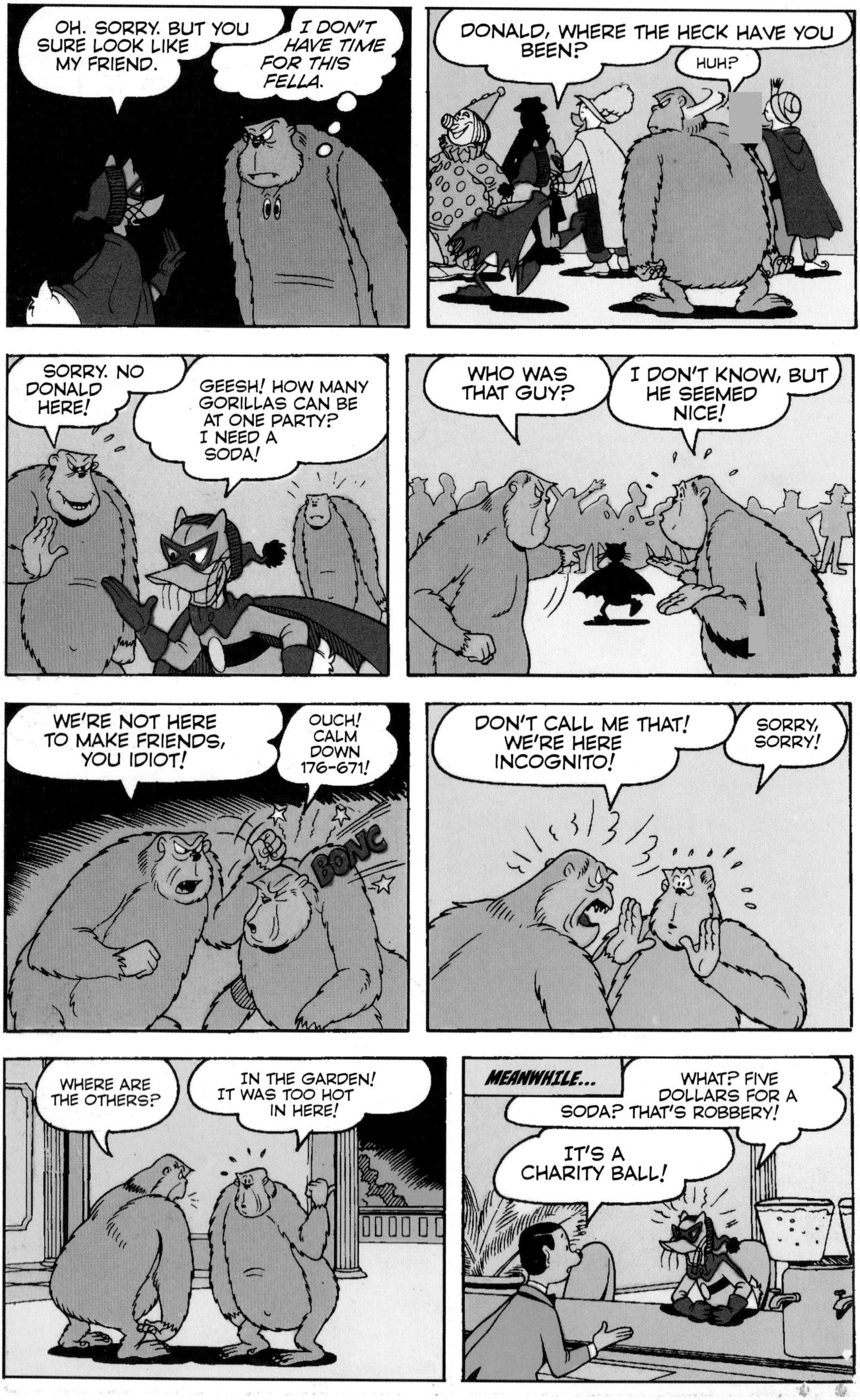

OH. SORRY. BUT YOU SURE LOOK LIKE MY FRIEND.
I DON'T HAVE TIME FOR THIS FELLA.
DONALD, WHERE THE HECK HAVE YOU BEEN?
HUH?
SORRY. NO DONALD HERE!
GEESH! HOW MANY GORILLAS CAN BE AT ONE PARTY? I NEED A SODA!
WHO WAS THAT GUY?
I DON'T KNOW, BUT HE SEEMED NICE!
WE'RE NOT HERE TO MAKE FRIENDS, YOU IDIOT!
OUCH! CALM DOWN 176-671!
BONC
DON'T CALL ME THAT! WE'RE HERE INCOGNITO!
SORRY, SORRY!
WHERE ARE THE OTHERS?
IN THE GARDEN! IT WAS TOO HOT IN HERE!
MEANWHILE...
WHAT? FIVE DOLLARS FOR A SODA? THAT'S ROBBERY!
IT'S A CHARITY BALL!

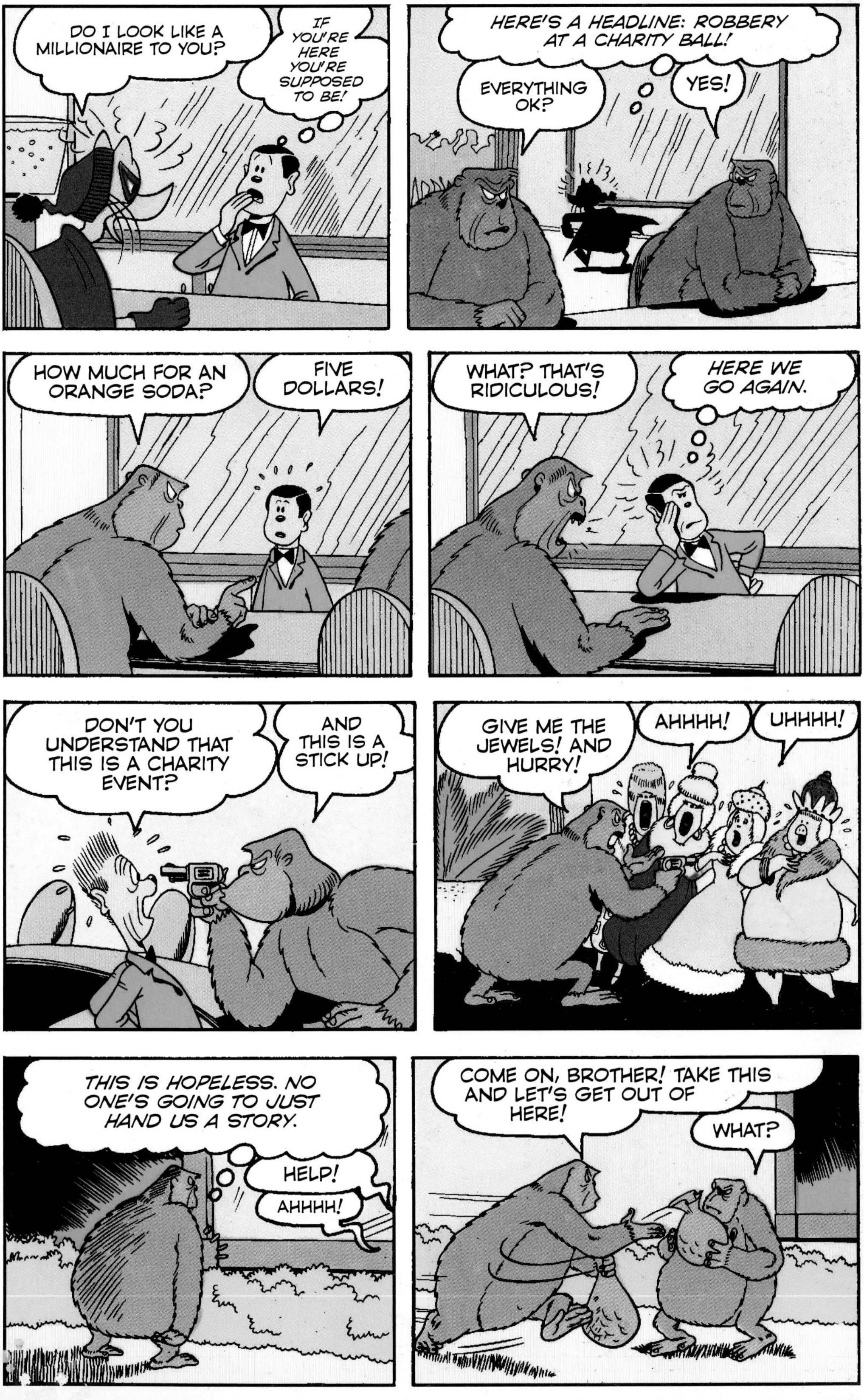
DO I LOOK LIKE A MILLIONAIRE TO YOU?
IF YOU'RE HERE YOU'RE SUPPOSED TO BE!
HERE'S A HEADLINE: ROBBERY AT A CHARITY BALL!
EVERYTHING OK?
YES!
HOW MUCH FOR AN ORANGE SODA?
FIVE DOLLARS!
WHAT? THAT'S RIDICULOUS!
HERE WE GO AGAIN.
DON'T YOU UNDERSTAND THAT THIS IS A CHARITY EVENT?
AND THIS IS A STICK UP!
GIVE ME THE JEWELS! AND HURRY!
AHHHH!
UHHHH!
THIS IS HOPELESS. NO ONE'S GOING TO JUST HAND US A STORY.
HELP!
AHHHH!
COME ON, BROTHER! TAKE THIS AND LET'S GET OUT OF HERE!
WHAT?

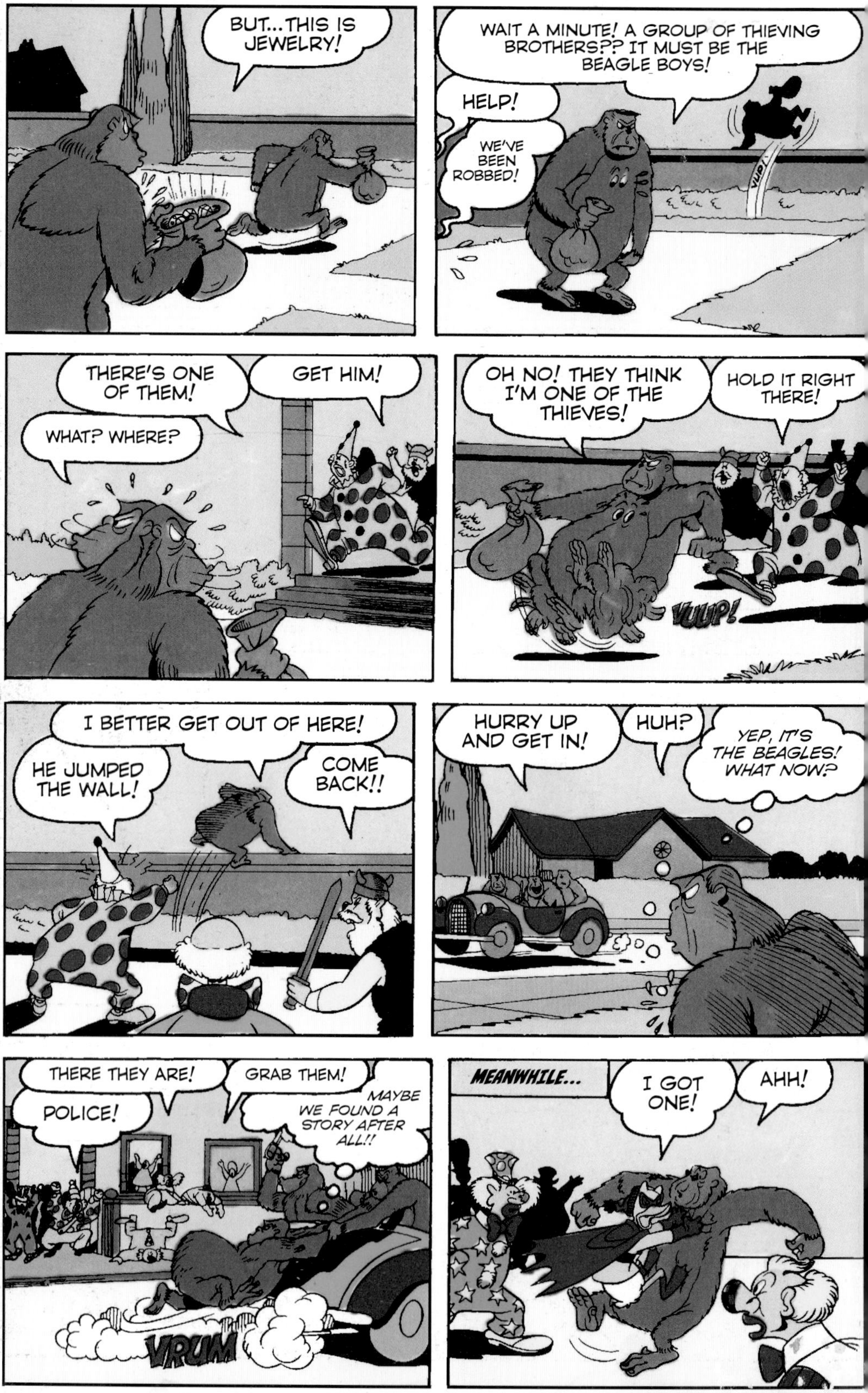
BUT...THIS IS JEWELRY!
WAIT A MINUTE! A GROUP OF THIEVING BROTHERS?? IT MUST BE THE BEAGLE BOYS!
HELP!
WE'VE BEEN ROBBED!
VUUP!
THERE'S ONE OF THEM!
GET HIM!
WHAT? WHERE?
OH NO! THEY THINK I'M ONE OF THE THIEVES!
HOLD IT RIGHT THERE!
VUUP!
I BETTER GET OUT OF HERE!
HE JUMPED THE WALL!
COME BACK!!
HURRY UP AND GET IN!
HUH?
YEP, IT'S THE BEAGLES! WHAT NOW?
THERE THEY ARE!
GRAB THEM!
POLICE!
MAYBE WE FOUND A STORY AFTER ALL!!
VRUM
MEANWHILE...
I GOT ONE!
AHH!

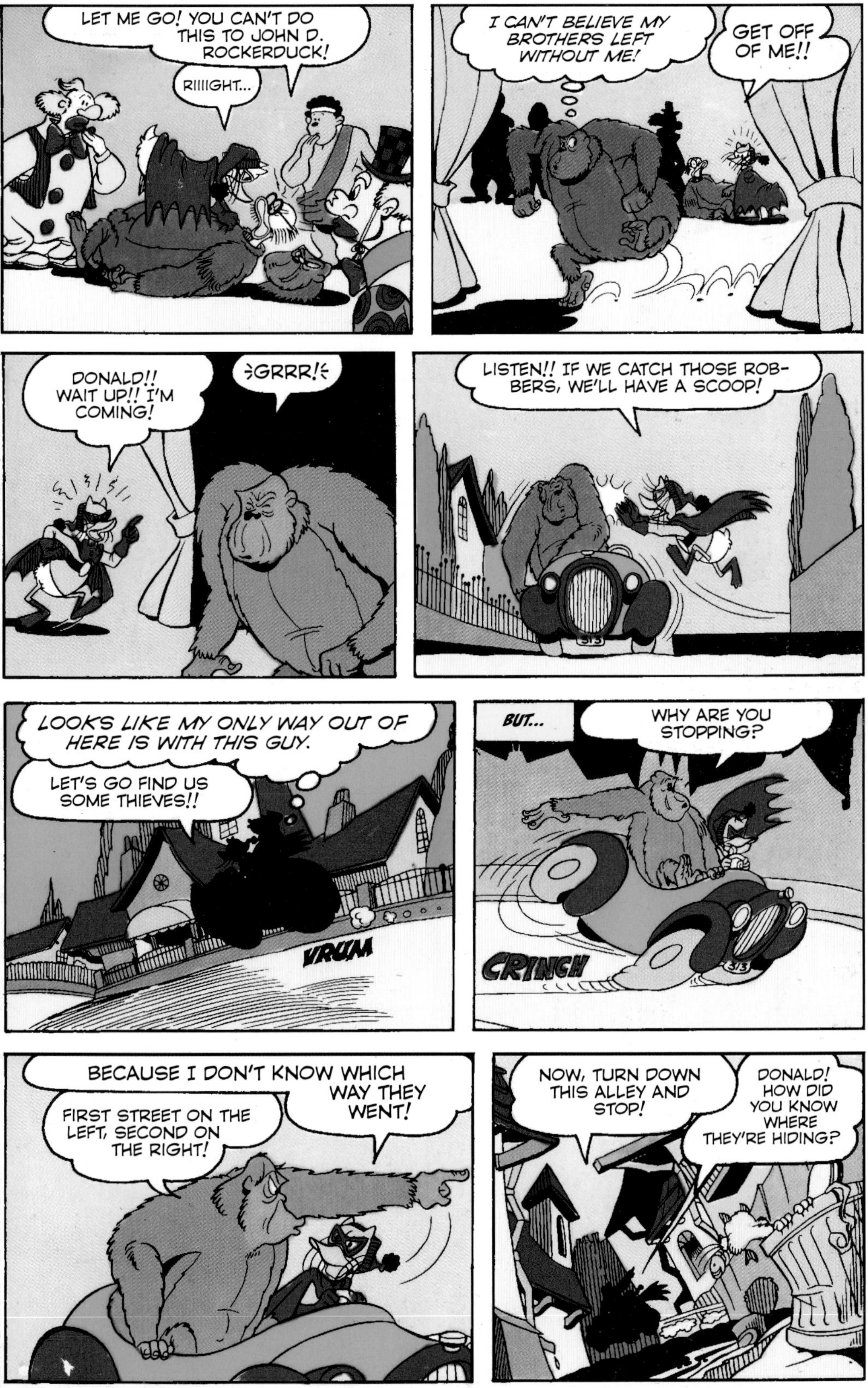
LET ME GO! YOU CAN'T DO THIS TO JOHN D. ROCKERDUCK!
RIIIIGHT...
I CAN'T BELIEVE MY BROTHERS LEFT WITHOUT ME!
GET OFF OF ME!!
DONALD!! WAIT UP!! I'M COMING!
GRRR!
LISTEN!! IF WE CATCH THOSE ROB-BERS, WE'LL HAVE A SCOOP!
LOOKS LIKE MY ONLY WAY OUT OF HERE IS WITH THIS GUY.
LET'S GO FIND US SOME THIEVES!!
VRUM
BUT...
WHY ARE YOU STOPPING?
CRINCH
BECAUSE I DON'T KNOW WHICH WAY THEY WENT!
FIRST STREET ON THE LEFT, SECOND ON THE RIGHT!
NOW, TURN DOWN THIS ALLEY AND STOP!
DONALD! HOW DID YOU KNOW WHERE THEY'RE HIDING?

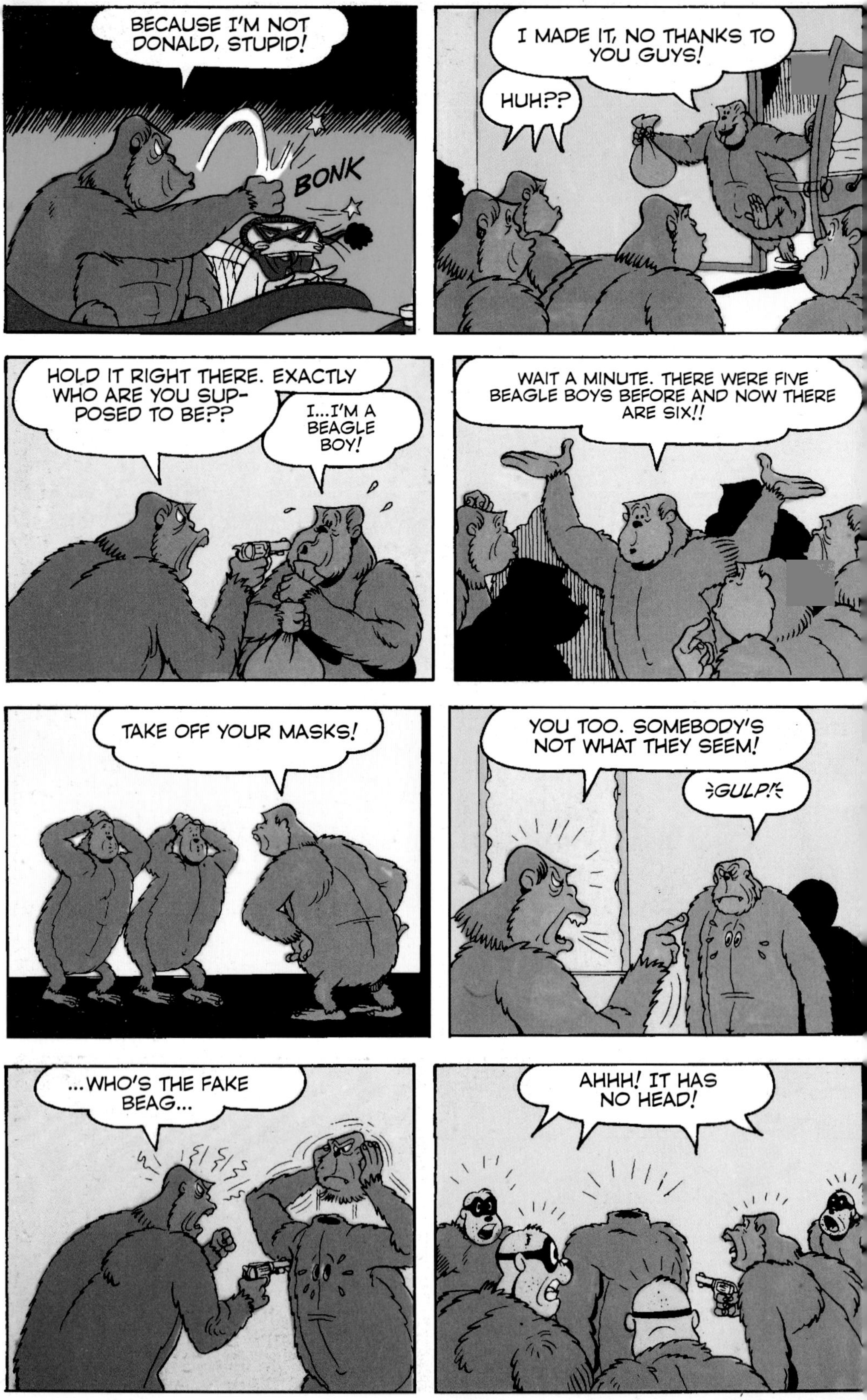
BECAUSE I'M NOT DONALD, STUPID!
BONK
I MADE IT, NO THANKS TO YOU GUYS!
HUH??
HOLD IT RIGHT THERE. EXACTLY WHO ARE YOU SUP-POSED TO BE??
I...I'M A BEAGLE BOY!
WAIT A MINUTE. THERE WERE FIVE BEAGLE BOYS BEFORE AND NOW THERE ARE SIX!!
TAKE OFF YOUR MASKS!
YOU TOO. SOMEBODY'S NOT WHAT THEY SEEM!
GULP!
...WHO'S THE FAKE BEAG...
AHHH! IT HAS NO HEAD!

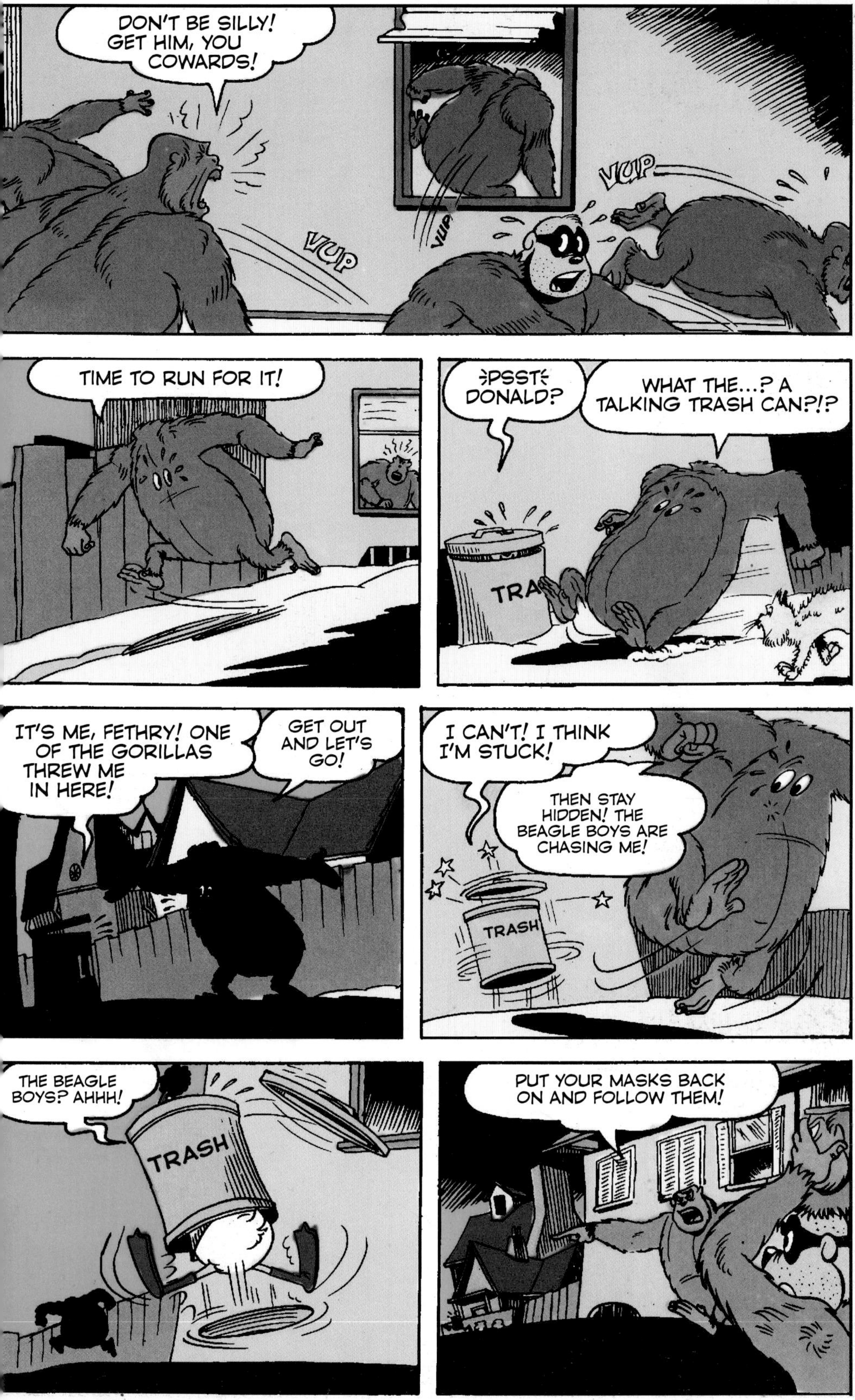
DON'T BE SILLY! GET HIM, YOU COWARDS!
VUP
VUP
VUP
TIME TO RUN FOR IT!
PSST! DONALD?
WHAT THE...? A TALKING TRASH CAN?!?
TRA
IT'S ME, FETHRY! ONE OF THE GORILLAS THREW ME IN HERE!
GET OUT AND LET'S GO!
I CAN'T! I THINK I'M STUCK!
THEN STAY HIDDEN! THE BEAGLE BOYS ARE CHASING ME!
TRASH
THE BEAGLE BOYS? AHHH!
TRASH
PUT YOUR MASKS BACK ON AND FOLLOW THEM!

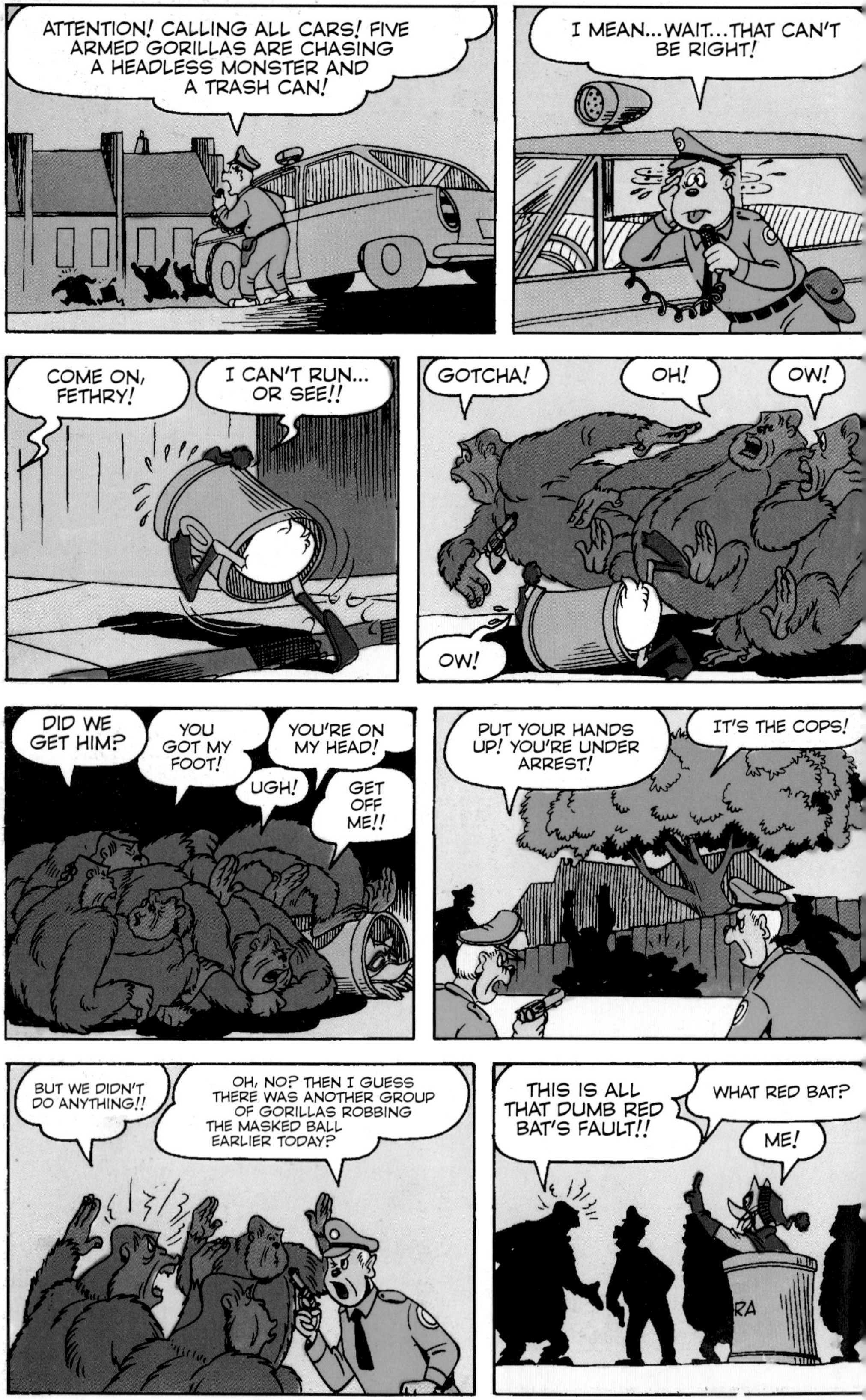

ATTENTION! CALLING ALL CARS! FIVE ARMED GORILLAS ARE CHASING A HEADLESS MONSTER AND A TRASH CAN!
I MEAN...WAIT...THAT CAN'T BE RIGHT!
COME ON, FETHRY!
I CAN'T RUN... OR SEE!!
GOTCHA!
OH!
OW!
OW!
DID WE GET HIM?
YOU GOT MY FOOT!
YOU'RE ON MY HEAD!
UGH!
GET OFF ME!!
PUT YOUR HANDS UP! YOU'RE UNDER ARREST!
IT'S THE COPS!
BUT WE DIDN'T DO ANYTHING!!
OH, NO? THEN I GUESS THERE WAS ANOTHER GROUP OF GORILLAS ROBBING THE MASKED BALL EARLIER TODAY?
THIS IS ALL THAT DUMB RED BAT'S FAULT!!
WHAT RED BAT?
ME!
RA

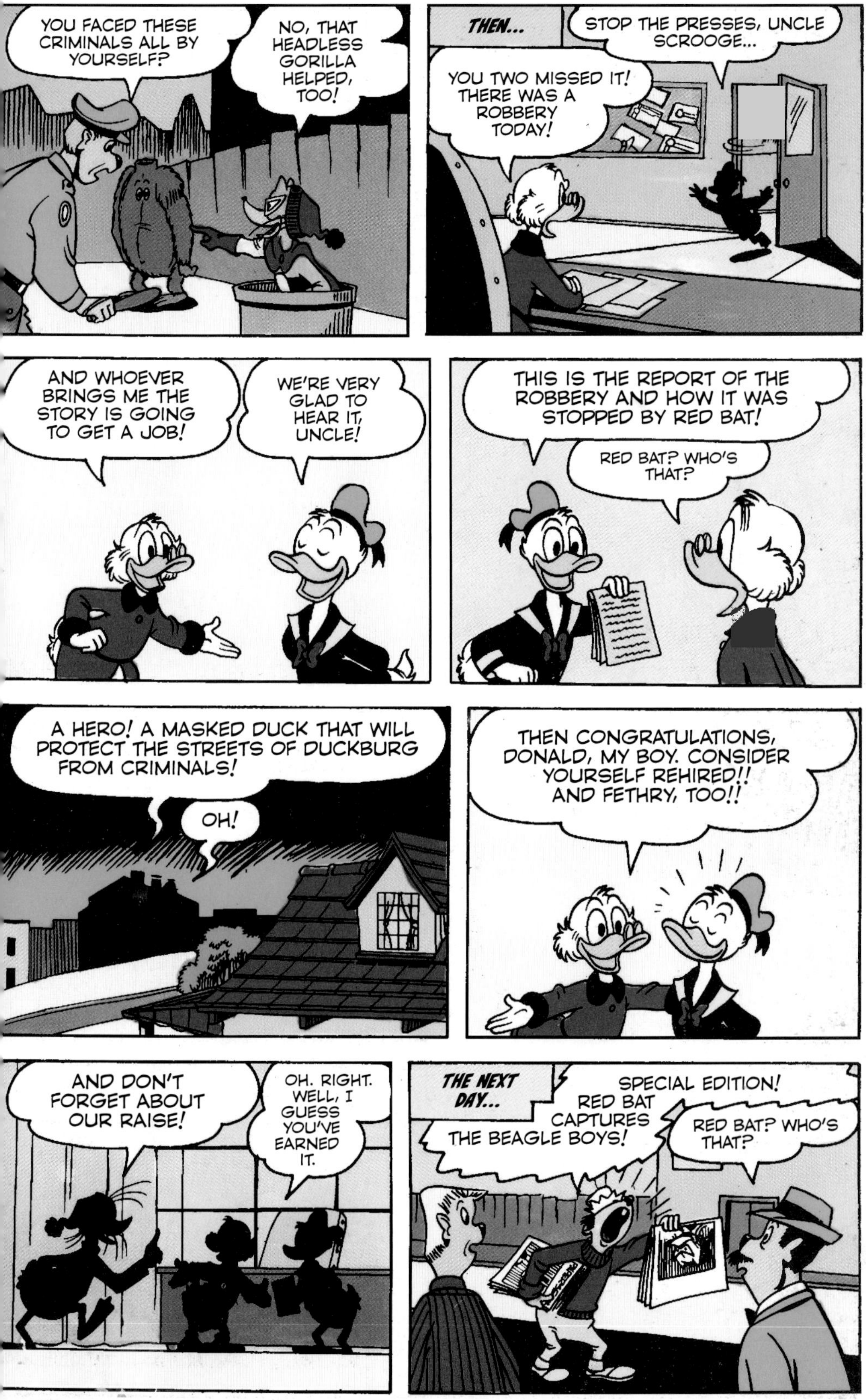
YOU FACED THESE CRIMINALS ALL BY YOURSELF?
NO, THAT HEADLESS GORILLA HELPED, TOO!
THEN...
STOP THE PRESSES, UNCLE SCROOGE...
YOU TWO MISSED IT! THERE WAS A ROBBERY TODAY!
AND WHOEVER BRINGS ME THE STORY IS GOING TO GET A JOB!
WE'RE VERY GLAD TO HEAR IT, UNCLE!
THIS IS THE REPORT OF THE ROBBERY AND HOW IT WAS STOPPED BY RED BAT!
RED BAT? WHO'S THAT?
A HERO! A MASKED DUCK THAT WILL PROTECT THE STREETS OF DUCKBURG FROM CRIMINALS!
OH!
THEN CONGRATULATIONS, DONALD, MY BOY. CONSIDER YOURSELF REHIRED!! AND FETHRY, TOO!!
AND DON'T FORGET ABOUT OUR RAISE!
OH. RIGHT. WELL, I GUESS YOU'VE EARNED IT.
THE NEXT DAY...
SPECIAL EDITION! RED BAT CAPTURES THE BEAGLE BOYS!
RED BAT? WHO'S THAT?

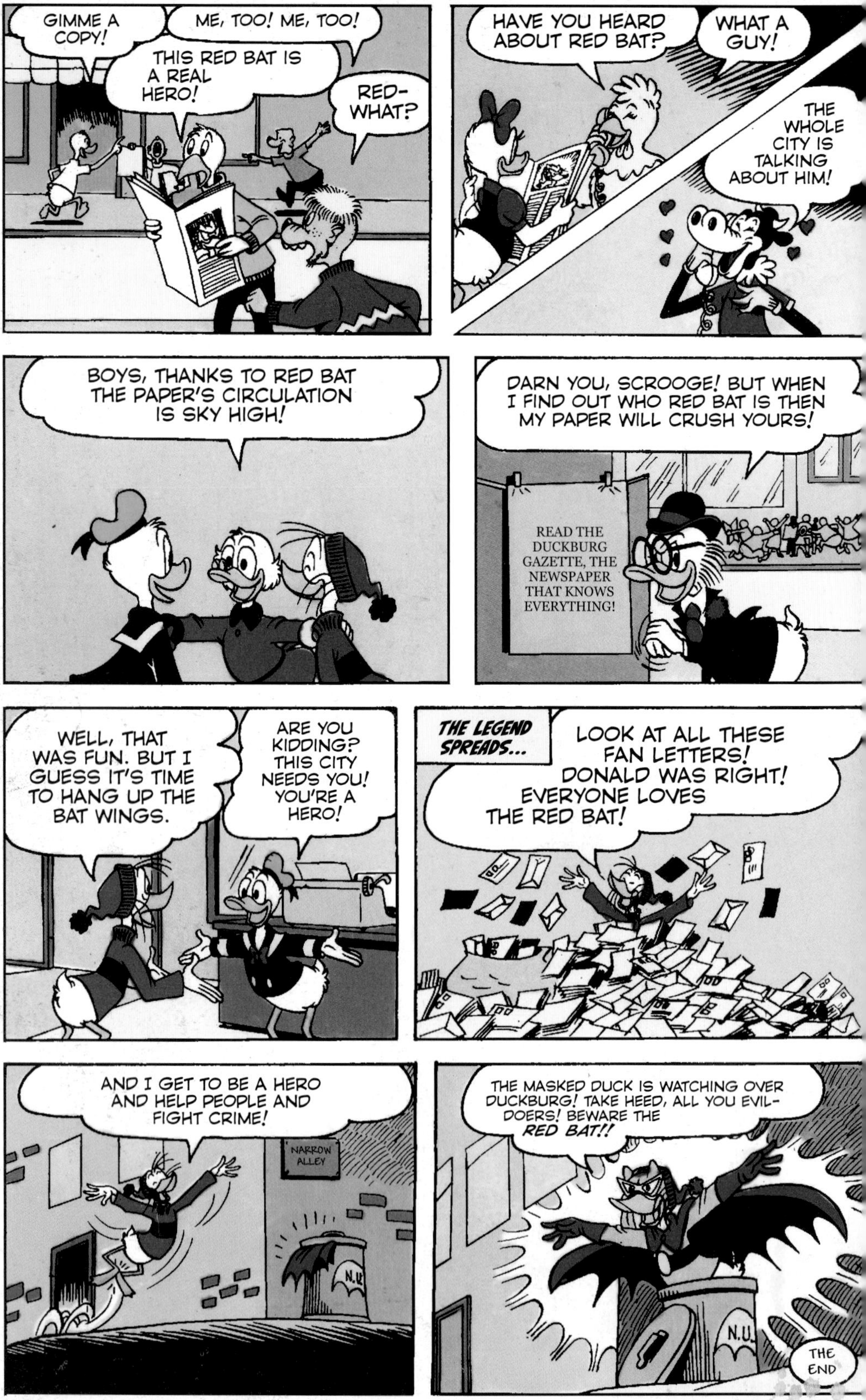
GIMME A COPY!
ME, TOO! ME, TOO!
THIS RED BAT IS A REAL HERO!
RED-WHAT?
HAVE YOU HEARD ABOUT RED BAT?
WHAT A GUY!
THE WHOLE CITY IS TALKING ABOUT HIM!
BOYS, THANKS TO RED BAT THE PAPER'S CIRCULATION IS SKY HIGH!
DARN YOU, SCROOGE! BUT WHEN I FIND OUT WHO RED BAT IS THEN MY PAPER WILL CRUSH YOURS!
READ THE DUCKBURG GAZETTE, THE NEWSPAPER THAT KNOWS EVERYTHING!
WELL, THAT WAS FUN. BUT I GUESS IT'S TIME TO HANG UP THE BAT WINGS.
ARE YOU KIDDING? THIS CITY NEEDS YOU! YOU'RE A HERO!
THE LEGEND SPREADS...
LOOK AT ALL THESE FAN LETTERS! DONALD WAS RIGHT! EVERYONE LOVES THE RED BAT!
AND I GET TO BE A HERO AND HELP PEOPLE AND FIGHT CRIME!
NARROW ALLEY
N.U.
THE MASKED DUCK IS WATCHING OVER DUCKBURG! TAKE HEED, ALL YOU EVIL-DOERS! BEWARE THE RED BAT!!
N.U.
THE END

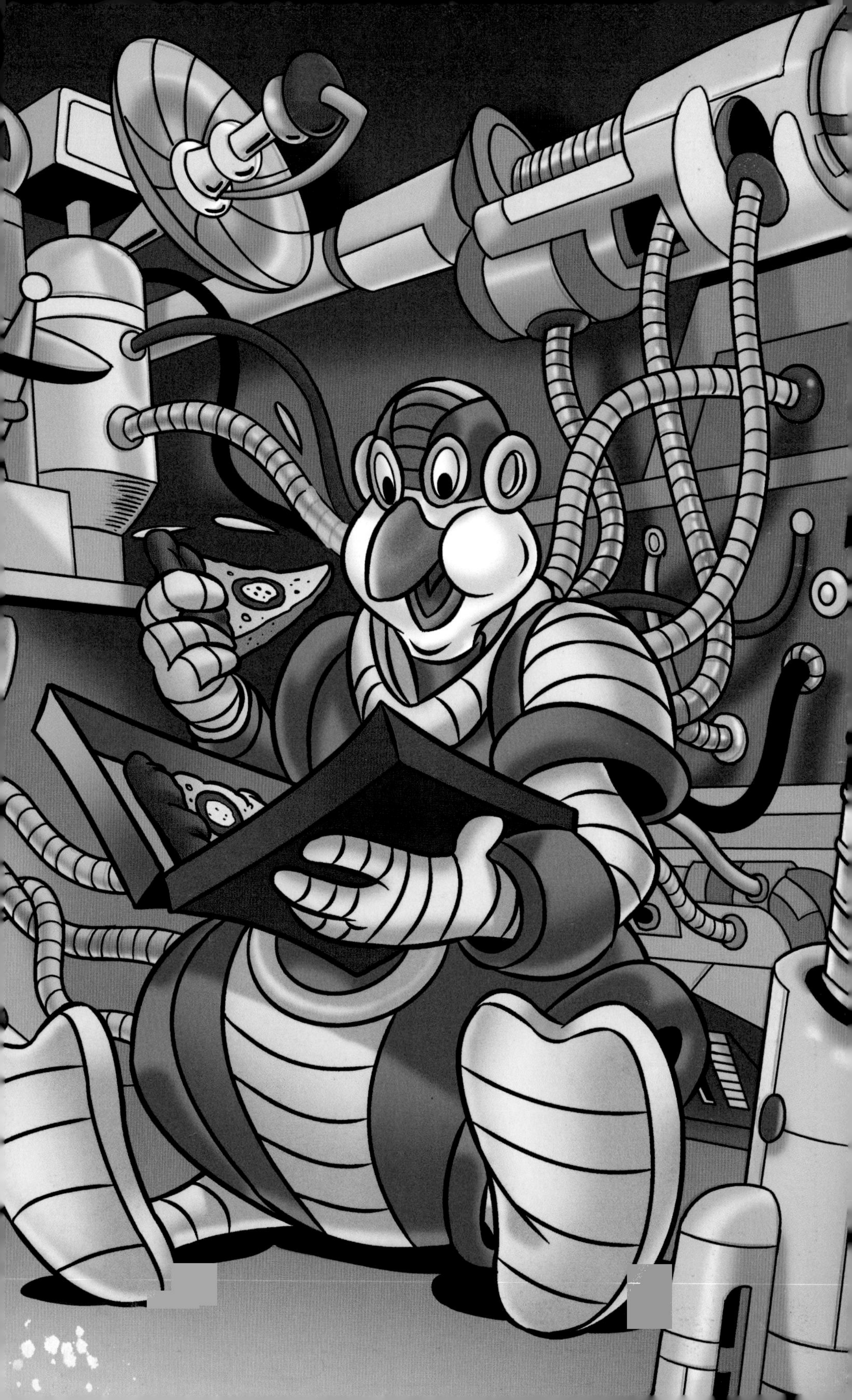

LOOKING FOR MORE FUN WITH YOUR FAVORITE CHARACTERS?

CHECK OUT THESE EXCLUSIVE PREVIEWS OF OTHER GREAT TITLES NOW AVAILABLE FROM

BOOM KIDS!

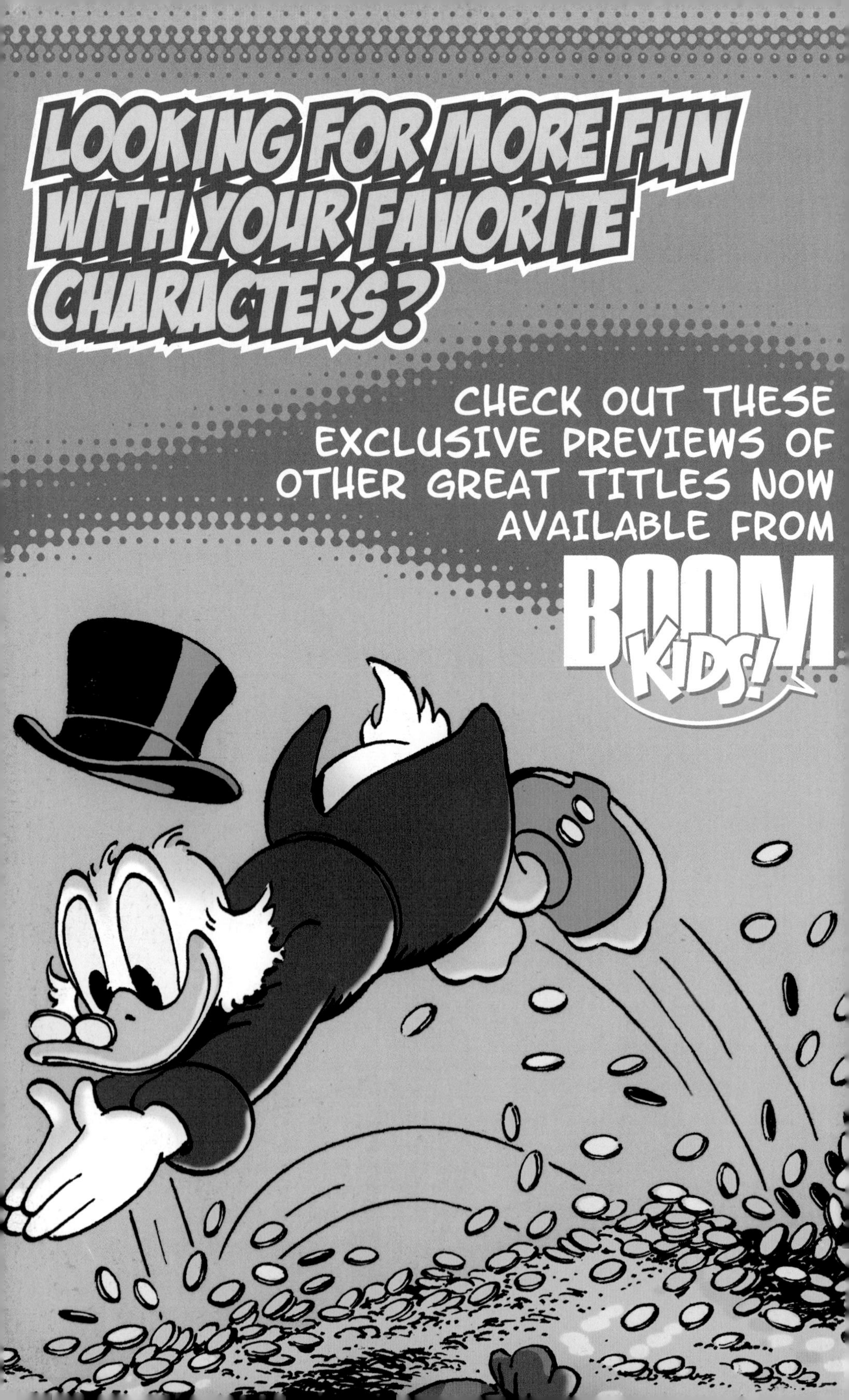

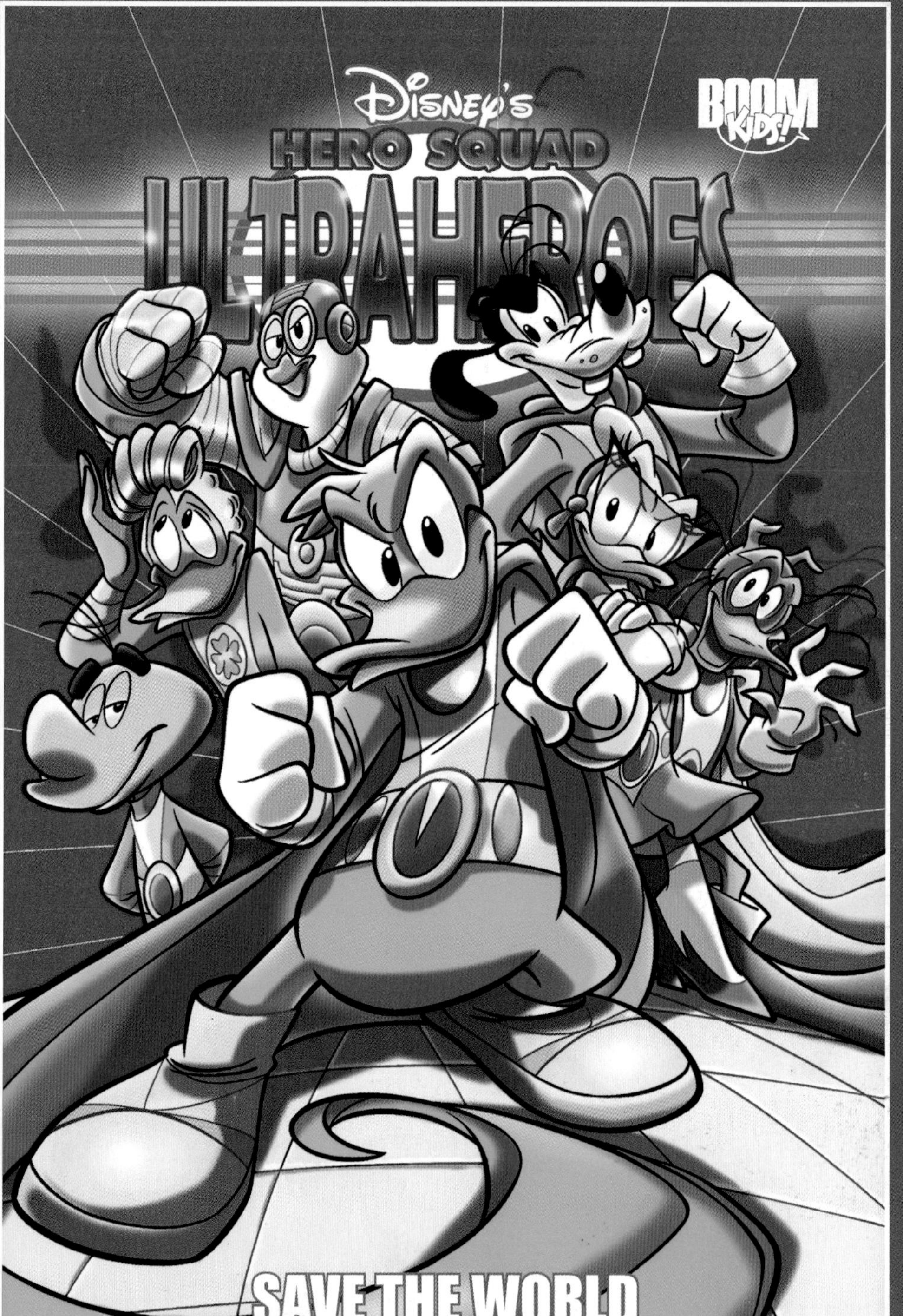
Disney's
HERO SQUAD
ULTRAHEROES
BOOM KIDS!
SAVE THE WORLD

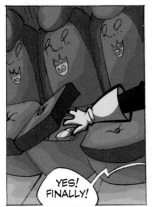

YES! FINALLY!

ULTRAPOD-2 IS MINE!

AND SOON THE WORLD WILL FOLLOW... HUH?!?

STOP!

SLOW DOWN THERE, SUPER-IDIOT!

CRASH

GIVE ME BACK THAT ULTRAPOD, YOU HOVERING HEAP OF TRASH!

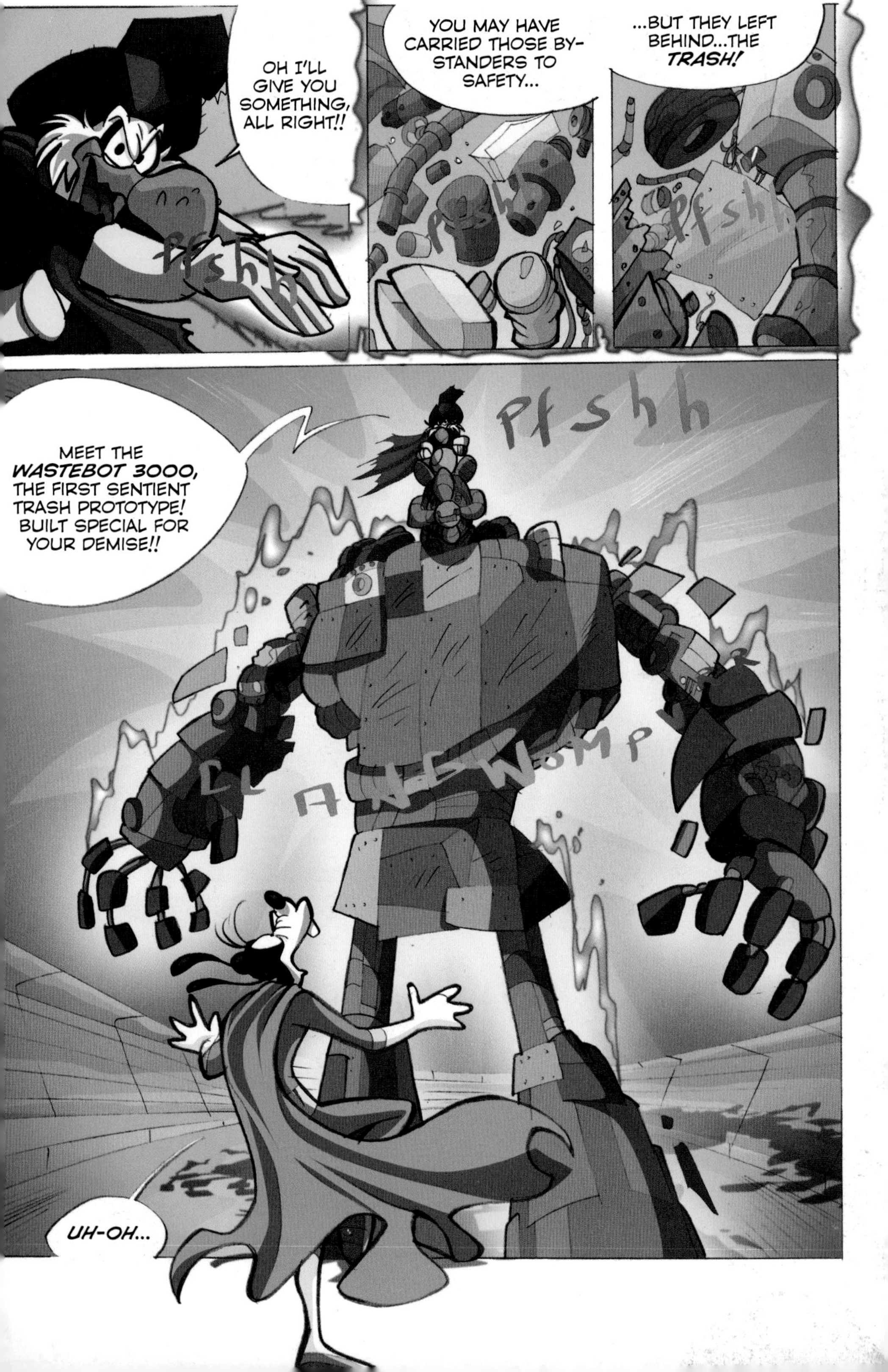
OH I'LL GIVE YOU SOMETHING, ALL RIGHT!!
Pfshh
YOU MAY HAVE CARRIED THOSE BY-STANDERS TO SAFETY...
Pfshh
...BUT THEY LEFT BEHIND...THE *TRASH!*
Pfshh
MEET THE *WASTEBOT 3000,* THE FIRST SENTIENT TRASH PROTOTYPE! BUILT SPECIAL FOR YOUR DEMISE!!
Pfshh
CLANG WOMP
UH-OH...

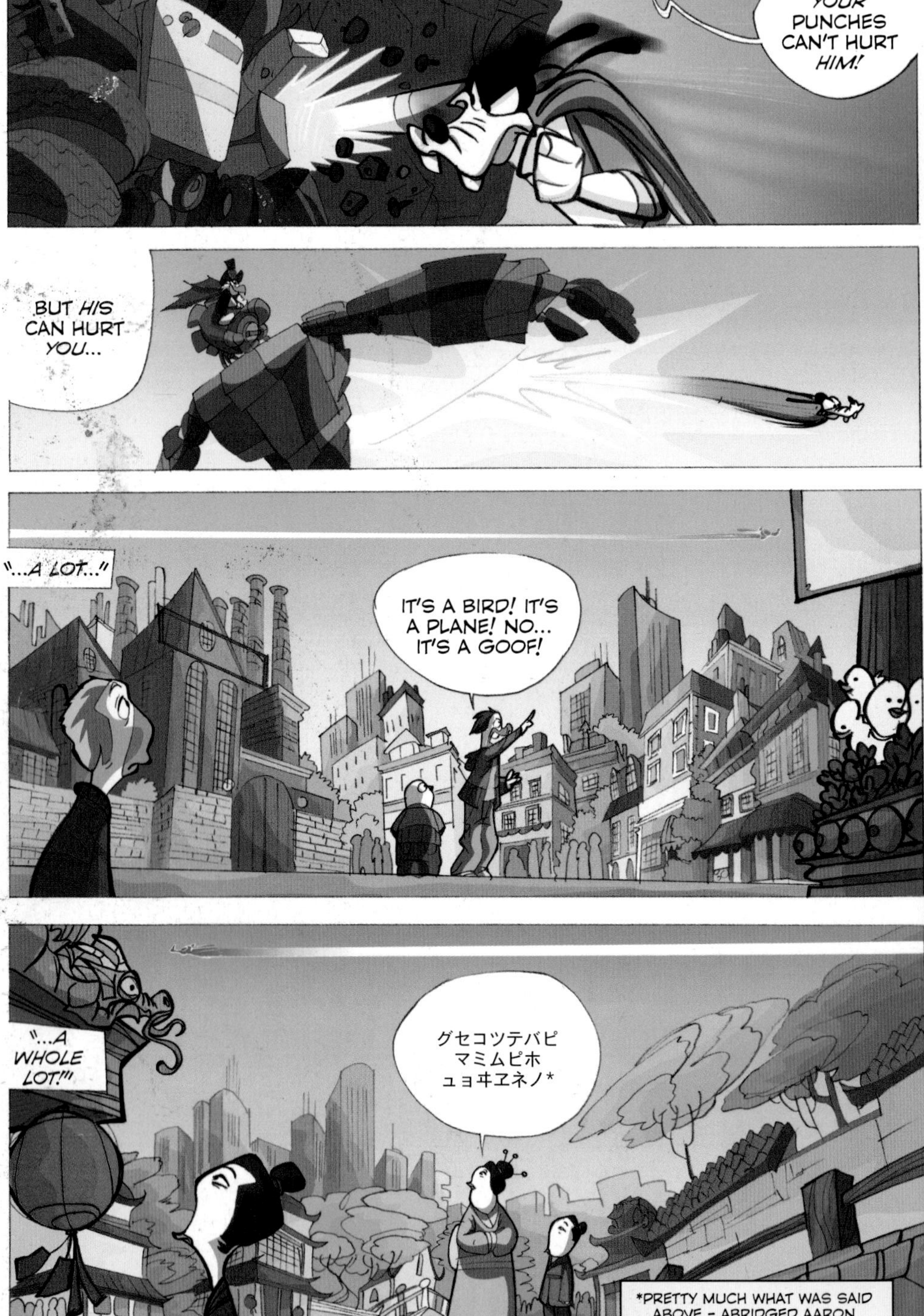
YOUR PUNCHES CAN'T HURT HIM!
BUT HIS CAN HURT YOU...
"...A LOT..."
IT'S A BIRD! IT'S A PLANE! NO... IT'S A GOOF!
"...A WHOLE LOT!"*
グセコツテバピ マミムピホ ュヨヰヱネノ*
*PRETTY MUCH WHAT WAS SAID ABOVE - ABRIDGED AARON

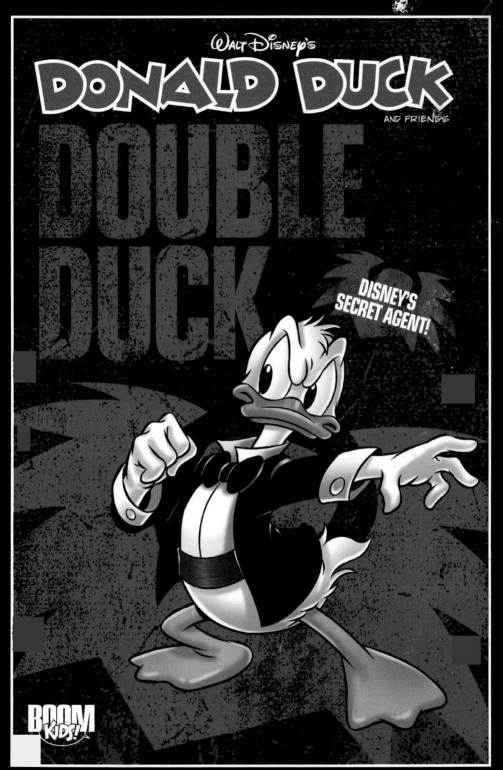

Donald Duck...as a secret agent? Villainous fiends beware as the world of super-sleuthing and espionage will never be the same! This is Donald Duck like you've never seen him!

DONALD DUCK AND FRIENDS: DOUBLE DUCK
DIAMOND CODE: DEC090752
SC $9.99 ISBN 9781608865451
HC $24.99 ISBN 9781608865512

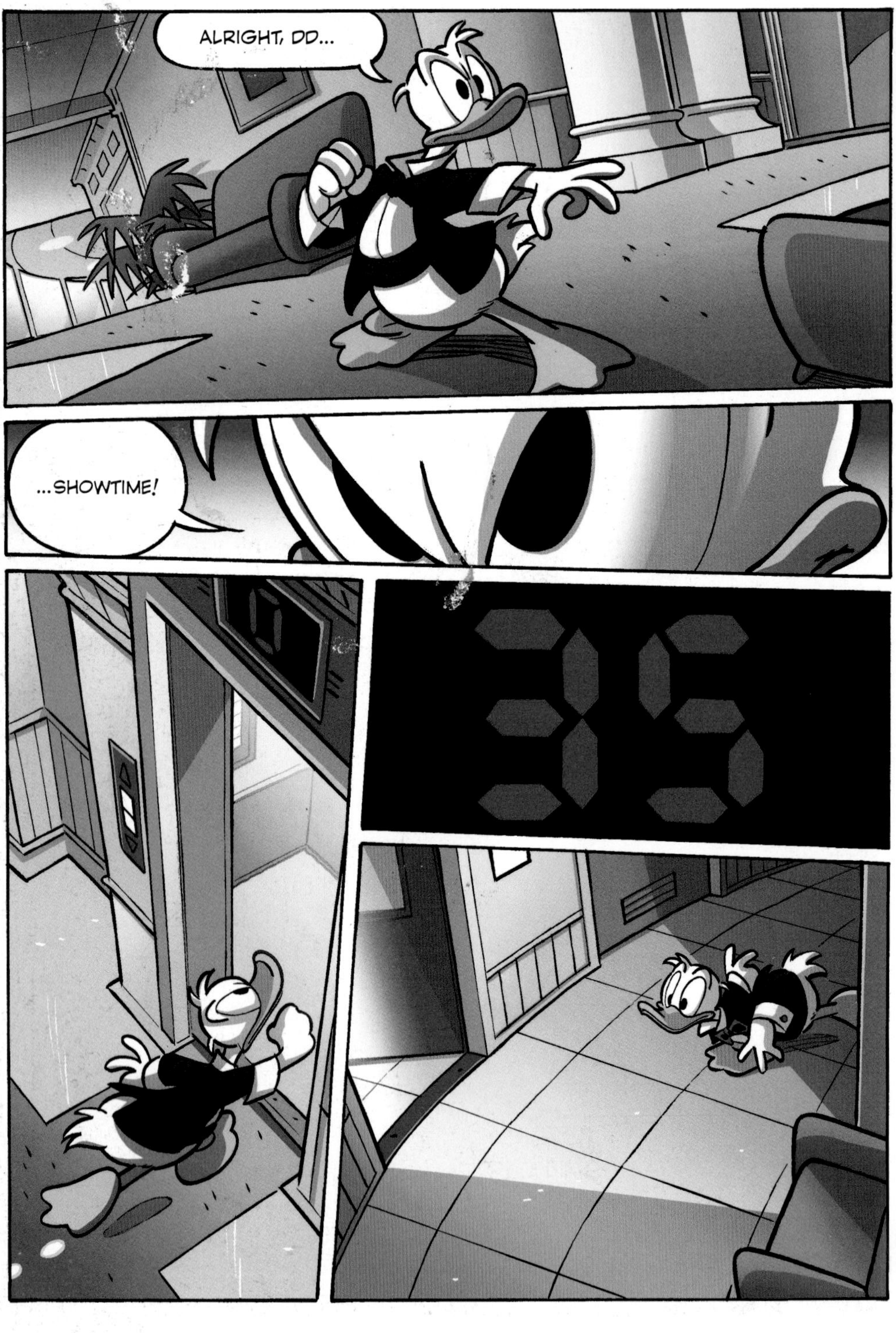
ALRIGHT, DD...
...SHOWTIME!

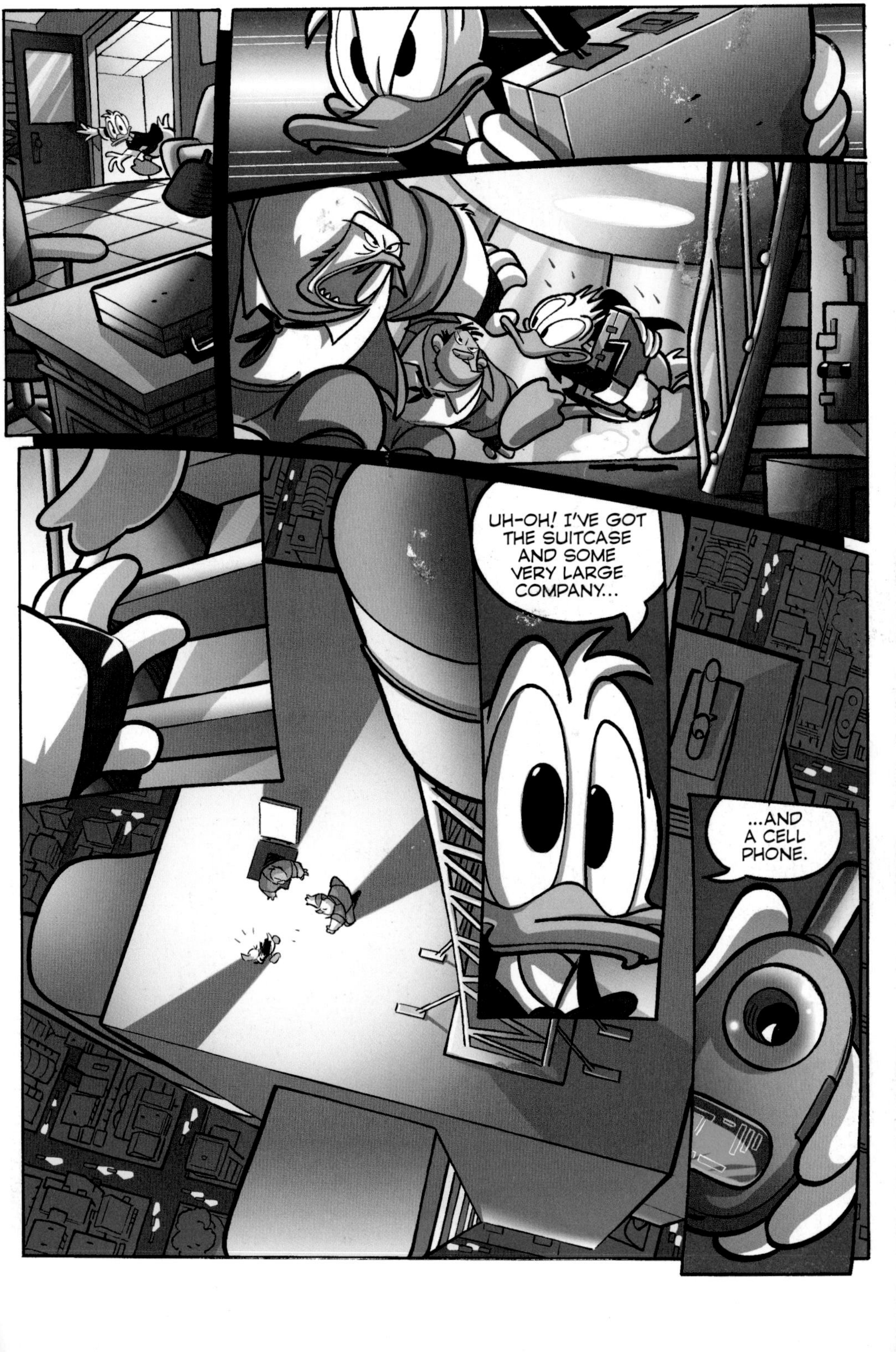
UH-OH! I'VE GOT THE SUITCASE AND SOME VERY LARGE COMPANY...
...AND A CELL PHONE.

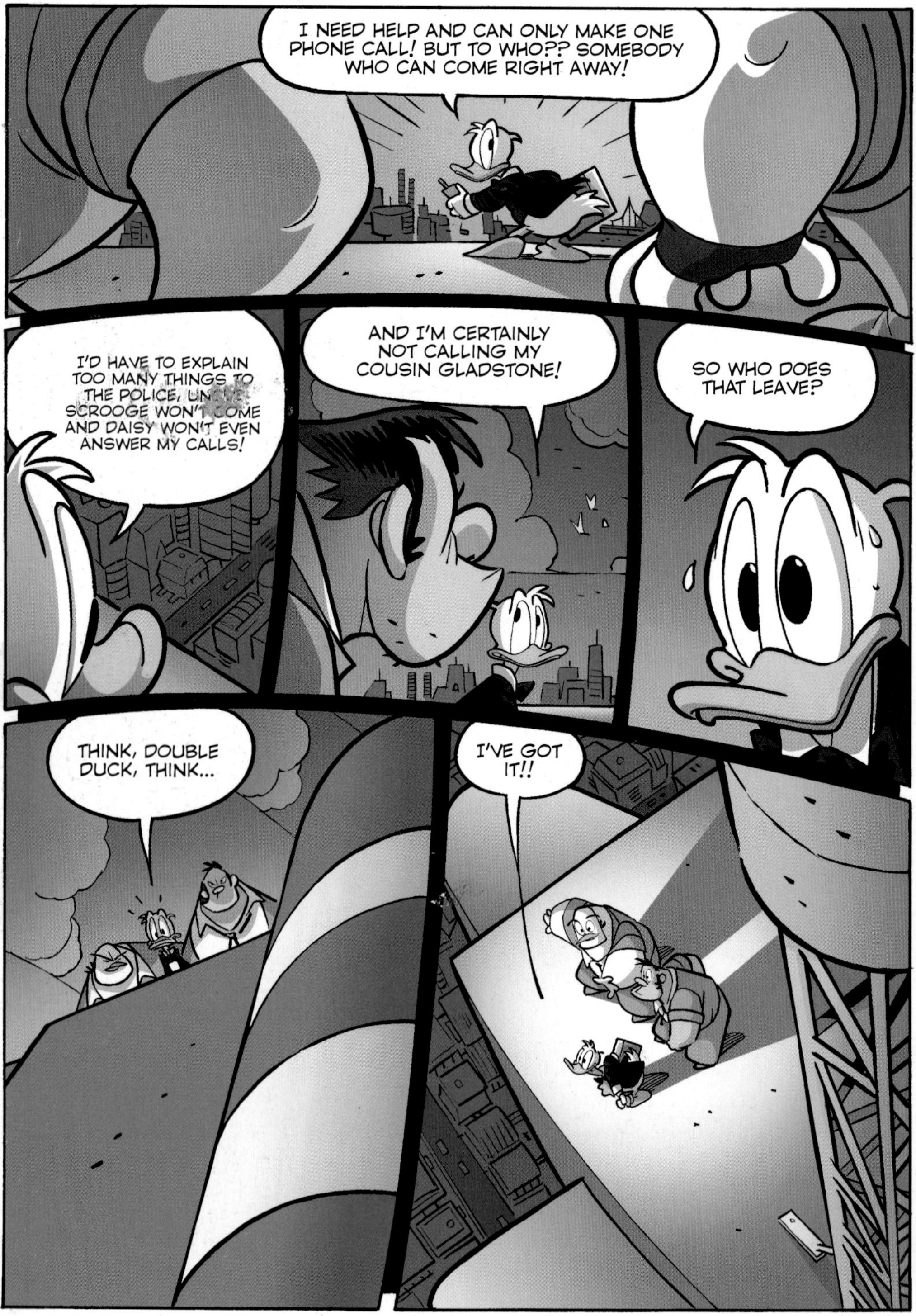
I NEED HELP AND CAN ONLY MAKE ONE PHONE CALL! BUT TO WHO?? SOMEBODY WHO CAN COME RIGHT AWAY!
I'D HAVE TO EXPLAIN TOO MANY THINGS TO THE POLICE, UNCLE SCROOGE WON'T COME AND DAISY WON'T EVEN ANSWER MY CALLS!
AND I'M CERTAINLY NOT CALLING MY COUSIN GLADSTONE!
SO WHO DOES THAT LEAVE?
THINK, DOUBLE DUCK, THINK...
I'VE GOT IT!!

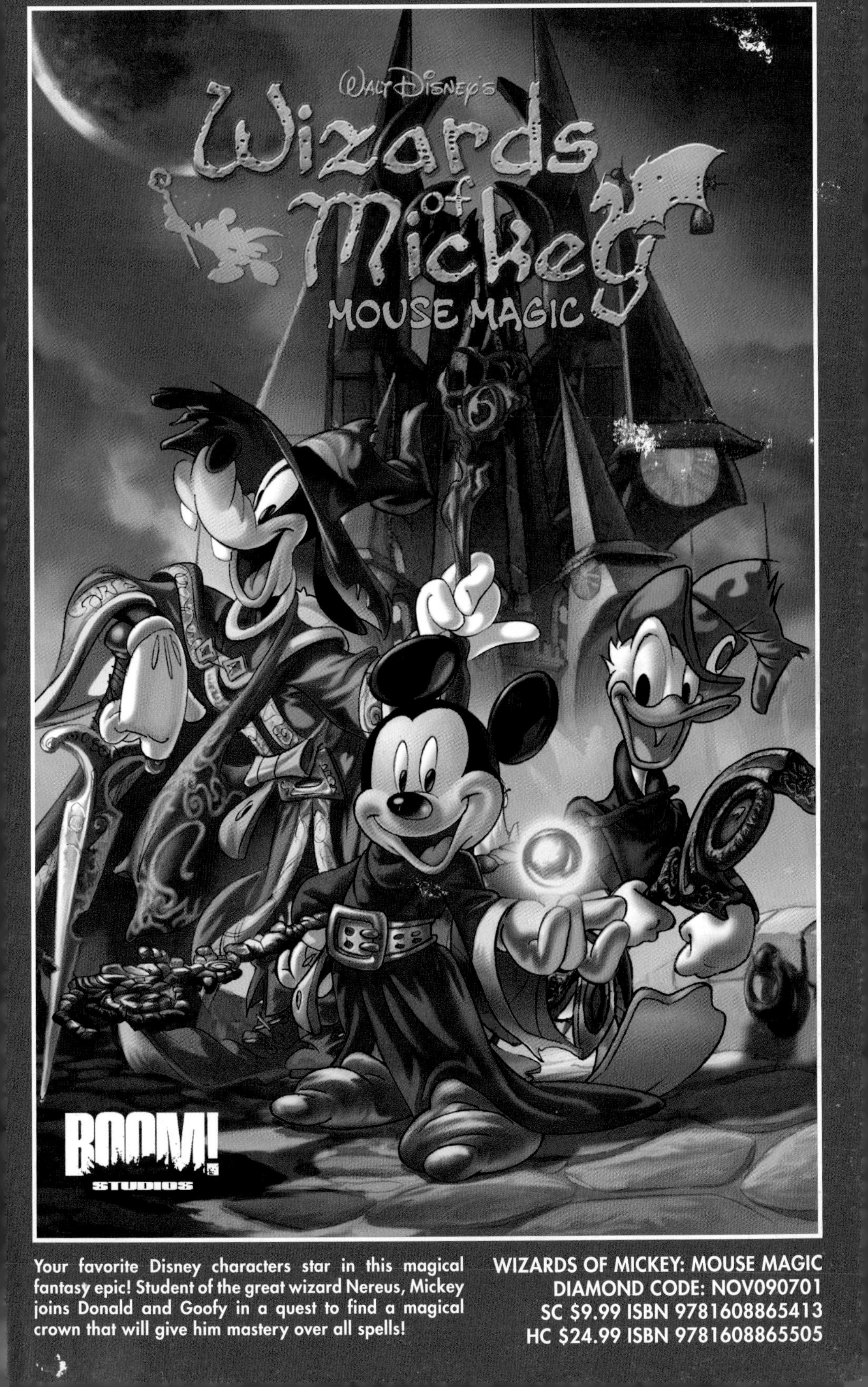
Walt Disney's
Wizards of Mickey
MOUSE MAGIC
BOOM! STUDIOS

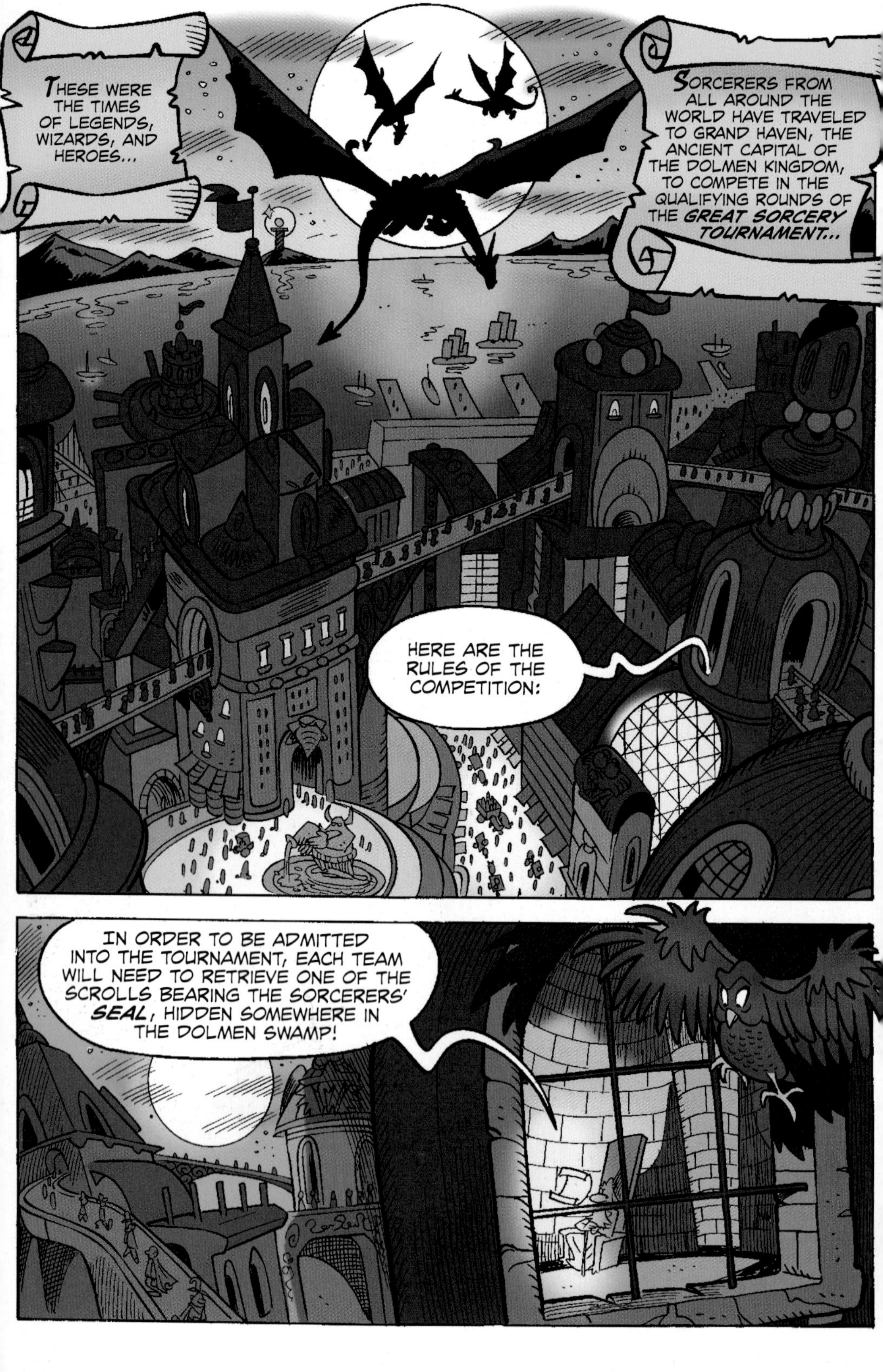
THESE WERE THE TIMES OF LEGENDS, WIZARDS, AND HEROES...
SORCERERS FROM ALL AROUND THE WORLD HAVE TRAVELED TO GRAND HAVEN, THE ANCIENT CAPITAL OF THE DOLMEN KINGDOM, TO COMPETE IN THE QUALIFYING ROUNDS OF THE GREAT SORCERY TOURNAMENT...
HERE ARE THE RULES OF THE COMPETITION:
IN ORDER TO BE ADMITTED INTO THE TOURNAMENT, EACH TEAM WILL NEED TO RETRIEVE ONE OF THE SCROLLS BEARING THE SORCERERS' SEAL, HIDDEN SOMEWHERE IN THE DOLMEN SWAMP!

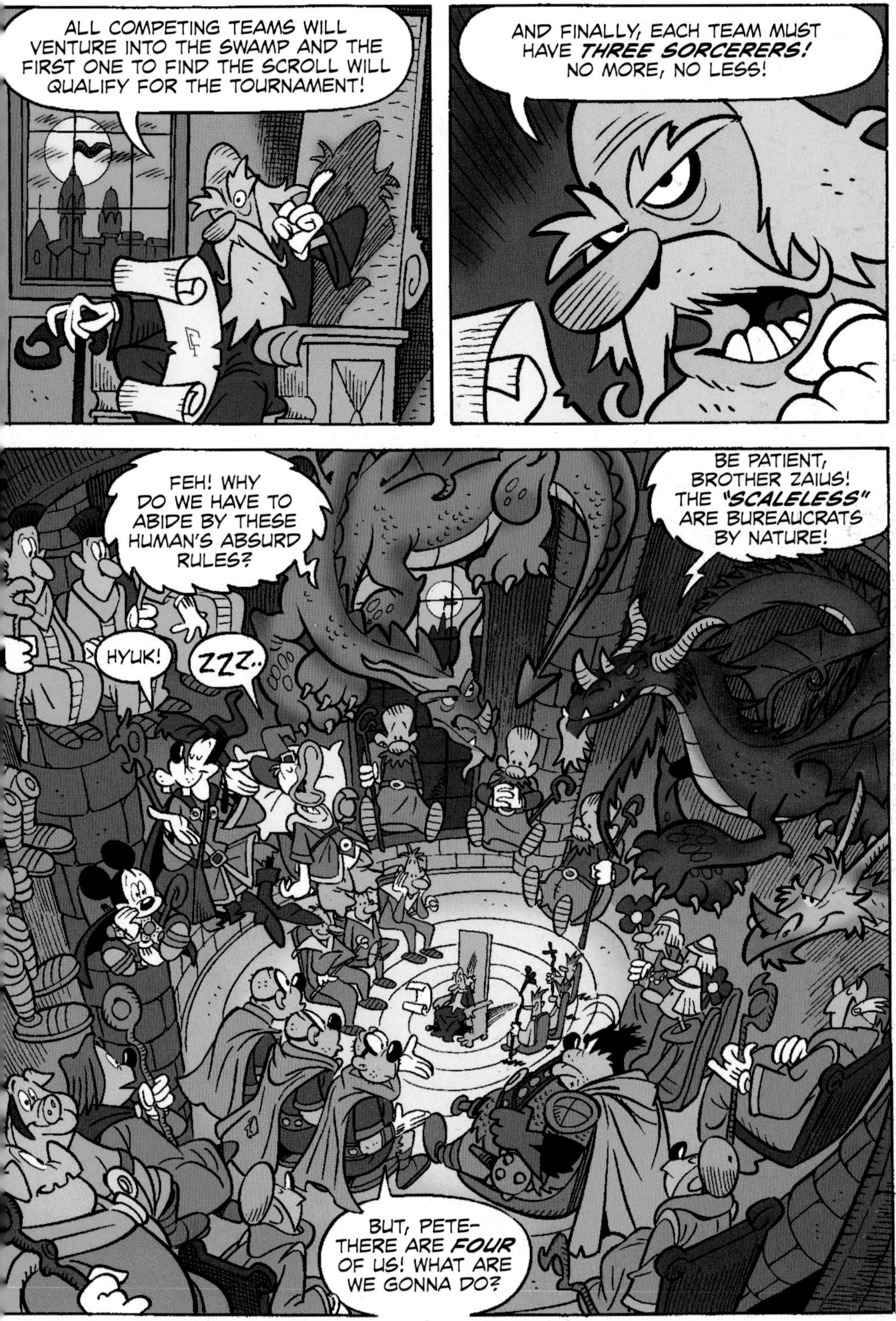
ALL COMPETING TEAMS WILL VENTURE INTO THE SWAMP AND THE FIRST ONE TO FIND THE SCROLL WILL QUALIFY FOR THE TOURNAMENT!
AND FINALLY, EACH TEAM MUST HAVE THREE SORCERERS! NO MORE, NO LESS!
FEH! WHY DO WE HAVE TO ABIDE BY THESE HUMAN'S ABSURD RULES?
BE PATIENT, BROTHER ZAIUS! THE "SCALELESS" ARE BUREAUCRATS BY NATURE!
HYUK!
ZZZ..
BUT, PETE-THERE ARE FOUR OF US! WHAT ARE WE GONNA DO?

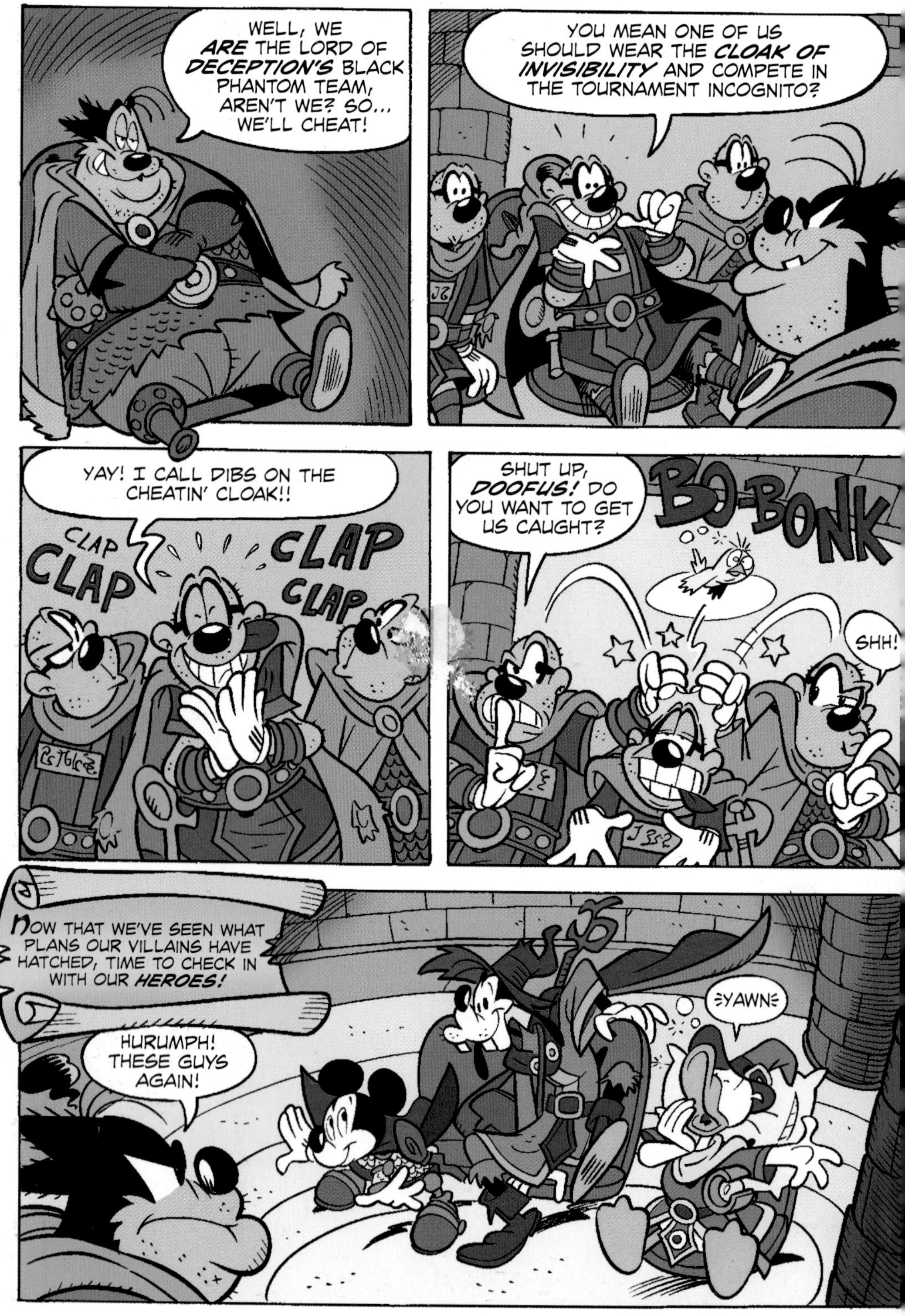
WELL, WE ARE THE LORD OF DECEPTION'S BLACK PHANTOM TEAM, AREN'T WE? SO... WE'LL CHEAT!
YOU MEAN ONE OF US SHOULD WEAR THE CLOAK OF INVISIBILITY AND COMPETE IN THE TOURNAMENT INCOGNITO?
YAY! I CALL DIBS ON THE CHEATIN' CLOAK!!
CLAP CLAP
CLAP CLAP
SHUT UP, DOOFUS! DO YOU WANT TO GET US CAUGHT?
BO-BONK
SHH!
NOW THAT WE'VE SEEN WHAT PLANS OUR VILLAINS HAVE HATCHED, TIME TO CHECK IN WITH OUR HEROES!
HURUMPH! THESE GUYS AGAIN!
YAWN

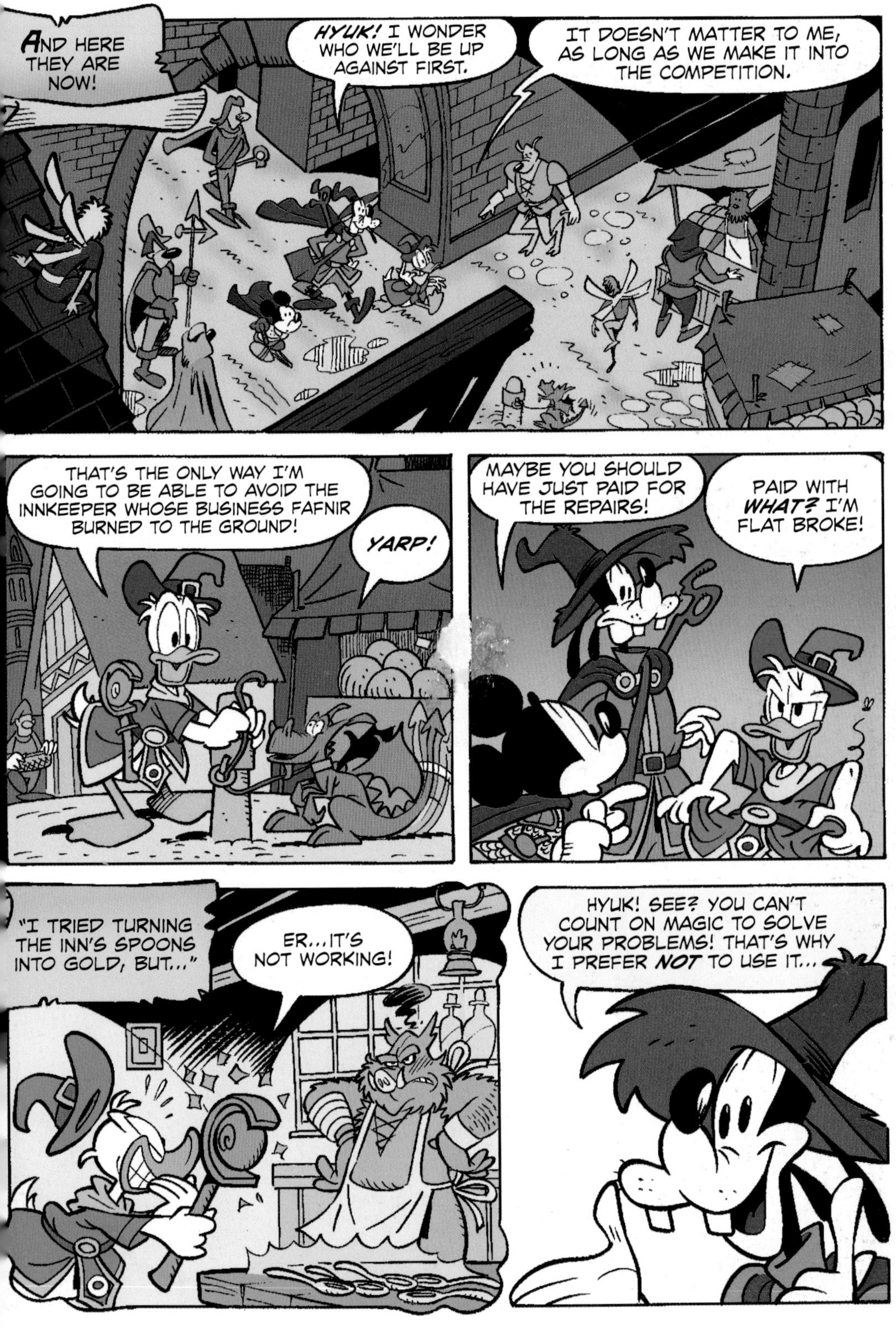
AND HERE THEY ARE NOW!
HYUK! I WONDER WHO WE'LL BE UP AGAINST FIRST.
IT DOESN'T MATTER TO ME, AS LONG AS WE MAKE IT INTO THE COMPETITION.
THAT'S THE ONLY WAY I'M GOING TO BE ABLE TO AVOID THE INNKEEPER WHOSE BUSINESS FAFNIR BURNED TO THE GROUND!
YARP!
MAYBE YOU SHOULD HAVE JUST PAID FOR THE REPAIRS!
PAID WITH WHAT? I'M FLAT BROKE!
"I TRIED TURNING THE INN'S SPOONS INTO GOLD, BUT..."
ER...IT'S NOT WORKING!
HYUK! SEE? YOU CAN'T COUNT ON MAGIC TO SOLVE YOUR PROBLEMS! THAT'S WHY I PREFER NOT TO USE IT...

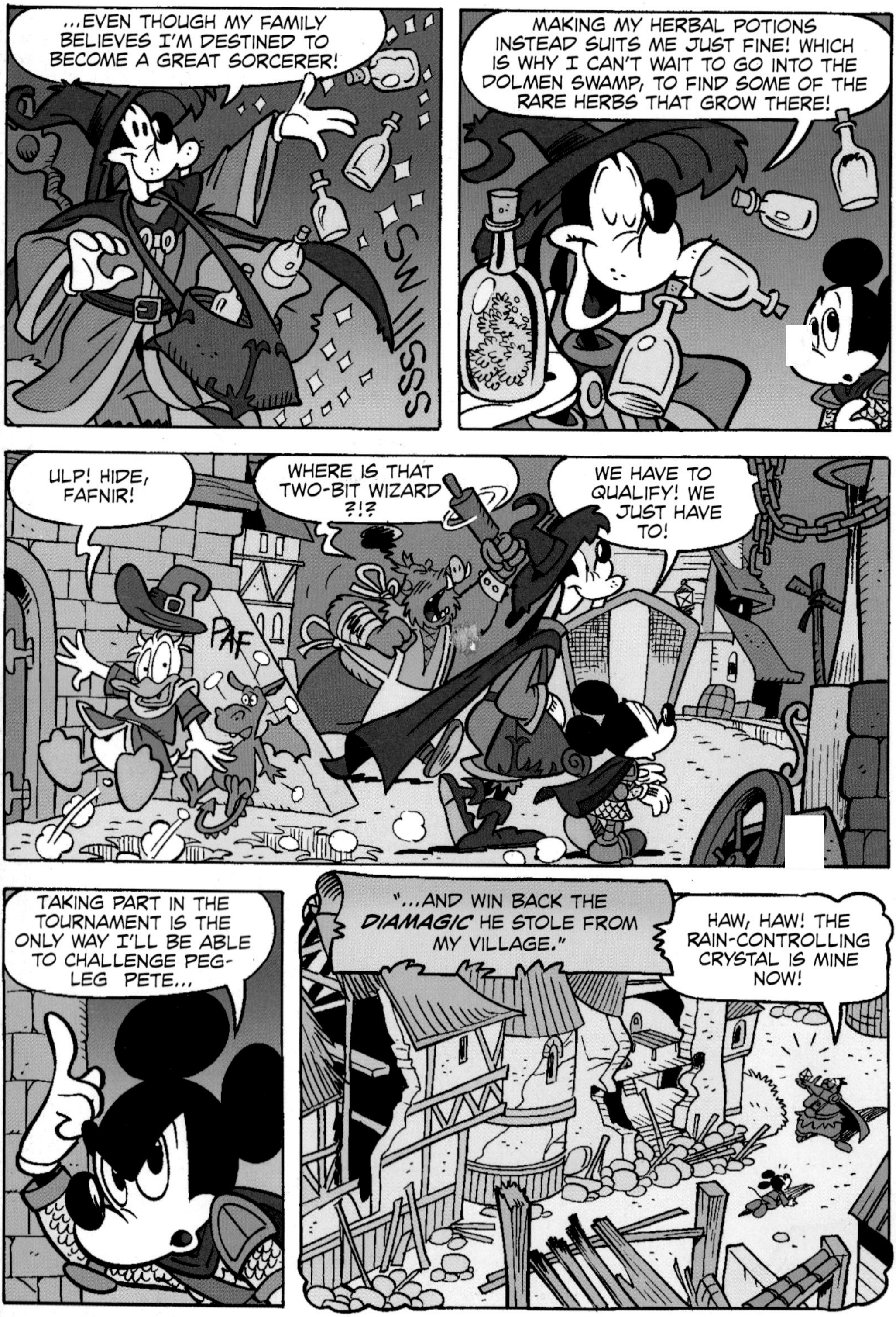
...EVEN THOUGH MY FAMILY BELIEVES I'M DESTINED TO BECOME A GREAT SORCERER!
SWISSS
MAKING MY HERBAL POTIONS INSTEAD SUITS ME JUST FINE! WHICH IS WHY I CAN'T WAIT TO GO INTO THE DOLMEN SWAMP, TO FIND SOME OF THE RARE HERBS THAT GROW THERE!
ULP! HIDE, FAFNIR!
WHERE IS THAT TWO-BIT WIZARD ?!?
WE HAVE TO QUALIFY! WE JUST HAVE TO!
PAF
TAKING PART IN THE TOURNAMENT IS THE ONLY WAY I'LL BE ABLE TO CHALLENGE PEG-LEG PETE...
"...AND WIN BACK THE *DIAMAGIC* HE STOLE FROM MY VILLAGE."
HAW, HAW! THE RAIN-CONTROLLING CRYSTAL IS MINE NOW!

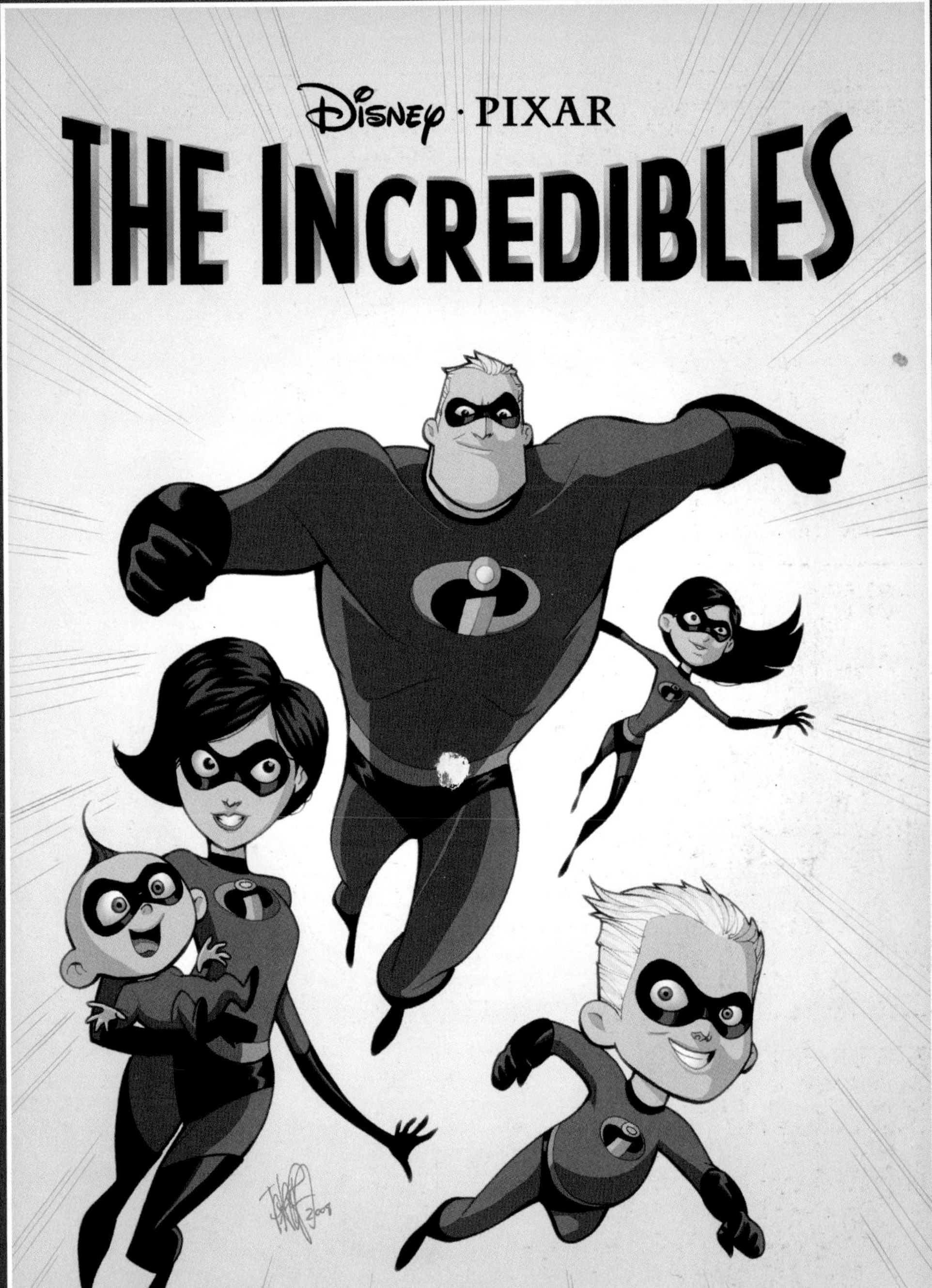
Disney · PIXAR
THE INCREDIBLES
FAMILY MATTERS

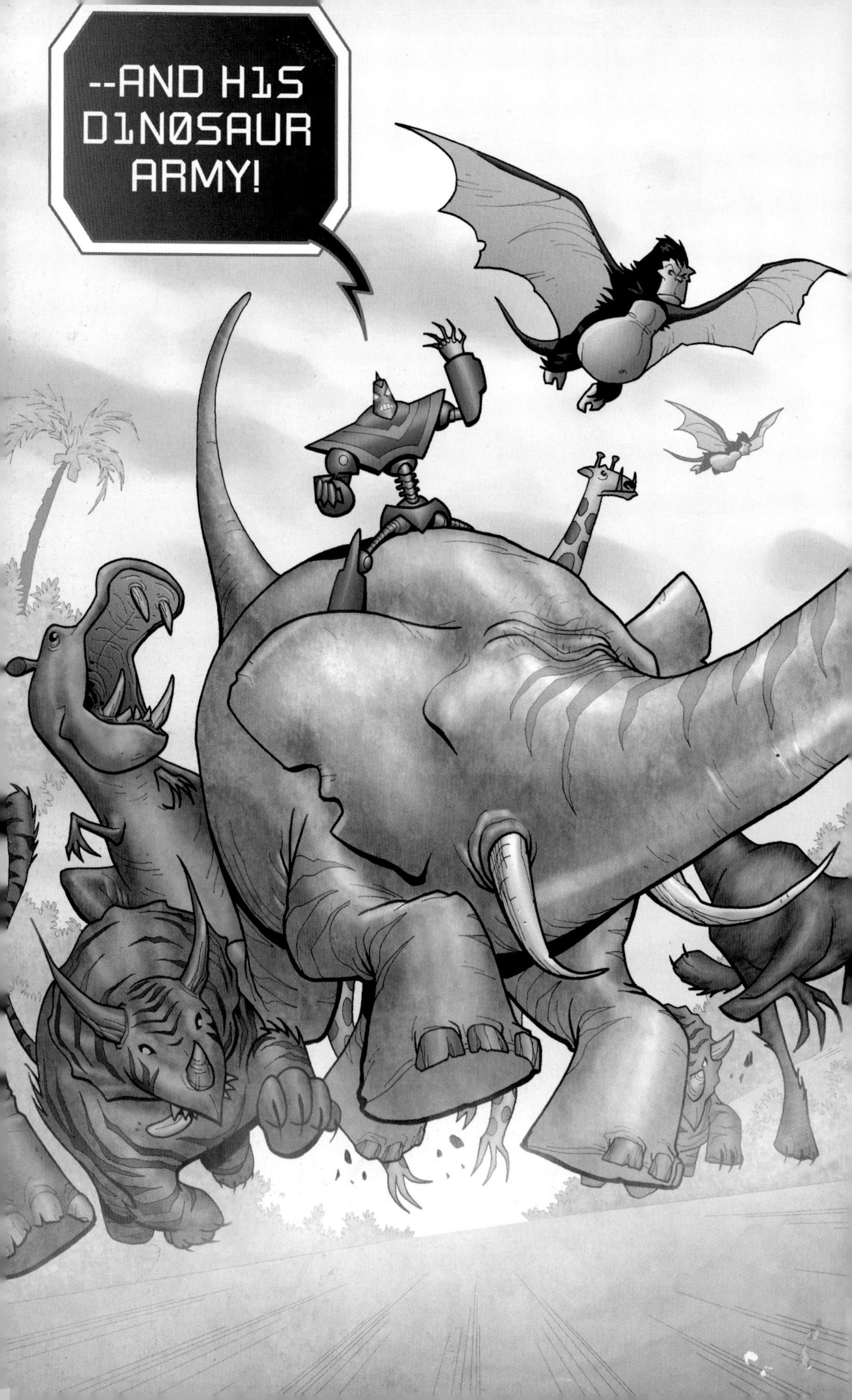
--AND H1S D1N0SAUR ARMY!

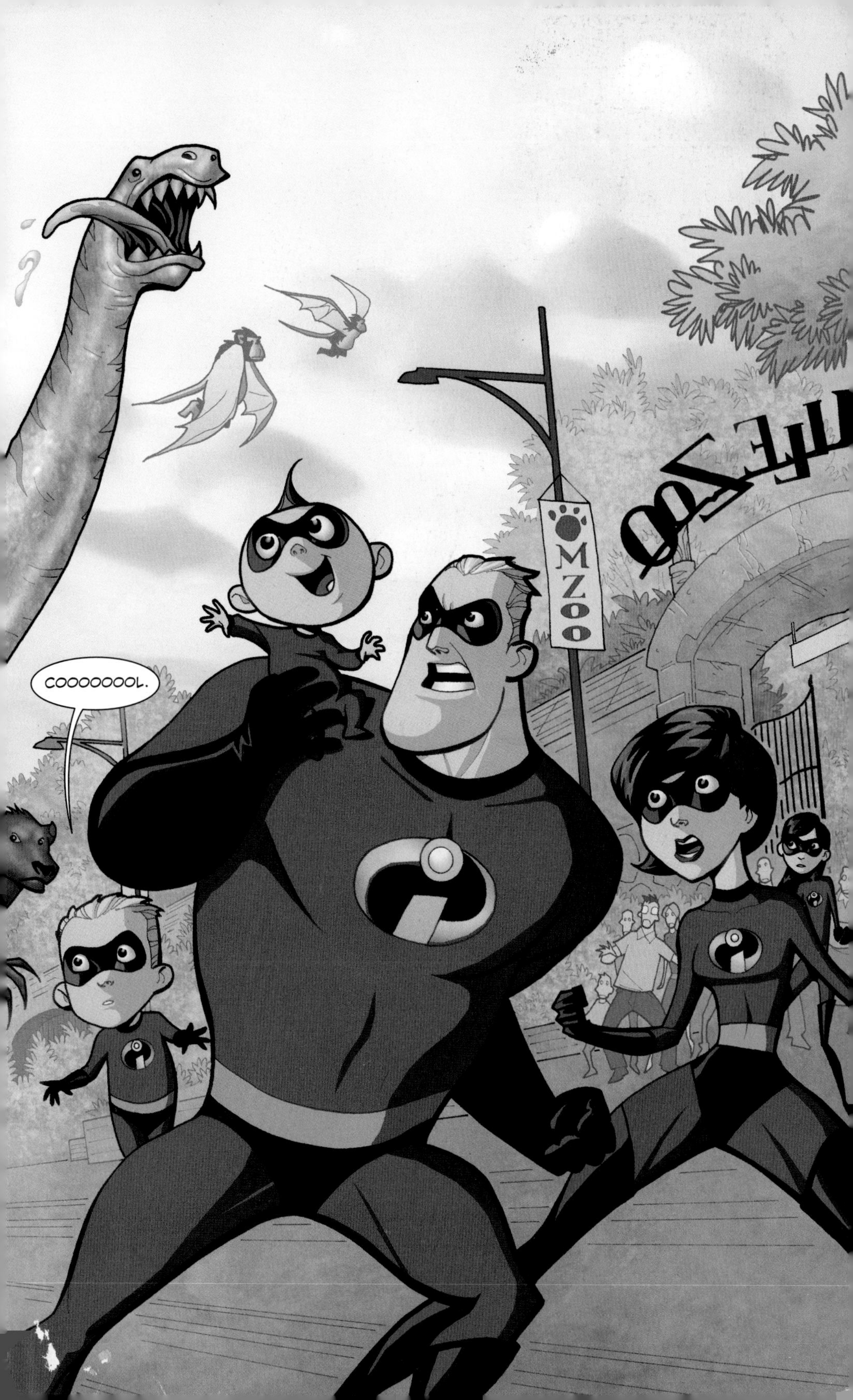
COOOOOOOL.
MZOO

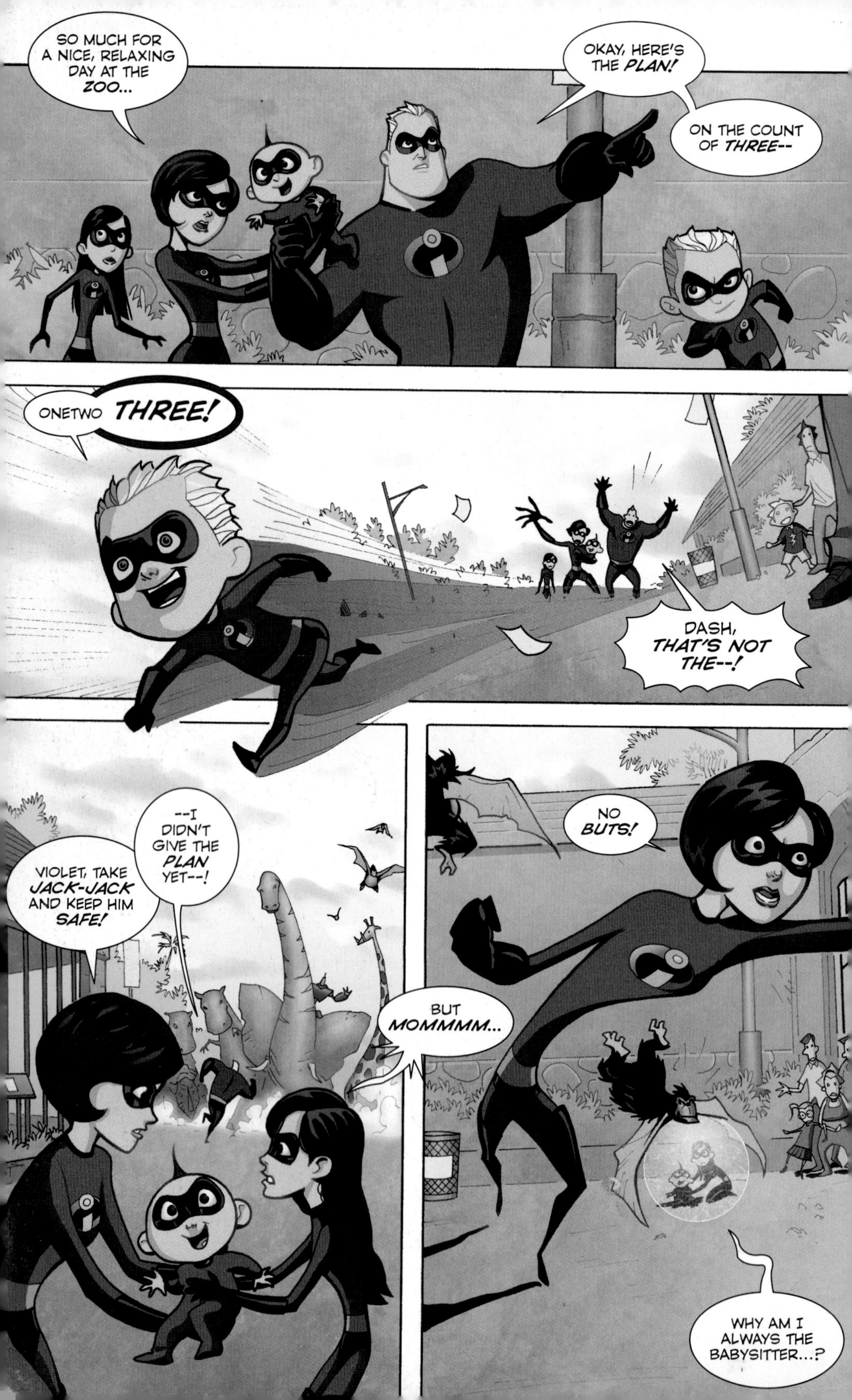
SO MUCH FOR A NICE, RELAXING DAY AT THE ZOO...
OKAY, HERE'S THE PLAN!
ON THE COUNT OF THREE--
ONETWO THREE!
DASH, THAT'S NOT THE--!
--I DIDN'T GIVE THE PLAN YET--!
VIOLET, TAKE JACK-JACK AND KEEP HIM SAFE!
BUT MOMMMM...
NO BUTS!
WHY AM I ALWAYS THE BABYSITTER...?

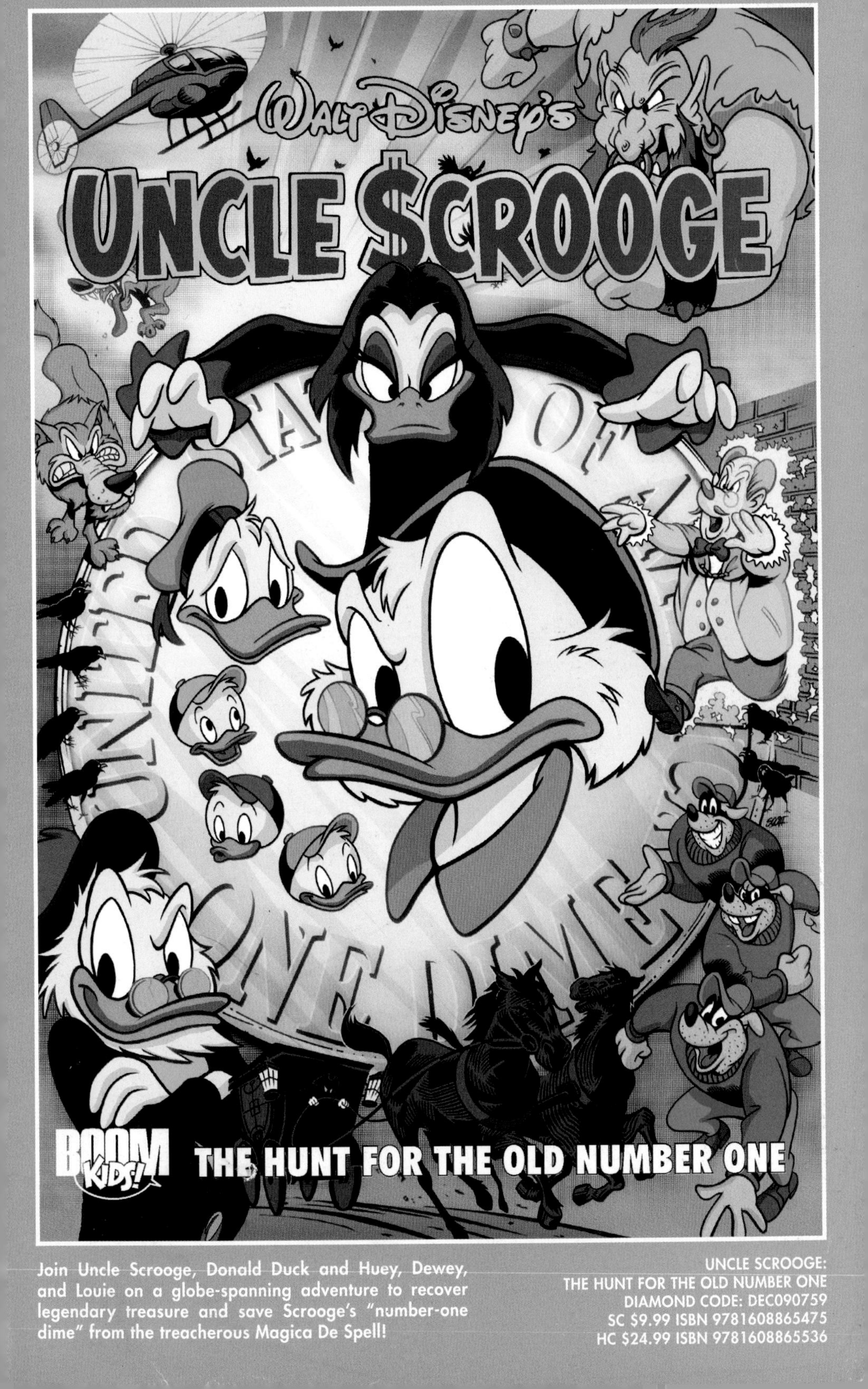

WALT DISNEY'S
UNCLE $CROOGE
BOOM KIDS!
THE HUNT FOR THE OLD NUMBER ONE

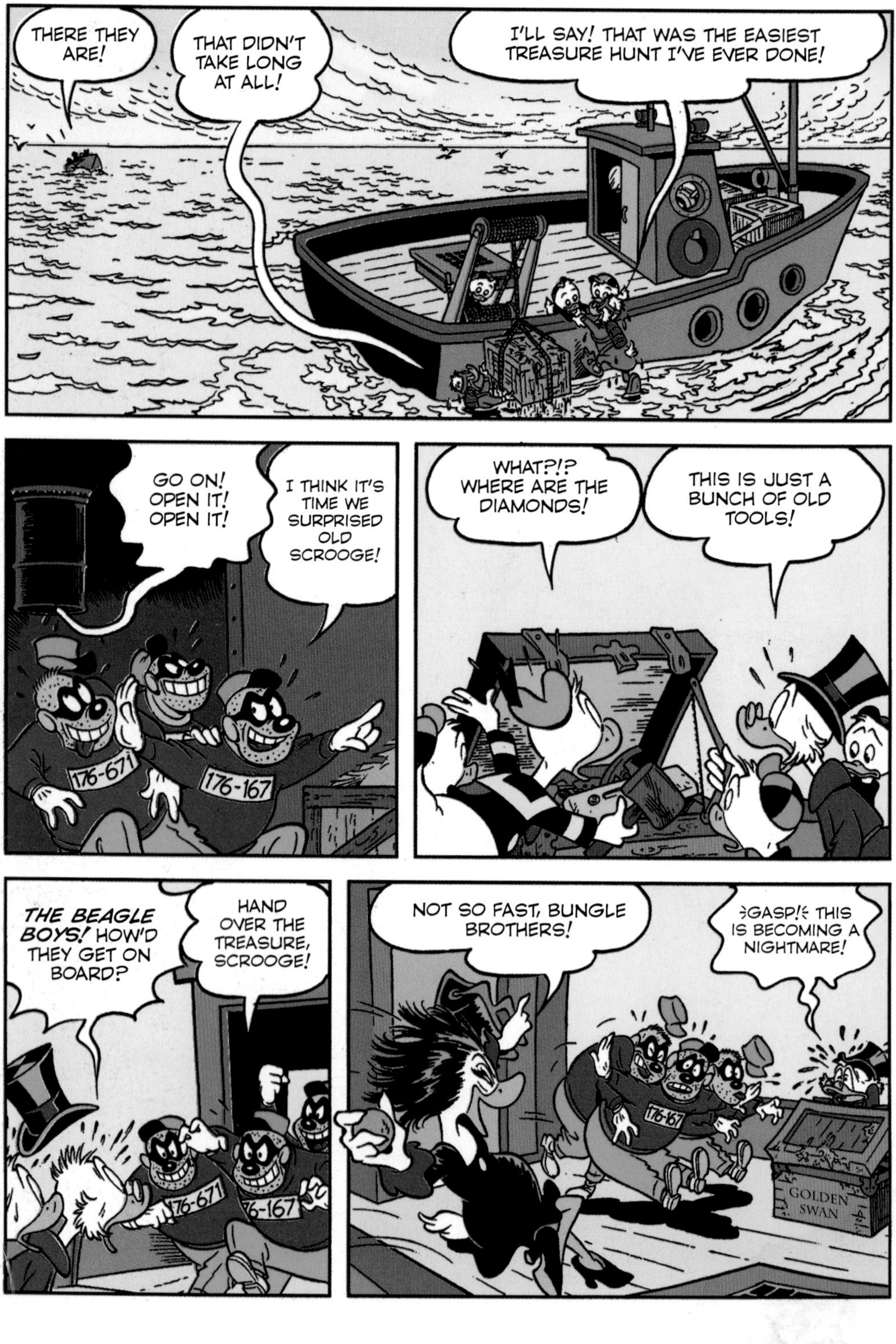
THERE THEY ARE!
THAT DIDN'T TAKE LONG AT ALL!
I'LL SAY! THAT WAS THE EASIEST TREASURE HUNT I'VE EVER DONE!
GO ON! OPEN IT! OPEN IT!
I THINK IT'S TIME WE SURPRISED OLD SCROOGE!
176-671
176-167
WHAT?!? WHERE ARE THE DIAMONDS!
THIS IS JUST A BUNCH OF OLD TOOLS!
THE BEAGLE BOYS! HOW'D THEY GET ON BOARD?
HAND OVER THE TREASURE, SCROOGE!
176-671
76-167
NOT SO FAST, BUNGLE BROTHERS!
GASP! THIS IS BECOMING A NIGHTMARE!
176-167
GOLDEN SWAN

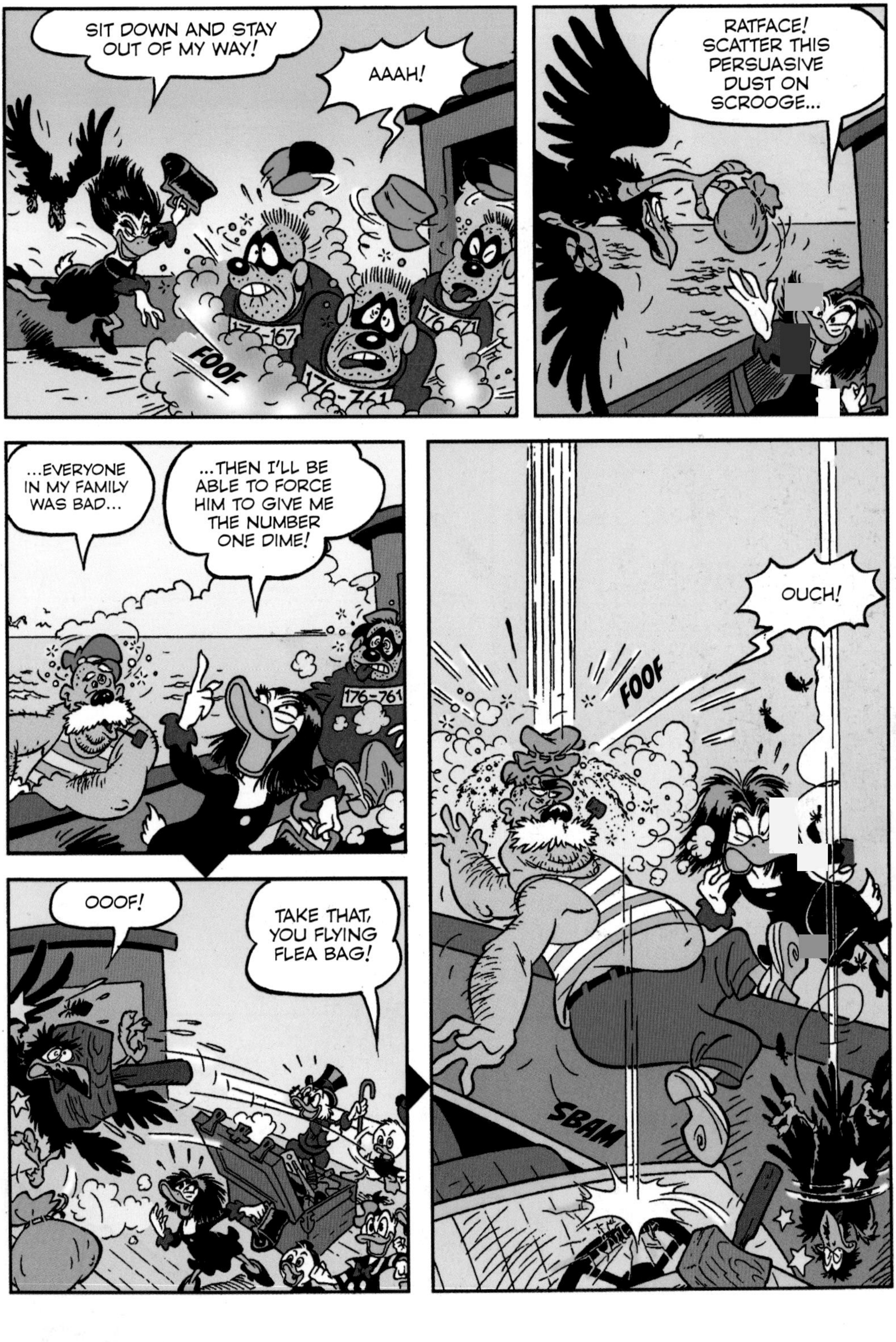
SIT DOWN AND STAY OUT OF MY WAY!
AAAH!
176-167
176-761
176-671
FOOF
RATFACE! SCATTER THIS PERSUASIVE DUST ON SCROOGE...
...EVERYONE IN MY FAMILY WAS BAD...
...THEN I'LL BE ABLE TO FORCE HIM TO GIVE ME THE NUMBER ONE DIME!
176-761
OOOF!
TAKE THAT, YOU FLYING FLEA BAG!
OUCH!
FOOF
SBAM

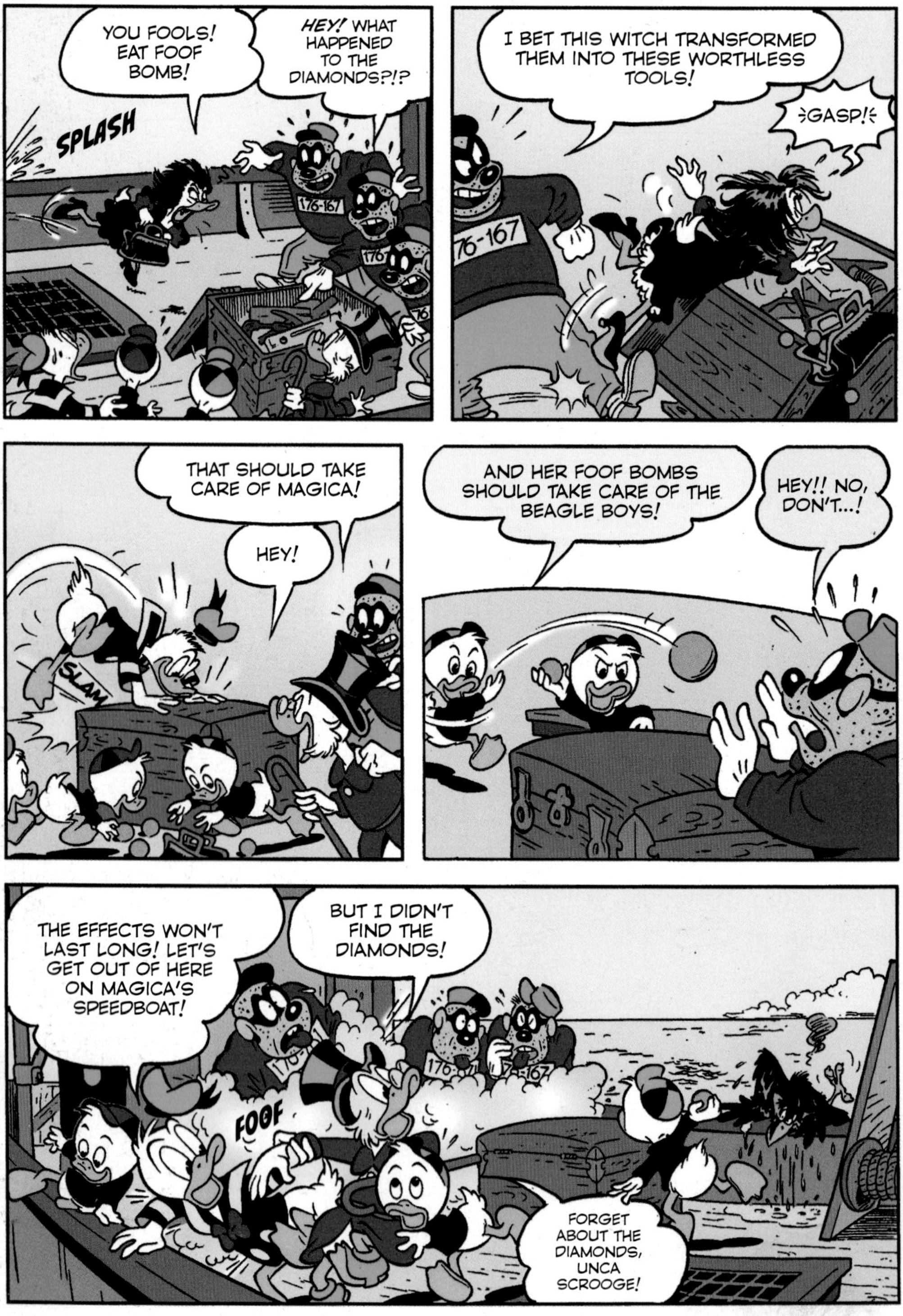

YOU FOOLS! EAT FOOF BOMB!
HEY! WHAT HAPPENED TO THE DIAMONDS?!?
SPLASH
I BET THIS WITCH TRANSFORMED THEM INTO THESE WORTHLESS TOOLS!
GASP!
THAT SHOULD TAKE CARE OF MAGICA!
HEY!
SLAM
AND HER FOOF BOMBS SHOULD TAKE CARE OF THE BEAGLE BOYS!
HEY!! NO, DON'T...!
THE EFFECTS WON'T LAST LONG! LET'S GET OUT OF HERE ON MAGICA'S SPEEDBOAT!
BUT I DIDN'T FIND THE DIAMONDS!
FOOF
FORGET ABOUT THE DIAMONDS, UNCA SCROOGE!

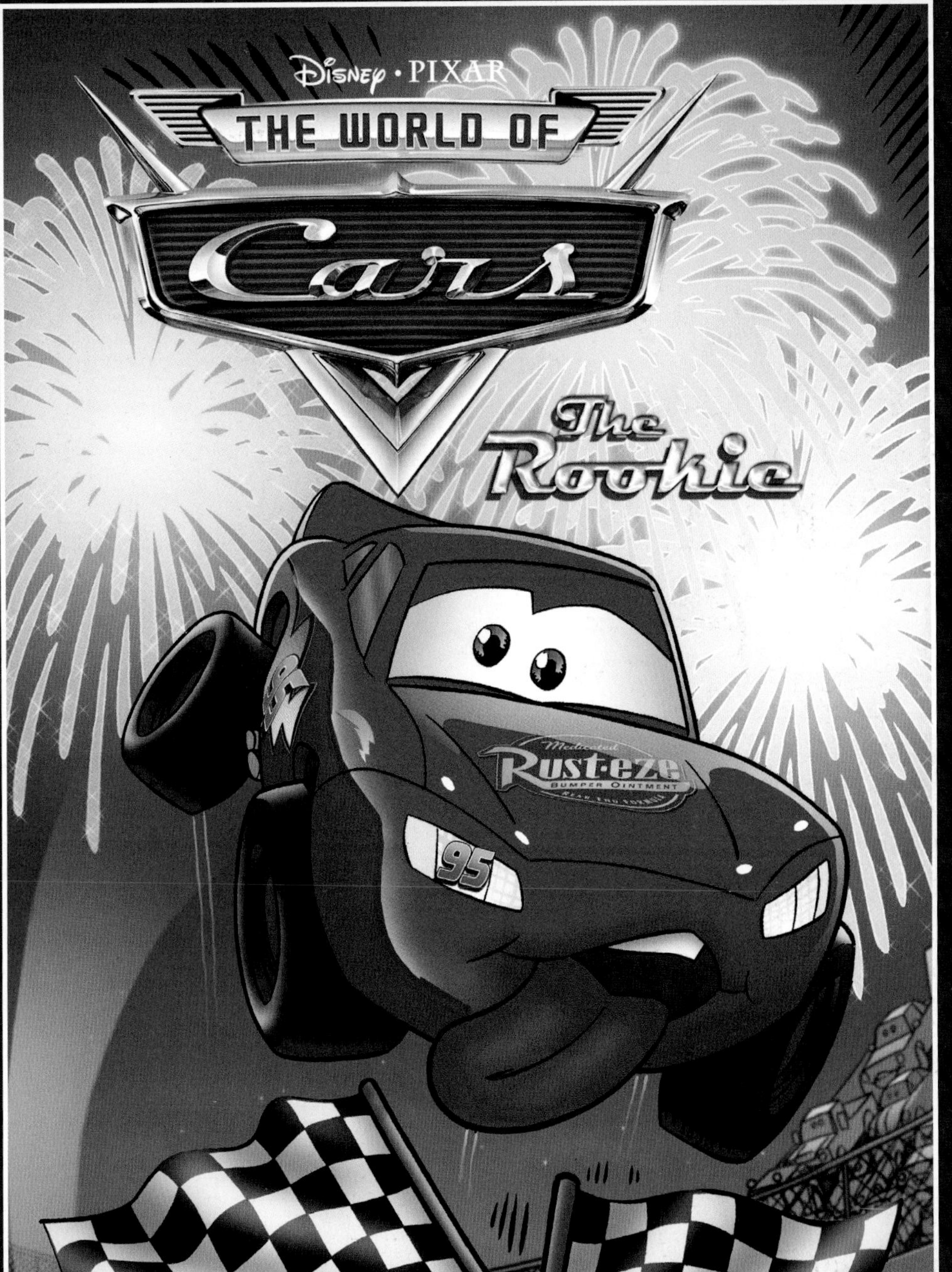
DISNEY • PIXAR
THE WORLD OF
Cars
The Rookie
Rust-eze
BUMPER OINTMENT
95

McQueen reveals his scrappy origins as "Bulldozer" McQueen—a local short track racer who dreams of the big time...

CARS: THE ROOKIE
DIAMOND CODE: MAY090749
SC $9.99 ISBN 9781608865024
HC $24.99 ISBN 9781608865284

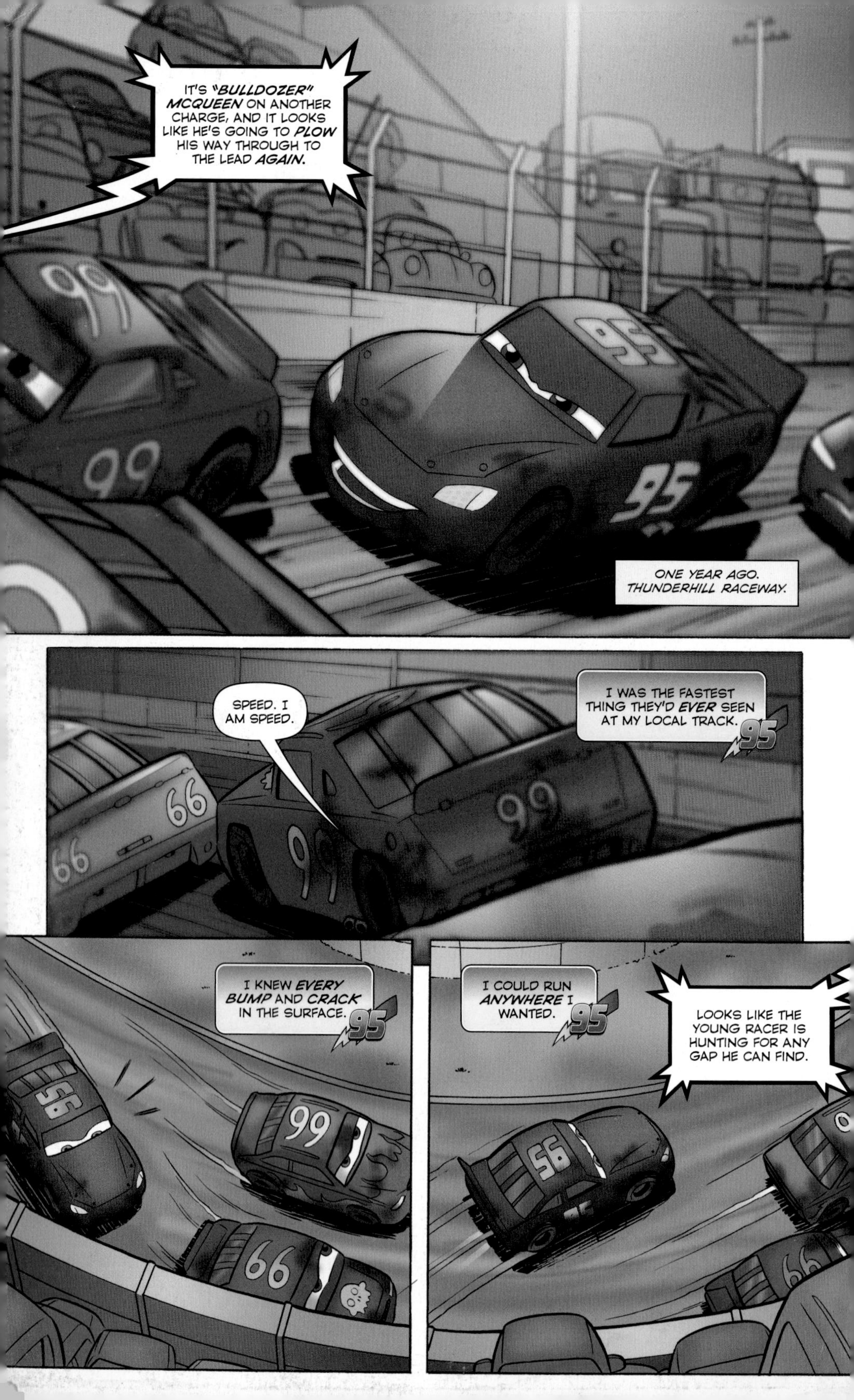
IT'S "BULLDOZER" MCQUEEN ON ANOTHER CHARGE, AND IT LOOKS LIKE HE'S GOING TO PLOW HIS WAY THROUGH TO THE LEAD AGAIN.
ONE YEAR AGO. THUNDERHILL RACEWAY.
SPEED. I AM SPEED.
I WAS THE FASTEST THING THEY'D EVER SEEN AT MY LOCAL TRACK.
I KNEW EVERY BUMP AND CRACK IN THE SURFACE.
I COULD RUN ANYWHERE I WANTED.
LOOKS LIKE THE YOUNG RACER IS HUNTING FOR ANY GAP HE CAN FIND.

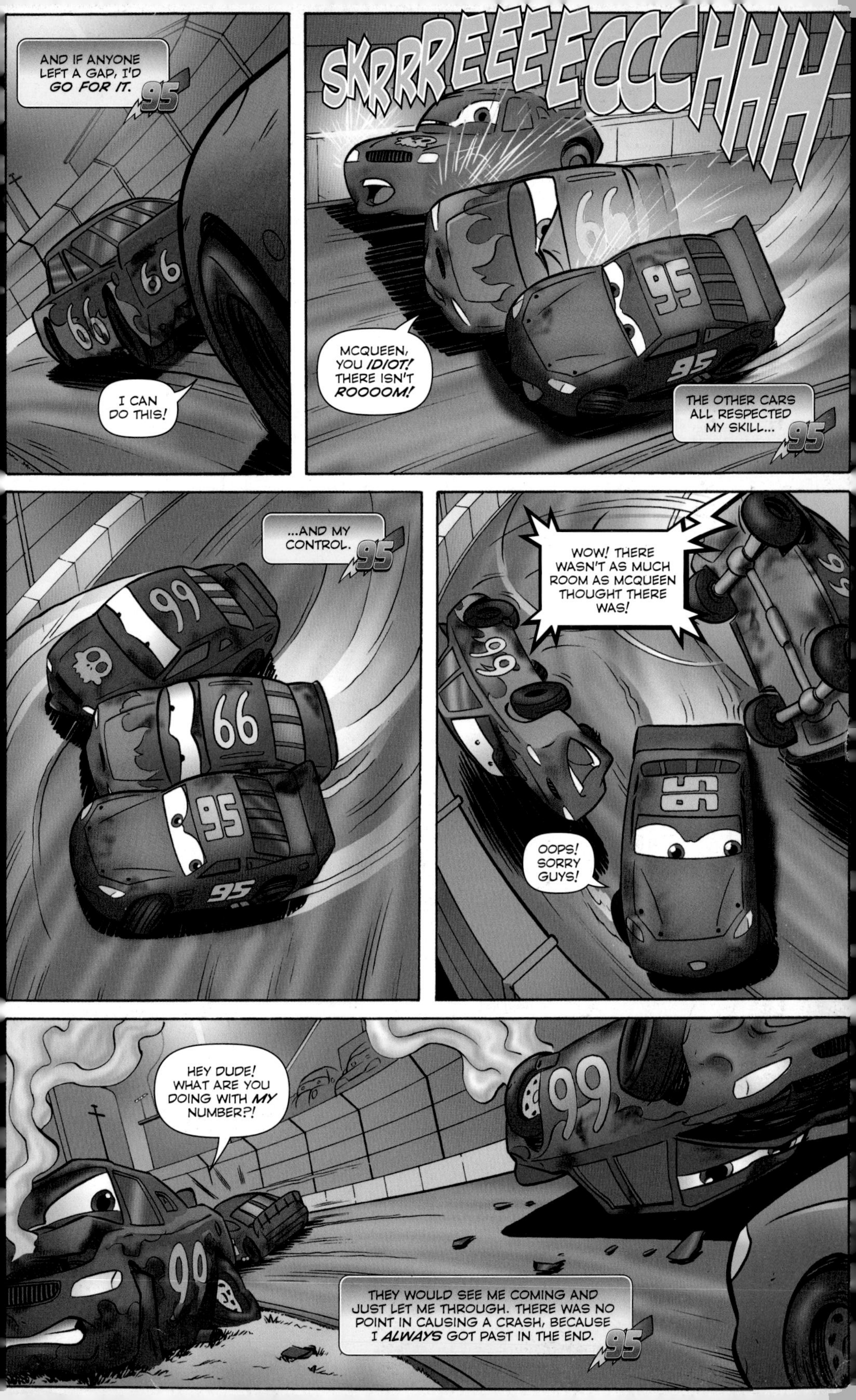
AND IF ANYONE LEFT A GAP, I'D *GO FOR IT.*
I CAN DO THIS!
SKRRREEEEECCCHHH
MCQUEEN, YOU *IDIOT!* THERE ISN'T *ROOOOM!*
THE OTHER CARS ALL RESPECTED MY SKILL...
...AND MY CONTROL.
WOW! THERE WASN'T AS MUCH ROOM AS MCQUEEN THOUGHT THERE WAS!
OOPS! SORRY GUYS!
HEY DUDE! WHAT ARE YOU DOING WITH *MY* NUMBER?!
THEY WOULD SEE ME COMING AND JUST LET ME THROUGH. THERE WAS NO POINT IN CAUSING A CRASH, BECAUSE I *ALWAYS* GOT PAST IN THE END.

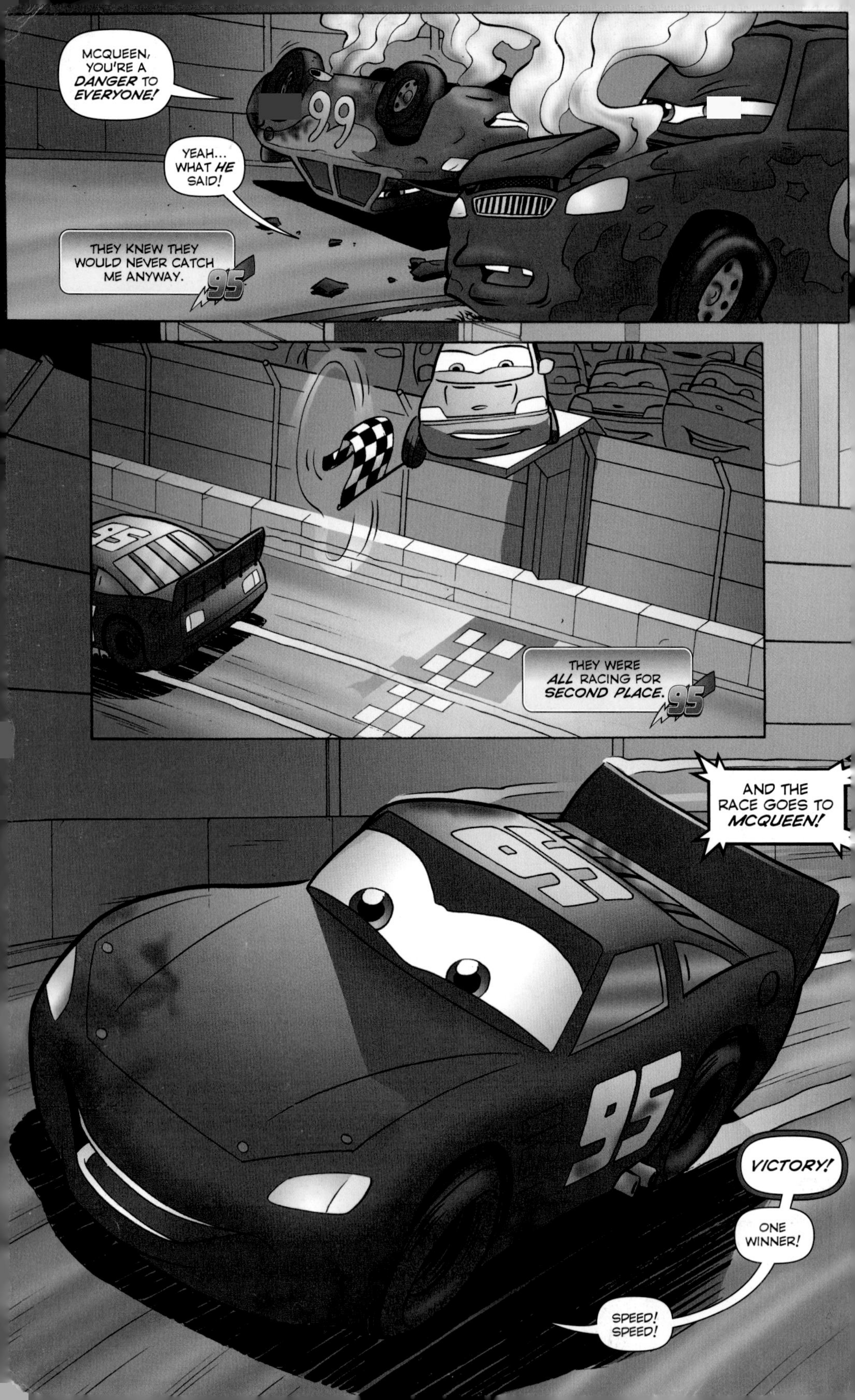
MCQUEEN, YOU'RE A DANGER TO EVERYONE!
YEAH... WHAT HE SAID!
THEY KNEW THEY WOULD NEVER CATCH ME ANYWAY.
95
THEY WERE ALL RACING FOR SECOND PLACE.
95
AND THE RACE GOES TO MCQUEEN!
95
VICTORY!
ONE WINNER!
SPEED! SPEED!

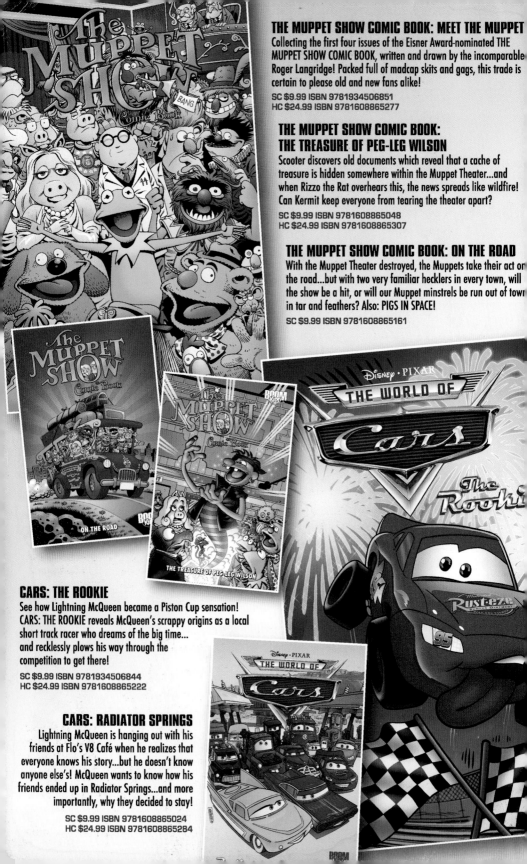

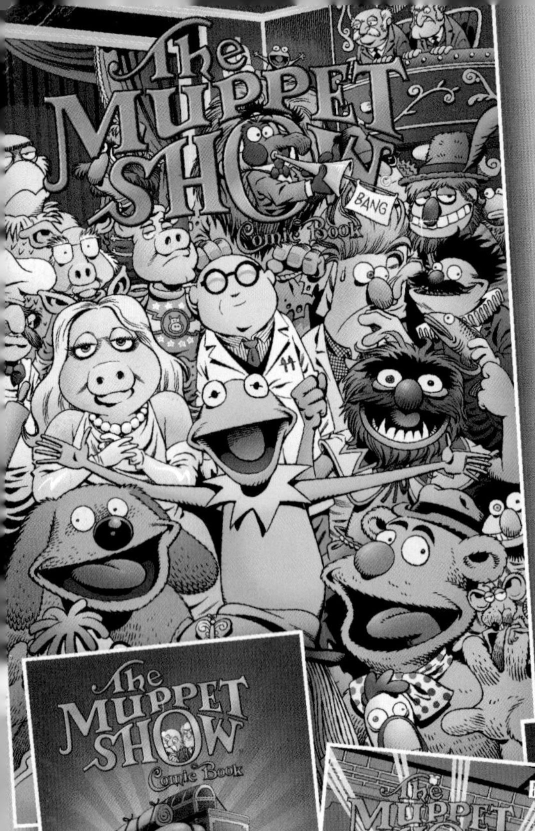
The Muppet Show
Comic Book
BANG

THE MUPPET SHOW COMIC BOOK: MEET THE MUPPET

Collecting the first four issues of the Eisner Award-nominated THE MUPPET SHOW COMIC BOOK, written and drawn by the incomparable Roger Langridge! Packed full of madcap skits and gags, this trade is certain to please old and new fans alike!

SC $9.99 ISBN 9781934506851
HC $24.99 ISBN 9781608865277

THE MUPPET SHOW COMIC BOOK: THE TREASURE OF PEG-LEG WILSON

Scooter discovers old documents which reveal that a cache of treasure is hidden somewhere within the Muppet Theater...and when Rizzo the Rat overhears this, the news spreads like wildfire! Can Kermit keep everyone from tearing the theater apart?

SC $9.99 ISBN 9781608865048
HC $24.99 ISBN 9781608865307

THE MUPPET SHOW COMIC BOOK: ON THE ROAD

With the Muppet Theater destroyed, the Muppets take their act on the road...but with two very familiar hecklers in every town, will the show be a hit, or will our Muppet minstrels be run out of town in tar and feathers? Also: PIGS IN SPACE!

SC $9.99 ISBN 9781608865161

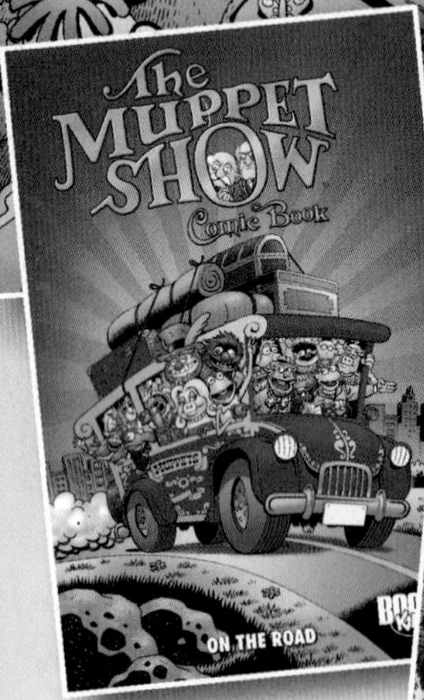
The Muppet Show
Comic Book
ON THE ROAD

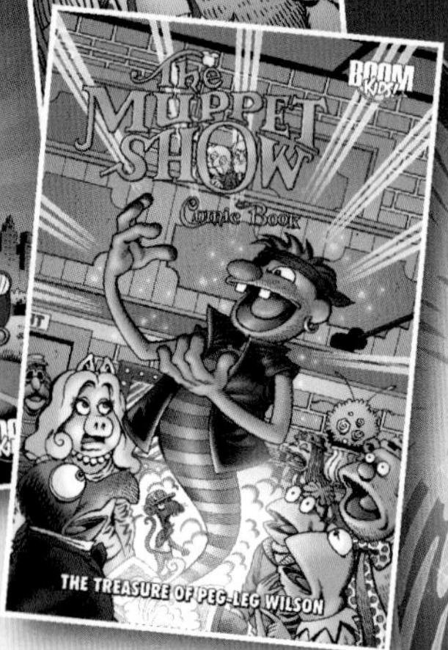
The Muppet Show
Comic Book
BOOM! KIDS
THE TREASURE OF PEG-LEG WILSON

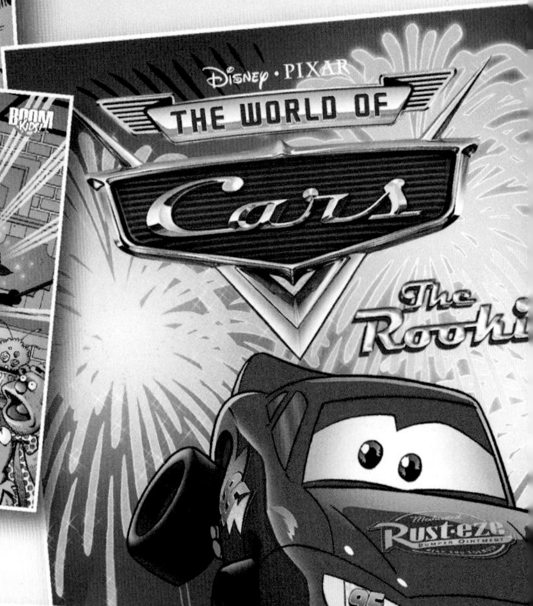
Disney • PIXAR
THE WORLD OF
Cars
Rust-eze

CARS: THE ROOKIE

See how Lightning McQueen became a Piston Cup sensation! CARS: THE ROOKIE reveals McQueen's scrappy origins as a local short track racer who dreams of the big time... and recklessly plows his way through the competition to get there!

SC $9.99 ISBN 9781934506844
HC $24.99 ISBN 9781608865222

CARS: RADIATOR SPRINGS

Lightning McQueen is hanging out with his friends at Flo's V8 Café when he realizes that everyone knows his story...but he doesn't know anyone else's! McQueen wants to know how his friends ended up in Radiator Springs...and more importantly, why they decided to stay!

SC $9.99 ISBN 9781608865024
HC $24.99 ISBN 9781608865284

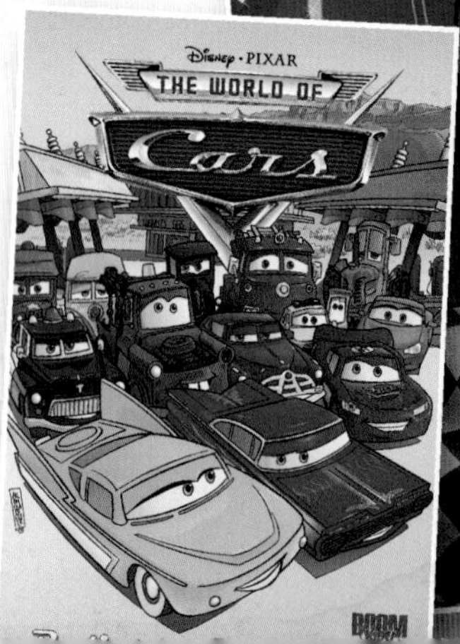
Disney • PIXAR
THE WORLD OF
Cars

WALL•E: RECHARGE

efore WALL•E becomes the hardworking robot we know and love, he ets the few remaining robots take care of the trash compacting while he collects interesting junk. But when these robots start breaking down, WALL•E must adjust his priorities...or else Earth is doomed!

SC $9.99 ISBN 9781608865123
HC $24.99 ISBN 9781608865543

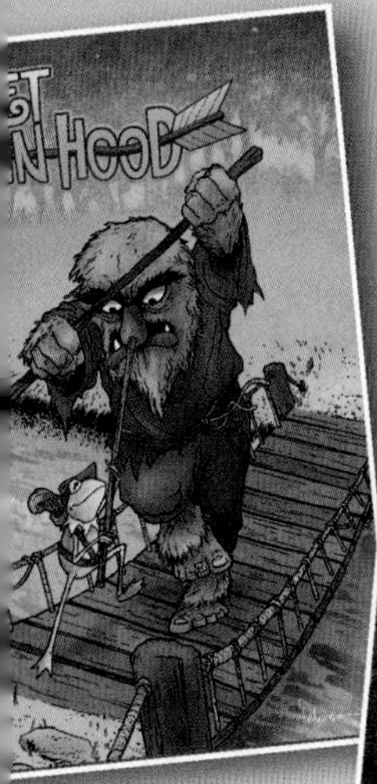

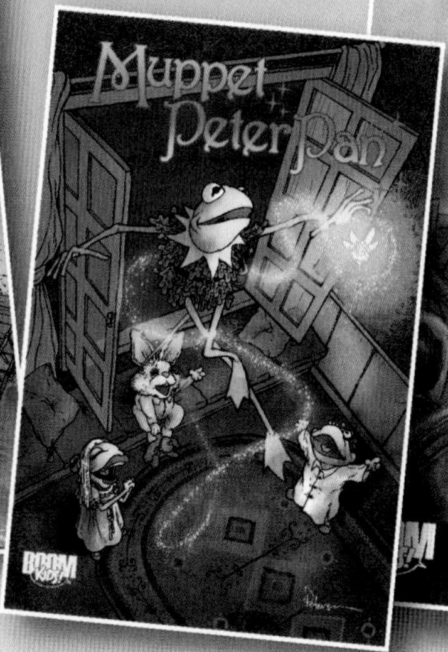
Muppet Peter Pan

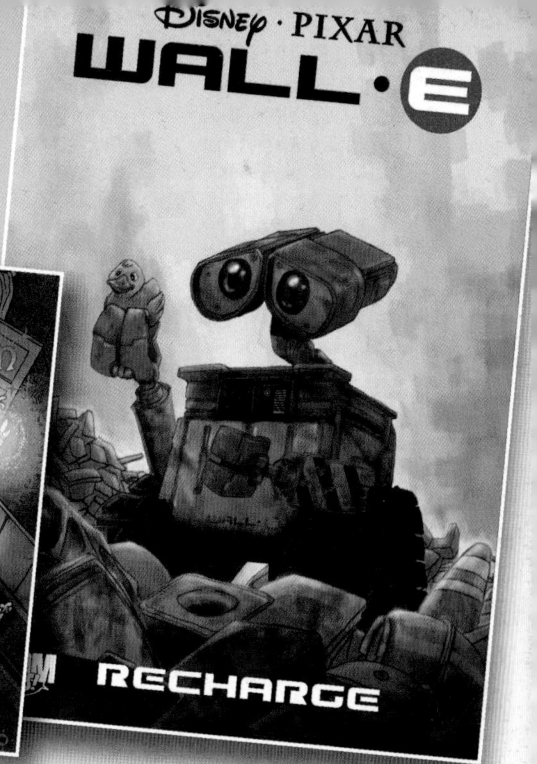
Disney · PIXAR
WALL·E
RECHARGE

UPPET ROBIN HOOD

e Muppets tell the Robin Hood legend for laughs, and it's the reader who will be merry! bin Hood (Kermit the Frog) joins with the Merry Men, Sherwood Forest's infamous gang of sfit outlaws, to take on the Sheriff of Nottingham (Sam the Eagle)!

$9.99 ISBN 9781934506790
$24.99 ISBN 9781608865260

MUPPET PETER PAN

When Peter Pan (Kermit) whisks Wendy (Janice) and her brothers to Neverswamp, the adventure begins! With Captain Hook (Gonzo) out for revenge for the loss of his hand, can even the magic of Piggytink (Miss Piggy) save Wendy and her brothers?

SC $9.99 ISBN 9781608865079
HC $24.99 ISBN 9781608865314

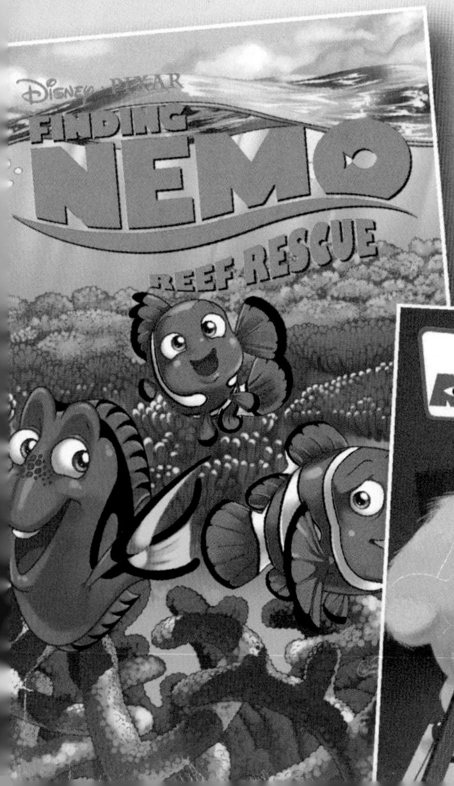
FINDING
NEMO
REEF RESCUE

FINDING NEMO: REEF RESCUE

Nemo, Dory and Marlin have become local heroes, and are recruited to embark on an all-new adventure in this exciting collection! The reef is mysteriously dying and no one knows why. So Nemo and his friends must travel the great blue sea to save their home!

SC $9.99 ISBN 9781934506882
HC $24.99 ISBN 9781608865246

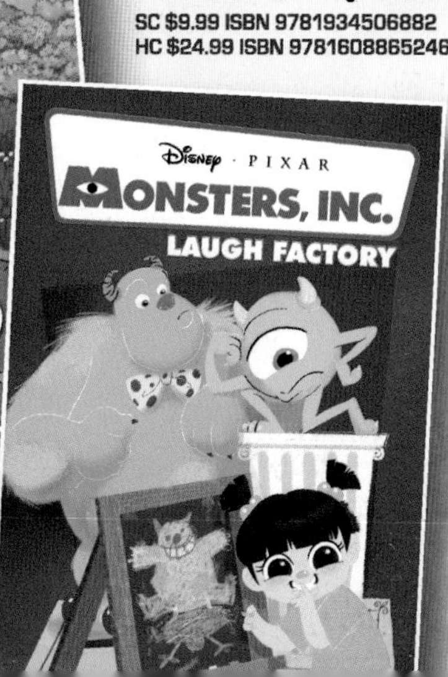
Disney · PIXAR
MONSTERS, INC.
LAUGH FACTORY

MONSTERS, INC.: LAUGH FACTORY

Someone is stealing comedy props from the other employees, making it difficult for them to harvest the laughter they need to power Monstropolis...and all evidence points to Sulley's best friend Mike Wazowski!

SC $9.99 ISBN 9781608865086
HC $24.99 ISBN 9781608865338

DISNEY'S HERO SQUAD: ULTRAHEROES VOL. 1: SAVE THE WORLD

It's an all-star cast of your favorite Disney characters, as you have never seen them before. Join Donald Duck, Goofy, Daisy, and even Mickey himself as they defend the fate of the planet as the one and only Ultraheroes!

SC $9.99 ISBN 9781608865437
HC $24.99 ISBN 9781608865529

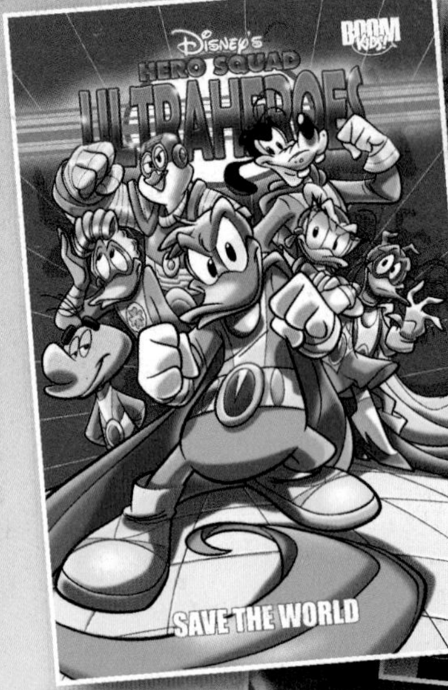
Disney's
HERO SQUAD
ULTRAHEROES
BOOM KIDS!
SAVE THE WORLD

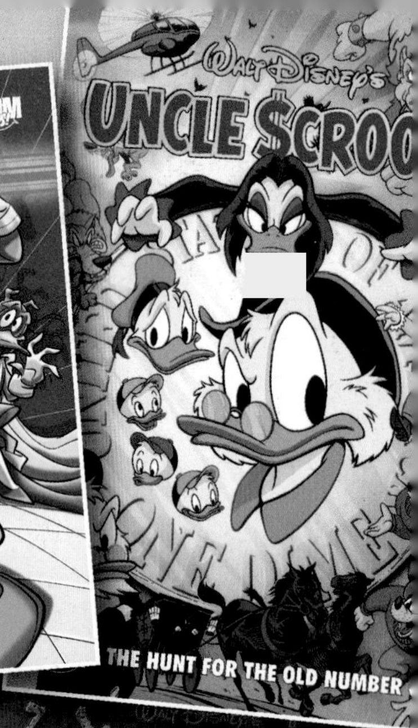
Walt Disney's
UNCLE $CROO
THE HUNT FOR THE OLD NUMBER

UNCLE SCROOGE: THE HUNT FOR THE OLD NUMBER ONE

Join Donald Duck's favorite penny-pinching Uncle Scrooge as he, Donald himself and Huey, Dewey, and Louie embark on a globe-spanning trek to recover treasure and save Scrooge's "number one dime" from the treacherous Magica De Spell.

SC $9.99 ISBN 9781608865475
HC $24.99 ISBN 9781608865536

WIZARDS OF MICKEY VOL. 1: MOUSE MAGIC

Your favorite Disney characters star in this magical fantasy epic! Student of the great wizard Nereus, Mickey allies himself with Donald and team mate Goofy, in a quest to find a magical crown that will give him mastery over all spells!

SC $9.99 ISBN 9781608865413
HC $24.99 ISBN 9781608865505

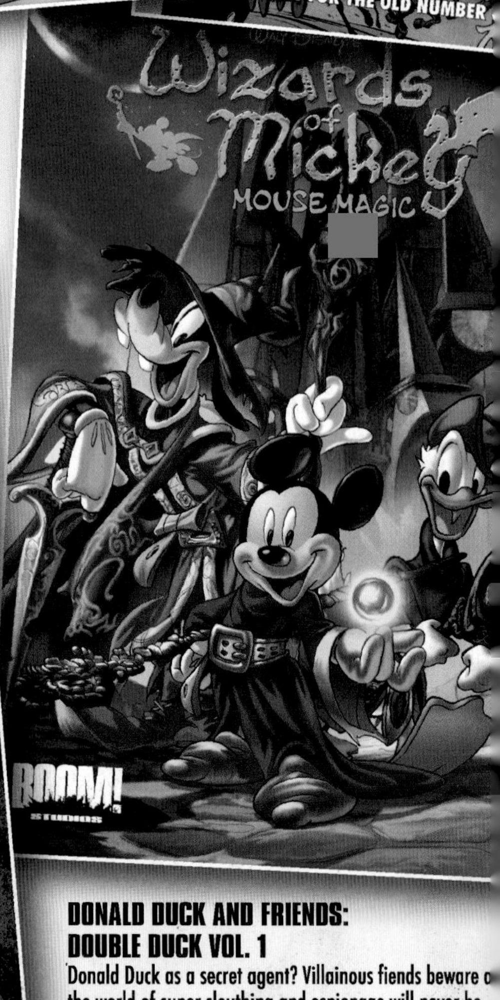
Wizards of Mickey
MOUSE MAGIC
BOOM! STUDIOS

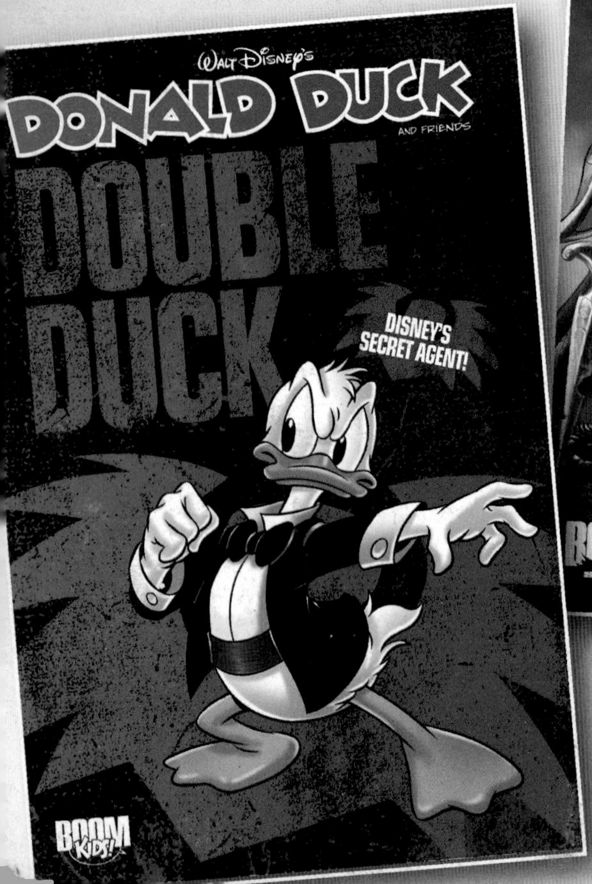
Walt Disney's
DONALD DUCK
AND FRIENDS
DOUBLE DUCK
DISNEY'S SECRET AGENT!
BOOM KIDS!

DONALD DUCK AND FRIENDS: DOUBLE DUCK VOL. 1

Donald Duck as a secret agent? Villainous fiends beware o the world of super sleuthing and espionage will never be the same! This is Donald Duck like you've never seen him!

SC $9.99 ISBN 9781608865451
HC $24.99 ISBN 9781608865512

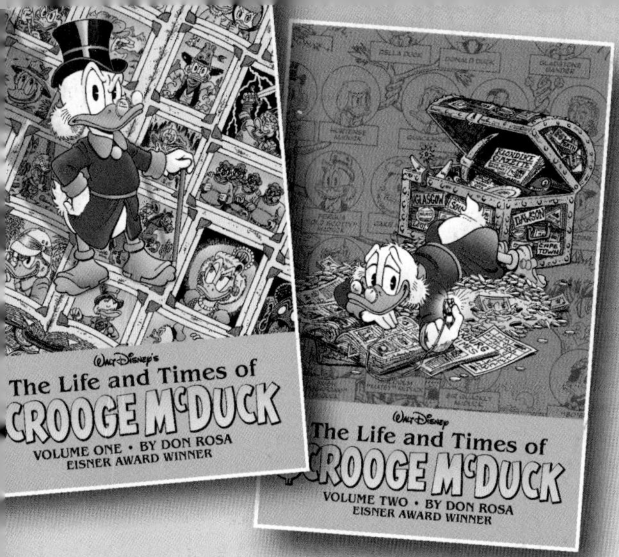
Walt Disney's
The Life and Times of
Scrooge McDuck
Volume One • By Don Rosa
Eisner Award Winner
Walt Disney
The Life and Times of
Scrooge McDuck
Volume Two • By Don Rosa
Eisner Award Winner

THE LIFE AND TIMES OF SCROOGE McDUCK VOL. 1

BOOM Kids! proudly collects the first half of THE LIFE AND TIMES OF SCROOGE MCDUCK in a gorgeous hardcover collection – featuring smyth sewn binding, a gold-on-gold foil-stamped case wrap, and a bookmark ribbon! These stories, written and drawn by legendary cartoonist Don Rosa, chronicle Scrooge McDuck's fascinating life.

HC $24.99 ISBN 9781608865383

THE LIFE AND TIMES OF SCROOGE McDUCK VOL. 2

BOOM Kids! proudly presents volume two of THE LIFE AND TIMES OF SCROOGE MCDUCK in a gorgeous hardcover collection in a beautiful, deluxe package featuring smyth sewn binding and a foil-stamped case wrap! These stories, written and drawn by legendary cartoonist Don Rosa, chronicle Scrooge McDuck's fascinating life.

HC $24.99 ISBN 9781608865420

MICKEY MOUSE CLASSICS: MOUSE TAILS

See Mickey Mouse as he was meant to be seen! Solving mysteries, fighting off pirates, and generally saving the day! These classic stories comprise a "Greatest Hits" series for the mouse, including a story produced by seminal Disney creator Carl Barks!

HC $24.99 ISBN 9781608865390

ONALD DUCK CLASSICS: QUACK UP

hether it's finding gold, journeying to the Klondike, fighting ghosts, Donald will always have the help his much more prepared nephews – Huey, Dewey, nd Louie – by his side. Featuring some of the best onald Duck stories Carl Barks ever produced!

C $24.99 ISBN 9781608865406

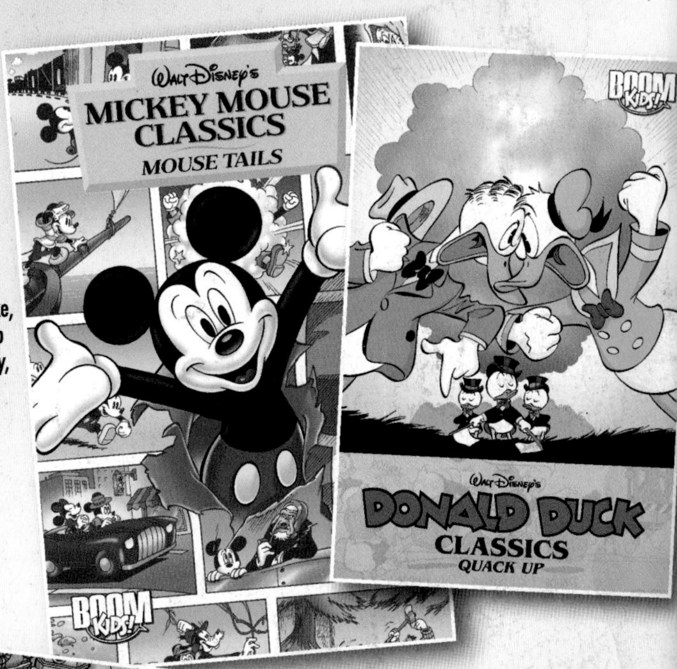
Walt Disney's
Mickey Mouse Classics
Mouse Tails
BOOM Kids!
BOOM Kids!
Walt Disney's
Donald Duck
Classics
Quack Up

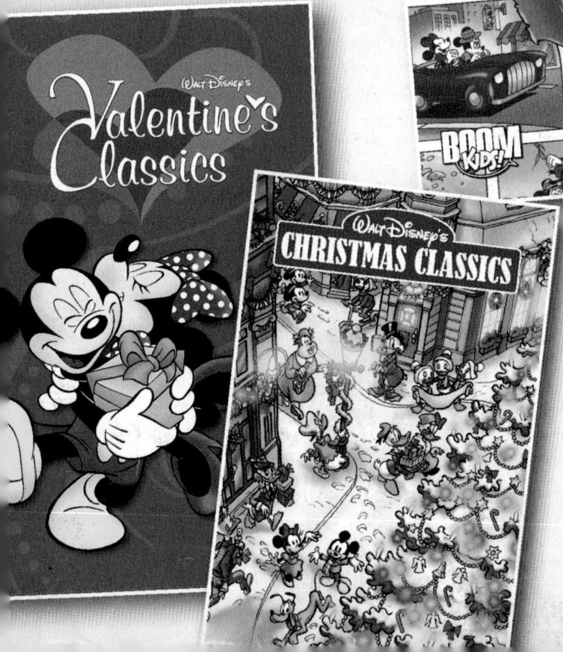
Walt Disney's
Valentine's Classics
Walt Disney's
Christmas Classics

WALT DISNEY'S VALENTINE'S CLASSICS

Love is in the air for Mickey Mouse, Donald Duck and the rest of the gang. But will Cupid's arrows cause happiness or heartache? Find out in this collection of classic stories featuring work by Carl Barks, Floyd Gottfredson, Daan Jippes, Romano Scarpa and Al Taliaferro.

HC $24.99 ISBN 9781608865499

WALT DISNEY'S CHRISTMAS CLASSICS

BOOM Kids! has raided the Disney publishing archives and searched every nook and cranny to find the best and the greatest Christmas stories from Disney's vast comic book publishing history for this "best of" compilation.

HC $24.99 ISBN 9781608865482

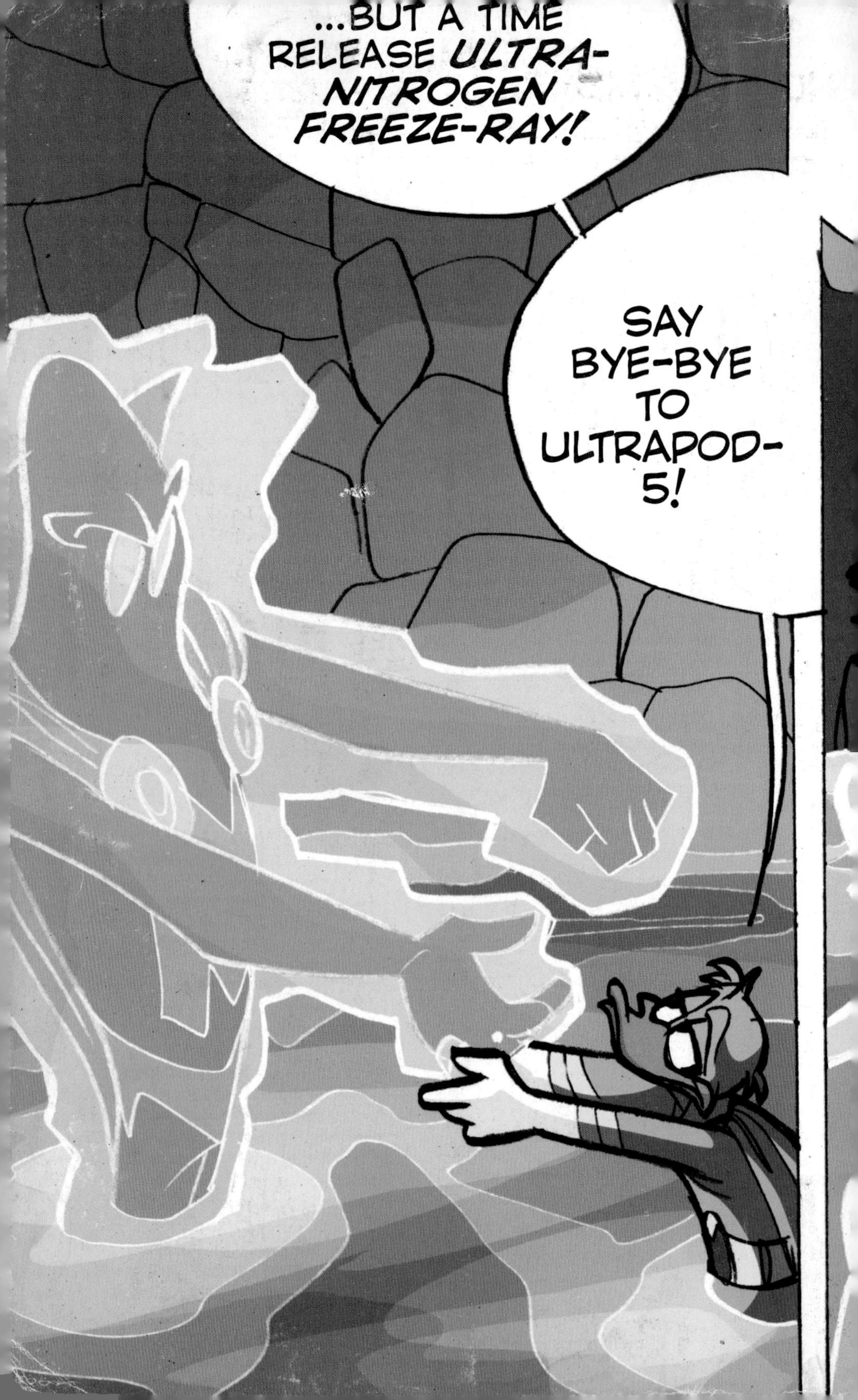
...BUT A TIME RELEASE *ULTRA-NITROGEN FREEZE-RAY!*
SAY BYE-BYE TO ULTRAPOD-5!